SNARED

OTHER TITLES BY ED JAMES

ED JAMES
SNARED

THOMAS & MERCER

Published by Thomas & Mercer, Seattle

www.apub.com

Amazon, the Amazon logo, and Thomas & Mercer are trademarks of Amazon.com, Inc., or its affiliates.

ISBN-13: 978-1477828441
ISBN-10: 1477828443

Cover design by bürosüd° München, www.buerosued.de

Library of Congress Control Number: 2014955026

Printed in the United States of America

For Allan

Wednesday
26th March 2014

Chapter One

"There he goes. He's just about ready." The man tugged his balaclava tighter before patting his companion on her shoulder. "You'll see why they call it doggy style."

The woman shrugged his arm off, twisting her body away from the cage, staring into the black of the rest of the large room. A tap dripped somewhere in the distance. "Right."

The man frowned at her. "What's up?"

"Nothing."

The man walked up to the cage and rattled it, the clank still echoing round the room once he stopped. "Go on, boy, get it up her."

The male in the cage moved away from the female, head bowed, avoiding eye contact with either of them, eyes locked on the dirty floor instead, on the mounds of their own excrement.

The man pointed at the cage, eyes on her. "What's he doing?"

The woman glanced back at the cage, then shook her head. "This is a bit too cruel."

"They're animals. There's nothing cruel about this." The man rattled the cage again, gloved hands gripping the steel.

The male's pupils contracted.

He pointed the Taser at the cage before sparking it. "Don't make me use this again."

The male focused on the weapon. It knew. It looked back at the female before groaning as it settled on its haunches near the edge of the cage between the female and them, protecting her. Its chest heaved as its breathing increased.

"Christ's sake. We'll never get these two to breed at this rate." He sparked the Taser again and jammed it through the bars, catching the male between the shoulder blades.

It jerked up then sprawled over the floor of the cage, its whole body shaking.

The female crawled into the far corner, pushing up against the bars, tucking herself into a foetal position.

The male's brown eyes pleaded with them as it lay prone in a pool of its own urine.

The man held out the Taser again, not quite reaching the male. "Want to be a good boy for me?"

The male growled at them, some motor control returning.

The man let out a sigh and looked around. He tapped her on the shoulder. "Do you want to help me here?"

The woman turned to look at the cage, at the pathetic animals inside, staring at them for a few seconds. "You using that thing isn't going to help, you know."

He inspected the Taser before nodding. "You're probably right."

"Come on, let's leave them to it. That might encourage them more than your battering-ram approach."

"You could be right."

The male sat up and started clawing at the bars at the front.

The man put his face up to the bars, eyeballing the male, before pointing the Taser at the cage, inches from its face, and sparking it again. "Don't worry, you'll be here for a while, Paul."

3

Thursday
27th March 2014

Chapter Two

Vicky Dodds pulled off the roundabout onto the North Marketgait, the dual carriageway giving her a clear run for once. The trees lining the road obscured a block of new flats in brown and blue climbing over the car park to the right, already half full.

Her phone started ringing as she shot through the green lights, past the pink brick of the Wellgate Shopping Centre, the towering multi-storey flats ahead of her surrounding a turreted building in the brown stone of old Dundee. She slipped into the half darkness of the tunnel just as her mobile stopped ringing.

"Shit, shit, shit." She hit the brakes. The road ahead was jammed solid, what passed for morning rush hour traffic in Dundee. Fumes leaked into the car. She flipped the air conditioning to recycle mode and picked up the phone from its cradle.

David Forrester. No voicemail. The clock on the dashboard showed 8.22. She wasn't late, yet. What did he want?

The cars ahead started trundling forward, their brake lights more on than off. She set off and dialled Forrester, phone on speakerphone, ringing and ringing.

She pulled left, more traffic queuing outside the long row of ancient jute mills, now all redundant and repurposed, opposite the brown and mustard ridges of the three-storey police station.

". . . please leave a message after the tone." The phone beeped.

Vicky held up the phone. "Sir, it's DS Dodds just returning your call. I'll be in soon." Eyes on the road, she fumbled for the red button before tossing the phone onto the passenger seat.

Setting off again, she passed the police station before hanging a left onto West Bell Street, the grand Sheriff Court with its flat doric columns almost outmuscled by the surrounding concrete buildings. She took another left, navigating the twisting back road into the car park at the front.

A blue BMW 1-Series sat in her parking bay, gleaming in the sunshine.

"Not again . . ." She parked in the nearest free space, teeth clamped together. She grabbed her bag and phone as she got out, zapping the lock on her black Fiesta as she stomped across the small car park. She entered the double doors, the Tayside Police lettering above still outlined by the weathering.

The desk sergeant glanced up at her approach, his thick beard patchy in places but covering most of his pink face.

"Morning, Tommy."

"I prefer Sergeant Davies but you know that, don't you?" He ran a hand over his bald head, shaved to the pockmarked skin. "But what a beautiful morning it is."

"Don't try to sweeten me up." Vicky held his gaze as she rummaged in her handbag. "Someone's taken my space again."

Tommy looked away, fingers combing his beard. "Aye, sorry about that. New lad started in your area. DI Forrester said it was okay today."

"Check with me first, Tommy, all right?"

"He said he'd called you. Didn't think you'd mind, what with you being so even-tempered and everything."

Vicky tugged her ID badge over her head before zipping her bag and slipping it over her shoulder. "I'll let it pass today, but tomorrow will be a different matter."

"No bother."

"Cheers, Tommy." Vicky stepped over to the door, using her security card to gain access to the guts of the station. She hurried down the corridor, already bustling with uniformed officers, before slowing to a halt halfway.

Forrester was heading straight for her, his long arms and legs eating up the distance. He stopped in front of her, arms crossed and fingers drumming on his white shirt. He ran a hand through his hair, the colour almost all gone. "Morning, Vicky."

"Morning, sir." Vicky moved aside to let the foot traffic past. "Tommy Davies let someone park in my space again."

Forrester leaned against the wall and nodded. "Aye, sorry about that. I did try calling. I've got that new DS starting this morning. Got to take him through his induction. Pain in the arse how he's starting on a Thursday, but there you go. Bloody holidays and moving up from Glasgow."

"So what's that got to do with me, sir?"

"Means we won't be having the briefing this morning. Got a couple of disappearances passed over from Local Policing. There's one out in Forfar as well but that looks like a waste of time. I need you to look at the one in Invergowrie, though — looks suspicious."

"Some Major Investigation Team we are. A disappearance isn't exactly a major incident."

Forrester laughed as he handed her an incident report. "Can't have murders every day. We can only do what's put in front of us."

"Right, fine." Vicky got out her notebook, folding the sheet and tucking it in. "So, who do I get? Tell me it's Karen Woods."

Forrester tilted his head to the side. "Well, actually, I was thinking young DC Considine needs a bit of coaching."

Vicky bit the inside of her cheek. "I'll eat him alive, sir."

"That's what I'm counting on." Forrester grinned, a row of perfect white teeth interrupted by a sliver of gold at the edge of a molar. "Cocky wee bugger needs brought down a peg or two. Thinks he's God's gift to policing after arresting that taxi driver last month."

"Fine, I'll see what I can do."

Forrester put a hand to her shoulder. "It's what being a sergeant's all about. You're my only leader on the pitch, Vicky, at least until I work out if this new boy's up to scratch."

Chapter Three

DC Stephen Considine turned left off Riverside Avenue, his dark grey Subaru passing through the leafy barrier separating town from motorway. He took a hand off the steering wheel to smooth his red hair over before scratching at his sideburns. He was solid but not particularly tall, maybe five ten. "Is Invergowrie actually in Dundee?"

Vicky looked up from her notebook. "No, it was Perth and Kinross before everything changed last year."

"So why are we getting this?"

"It's our patch now. It's inefficient to have Perth officers come all the way over, isn't it? Besides, Dundee's got an MIT. Perth hasn't."

Considine drove them through Invergowrie, low stone walls and beech hedges lining the dark brown stone cottages and modern council houses of the main road, a couple of church spires rising up in the distance.

"You've still not mentioned how late you were this morning, Stephen. You're just lucky the briefing was cancelled."

"Whatever."

"Don't whatever me."

Considine exhaled as he took a left past one of the churches, a sprawling school opposite. "Sorry. I was working late last night. Thought it'd be okay."

"Did Forrester see it?"

"No."

"Then you weren't in late."

"But I've got the OT form signed by that old desk sergeant guy."

"Doesn't matter. You still need to be in on time. I had to wait almost half an hour for you. I was close to taking DC Kirk with me instead."

"Be my guest."

"DI Forrester requested I take you, Stephen. I'd like to see you explain it to him."

Considine continued down the long road dotted with mismatched houses — low cottages hidden by tall trees opposite two-storey semis. Halfway down, he bumped up onto the pavement and pulled in behind a squad car before killing the engine. "So why did Forrester cancel the briefing, then?"

"He's got a new DS starting today." Vicky looked over at the houses — little squares with tiled pyramids resting on top — trying to spot a number. "He needs to get him up to speed."

Considine tugged at the collar of his dark grey suit. "Don't see why we need another DS. After Ennis went on long-term sick, I thought I'd get at least an Acting gig."

A uniform came out of one of the houses and waved at them.

Vicky arched an eyebrow at Considine. "You really think you're ready for a DS role?"

"You saying I'm not?"

"I'm saying you need to have a serious think about whether you are. An honest one." Vicky got out, leading them to the panda car, the uniformed officer now leaning against it, arms folded. She held up her warrant card. "DS Vicky Dodds. This is DC Stephen Considine."

"PC Stuart Melville." Tall, goateed, hair receding at the temples. His stick-thin arms made him look like he ran a lot, maybe competitively.

"What's happened, then?"

Melville stood up straight. "Boy's wife didn't come home from walking the dogs last night. He's going spare. Got a Family Liaison Officer in with him just now."

Vicky looked at the sheet. "Derek Hay, right?"

"Aye. Wife's called Rachel."

"I've got the incident report." Vicky held up the page before refolding it. "Why did this get bumped to Specialised Crime Division?"

"We were doing okay on our own. Standard MisPer case, you know how it is." Melville retrieved an evidence bag from his pocket, a sheet of paper inside. "Then this note came this morning."

Vicky inspected it. Classic poison pen style — cut-up letters from a newspaper glued to a sheet of paper. *We have your wife. She is safe. Do not worry. Much.* She handed it to Considine. "It's not signed."

"I know that." Melville shrugged. "You think it's important?"

"Maybe." Vicky nibbled at her top lip. "When did it arrive?"

"Found it with their *Courier* this morning. The FLO was just wanting to check the *Garfield*."

Considine frowned. "This was folded up in it?"

Melville shook his head. "Underneath. She got a bit of a shock, I can tell you."

"Have you got the paperboy?"

"Paper *girl*. She's giving a statement down the station."

Vicky frowned. "Is that Longforgan?"

Melville nodded. "Aye. We're Carse of Gowrie out here."

"Have you got a trace put on her mobile phone?"

"Not yet."

Vicky nodded at Considine. "Stephen, could you speak to Jenny Morgan? Tell her it's for me."

Melville held out a Post-It note. "Here's her number."

"Fine." Considine got out his phone and sloped off back to his car, eyes locked on the Post-It.

Vicky waved at the house. "After you."

Melville led inside the house, the grey-harled villa pockmarked with at least two attic conversions, before walking down the hallway, busy with multiple doors and little in the way of wall space, and entering through a door.

The living room had the bitter tang of filter coffee kept on the heat too long, coming from the adjoining kitchen door. A dark wood mirror sat above a tiled fireplace, a gas fire burning away beneath.

A man sat on a settee, clutching a mug, scratching at the stubble on his face. He had beige cargo pants on, a plain green t-shirt covering his pot belly.

A female officer sat on a chair opposite, hat in her lap, blonde hair all mussed up. "These officers are detectives, Derek. They're going to help find Rachel."

Hay didn't look up. "Thanks."

The FLO got to her feet and walked to the front window, nodding at Vicky to take over as she rested her hands against the wide radiator.

Vicky sat on the now-vacant armchair. "I'm DS Dodds. My colleague DC Considine is just outside." She got out her notebook and biro, fixing a stare on Hay — treat him as a suspect for now. "I believe your wife has gone missing, is that correct?"

"It is, aye."

"I appreciate you'll have been through this with my colleagues, but could you go through what's happened for my benefit?"

Hay leaned forward on his seat, the springs underneath creaking as he placed the mug on a wooden coaster on the coffee table. "Rachel was out walking the dogs yesterday afternoon, as usual. She didn't come back."

"Are the dogs okay?"

Hay nodded. "Aye, they ran home. I heard them rattling at the back door, so I let them in." His fingers twitched as he reached for his mug again, wrapping his thick fingers around it. "I was worried someone had kidnapped them."

"Why would that be?"

"Rachel breeds pugs. She was out with the main breeding pair last night and their two sisters. They're prizewinning, worth a lot of money."

Considine entered the room, perching on a recliner next to Vicky. "Where are the dogs now, sir?"

"I put them in the kennel last night." Hay got to his feet. "I can show you, if you'd like?"

Considine nodded. "Thanks."

"This way." Hay took them through the back of the house into a room lined with dark oak bookshelves, a dresser at the back covered in rosettes and trophies. He twisted a key in the French doors and led outside, propping the door with a small gnome, the wind knocking the casing against it.

The long Victorian garden was filled with ten dog kennels, the pugs sitting in the cages staring at them, their faces lined and creased.

Hay pointed to the first two cages, two beige dogs sitting up, heads tilted to the side, eyebrows up in the middle and arching down, their dark muzzles almost pouting. "These are the ones Rach was out with last night. Benji and Jemima. They're her breeding pair." He waved at the next two cages. "That's Lucy and Susie, the other two she was out with."

Standing in the cold air, Vicky couldn't look at them for long. She rubbed at her arms. "Can we go back inside?"

"Sure." Hay gestured for Considine to lead, the gnome toppling over as he shut the door.

Vicky sat on her armchair, the wooden arm clunking as she rested against it, the room feeling a few degrees cooler. "What time did Mrs Hay set out last night?"

"Half four, something like that." Hay glanced at his watch. "The dogs got back about six? Maybe twenty past?"

"Does she usually go on such long walks?"

"Aye, every day. Likes to make sure they get a lot of exercise."

"When did you call the police?"

"Just after half six. I waited a while to see if she'd come back but she didn't."

Vicky noted it down on a timeline. "And you were here at the time?"

"Aye. It was my day off. I work at Downfield golf course. I'm a greenkeeper there."

Vicky turned to a new page in her notebook. "There was a note found with the newspaper this morning. Did you see who delivered it?"

Hay shook his head. "No. I've been on the phone since I woke up this morning, not that I slept much."

"Who were you speaking to?"

"As many people as I could think of. Everyone we know, really." Hay picked up his mug, lifting the coaster with it, and took another drink, grimacing. "Her friends, her parents."

"Has anyone heard from her?"

"No. They all sounded really worried."

"Can you think of anyone who'd want to harm your wife? Any enemies?"

Hay scratched his neck. "Well, there was a couple who bought a dog from Rach that died of PDE."

"What's PDE?"

"Pug Dog Encephalitis, I think. It's like meningitis for dogs. Pugs can be prone to it, hence the name." Hay tugged at the collar of his t-shirt. "We've had a few over the years."

"And what happened to this particular dog?"

"Had to get put down. They were threatening to sue Rach."

"How much did the dog cost them?"

"Over a grand, but they were suing for distress and vet bills and things like that." Hay took another sip, the coaster dropping into his lap. "We settled out of court. Gave them a refund. They seemed happy with that."

"Do you still have their contact details?"

Hay nodded before reaching over for a mobile phone. "Here you go. Guy called Gary Black."

Vicky noted it down before handing the phone to Considine. "Why did you mention them?"

"They got really angry, started threatening Rachel." Hay retrieved his phone, clasping it tight. "She's just trying to make an honest living out of this, you know?"

Vicky smiled at Hay. "We're tracing her mobile number now. It might help."

"Thanks."

"Was there a set route your wife would walk the dogs?"

"Rachel's a creature of habit." Hay stared at the window. "She used to go through the fields out the back, same route every day. She walks to the end of the village then just keeps on going the edge of the fields and the wood by the motorway. She comes home through the James Hutton Institute."

Vicky noted it — would the regularity have allowed for easy capture? "Seems a long route for pugs."

"Need to keep them in shape. She took that breeding pair to Crufts last year. Proudest day of our lives."

"I see." Vicky got to her feet and gestured to the FLO, still standing in the window. "I'll leave you with my colleague here. We've got a few avenues of investigation just now but we may be back for further questions."

"By all means."

Melville led them back out.

Vicky stopped by the gate and squinted at the house. "Did that tally with what you heard earlier?"

Melville shrugged. "Well, you asked a few more things than we did but there were no inconsistencies."

"Okay."

Considine zapped his car with his key fob. "Where next, then?"

Vicky looked down the long street, almost completely silent save for the cars in the distance and the rustle of the trees in the wind. "Let's start with the paper girl. This note seems a bit dodgy. She's probably innocent, but you never know."

"You sure?"

"Not really." Vicky's phone rang. She reached into her bag to get it — an unknown number. "DS Dodds."

"Hey, Vicks, it's Jenny."

"I almost didn't answer because of the unknown number."

"Sorry. It's these new Police Scotland phones. You with a DC Considine? Sounds like he fancies himself."

"Aye."

"Right. He asked me to call you. I traced Rachel's mobile. Got a last location yesterday afternoon at the back of six just before it was switched off."

"Where?"

"Google Maps tells me it's near the James Hutton Institute, just by Invergowrie. Place called the Living Garden."

"Cheers, Jenny." Vicky dumped her phone in her bag and nodded at Considine. "Come on, Stephen, we've got something."

Melville put his hat on. "Want me with you?"

Vicky shook her head. "Stay here. See if you can call around their family again. Keep on top of it. And let me know the outcome of the interview with the paper girl."

Chapter Four

Considine slowed to a crawl as they rumbled over the gravel, passing a large field segregated into multiple areas, looking like different crops in each. A team of twenty or so people were dotted around the various areas. Nearby, two burly men were locked in conversation, arms folded and brows creased.

He pulled into the car park, crunching the handbrake on. "See what you were saying about me having a think about whether I'm ready?"

"I meant you should think about it when you're not driving. Off duty." She undid her buckle. "I'm happy to do some coaching."

Considine let his seatbelt ride up, a smirk on his face. "What makes you think you can coach me?"

"You don't think you need any?"

"I don't. I'm ready for it. I told Ennis I was ready and I'm telling you."

"Stephen, you actually need to *be* ready, not just think it."

"What about catching that taxi driver last month?"

"What about it? You were doing your job. Well done."

"I did that all on my own, though."

"That might be the problem." Vicky got out of the car. She walked through the almost-full car park, a few steps ahead of Considine, heading for the James Hutton Institute, a low-slung set of dark-brown brick buildings. The doors swooshed open as they approached. She stamped her feet on the strips of mat near the door.

The receptionist looked up from a magazine. "Can I help?"

Vicky went over to the desk and flashed her warrant card. "We're investigating a disappearance." She showed her a photo Melville had given them. "Rachel Hay. We believe she was abducted near here. Do you recognise her?"

"Sorry, no."

"You sure?"

The receptionist scowled. "Hang on. Is that the woman whose dogs ran all over the garden?"

Vicky frowned. "Go on?"

"You'll need to speak to Marianne about it. Marianne Smith. She's the curator of the Living Field. It's just back there."

Vicky smiled. "Do we need to sign in?"

"Not if you stay outside, you don't."

"Thanks." Vicky left the building and walked towards the field, back the way they'd come.

A figure knelt at the flower bed nearest them, stabbing a trowel into the earth.

Vicky cleared her throat. "Excuse me."

The woman thrust the trowel into the ground and got to her feet, rubbing her wrist against her temple, eyebrows raised. "Yes?"

"We're looking for a Marianne Smith?"

"That'll be me." Marianne tore off her garden gloves and held out a hand, her skin rough and pale.

Vicky shook it. She was maybe mid-forties, greying hair in a long ponytail snaking down her back. She wore shorts and a vest top — despite it being late March and in Dundee — and there was no sign of a bra.

She looked Vicky up and down. "To whom am I speaking?"

Vicky showed her warrant card. "DS Vicky Dodds and DC Stephen Considine of Police Scotland's Specialised Crime Division."

"How can I help?"

Vicky noticed a few other workers were starting to look over. "What are you working on here?"

"I'm the curator of the Living Garden." Marianne dusted off her hands. "It's the institute's outreach project on biology and environmental science. We grow lots of diverse crops and perform safe experiments."

"Such as?"

"Well, we now know which plants bees like best, for example. Our work's helping farmers in the States repopulate their lost colonies." Marianne chewed on a fingernail, slightly torn down the middle. "How can I help?"

"We're investigating the disappearance of a Rachel Hay. We believe she was walking her dogs near here yesterday."

Marianne frowned. "The name doesn't ring a bell, I'm afraid."

"Used to walk this way every day." Vicky held up the photo. "This is her."

"Nope, sorry."

"Strange." Vicky pointed back to the main building. "The receptionist just told us her pugs ran all over the garden."

Marianne stared at her for a few seconds, jaw clenched. "Ah, yes, I remember her now."

"Did you see her yesterday?"

"I don't recall."

Vicky held her gaze before nodding and looking away. "What happened with her dogs, then?"

Marianne sighed then gestured around the space. "They ruined half of the garden. Those little buggers trampled all over a crop. We'd had seeds flown over from Malaysia. It was crucial to one of our PhD students' projects. Ingrid had to start again from scratch." She shook her head slowly. "Pugs are the most despicable breed of dogs."

"In what way?"

"Oh, nothing to do with them per se, just the breeders. I love dogs but I hate dog breeders."

Vicky got out her notebook and wrote Marianne's name, underlining it twice. "Have you done anything to her?"

Marianne narrowed her eyes. "I wouldn't do anything to harm a living creature."

"Where were you between four and seven p.m. yesterday?"

Marianne folded her arms. "I was at my home. In Fife. I'd been doing a talk at the local high school in the morning."

"And after that?"

"I was reading."

"Can anyone verify this?"

"I'm afraid not. I live alone."

Vicky made a note then handed her a card. "If anything jogs your memory, please don't hesitate to get in touch." She led Considine back towards the car, glancing back at Marianne as they walked. "I wish she'd wear a bra."

"I didn't know where to look."

Vicky took a deep breath as she stopped by the Subaru. "I need more manpower on this. This is too much for just us."

"Agreed. What about the Three Amigos?"

"I'll need to speak to Forrester about it."

Considine's phone rang. "Do you mind?"

"Go for it."

He answered it and walked round to the driver's side of the car.

Vicky looked back at the Living Garden. Was Marianne Smith involved?

Considine ended his call and tossed his phone in the air. "That was Gary Black, the boy who bought that defective dog from Rachel Hay? He can meet us now."

Chapter Five

What sort of name is Perspect?" Finger on the intercom buzzer, Considine shook his head at the brass plate, the purple and lime logo curved almost to the point of illegibility.

"A bad one." Vicky looked down Whitehall Street, lined with old townhouses now turned into city centre shops — a bakery and a camping shop sat either side of Perspect. She pointed across the road. The ground floor was stuffed with a range of bookies, pizza restaurants and Chinese buffets. "I remember when that was all Debenhams."

"Showing your age there."

Cheeky bastard. Vicky nodded towards the office. "You're leading here, okay?"

"Perfect."

The door clicked open. A tall man in a light grey suit beamed out at them, pale skin shaved close. "How can I help?"

"Police." Considine showed his warrant card. "We've got an appointment with a Gary Black."

"Certainly. He's expecting you." The man pointed inside, both hands outstretched. "If you'll just follow me?" He led them inside, the unit small but almost completely filled with offices, everything gleaming in chrome and glass. He indicated to a glass-fronted room. "If you could just wait in here, Mr Black will be along shortly." He gave a tilt of his head then returned to a small reception desk.

Vicky sat in front of the desk, the seat back jerking back. Modern art paintings filled the white walls, splashes of oranges and reds in a series of three large canvases. "Feels like I'm applying for a mortgage all over again."

Considine laughed. "Tell me about it."

Gary Black stormed into the room, clutching a tall beaker of coffee. He shrugged off his suit jacket and put it on the back of his chair, his pink shirt looking box fresh. "Sorry I'm late. Had a client meeting in the Overgate."

Vicky smiled as she got out her notebook. "Thanks for seeing us, Mr Black."

Black collapsed into his seat, breathing hard. He took a long pull at the coffee. "You said on the phone this is about the dog we bought, aye?"

Considine nodded. "What can you tell us about it?"

"My daughter called him Boab. Wee guy just wasn't himself after about six months. He'd have been about a year old by then, so he was pretty much fully grown. We took him to the vet and he reckoned he'd seen it before. Said it was NME, like the music paper."

"NME?"

"Necrotizing meningoencephalitis. It's also known as PDE." Black took great care pronouncing the words. "I've since become something of an expert on the matter, shall we say. He gave us some tablets but it didn't help wee Boab any. After another few months, we had to put the wee guy to sleep. He could only confirm it was this NME after the autopsy."

"And what did you do?"

"I went ballistic. Rocked up at that Hay woman's house and had it out with her. She denied all responsibility. Said the dog must have caught it." Black clenched his fists, pressing down on the wooden desktop. "Can you credit it? NME's hereditary in pugs. She's breeding those dogs far too close. She's got three bitches she breeds from and the boy's the father of two of them. That's just not right."

"Did you do anything else?"

"I'm not a violent man but I swear I came close to swinging for her husband. We'd paid them a grand for that dog. The medication and vet bills came to another grand, even with insurance."

Considine scribbled in his notebook. "What happened next?"

"There was quite a fuss in the paper at the time. There'd been a few other defective dogs over the years, not just ours." Black toyed with his silver fountain pen. "They were pretty difficult about it. We just wanted a refund and our fees reimbursed. In the end, we sued them. Settled out of court." He let out a deep breath. "Got another dog from that animal rescue place on Brown Street, not the council one. God knows what it's crossed between but it's a lovely dog. I gave them the money we got off the Hays."

"Is there any lingering animosity on either side?"

Black gripped the edge of his desk. "My wife and daughter loved wee Boab. Him dying hit them hard. After months of him being in and out of the vet's, I had to tell my wee girl that Boab wasn't coming home. Do you know what that's like?"

"So there was some animosity on your part, then?"

"Aye." Black took another drink of coffee. "They shouldn't breed those animals so closely. It's unnatural."

Considine folded his arms. "We believe Mrs Hay's been abducted."

Black blinked a few times. "Really?"

"Do you know anything about it?"

"No."

"What about your wife and daughter?"

"I'd have to check."

"Can you give us your whereabouts yesterday afternoon?"

"What are you suggesting?"

"We're looking to eliminate you from our inquiries, Mr Black."

Black tapped at his computer. "I was working till eight doing client meetings all across the town. Happy to share my itinerary with you."

"That'd be useful." Considine smiled. "When was the last time you saw Rachel Hay?"

"Not since she handed us the cheque."

Considine gave him a card. "Give me a call if anything else comes to mind, okay?"

Chapter Six

Vicky set off down Whitehall Street towards the bus stops, glancing at Considine as they walked. "Look into Black's background, will you? I want to know if the police were involved. He says it was all over the press. Get copies of the old newspapers and try to find the journalist. And get someone to check out his wife and kid."

Considine let out a deep breath, his lips vibrating. "Is that really all I'm good for?"

Vicky stopped by the car. Give me strength. She locked onto his grey eyes, dark rings surrounding them. "Stephen. I've been over this with you —"

"Look, I'm a wee bit resentful of the fact you're bossing me around here."

"I'm your boss, Constable. I'm the sergeant allocated to this case and you're my DC. Deal with it."

Considine looked up and down the street. "Come on, Vicky. It should be me getting that DS gig, not some new punter from Glasgow or Edinburgh or wherever." He stabbed a finger in his chest. "Me. I know the team, I know the area."

Vicky smiled, trying to disarm him. "Look, DI Forrester asked me to coach you, okay? If the DI's asking that, something needs to be done, okay?"

"What's that supposed to mean?"

"It means you might need to tone it down a bit. Nobody wants to constantly hear about how you need a promotion or highlights of you arresting a taxi driver all on your own or how your daddy never really loved you."

Considine leaned back against the Subaru, breathing hard through his nostrils, jaw twitching. "So you're saying I need to stop going on about it?"

She stared down at the pavement, sucking in the sharp smell of Chinese cooking, a nerve at the back of her neck thudding, then looked back up at him. "Something like that. If you want to become a DS, you need to *show* you're a DS, not *tell* everyone you're a DS. Actions speak louder than words, as they say."

"Okay."

"And start with being a competent DC."

"Are you say —"

She patted his shoulder. "Relax, I'm not saying you're not. I'm just asking you to do your job. Show me you can do it and I'll see what else I'll let you do, okay?"

"Fine."

"And call me 'Sarge', not Vicky."

"Okay, Sarge." Considine unlocked his car. "Where next?"

Vicky got out her mobile. "I'm going to get an update from Melville. Derek Hay's still top of my list of suspects." She leaned against the car and waited for Melville to answer.

"Morning, Sarge."

"Morning. How's it going out there?"

"Sounds like this dog isn't an isolated incident. I've been having a word with him. Reckons there've been a few had this PDE thing. Says it's the cost of having a pug."

"Do you think her husband's had anything to do with her disappearance?"

Melville paused for a few seconds. "All we've got on it seems to have come from him. He swears he's got nothing do with it."

"But?"

"Let's just say I'm thinking of taking him down the station, you know?"

"I do." Vicky watched the shoppers walk the street. "How did it go with the paper girl?"

"Just spoke to Dave, the interviewing officer. Dannii Patterson — that's Dannii with two i's — reckons she just delivered the paper, knows nothing about a note."

"Did he believe her?"

"No reason for her to lie, is there?"

"I suppose not."

"She did see a car, though, a black one. Never seen it before."

"What kind was it?"

"All I got was, and I'll quote, 'Kind of a big thing, y'know? Like on that Mercedes advert on the telly with Tinie Tempah. *We bring the stars out.*'" Mean anything to you, Sarge?"

"Yes, it does." Vicky hated it — some guy getting mic'd up so sound went through a set of lights stuck to his chest, listening to the sort of urban music she couldn't get her head around. "That car's white, though."

"Is it? Well, if it was black."

"Definitely a Mercedes?"

"No, just that it was like it."

"So, a big, black car?"

"Aye."

"Great." Vicky noted it down — something for Considine to check later. "Nothing else from her?"

"Not sure what you were expecting?"

Vicky flicked her notebook shut. "Anything else been happening there?"

"It's maybe nothing but I've been trying to call Rachel's brother in Forfar all morning."

"I thought Derek had tried everyone?"

"Aye, well, she doesn't really speak to her brother." A pause. "His wife finally answered just then. Sounded like shit. Turns out he's not been seen since yesterday either."

Chapter Seven

Considine weaved in and out of traffic as they drove into Forfar, spending more time on the wrong side of the road than the correct one.

Vicky clutched her mobile in her hand, the display still blank. "Slow down."

"It's taken forty minutes to get here. That feels like a failure."

"You're such a boy racer."

Considine pulled up outside the house, parking behind a panda car. "It's just a car."

"I'll remind you of that later." Vicky got out and led up the drive. No sign of uniform other than the empty car. She knocked on the door. "I don't know Forfar too well, but this doesn't look like one of the better parts."

"I live here and it isn't."

"His sister's house in Invergowrie was a lot nicer than this."

The door was opened by a uniformed officer, medium height and slightly overweight, dark sideburns creeping under his jawline. "You pair from the MIT?"

Vicky nodded and got out her warrant card. "DS Dodds, DC Considine. And you are?"

"PC Murray Watson."

Vicky pocketed her card. "We're dealing with his sister's disappearance. What's happened here?"

Watson got out an evidence bag containing a letter. "Kirsty Joyce — that's his wife, by the way — found this."

Vicky checked it — the same style as the other one. *We have your husband. He is safe. Do not worry. Much.* She took a deep breath. "It's a match. Where did she find it?"

"Underneath her paper. *The Sun.*"

"Have you spoken to the paperboy?"

"Aye. Lad swears he didn't do anything. Said he was half asleep and listening to Slayer."

Considine took the note from her. "Thought this case was given to uniform?"

Watson nodded. "It was."

Considine held up the evidence bag. "But there's a letter?"

"Aye, we only just found it, son. Mrs Joyce didn't check the paper until an hour ago. That's why it wasn't flagged for you lot."

"So she called it in last night?"

"Not till this morning, son. Thought he was out on the piss." Watson shook his head. "She's not in a good way."

"I gathered that when I was on the phone to her."

"Come on in, then." Watson led them inside, straight into the living room, a small space crammed with two sofas and lots of furniture, pretty much all lacquered wood. A TV hanging off the wall played a news channel on mute, one of those white-background photos next to it, the whole family in an action pose.

Kirsty Joyce was slumped on the dark green sofa, a wad of paper tissues in her hand, her red face slicked with tears. She wore a grey tracksuit, her cream t-shirt stained brown in the middle.

Vicky sat on the adjacent sofa. "Mrs Joyce, we're looking into your husband's disappearance. I spoke to you on the phone."

"I remember." Kirsty nodded as she dabbed at her eyes. "Will you find him?"

"We certainly hope so." Vicky motioned for Considine to sit next to her. "What can you tell us about your husband?"

"Paul's a good man. A great dad." Kirsty bit her lip.

"But he didn't come home last night. Is that odd?"

"It wouldn't be the first time. He likes a drink does Paul."

"How often does this sort of thing happen?"

"Every few months. Just loses track of time when he hooks up with some strangers. Usually when he's watching the football."

"Is it people from work?"

"Sometimes. Occasionally some Polish boys or other foreigners. He works in a factory, packing tatties. Murison's Prepacks, just off Montrose Road."

"When did you start to get suspicious?"

"Well, I called it in first thing this morning. Just thought I'd be on the safe side. But when I got that letter . . ." Kirsty broke off in tears, springs in the sofa heaving under her bulk as she rocked back and forth.

Vicky waited for her to make eye contact again. "So, you weren't particularly worried when you called it in?"

"Aye. I just wanted to check he wasn't in the cells or hospital."

Vicky noted it down. "Have you noticed anything funny in the street recently?"

"Not that I can think of."

"What about this morning?"

"Nothing. Sorry."

"You haven't seen any strange cars or anything like that?"

Kirsty frowned. "Why do you ask that?"

"Have you seen one?"

"Well . . . First thing this morning, just after I got the kids to school, I saw a car outside."

"What was it like?"

"Black. Quite big, too. Just shot off when I got to the end of the road. It was driving pretty fast."

"What was the make and model?"

"I've no idea. Just saw the colour." Kirsty shook her head. "Why did you ask if I'd seen one?"

Vicky focused on the painting behind her, a washed-out still life of some flowers. "Paul's sister, Rachel, has gone missing."

Kirsty shut her eyes. "I see."

"I take it they weren't close?"

"Not really. They didn't have much to do with each other, not since Rachel moved to Dundee when she was eighteen. Paul says she's getting above herself."

"Was there anyone who might've wanted to harm them or their family?"

Kirsty nibbled at a knuckle, the skin stretching as she gripped it. "Not that I can think of."

"Any family?"

"Their parents died about ten years ago. Their dad worked at Murison's like Paul does. Their mum was a cleaner."

Vicky made a note — it looked like an attack on Rachel rather than her brother. "And there's nobody who'd want to harm Paul?"

"Look, Paul's a model citizen. He keeps himself to himself. He likes a drink but nothing too bad."

Vicky nodded as she got to her feet, business card out. "We'll do everything we can to find him."

Chapter Eight

Vicky walked up to the front desk at Murison's Prepacks, flashing her warrant card at the security guard. "We're looking to speak to the owner or the manager."

"Same person." The guard checked his watch. "Think the gaffer'll be on his break up in the canteen." He thumbed behind him towards a stairway rising up to the giant corrugated iron roof. "Up the stair there, end of the corridor, can't miss it. The name's Michael Murison. Just ask around if you can't find him."

Vicky smiled a thanks before walking down the corridor running along the outside of the building. "That's some security they've got here."

Considine shrugged. "You showed him your warrant card. What else is he going to do?"

Vicky stopped at the entrance to the canteen and looked around. The deserted factory floor was littered with conveyor belts and forklifts, all now static. A couple of men leaned against a van, chatting as they ate. "I worked in something similar in Carnoustie one summer. A lot more basic than this."

"Surprised they've got factories in Car-snooty."

"It's hardly Broughty Ferry." Vicky pushed open the door and entered the busy canteen, the place stinking of frying meat and onions. She headed for the nearest occupied table, where a man was reading a book. "Excuse me, we're looking for Michael Murison."

Without looking up, the man waved behind him. "Two tables back. Boy fiddling with his mobile."

"Thanks." Vicky clocked him immediately. Mid-fifties, red-faced, glaring at his phone and shaking his head. "Mr Murison?"

"Who's asking?" Murison jolted upright when he saw her warrant card. "Christ, who let you in?"

"The security guard."

"I'll need to have words with him." Murison shook his head, before picking up a roll and taking a bite, clear fat dribbling down his chin.

Vicky smiled — mince on a roll. "We're looking for Paul Joyce."

Murison swallowed his mouthful, ran his tongue over his teeth. "Paul's not been in the day."

"We believe he's possibly been abducted."

Murison nudged the plate away, the porcelain screeching against the laminate. "Seriously?"

"Aye."

"Come with me." Murison picked up the plate as he got to his feet, leading them out of the canteen into the room next door. He sat behind the desk, clattering the plate down in front of him. "Have a seat."

Vicky sat on a chair opposite, the plastic cold beneath her, and got out her notebook and pen. "When was the last time you saw Mr Joyce?"

"Yesterday afternoon. Paul got called out on a delivery last thing."

She made a note. "What sort of delivery?"

"Tatties. It's all we do here." Murison fiddled with his computer. "We had an order for three hundred kilos."

"When?"

"Call came in about half four. Paul went out not long after."

Vicky noted it down on her timeline — the area to the left was becoming crowded. "Was there anything strange about the order?"

"Not really."

"Him not coming into work this morning didn't strike you as odd?"

"Seen it all in this game, hen. Thought he'd just pissed off to the boozer last night. Liverpool were on the telly. As I say, he's not been in the day, but that happens with some of our boys, especially when there's football on in a pub."

"Did this happen often with Paul?"

Murison shrugged. "Occasionally."

"Where was this delivery going to?"

"Dundee somewhere. I'll need to check and get back to you." Murison lifted up his keyboard and dropped it, a cloud of dust shooting up. "We're a bit disorganised just now. My PA's just gone on maternity leave and the temp's not exactly hit the ground running. I can't really afford to pay somebody who knows what they're doing."

"When he did this delivery, I assume Paul would've taken one of your vans?"

Murison nodded. "I'm one down. Happens a fair amount. I trust my lads until they start taking the piss. Then I come down on them like a ton of tatties."

"Is Paul well liked here?"

"He is, aye." Murison cackled. "Not all of my boys are, but he's a good lad. Everybody likes him."

"Anyone want to cause him harm?"

"Hardly." Murison stared at the desk. "Gets on with all the lads. Scots, the couple of English boys we've got and all the foreign laddies."

"You said he's a drinker?"

"Aye. Few pints of lager a couple of nights a week. Occasionally, he'll go off on one. That's it. Boy isn't a fighter if that's what you're getting at."

"Does he gamble?"

"Not that I know."

"Fine. Please get in touch with DC Considine when your memory's jogged."

Considine handed him a business card. "Any time, day or night."

"That right, son?" Murison laughed as he reached for the plate. "We done here?"

Vicky got to her feet. "We will return if we don't hear from you."

"First thing after my roll, I swear."

Vicky led them back out of the office. "I haven't had a mince roll in years."

"A mince roll?" Considine scowled. "That's just rank."

"My granny used to make them. Fry some mince, shove it on a roll with butter. Perfect."

"Surprised you've made it to forty."

Vicky stopped at the top of the stairs, hands on hips. "I'm thirty-five."

Chapter Nine

I'll need to drop these off in the lab." Considine held up the notes, the evidence bags flapping in the wind.

"See you up there." Vicky scowled at the blue 1-Series squatting in her space again, then marched across the car park, entering the building and parting ways with Considine.

Sergeant Davies was dealing with an elderly couple as they stabbed fingers at him. "You need to have a word with him, sonny!"

She swiped through the security door and dodged her way along the corridor, busy with uniform coming back from their lunch breaks. She climbed the stairs at the end, the metal resonating with each step, then swiped through to their office space, Forrester's office and ten desks overlooking the car park. The place was almost empty, the usual smell of body odour replaced by print toner and damp.

Vicky stopped by her desk, hand on hip. A blue overcoat was folded on her chair. A navy leather document pouch embossed with *EMac* lay on the desk. She looked across the room. The door to Forrester's office was shut, the lights off.

She leaned across the desk and waved her hand in front of Karen's face. "Seen Forrester?"

"Not for ages." Karen took her earphones out and sighed. She stretched out, her green blouse riding up her slight belly, and tugged her brown hair back into a ponytail, tying it with a scrunchie. "He's had that new DS in his office all morning. They've gone for a meeting with the big knobs, I think."

"DCI Raven?"

"Think so." Karen rested the headphones on the desk, the plastic tapping on the wood as it settled. "You had lunch yet, Vicks?"

"Not yet. You?"

"Nope. I'm starving." Karen grabbed her jacket while Vicky retrieved her purse, checking she still had some money. "Been out in Forfar, haven't you?"

"Think my wild goose chase now has two geese."

"We've got a briefing at two."

"Have we?"

"It's called email. You could check yours once in a while."

"I've been chasing wild geese."

Karen walked towards the stairs. "Shall we just go to the canteen?"

"Why not?" Vicky started up the steps, sniffing at something spicy in the air. "Hope they've got mince rolls on today."

"*Mince rolls?*"

"Long story. It's a Dundee thing. A Fifer like you wouldn't get it."

Vicky entered the canteen, picking up a couple of tubs from the fridge — cheese and coleslaw — and a bottle of Diet Coke before joining Karen at the end of the queue. "Baked tattie today, I think."

"As ever."

Vicky shrugged. "I know what I like."

"And you like what you know." Karen smiled at the server. "Chicken curry, thanks."

"Baked potato, cheers." Vicky put her tubs down, a torn fiver next to them. "I'm not a big fan of curries. Too spicy. I only like proper British food."

Karen shook her head.

"Well, it's true." Vicky collected her change, juggling the tubs and bottle with the polystyrene container. She looked around, spotting a table in the window. "There!" She marched off, securing the table overlooking the car park and the steady steam of traffic on the Marketgait, the mill behind it blocking out the skyline.

Karen dumped her tray and started stirring her curry and rice together, her plastic fork bending. "It's Cameron's birthday party a week on Saturday. Can't believe he'll be five. Are you definitely coming?"

"I'll be there. I'm sure he'd love to see his Auntie Vicky."

"The joys of being single. You can just decide like that." Karen clicked her finger and laughed.

Vicky opened the container and tipped in the cheese before shutting the lid again. "It has its downsides, believe me."

"You're not thinking of getting back on the scene again, are you?"

Vicky used her fork to stir the coleslaw in the pot, the mayonnaise sticking to the side. "I can't be arsed, Kaz. I really can't."

"Fair enough."

Vicky lifted the lid and started mashing the potato and cheese together. "Forrester's stuck me with Considine."

"The boy's an idiot."

"Tell me about it." Vicky tipped the coleslaw onto the potato, steam wafting up from it. "I don't know what Ennis was telling him but he thinks he's the big man just now. Driving his Subaru around and solving taxi murders. Reckons he should be a DS."

"Unreal." Karen took a mouthful of curry. "So what did Forrester say about him?"

"Coach him. Go hard on him."

"And have you?"

"Of course."

"You're a pussycat, really."

"Like hell I am." Vicky rubbed a thumb across her neck, the vein throbbing again. "To tell you the truth, he's doing my head in already. Promotion this, promotion that." She let out a sigh, the vein losing a few BPM in tempo. "I just don't find this sort of thing easy. It's the one bit of the job I hate. I'm okay dealing with most of the shit we get but having to be hard on him like that . . . It's not in my nature."

"You sure?"

"I don't know. I don't need the stress and the confrontation really wears me down. He's one of these people that just rubs me up the wrong way. I had to tell him to call me 'Sarge'. What sort of person does that?"

"Someone dealing with an arrogant wee laddie?"

"Maybe." Vicky mashed the potato, her fork clicking off the plate. "It'll be interesting to see how much he sucks up to Forrester at the briefing today."

"He'll be right in there, guaranteed."

Vicky opened her Diet Coke and took a drink. "He's not an idiot. He just needs a bit of shaping."

Karen turned her head to the side, her eyebrows pulled down. "You don't fancy him, do you?"

Vicky wagged a finger in the air. "No, and that's the last time the topic will be mentioned." She chuckled. "He thought I was *forty*."

"Cheeky bastard."

"Exactly." Vicky took another mouthful of potato, almost down to the charred skin. She spotted Forrester at the far end of the room, tucking his tie over his shoulder as he sat down, and she leaned over the table. "Who's that with Forrester?"

Karen squinted. "That's the new DS. MacDonald, I think."

Vicky checked him out — tall and athletic with a broad grin on his face, his hair gelled to the side, a small tuft sprouting up mid-parting. Black suit, blue tie, white shirt. "Bit of an improvement on old Ennis."

"Aye." Karen put her fork down on the half-empty plate. "Tell me you've not fallen for him already?"

"Hardly." Blushing, Vicky finished her potato skin and set her cutlery down. "You done?"

"Aye."

"Need to get back and see what Considine's been up to." Vicky got up and crossed the canteen, carrying her tray in front of her, the wood digging into her stomach, pulling her blouse tight.

Forrester patted her on the arm when he saw her. "DS Dodds, good to see you."

"Been trying to call you since we finished in Forfar, sir."

"Right, sorry. I've been busy." Forrester gestured across the table. "This is DS Euan MacDonald."

MacDonald grinned as he flattened down his hair. "David's told me a lot about you."

Vicky raised an eyebrow. "All good, I hope."

"No comment." MacDonald laughed as he held out his hand. "Please, call me Mac."

Vicky took the weight of the tray in her left hand and shook his. "Pleasure to meet you."

"We'll be a minute, Vicky." Forrester's smile was polite at best, eyes gesturing to the door. "Go prepare yourself for the briefing."

"Will do, sir." Vicky waved at MacDonald before catching up with Karen as she dumped her tray. "MacDonald's even better up close."

"He looks well dodgy, Vicks." Karen shook her head. "Wouldn't trust him an inch."

"You know I like a bad boy."

"I seriously don't get that. Besides, what sort of person gives themselves a nickname?"

Chapter Ten

D I Forrester stood by the window running the full width of their office space, the early afternoon sun almost silhouetting him from behind. "Apologies for not having a briefing this morning but we've got a new officer joining the team. DS Euan MacDonald. Mac, go on, introduce yourself."

"Afternoon. Very pleased to be joining MIT North." Standing next to Forrester, MacDonald beamed at Vicky then at the six DCs spread around the whiteboard. "Been working in the Glasgow North Major Investigation Team for the last year since the change-over. Before that, I was in Strathclyde CID. Actually started my career in Tayside Police. Four years on the beat in Dundee and Arbroath before moving south." He peered at each of the officers. "Don't think I know any of you lot, though."

Forrester patted him on the back. "Mac brings in a wealth of experience we simply don't have in either this team or DI Greig's. You'll know we've been seriously shorthanded of late, relying on DS Dodds' solid work covering two roles while DS Ennis has been off ill. It's doubtful he'll be back any time soon and DCI Raven gave me the go-ahead to increase my headcount. We'll obviously review the situation in six months but for now it feels good to be back up to two sergeants."

MacDonald grinned. "Feels good to be here."

"That's your fun over, Mac. You understand that, right?"

MacDonald laughed, maybe a little too hard.

Forrester tapped the whiteboard. "Now, on with the proper briefing. First, there's still nothing on the Airwave scanner believed to be in Dundee."

"What's that, sir?" MacDonald was frowning.

"Our Airwaves may have been compromised. We've received intelligence pointing to some criminals potentially having access to a scanner that can hack into the Tetra network."

"But it's nothing without the access codes?"

"Who says they don't have them?" Forrester's grin faded as he looked around the room. "Be very careful what information you put out there, okay? Mobile phones are our primary mode of communication now." He stared at the floor. "We're trying to bring the old team back in. Looks like we'll need to reconfigure our entire network from the handsets up."

Vicky raised a hand. "And meanwhile someone's listening in to our radios?"

"We don't know that." Forrester held out his hands. "We've got suspicions but nothing concrete."

"The Tetra system was supposed to be totally secure but we found out pretty quickly that it's not necessarily the case. Ways and means, usually backhanders." MacDonald cleared his throat, hands flicking up briefly. "Worked on the team installing the Airwaves in Strathclyde back in the day. Specialist subject, so apologies if I bore you."

"Let's keep that to ourselves, Sergeant. Don't want to lose you to that team already."

MacDonald zipped his lips shut.

"Right, moving on." Forrester looked at the whiteboard next to him. "The caseload from last night. Had a rape in Tannadice, near Forfar, an assault in Menzieshill and one on Dens Road. There were three muggings in the town centre and a burglary in Broughty Ferry. I've allocated the burglary to DS MacDonald but everything else has been bounced back to Local Policing's CID team or uniform." Forrester shifted his gaze to Vicky. "Do you want to give us an update on your cases?"

Vicky put on her deep voice, trying to add gravitas. "Well, it's actually two cases but they might be connected. Rachel Hay and Paul Joyce were both abducted yesterday evening. Brother and sister. Rachel was walking her dogs in Invergowrie and didn't return home. Her dogs are all fine. Paul, however, was on a delivery run to Dundee."

Forrester frowned. "Do we know where?"

Considine shook his head. "Still waiting on confirmation, sir."

"Be a pain about it if you don't hear back soon, okay?"

"Will do, sir."

Vicky held up a photocopy of the note from Forfar. "Anyway, their spouses received notes like this one. *We have your husband. He is safe. Do not worry. Much.* They're undergoing forensic analysis in the lab just now."

Considine held up a copy of the other one. "Should be back tomorrow."

Forrester made some notes on the board. "Good work."

"It appears she sold a dog with a congenital disease. The story was all over the papers." Vicky eyed Considine. "Did you look into the journalist who broke the story?"

"I did, Sarge. Story all checks out." Considine showed her a page of newsprint. "I've got the original article. Not sure what else we can do."

"Leave it for now." Vicky walked up to the whiteboard and started writing. "We've got an active trace on Rachel's mobile and we're in the process of tracing Paul's personal and work phones."

MacDonald joined them at the board. "Anyone seen anything in the vicinity?"

Vicky tapped at her scribbles. "We've got sightings of a black car at both addresses when the letters might've been delivered."

Considine held up a sheet of paper with a car on it. "The paper girl in Invergowrie reckons it's a Mercedes E63 AMG."

Vicky wagged a finger. "She said it was *like* a car in an advert. She didn't say it was that specific model. We need to get her to identify which car it actually was."

Forrester pinned the photo of the car to the board. "Any suspects?"

Vicky checked her notebook. "I've got three so far. First, there's her husband, Derek Hay."

"Any reason why?"

"Nothing in particular. Just covering all bases." Vicky shrugged. "Second, Marianne Smith. She works at a garden at the James Hutton Institute near where Rachel walks her dogs. Apparently, the dogs trashed part of the garden a while back, causing a whole load of rework. Third, Gary Black. He bought a defective dog from Rachel. The poor thing died within a year and they sued her. Settled out of court."

Forrester gazed at Considine. "Anyone else from you?"

"No, sir. Sorry."

MacDonald rubbed his chin. "Anyone taken credit for this?"

"No."

"Ransom demands?"

"None. Just the notes, which are fairly abstract."

Forrester took a step back and reviewed the board. "So, next steps?"

"We need street teams in Invergowrie and Forfar." Vicky scribbled them on the whiteboard. "See if anyone saw the driver of this car, assuming that's how it happened. Additionally, we should look at when they were abducted. If the cars were there, we may be able to use CCTV to get plates or a better description than 'it was like one on an advert'. We should get the street teams armed with the possible photos of the car."

"Sounds good. Anything else?"

Vicky put a hand on her hip. "Do you think we should go public with it?"

"Not sure." Forrester narrowed his eyes. "I'm not against it, per se, but I'll have to speak to DCI Raven about it."

Vicky let her hand drop. She didn't agree but wasn't going to say so in a briefing. "Okay, so actions, sir?"

Forrester joined her at the board and drew a box for *Actions*. "Mac, that burglary is pretty much on pause just now, right?"

"Waiting on uniform to get back to us, sir."

"Fine. You're managing the street teams. You've got Woods, Kirk and Summers plus any uniform you can rustle up. Vicky, can you get the photofit sorted and get the suspects in a room?"

"Will do."

"Considine, can you get back out to Murison's and check out this order of tatties? Who placed it, phone number, all that jazz?"

"Sure thing, sir."

"Right. Dismissed."

Vicky leaned against the window sill, lost in thought as the officers broke off and returned to their desks.

"Penny for them." MacDonald stood there, hands in pockets, eyebrow raised.

She got to her feet, smoothing down her black skirt. "Just trying to process everything, that's all."

"Looks tough, this. Hard to tell which way's up. Weird how nobody's taking credit for it, though."

"Agreed."

"Sorry I've not introduced myself yet. Got time for a coffee?"

"Definitely." Vicky felt the nerve twanging again. "Not today, though. Sorry."

"Sure, sure. Forrester's shoved me right into the thick of things."

"Better that than being bored, right?"

"Absolutely."

"Catch you later." Vicky went back to her desk, face flushed. Diet Coke time.

Considine wheeled his chair over. "You'll love this, Sarge. Your mate Jenny Morgan's just got back to me."

"What is it?"

"She's found Paul's phone."

Chapter Eleven

H ere." Karen pointed across the road, slicing through the Dryburgh Industrial Estate, a variety of units either side.

Vicky pulled in at the end of a line of four cars.

MacDonald and Forrester stood by a burger van, Mac handing some money over.

Vicky got out. "Doesn't look obvious, does it?"

Karen darted around, still clutching her mobile. "Agreed."

Vicky headed over. The van had a decent view of the units across the road. "Sir."

Forrester was squinting at the building. "Which one is it again?"

Karen pointed down the street. "That blue one. Number seventeen."

A warehouse, reasonably narrow but taller than most others on the estate, save the Jewson round the corner, and surrounded by a heavy-duty fence, currently padlocked shut.

Forrester thumbed behind them. "Got some bolt-cutters on the way."

Vicky frowned. "You've got approval for entry?"

"Aye. Raven gave us the all-clear. Warrant's been agreed." Forrester frowned at Karen. "Is his phone still on?"

Karen checked her mobile. "It is. I'm monitoring the tracker web page on my phone now. It's not moved in the last hour since it was switched on."

MacDonald handed Forrester a coffee cup from the burger van. "How do you want to play this, sir?"

"Okay." Forrester took a slurp of coffee, the breeze rippling the surface. "We've got no idea what's in there. I want grid searches done on each floor. MacDonald, you take ground. Vicky, you take the first."

MacDonald tore the lid off his coffee. "We should be armed, sir."

Forrester took a sip of coffee, screwing up his face. "Got an Armed Response Unit on standby but I don't want to use it until we know we need to."

A meat wagon ploughed along the road, stopping just outside the building, officers piling out, all in full riot gear.

Forrester replaced the lid and dumped his coffee on top of a bin before leading them across the road, the padlock already being cut open. "Vicky, you take DC Woods and four of the uniform upstairs. Mac, you're with me, we'll get downstairs secured. I want two officers guarding the exits and the van's engine on continually." He surveyed the group, splitting them in three with chops of his hand — four, four, two. "Let's go."

The officer with the bolt-cutters ran up to the front door, the padlock taking longer to open than the one on the gate. It snapped open and another officer pushed inside, holding the door open for the rest of them.

Forrester pointed at them in turn. "You pair stay here, okay?"

Vicky followed him inside, her team close behind. The floor was open, with rows of ceiling-height shelves now sitting empty, some forklifts left in the middle of the aisles. She made for a set of stairs to the left, waving her team to follow. As she climbed, she mentally divided the floor into six based on the layout of the ground floor. One each.

Stopping at the top of the stairs, she signalled for her team to wait and stay quiet.

The only sound was a tap dripping somewhere to the right. The place looked empty but it was hard to tell — there was a different layout up here. A series of corridors twisting around, the windows in a side-on wall showing an office or storage room behind, another revealing just more corridor.

Her plan was shot. Vicky gestured to the team, she and Karen forming one group and the other four officers making two pairs. "Split up. Take a third of the floor per group. Meet back here in ten minutes on my mark. Now." She glanced at Karen. "Come on."

"I'm coming."

Vicky led down the corridor, the windowless grey wall looking like it went right to the back of the building. As they crept forward, a clanking sound joined the dripping tap. She leaned over to Karen and whispered. "What's that?"

"Dunno. A broken radiator, maybe?"

Vicky made for the sound, coming to another wall, six big windows roughly cut into the plasterwork. A large room sat behind, filled with crates and shelves. "It's coming from through there."

Karen tugged at her sleeve. "Can you smell that?"

Vicky sniffed — nothing. Wait, something sweet and tangy. "What is that?"

"I think it's shit."

"Let's split up." As Karen headed left, Vicky took the right, opening a door and inching forward into the room, the rattling sound getting louder and more insistent with each step. Seemed to be coming from a cage at the back of the room. She almost gagged at the stench. Excrement mixed with ammonia. Urine?

She ran for it, hand clasped over her mouth and nostrils, stopping dead when she saw what was inside — two people lay naked, legs and torsos smeared brown, the base of the cage wet and filthy underneath them. A man and a woman. She couldn't tell if it was Paul and Rachel.

The man was doing most of the rocking, pushing against the bars with the filthy soles of his feet, face contorted with the effort, getting increasingly agitated. His mouth was taped up but sound came out. "Mmmf!"

Karen appeared and started tugging at the cage. "Oh my God."

Vicky searched the front of the cage for a catch, a keyhole, anything. "I can't see a way in." She circled around the sides for a way in, the metal almost lifting off the ground as the man rocked it harder.

At the back, she froze. "Shit, shit, shit." There was a note pinned to the cage at the far side.

See? They're fine. Not so nice, though, is it?

Chapter Twelve

Vicky stood in the corridor of Ninewells hospital, drinking from a can of Diet Coke. She sucked in the nothing smell of the drink and the stench of the cleaning fluid in the hospital, trying to get rid of the reek from the cage. She could still smell shit.

Karen appeared from Rachel's room, tugging at her hair. "The doctor's still in with them."

"How are they?"

"Not good." Karen leaned against the wall beside Vicky. "She thinks Paul's injured himself with all that rocking."

Vicky took a long drink. "Figures. Took ages for the fire engine to get there."

Karen walked over to the vending machine and put coins in. "Dr Rankine said she was going to come speak to you when she was finished."

"Right." Vicky shook her head. "I can't believe this. It's barbaric."

"Tell me about it." Karen knelt down to collect her can. "Reckon they'll go public with this?"

"Just a case of when."

A small doctor came out into the corridor and took a deep breath, eyes eventually settling on Vicky. "DS Dodds?"

Vicky nodded. "Yes."

"Dr Alison Rankine." She offered a hand.

Vicky shook it, looking down at her. "Call me Vicky."

She looked late thirties and was barely five foot tall, and most of that seemed to be hair, a wild, dark brown frizz creeping down her back. "I've never seen anything like this."

"Even in Dundee?"

"Even in Dundee."

Vicky smiled. "How are they doing?"

"Well, I'll start with Rachel. The good news is there aren't physical injuries, certainly nothing serious. Paul, on the other hand . . . Well. He's been throwing himself against that cage as much as possible, not that it's done them any good. He's got a sprain in his ankle and some bruising on his shoulder."

"And the bad news?"

"Well, they're just not in a good way."

Vicky finished her can. "Can we speak to her yet?"

Rankine nodded. "I'll clear Rachel to speak to you."

"What about Paul?"

Rankine looked away. "He's still not speaking, I'm afraid. I'm not sure if he's suffered a brain injury or what." She brushed her thick hair away from her eyes and stared at Karen's can. "He's just not talking to us or anyone."

"Thanks." Vicky took a deep breath. "Let's speak to Rachel then." She entered the room, the third-floor window looking into the garden in the middle of the building, and sat on the seat by the bed. "Mrs Hay?"

Rachel didn't speak, her eyes moist with tears.

"My name's DS Vicky Dodds of Police Scotland. DC Woods and I are investigating what's happened to you. Can you understand me?"

Rachel nodded, fingers screwing a tissue tight. "Are my dogs okay?"

"They're fine. They ran back home last night. Your husband's got them."

Rachel adjusted her position on the bed, the frame crunching as she moved. "Where's Derek?"

"Your husband's being brought in just now. You'll get to see him soon."

"How's Paul?"

"He's not doing so well, I'm afraid. He's either unable to speak or is refusing to."

Rachel closed her eyes. "Oh."

"Mrs Hay, we want to catch whoever did this to you. Do you know who abducted you?"

Rachel shook her head.

"Did you see them?"

"No. They wore masks." Rachel clicked her fingers, trying to find the words. "Balaclavas."

"Did you hear their voices?"

Rachel nodded. "They'd done something to them, though. The voices were deep, like when the IRA spoke on the news years ago."

Vicky noted it. "Tell us what you remember when you were abducted?"

Rachel took a few seconds to compose herself. "I was walking my dogs just outside of Invergowrie, just past the Hutton Institute, when I was grabbed from behind. I dropped their leads and the dogs ran off." A tear slid down her cheek. "I thought that was the last time I'd see my babies."

"How did they abduct you?"

Rachel turned her head to the side and looked out of the window, her jigging leg making the bed rattle. "I remember hearing a car approach. I thought nothing of it — it's a fairly busy route. There was a noise and they blindfolded me. I didn't know where we were taken."

"Were you there before Paul?"

"He was already there. They forced us to strip then locked us in the cage. They welded it shut. I thought we'd die in there. Paul started kicking at it."

"When did you last see your abductors?"

"I lost track of time. They left us maybe a couple of hours ago. I kept thinking we were going to die."

"It's okay. You're safe now." Vicky gave her a fake smile. "Do you have any idea why anyone would want to do this to you?"

Rachel rubbed a tear from her cheek. "None whatsoever."

"What about the dogs you sold with PDE?"

Rachel's eyes widened as her hands tightened on the tissue. "The Blacks wouldn't do this to us, would they?"

"You sure about that?"

"We settled everything. It was all amicable at the end."

"Anybody else spring to mind?"

Rachel shook her head. "I kept thinking it was Paul they were after. He lives out in the countryside. They do this sort of thing out there, don't they?"

"I'm not so sure. This feels fairly well organised. I wouldn't assume it's some country boys having fun."

"That's the only conclusion I can draw from this." Rachel shrugged. "I'm sorry."

"What happened to you in the cage?"

"I don't want to talk about it."

"We need to know everything if we're to catch who did this to you."

Rachel sat staring at her hands, silent. The door opened. Derek Hay ran in and held his wife close.

Vicky nodded at him then backed out of the room.

Chapter Thirteen

Vicky stood by the drinks machine. Another can of Diet Coke would wash the taste away. She took a long swig and headed back to where Forrester and MacDonald stood talking to Dr Rankine.

Forrester spotted her and let the doctor go, pacing over. "Hell of a business, this. There are some sick people out there."

Vicky tightened her grip on the can, denting the cold aluminium. "Did we get anything on the call made to Murison's that sent Paul out there?"

MacDonald got out his notebook. "Considine's up there just now chasing this Murison guy. Reckons the call specifically asked for Paul."

Vicky furrowed her brow. "That makes sense. They've targeted him."

"Absolutely. Sent to the address we found them at, as well." MacDonald inspected a page. "Murison reckons the order was placed by someone with an Angus accent, Arbroath or Forfar maybe. Nondescript. Definitely male, could be twenties or early thirties."

"Was the delivery to a company?"

"Need to check with him."

"What about his wife?"

"Still in Forfar." MacDonald patted down his hair. "Family Liaison reckons she's not in a good way. Relieved, though."

Forrester folded his arms. "So we're pretty much nowhere?"

MacDonald put his notebook away. "Maybe. Considine's getting the phone logs from the company to see if we can get a number."

Dr Rankine stormed out of the nurses' station and headed straight for them, clutching a sheet of paper, waving it in front of them. "We found traces of GHB in Paul's blood test."

"The date rape drug?"

Rankine nodded. "And Sildenafil citrate. Viagra."

"Christ." Vicky's skin tingled, her mouth now bone dry. "Were they trying to get them to have sex?"

"Not for me to say. I could only tell you if it succeeded. She didn't consent to a rape kit on the grounds she hadn't knowingly been raped."

MacDonald narrowed his eyes. "Mind if I speak to her?"

"I've not got a problem with that."

"Need to get the husband out of there, of course."

"I'll see what I can do."

Vicky folded her arms and looked at each of them. "Has anyone got any objections to me trying to get something out of him?"

Rankine shrugged. "By all means. We'll need to monitor his condition, though. If he becomes agitated again, he'll need to be sedated."

Vicky raised her eyebrows at Forrester. "Sir?"

"Go for it."

Chapter Fourteen

Paul Joyce lay in his bed, absolutely still, eyes fixed on a single point on the ceiling.

Vicky glanced at Rankine. "Has he been like this since he got here?"

She nodded. "The nurses cleaned him up, which took a bit of effort. He didn't move when they were doing it."

"He didn't move at all?"

"Not an inch."

"What's wrong with him?"

"Well, he's displaying symptoms similar to catatonia. I don't think that's what he's suffering from. I'm concerned it's a brain injury — he could've head-butted the cage, for instance."

Vicky sat in the seat next to him. "Mr Joyce, my name's DS Vicky Dodds. I'm investigating what happened to you and your sister. I want to help, but I'll need your co-operation."

No reaction.

"Paul, you were abducted, weren't you?"

Nothing.

"Someone kidnapped you."

No response.

"Whoever kidnapped you took your sister, as well."

A brief flicker of the eyelids.

Vicky leaned forward, the chair tipping up at the back. "Paul, what did they do to you?"

No reaction.

"Paul, did they try to make you do something?"

Moisture formed in his eyes. "My *sister*."

"What happened?"

Paul's eyes shot up to Vicky's. He didn't speak.

"You need to tell us, Mr Joyce."

He swallowed. "My *sister*." Blinking, he flared his nostrils and clenched his teeth. Swallowed again. "My *sister*."

"We want to catch the people who did this to you. Can you help us?"

Paul opened his cracked lips again and spoke in a whisper. "They tried to force us to do it."

"Do what?"

A tear slid down the side of Paul's face, hitting his ear.

"What did they do to you?"

"They had a thing that gave out electric shocks. Like a cattle prod. They kept zapping me." Paul bucked with sobs, his raised knees forming a tent with the blankets.

Rankine took a step forward, her brow creased.

Vicky held out a hand to pause her. "What did they make you do?"

Paul's breathing quickened. "They tried to make us have sex."

"Did they succeed?"

"Of course not." The bed made a grinding noise as Paul sat up, clasping his fists around his knees. "She's my *sister*. They kept prodding that thing into me, like I was a cow or a sheep or something." He slammed a fist on the bed. "I thought they were going to kill us."

"Do you have any idea why this happened?"

Paul shook his head, eyes locked shut.

"Sometimes people who do these things pick the most trivial of reasons. Can you think about it for me?"

He laughed. The sound was cold and devoid of humour. "Believe me, I've thought about it. I've done nothing else." He let out a deep breath. "I don't have any enemies. I don't follow Scottish football, I'm not religious, I'm not gay, I'm not black, I'm not Polish, I'm not racist. I've no idea why anyone would attack me like this."

"Could they have been targeting Rachel?"

"That's the only conclusion I can come to."

"What happened when you were attacked?"

"I got called out on a delivery. Mr Murison told me to do it."

"Dryburgh Industrial Estate?"

"Aye."

"Have you been there before?"

"Once, to get some wood from Jewson when I was doing our attic a few years back, but never to drop tatties off." Paul pointed to his bandaged head. "See this? They knocked me out. They got me from behind."

Rankine adjusted her coat. "His injuries are certainly consistent with a blunt trauma to the head."

"When I woke up, I was in an empty room. Not long after, they brought Rachel in and put us in that cage."

Vicky stared at the floor. "Did you see anything when you woke up?"

"Just Rach and the cage. Nothing else. It was dark and the light kept shining at us."

"A light?"

"I think it was from a camera." Paul shut his eyes, stomped a foot on the bed. "I think they were filming us."

Vicky swallowed, the metallic taste of Diet Coke still in her mouth. "What did you see of your attackers?"

"Nothing. They wore balaclavas and they did that thing with their voices like in that *Arrow* show on Sky, made them all deep and that."

"You say *they*?"

"Aye, there were two of them."

"Male or female?"

"Definitely one male." Paul rubbed his nose. "I've no idea about the other one. Didn't really see them."

Chapter Fifteen

Forrester leaned against the whiteboard, yawning as he rolled up his sleeves. "Let's summarise where we've got to, okay?"

Vicky looked at the other officers. Considine, Karen and MacDonald didn't say anything.

Forrester tapped at the large-scale map, circling the Hutton Institute with a finger. "Rachel Hay was abducted near her home in Invergowrie." His finger switched to Forfar. "Paul Joyce was called out on a delivery to Dryburgh Industrial Estate in Dundee." He moved down to the north side of the city. "He was attacked here. Next thing we know, Paul's mobile gets switched on and by the time we get there, whoever switched it on has pissed off." He scratched the back of his head. "I need some inspiration here."

MacDonald got to his feet, the chair rattling backwards. "This is meticulously planned."

"Go on."

"They knew precisely when and where to abduct them. Knew Rachel's walking pattern. You'd need to monitor her over a few weeks to assess whether she'd follow the same route every day. Quick, too — they jumped Rachel an hour after they got Paul."

"Seems a bit risky."

"Absolutely." MacDonald nodded. "DC Considine investigated the order — looks like it could be a lure. Agreed?"

"Aye, Murison's stock system wasn't the best, shall we say." Considine inspected his notebook. "The order was from a new company on their system. Wasn't properly set up, just had a mobile number and the address of the unit at the Dryburgh Industrial Estate. I've dug into it a bit more. Looks very much like it's a bogus company."

"It's the fact they asked for Paul by name . . ." Forrester folded his arms. "Did you get anything on the mobile, Stephen?"

"It's a burner, sir. Sorry. Pay-as-you-go."

"Right." Forrester rubbed it out on the whiteboard before looking at MacDonald. "Has anything come back from the street teams going round the industrial estate?"

"Got a sighting of the black car, sir."

Vicky joined them at the whiteboard. "Did you get a make or a model?"

"Guy reckoned it was a Lexus or a Merc."

Forrester underlined *Black Car* on the board before prodding it with the pen. "We need to find this car. Considine, have you finished with the CCTV yet?"

"Aye, sir. There's a camera by the building. Just shows Paul going up to the gate. The field of view didn't cover the entrance. Boy didn't come back out. His van was unlocked when we searched it."

"Who owns the building?"

Considine flipped back a few pages. "Karen Woods has got a request out with the letting agent, but it'll be tomorrow before we hear anything concrete from them. Doubt it'll get us anywhere."

Vicky frowned. "You think they were squatting?"

"I have my suspicions, aye."

Vicky nodded — decent effort for once. "Good work, Stephen."

Considine shrugged. "Cheers, Sarge."

Forrester looked at Vicky. "What happened in this industrial unit?"

Vicky rubbed her hands together, still feeling dirty from the interviews. "It looks like they were held in a cage. It was welded shut and we had to get the fire service to open it. They didn't see anything of their captors. It appears they were attempting to force them to have intercourse. Dr Rankine just called me — Rachel definitely hasn't been raped, so it looks like they were unsuccessful."

"Small mercy." Forrester shut his eyes briefly. "Where are we with any suspects?"

Vicky checked the *Suspects* area of the whiteboard, not touched since they'd discovered Paul's mobile. "I had three earlier. I still want to speak to Rachel's husband again. The curator of the Living Garden is looking less likely, I'd say. As it stands, the man who bought a dog from her, Gary Black, he's probably the likeliest." She smiled at Considine. "Don't suppose you managed to look into that any further in amongst your whirlwind of activity this afternoon?"

"I did, actually. Turns out some uniform guys investigated it after the dog was put down. Black called them out. They couldn't find a crime, so they handed it to Trading Standards and the SSPCA. Neither progressed it past warning Rachel on her future behaviour."

Forrester rubbed his forehead. "So you're saying she's been breeding and selling dodgy dogs and she's still allowed to do it?"

"Aye. If there were any further instances, the SSPCA were going to prosecute. As far as they're aware, the recent sales have been clean. I don't know if she's using a wider breeding stock or what."

Forrester stared at the board again. "Forget Rachel for a moment. What about if it's Paul they're targeting?"

Vicky shrugged. "The only possible lead would be his boss, Michael Murison. The instruction to head out there came from him."

Forrester stared at Considine. "Do you think he's a suspect?"

"I seriously doubt it, sir. He's got alibis for starters and Paul's a good mate of his. Checked it with a few people there, plus a bar they go to down the road."

"Let's keep an open mind on it, okay?" Forrester tapped at *Notes* on the whiteboard. "It seems like there's some sort of connection to these dogs, right?"

"I agree." Vicky held up a photocopy. "'*Not so nice, is it?*' I'd say someone's trying to send Rachel a message."

"Think it's this Gary Black boy?"

"Could be. Other than the fact he's got his money back and he donated the cash to an animal charity, he's still got a motive." Vicky drew a ring around his name. "He's been doing some research into it and he could've got angrier with them."

"Interesting." Forrester clicked his tongue. "Has any terror group claimed ownership? PETA or anything like that?"

"The letters were unsigned, sir, and I'm not aware of any phone calls or anything like that."

"We should speak to the National Crime Agency about this, Vicky. We may be dealing with a group we've never heard of."

"Had experience with the NCA myself. SOCA, formerly." MacDonald shrugged. "Happy to help."

"Done." Forrester wrote *Mac — NCA* on the *Actions* list. "Anything else, Vicky?"

"I'd like to bring in an IT analyst, if that's okay."

Forrester scowled. "Why?"

"Given there's a possibility of a terror angle, we need to scour the internet. Some group might've already taken credit and we just don't know. Someone might've been mouthy on Facebook or Twitter. Besides, Paul Joyce said there was a camera involved."

"They were *filming* them?"

"Aye."

"Bloody hell." Forrester pinched his nose. "I'll see what I can do about an analyst, okay? Probably only got budget for tomorrow." Forrester scanned the room. "Is there anything else we can get on with?"

"I think it's a waiting game, sir." Vicky grimaced. "We've got detectives and uniformed officers going round the various locations. We might get something tomorrow, we might not."

Forrester put the pen back. "Right. I'll need to give DCI Raven an update on this. I want a briefing at nine tomorrow but I expect you all to be in earlier, okay?" He marched towards the corridor.

MacDonald turned to Vicky. "Didn't get that coffee, did we?"

"It's been a day from hell. Probably nothing compared to what you're used to in Glasgow."

"Don't know — rescuing two kidnap victims is a pretty good result."

"I'm not sure we really rescued them, though. The mobile led us there. They'd have known we'd be monitoring it." Vicky stood up. "Let's get that coffee tomorrow, okay?"

MacDonald patted her shoulder. "Look forward to it."

Chapter Sixteen

Vicky entered the Spar on Barry Road in Carnoustie, wandering around the small shop looking for inspiration. It still had a sickly sweet smell from the bakery section, mixing with the smell of off oranges. She reached into the fridge and picked up a bottle of South African Chardonnay.

"Still tanning the wine, I see?" Liz stood next to her, a grin on her face.

Vicky tilted her head at Liz's basket, where three bottles of red nestled underneath a bag of bagels. "You can hardly talk."

"Still, I'm not a police officer."

"We're not all alcoholics, you know." Vicky laughed. "Haven't seen you in a few weeks, Liz. How's it going?"

"You know how it is." Liz rubbed a hand down Vicky's arm, a frown etched on her forehead. "How are you coping?"

"I'm fine."

"I mean really. Bottles of wine aren't the answer."

Vicky sighed, looking around the shop for prying ears — the closest was a man in a dress shirt and tracksuit bottoms checking out the strong cider, holding a can at arm's reach, glasses over his white hair. "I'm still finding it tough."

"You can always talk to me, you know?"

"I know. Thanks for that." Vicky nodded, shifting the weight of the basket to the other hand. "I'm still trying to do that 'don't take your work home with you' thing."

"It's not easy."

"Nope." Vicky nibbled at her bottom lip, rolling the flesh between her teeth. "Just so many things to juggle on my own."

A grin crept across Liz's face, eyebrows flicking up and down a couple of times. "Dave's got a new best mate. Our new neighbour. They're getting on really well."

Vicky didn't like the insinuation. "Are you suggesting anything, Lizzie?"

"No!" Liz rested her basket on the floor. "Well, maybe I am. We were going to go out with him on Saturday . . ."

Vicky put her free hand to her hip. "So you're suggesting a double date, right?"

"No! . . . Well, aye." Liz reached into the chiller for a bottle of Prosecco. "How about it?"

"What's he like?"

"He's really nice. He's a teacher." Liz raised an eyebrow as she put the bottle back. "You'd like him."

"I'll think about it."

"We're going up to the Ferry for a curry then maybe go for a couple of drinks afterwards."

Vicky laughed. "You've still got a downer on Carnoustie, right?"

"Oh, come on. The Ferry's a lot better. So, how about it?"

"We'll see."

Liz's forehead wrinkled. "I do worry about you still being single at your age."

Vicky scowled at her — what was it with everyone today? "I'm hardly decrepit, am I?" She took a deep breath. "Look, I'll think about it, okay?"

"You do that."

Vicky checked her watch. "I'll need to shoot off. Got to pick up Bella."

Chapter Seventeen

Vicky knocked on her parents' front door, looking back along Bruce Drive as she waited. The old street looked the same, except for the absence of children — the parents of her youth were now the grandparents of the present. How many of her old friends were as reliant on their parents as she was?

Her mum opened the door. She wore black trousers and a short-sleeved top with blue and white hoops. Her hair was still long, though trimmed on the top. "Good evening, Victoria. Nice of you to finally show up."

"I'm not late, Mum. Besides, I've got a big case on just now."

"I see."

"How's Bella been today?"

"Fine, I suppose. I do worry about the pair of you. She barely gets to see you. If it wasn't for us, you'd be in real trouble. You need to get yourself a man, Victoria."

Vicky took a step back onto the paving slabs lining the front lawn. "Is this my day for getting unsolicited advice about what to do with my life?"

"I'm just saying." Mum folded her arms, loose skin hanging from her upper arms. "You know best, don't you?"

Vicky pressed her teeth together. "Has Bella had her tea?"

"I gave her a plate of soup when she got in but you know what they're like at that age."

"Okay."

Mum reached to the ledge in the porch. "Here's a DVD from your brother. Said you'd like it."

"I told him to stop doing that for me." Vicky took the disc. *Breaking Bad series 4* was written in black marker. "Is he still up?"

Mum put her hands in her pockets. "He's gone to bed."

"Well, I'll speak to him on Sunday, I suppose."

"You'll thank him, I hope. He doesn't do much these days. Giving people CDs and DVDs really helps him."

"Shame he's pirating them off the internet."

Mum ignored the comment. "Your father's going to put up those shelves for you on Saturday."

"Is he in?"

"He's away playing snooker with Eric." Mum descended to the bottom step, resting a hand on Vicky's shoulder. "Victoria, what are we going to do with you? You really need a man, you know that?"

Vicky stared at the hand stroking her arm. "I'm fine, Mum. *We're* fine."

Bella came bouncing out of the door, easily side-stepping her grandmother, grabbing Vicky by the waist, burying her head in her mother's midriff, wide eyes and cheeky cheeks looking up. "Mummy!"

Vicky picked her up, resting the wriggly little legs against her hip. "Oh, you're almost too heavy to be carried, my girl." She kissed her on the head before spinning her around. "How's my baby?"

"Granny made me tablet!"

Vicky put Bella down, rolling her eyes at her mother. "Mum, I told you not to give her that stuff."

"I don't remember you complaining when you were her age."

"With the number of fillings I've got, I wish I'd hated the stuff."

Bella tugged at Vicky's coat. "What's for tea, Mummy?"

"Cheesy pasta, your favourite." Vicky smiled at her mum. "I'll need to drop her off tomorrow at half seven. Got to get in early."

Mum climbed back up to the top step. "That's fine, I suppose."

"Thanks, Mum. Bella, say goodnight to Granny."

"Night-night, Granny!"

Vicky led Bella back to the car, the child's little hand tugging at her pinky, the skin soft and unblemished. She put Bella in the car seat and kissed her forehead, drinking in the sweet smell for a few seconds. She got behind the wheel and started the engine, following the loop round before heading down North Burnside Street, the tall post-war houses standing between them and home. "How was your day, Bella?"

"Good, Mummy. After playgroup, we went up to Arbroath and walked along the cliffs. Grandad saw a friend and he let me walk his dog! Can I get a doggie?"

Vicky turned right at the end, chip shop smells making her mouth water. "We'll see when you're a bit older, Bells. You've got Tinkle. You like cats."

"I love Tinkle, Mummy, but I'd love a doggie just as much."

"Let Mummy think about it." Vicky drove on in silence, adjusting the mirror to keep an eye on her daughter, hoping it would be another thing she'd eventually forget. School next year — peer pressure had been bad enough in the eighties . . .

She turned left into Westfield Street, pulling up in front of her house. She got out and helped Bella from her car seat.

Bella hopped out of the car then skipped down the path. "Hello, Tinkle!" A small tabby swarmed around her feet, the purring audible from the gate.

Vicky joined her at the door, fishing around in her bag for keys. She hung Bella's possessions on a peg, draping her own coat and bag over the top, then joined them in the kitchen. "Come on, Bells, let's get your tea on."

"I'm not that hungry, Mummy." Bella perched by the cat bowl, an open sachet in her hand, stroking Tinkle as she ate. "My wee tummy's full up."

"Did Grandad teach you that?"

Bella closed a zip over her lips.

Vicky knelt and kissed her, holding her close for a few seconds, wishing she had a lot more time with her.

Friday
28th March 2014

Chapter Eighteen

E xcuse me. I'm looking for DS Dodds. Is he around?"

Vicky looked up from her desk. A young girl, maybe sixteen at most, stood there — red hair, freckles. Glasgow accent, lilting and slightly nasal. She held out a hand. "DS Vicky Dodds."

"Oh, sorry." The girl blushed then shook it. "Good morning, ma'am. I'm Zoë Jones."

"How can I help?"

"I'm the IT analyst. DCI Forrester said to ask for you."

"Okay." Vicky examined her for a few seconds. The strap of the girl's laptop bag scythed between her breasts and bumped off her exposed midriff. Definitely older than sixteen — despite the face, Zoë had the body of a grown woman, curves and all.

Vicky patted the empty chair next to her. "Take a seat."

Zoë perched on the edge of the chair, barely denting the fabric, and started emptying her bag, placing the laptop and charger on the desk. She slid the desk forward to reveal the power supplies behind and leaned over to plug in her laptop. She sat back and crossed her legs before opening the machine.

Vicky tapped the computer. "Well, you've already done better than me. Usually takes me an hour to plug it in."

"I'm sure you're not that bad, ma'am."

"Don't count on it."

Zoë looked around the room, one hand tugging her hair back. The four male DCs at the next desk looked back at their laptops. She smiled and shifted the seat closer to the desk. "So, what are you looking for?"

Vicky got out a sheet of paper. "This is a list of actions I think we need to do. I'll give you an overview of the case and tell you what we're looking for. Okay?"

"DI Forrester's already briefed me."

"He has, has he?" Vicky pushed the sheet of paper across the desk, crumpling the edge. "Well, I want you to trawl social media for these people. I think it'd be a good idea to do an idiot search, too."

"A what?"

"You know, looking for the sort of idiot who posts on Facebook saying they're going to go out and kill someone just before they go out and kill someone."

Zoë noted it down in an app. "I'll see what I can do."

Vicky tapped a finger against the sheet. "We're more likely to get something from this list of names."

"What about the dark net?"

"What's that?"

"It's the secret side of the internet, where all the paedophiles and pirates hide their stuff."

"I vaguely remember that from a training course."

"Want me to check?"

"Please."

"Our search algorithms and access aren't perfect, but you never know. Might turn up something."

"So what brings you to bonny Dundee?"

"Opportunity, ma'am."

"You don't need to call me 'ma'am', okay?"

"Okay." Zoë winked at her. "My manager in Glasgow sold me this as an opportunity. You've not got many experts left after the restructure. Said it's a much better chance of getting the experience I need to progress. The North MITs are understrength in terms of IT support, or so the story goes."

"I see."

MacDonald appeared, eyes only for Zoë. "Miss Jones, you're definitely stalking me."

Zoë's eyebrows shot up. "What are *you* doing here?"

"Transferred up. First day yesterday."

"Oh, I see." Zoë curled her hair round a finger. "Good to see you again, sir."

MacDonald stood between them, his gaze shooting over to Vicky. "DS Dodds, can I have a word?"

Vicky got to her feet, smoothing down her skirt as she stood. "Certainly."

MacDonald led them out into the corridor. Coffee and bacon smells wafted down from the canteen. "Zoë's good, by the way. Trained in Strathclyde the proper way. Used her a couple of times over the last year."

"That's a relief. The last guy we had was an idiot once he stopped looking down my top."

MacDonald laughed then waited for a uniform to pass by. "Knackered. First day ended with a sixteen-hour shift supervising the street teams in Dryburgh and Invergowrie."

Vicky nodded as she leaned against the wall. "How was it?"

"Confirmed the sighting of the black car in all three locations now. Had the phone call information verified by our Forensic Support Unit — the call used to lure Paul Joyce to that building came from a burner. Dead end."

"So they are targeting him."

"Correct. Just got off the phone to the National Crime Agency. Nothing so far but they're checking for me."

Vicky tugged at her ponytail. "What was it you wanted to see me about?"

"Got a few minutes before I head back to Dryburgh. How about that coffee?"

Chapter Nineteen

MacDonald held open the door to the Old Mill Café, which nestled in the bowels of one of Dundee's long-dead jute mills just across the Marketgait from the station. The icy wind blew his tie around. "After you."

"Thanks." Vicky entered the café and made for the counter, the morning rush now cleared. The mirrors filling the walls were covered in steam from the espresso machine.

MacDonald rested his hands on the counter, raising a finger to attract a barista. "What can I get you —" He laughed. "Can I call you Vicky?"

"Vicky's fine. Vicks I'll tolerate. *Never* Victoria."

"What can I get you, *Vicky*?"

"A Diet Coke."

MacDonald scowled. "With all those sweeteners?"

"Got to be better than sugar."

MacDonald nodded to the server, a skinny man in jeans and a black turtleneck. "Diet Coke. Glass with ice, please. And an Americano, black with cold milk on the side. Cheers." He turned back to Vicky. "Don't drink coffee?"

"It totally *breaks* me. If I have a coffee, I just won't sleep. I can manage a cup of tea if forced, but I'm fine on the Diet Coke."

MacDonald took his change from the barista then winked at Vicky. "I'll bring them over."

"Thanks." Vicky sat in a table by the window, staring out to avoid looking at MacDonald as he fiddled with his phone.

What was she playing at? Acting like she was fifteen again, blouse pulled tight, flirting with Craig Norrie in the year above.

Play it cool, girl.

MacDonald sat opposite, laying their drinks on the wooden surface. "Don't want to make a habit of sitting around, drinking coffee. Usually quite a grafter, don't take many breaks. You've probably gathered that, though?"

"I have."

"Just wanted to spend some time getting to know you, really. We'll probably be working closely together."

"No worries. What do you want to know?"

MacDonald smiled as he wrapped his fingers around his coffee. "Think I'm after inside gen, do you?"

"Well, you paid."

MacDonald leaned back, a wide grin on his face. He rubbed at his nose. "That's pretty perceptive, DS Dodds."

"I like to think I am. Might make detective one of these days."

MacDonald tore open a sachet of sugar and tipped it into his coffee, before stirring in just enough milk to alter the colour. "What's Forrester like?"

Hands wrapped around her can, Vicky took a few seconds to choose how to answer. Brutal honesty — why not? "I like David, but he can be officious at times. Bureaucratic. He's very by the book, if you know what I mean."

"Not necessarily a bad thing?"

"Didn't say it was." Vicky poured her can into the glass, the ice cubes bouncing to the top and clinking off the edges. "He's good at politics, unlike me. I'm shi — really bad at that side of things. He's very well connected in the force."

MacDonald took an experimental sip before reaching for another sachet. "You like working for him?"

"I do. I've had some really bad bosses and some okay ones. He's good."

"What's the team like?"

"The team?" Vicky took a drink as she thought. "DC Woods is the best."

"Karen, right?"

"Right. She's been a DC ten years. She's not going anywhere but she knows what she's doing and she's reliable."

"And Considine?"

Vicky licked her lips. "He'll be good once I've kicked him into shape."

"So Forrester tells me. Bit up himself, that one, right?"

"He solved a taxi murder recently. Thinks he caught Jack the Ripper."

"I'll bear that in mind." MacDonald blew on his coffee before taking another sip. "What about the others?"

"Summers, Buchan and Kirk?" Vicky ran a hand through her hair. "I try and keep away from the Three Amigos. They're thick as thieves. Decent officers, but they don't exactly respect a female boss."

MacDonald rubbed his smooth chin, his finger catching in the cleft. "Let me get my feet under the table then we'll see about divvying the team up a bit."

"I'd take Karen any day."

"If she's the only good one then we'll need to sort something out."

"I'll arm-wrestle you for her."

MacDonald smirked. "Don't want to lose."

"You look like you work out."

"Like to keep in shape. Helps with the job if nothing else."

Vicky crushed an ice cube with her teeth. A filling jolted out pain. "I haven't been to the gym in years."

He gave a curt nod. "What about this Ennis guy?"

"What about him?"

"Stepping into dead man's shoes here. Want to know what I'm facing up to."

Vicky took a sip. "I don't know what it's like in the old Strathclyde but since they formed Police Scotland it's got worse up here."

"In what way?"

"It's all stats, stats, stats. They want to report on everything all of the time. *Now.* That's why Forrester does so well. His bureaucratic streak means he's perfect for it."

"That not just knowing what's happening?"

"Maybe. I think it's been worse than that, though. With Ennis, it just got really bad. He's old school — likes his snouts and his scrotes."

"Was he in *The Bill*?"

"Exactly. He couldn't cope with being out in Stonehaven one minute and in deepest, darkest Perthshire the next, then getting flung down to Fife or up to Inverness at a moment's notice. He was Dundee through and through."

"How do you cope?"

"Not sure I do."

MacDonald took another drink of coffee. "Good coffee in here."

"Beats the canteen, that's for sure."

"You work in Tayside before the reorg, Vicky?"

"I did." Vicky finished the drink, leaving ice cubes at the bottom. "Had a fairly standard career, to be honest. Two years in uniform before applying for CID. Did three years as a DC then I got my DS position. Eight years later I'm still there."

"Like I said earlier, dead man's shoes?"

"I'm not a particularly ambitious officer."

"Really? DS within five years is impressive, especially in a small force like Tayside. Guys I know in the old Lothian and Borders and Strathclyde managed it but there's more opportunity there. You've done well."

"Thanks." Vicky pushed the glass away, trying to avoid the temptation of crunching more ice. "So, why've you come here, Euan?"

"From Coupar Angus originally. Just want to settle down, really. Sold the flat in Glasgow. Renting a place just now but a house would be ideal."

"What does your wife do?"

"Not married." He finished his coffee. "All part of the plan, I suppose. Looking to make DI in the next eighteen months."

"Sounds ambitious."

MacDonald leaned towards her and spoke quietly. "Working in Glasgow was tough. Lot of murders, assaults and brutal rapes. Scars you. Don't want to become one of those embittered old cops, you know?"

"Yeah, I know. Was that the MIT you worked in?"

"Glasgow North, aye. That said, we were all over the place, supporting other MITs. Had that shooting in Edinburgh, a murder in the Highlands, all over and above our usual caseload."

"Sounds tough."

"Absolutely." MacDonald pushed the coffee away. "How can I help you with this case?"

"Getting the information from the NCA would be useful. That sort of thing can seriously eat up time. Layers of bureaucracy and all that."

"Sensing a trend here."

"Don't get me wrong, I like to do things properly but I'm just not the sort to go filling out forms for the sake of it."

"Me neither." MacDonald picked up a sugar sachet and pulled at the opposing edges. "What about that case in Cupar a few months ago?"

"Which one?"

"Woman shoved in a bin?"

"I don't remember it."

"Was all over the papers at the time."

"I don't really read the papers." Vicky tugged at her ponytail, trying to flatten her hair down. "Anyway, what about it?"

"Maybe nothing, but it's got vague similarities to our case." MacDonald pushed his empty cup to the side. "Remember that woman who shut a cat inside a wheelie bin down south somewhere?"

"Worked for a bank, right?"

"Aye. Woman in Fife did the same thing a few years back. Got dredged up in the local press last summer, don't know why. Few months ago, she turns up in a rubbish bin herself."

Vicky thought about it for a few seconds before crushing her can. "We need to speak to her."

Chapter Twenty

Considine slowed as they entered Cupar, his dark grey Subaru hitting heavy traffic. "I still think you should have spoken to the boss about us going to see these boys."

"He was away." Vicky cleared her throat. "What's the point in having sergeants if you don't let them get on with it?"

"Your grave."

Considine drove past the council buildings, the new home of the police station, turning left onto what passed for a main shopping area in the town, parking outside a bakery.

Vicky got out and raced ahead to the station.

Considine caught up with her. "That baker's back there looks amazing. I'm getting a sausage roll for my piece today. Maybe get a pie as well."

"It's your cholesterol."

"Hey, I work out."

"Really?"

"Aye. Hulk's Gym in Forfar. Free weights three nights a week."

"I didn't know that." Vicky opened the door to the station, eyes sweeping around the waiting room.

A large man got to his feet. Shaved head, dark suit filled by his bulk. "Sergeant Dodds?"

Vicky nodded. "DC Reed?"

"Aye." Reed motioned to the security door. "Got us a room through the back." He led them through the station. The wallpaper was already torn and frayed beside fist-sized holes in the plaster. He opened the door to an interview room and collapsed into the nearest chair. "Take a seat."

Vicky sat opposite. "You came up from Glenrothes?"

"Aye, the least I could do given you're coming down from Scumdee."

"Says a man from Glenrothes."

"Aye, but I live in Anstruther."

"Must eat a lot of fish suppers."

Reed scowled at her. "Are you wanting me to help or what?"

"Tell us about the case."

Reed got out a notebook and flicked through it. "The victim's name is Irene Henderson. Back in 2010, November fifteenth to be precise, she was abducted from outside her home and chucked in an industrial waste bin at a factory on the outskirts of the town."

Vicky crossed her legs. "Did you catch anyone?"

"At the time, we thought it was just some local neds who'd maybe been egged on by their girlfriends."

"At the time?"

"Aye."

"Well, what about now?"

"I'd say the same. We never caught anyone."

"Was there a note?"

"What do you mean?"

"Anyone leaving a message? Maybe taking credit for it?"

Reed shrugged. "Mrs Henderson got a lot of notes through the post, as I'm sure you can imagine. Over a hundred. Luckily it wasn't me who had to go through them."

Vicky winced — another job for Considine. She raised an eyebrow at him. He nodded. She looked back at Reed. "Was a black car spotted near her house?"

"No."

"What about by the bin?"

Reed shook his head. "Not that I recall."

"We're talking about an exec saloon, like a Mercedes or a Lexus."

"Sorry, but no."

Vicky scribbled it down just as her mobile rang — Forrester. She held a hand up in apology.

Reed got out his own phone, chubby fingers stabbing at the screen.

She left the room, pressed her mobile to her ear. "Sir?"

"Where are you, Vicky?"

"In Cupar."

"What on Earth are you doing over there?"

"We're investigating a case potentially linked to ours. DS MacDonald raised it."

"Well, can you get back here? I've just finished up with Raven and I need to get an update from you."

"Fine. It doesn't really look like it's linked anyway." Vicky ended the call and re-entered the room. "Sorry about this but we've been summoned back to Dundee."

Reed stood up. "No problems. I've got to take a statement in St Andrews anyway, so it's not like it's a wasted trip."

Considine got to his feet. "Have you got the original case file with you?"

Reed chuckled. "I'm not in the habit of carrying cold case files on my person."

Considine stood taller, towering over Reed. "Any chance you could bring yourself to sending it up to us?"

Reed sighed before making for the door. "Aye. I'll get it sent up this afternoon."

Chapter Twenty-One

"You've been quiet." Karen put her cutlery down.

Vicky took a drink, finishing her can, and put it back on her tray. "Sorry. I'm just preoccupied."

"What with?"

"I couldn't find Forrester and decided to go to Fife. Considine was being a wanker about it."

"Do you think Forrester minded?"

"Doubt it." Vicky rubbed at the knot in her neck. "I don't trust Considine, though."

"Me neither." Karen took a drink of Dr Pepper. "You owe me one for the CCTV, by the way."

"Have you got anything?"

"Nothing. Been through the CCTV and the Auto Number Plate thingy. And nothing on the building owners either. They said they've been looking for new tenants for that unit for over a year. The security guard was supposed to have gone round it once a week to check on it."

"Okay. That'll be your hourly update for Forrester to pass up the way, I suppose."

"Can't believe they're making us do that."

"It's a big case, Kaz. You know the rules."

"I still think you owe me one."

"That's what a DC does. Sorry."

Karen smirked. "I know what a DS does."

"What?"

"Flirting. I saw you with MacDonald over the road."

Vicky coughed. "It was just coffee."

"You don't drink coffee."

"Okay, it was just coffee and Diet Coke."

"I'll remind you when you shag him."

Vicky sat back and folded her arms. "We're going to be working quite closely together. We were establishing a rapport."

"Is that what you call it? You're blushing."

"Stop it." Vicky picked at her pasta, eating a final mouthful before dumping her cutlery onto the plate. "Can I ask you something?"

"Sounds personal."

"It is."

"Fire away, then."

Vicky took a moment. "I bumped into my friend Liz last night. You know her?"

"Think so."

"Well, she's trying to get me to go on a date with some guy who's just moved in next door."

"How do you feel about that?"

"I don't know." Vicky clenched her fists, tugging nails along her palms. "Liz tries to do the best, you know? I just wish she'd stop interfering. It's like people think I can't cope."

"You can cope, Vicks."

"Can I?"

"You've done this all of Bella's life. It's not easy this job, especially having to babysit clowns like Considine. Looked like you've got him whipped into shape at the briefing."

"Well, there's that, I suppose."

Karen shook her bottle of Dr Pepper, the dark liquid fizzing up to the lid just before she tightened it. "What's this guy like?"

"I don't know much. He's a teacher. Liz says he gets on well with her husband."

"Dave Burns, right?"

"Aye, him."

"Dave's all right. My Colin used to play squash with him. He's a good judge of character. Can't play squash for toffee, though." Karen pushed her hands across the table. "But, of course, you're interested in DS MacDonald?"

"No!"

"Shut up, of course you are."

"Seriously, I'm not." Vicky stared up at the ceiling, thick extract pipes leading from the kitchen to just above the nearest window. "What do you think I should do?"

Karen shrugged. "Nothing ventured, nothing gained."

"She was talking about tomorrow night."

"Go for it."

"What about Bella, though?"

"We can take Bella, Vicks. Give your mum and dad some time off."

"I'd appreciate it." Vicky smoothed down her skirt leg. "Look, I don't know if Bella's ready for it."

"Focus on yourself for once, Vicks."

"You know me. I can't think of anything but the distant future." Vicky tried to swallow and failed, her throat tight and thick with tears. "I always think about how I'm letting her down with it just being me on my own."

"Hey, hey, it's okay." Karen reached across the table, warm fingers wrapping around Vicky's blocks of ice. "Think of it this way. Bella could maybe do with having a father figure around."

"I never thought of that."

"Just make sure you get some action, okay?" Karen laughed. "Your knicker drawer must be like an Ann Summers clear-out sale. You must get through a lot of batteries."

Chapter Twenty-Two

Vicky picked her phone up from the desk. No more prevaricating. She texted Liz. *About date — can make it.*

The phone lit up with a reply. *Gulistan at 7. OK? L*

Vicky replied, *Okay*, before chucking her mobile in her bag. She cleared her throat to loosen the knot in her neck.

She looked around — the adjacent desks were empty. Still no Zoë or Considine. She got out a sheet of paper and jotted down everything she knew about the case.

Animal cruelty seemed to be the clear motivation, at least from the notes left at the crime scenes. That they were all sent by the same people was a fairly safe assumption, even ahead of Considine's forensic searches. She'd nothing to dispute the fact they were linked, and the sighting of the black car at all three sites backed it up.

The Cupar case, though . . . She just didn't know. Assuming a link, they were both motivated by revenge against people who'd committed publicly known acts of animal cruelty.

Dumped a cat in a bin? You get stuck in a bin.

Made your dogs breed too closely? You get forced to have sex with your brother.

Thinking of it that way, Rachel had to be the target. They hadn't found anything on Paul so far — he just seemed like an ordinary bloke, with no enemies and nothing against him on public record.

She picked up the photocopies of the notes and read through them again.

We have your wife. She is safe. Do not worry. Much.
We have your husband. He is safe. Do not worry. Much.
See? They're fine. Not so nice, is it?

The first two were ambiguous. No political or moral messages there. *Not so nice, is it?* It had to be against Rachel. Rachel was a dog breeder. Attempting to force her to have sex with a close family member — genetically, even if they weren't necessarily on friendly terms — seemed close to what Gary Black said she was making her dogs do.

She dug out her copy of the newspaper articles relating to the case. The top one had an interview with the manager of a dog rescue centre, Alison McFarlane. She seemed to insist dog breeding was a form of cruelty. " *'They should be strung up.'* "

Vicky stared out of the window for a while, watching the traffic slowly shift down the Marketgait. Definitely worth speaking to her.

Considine slumped in his chair, chewing gum, his face flushed red. "Afternoon."

"Have you been to the pub?"

Considine smirked. "Just been out for a ramble."

"A ramble?"

"Yeah, Friday afternoon rambling club. Me, Kirk and Summers go for a ramble every week."

"Sounds like a pub trip to me."

"Okay, fine but it was just the one. I'll be fine by the time we knock off."

Vicky pointed to the desk next to her. "Seen Zoë?"

"Who?"

"The IT analyst."

"I thought that was your daughter and it was 'bring your kids to work day'."

"Christ, Stephen, Bella's only four."

"Sorry." Considine yawned. "Do you need me this afternoon?"

"It just so happens I do."

Chapter Twenty-Three

The Tayside Animals! kennel was just round the corner from the police station on Brown Street, the side of the building filled with the *Ta!* logo in purple.

Vicky nodded at the sign as they walked up. "Says a lot about Dundee that it's got two kennels really central in the town."

"Aye, but the dogs are making an absolute racket." Considine stopped and pointed at the sign next door for a halal meat packer. "Suppose they can just chuck them in there when they don't get rehomed."

Vicky grabbed his shoulder. "If you ever say that again, I'll get you done on a disciplinary."

Considine held up his hands. "Sorry."

"Don't you even think of *speaking* in there, let alone joking like that. It wasn't just the one pint, was it?"

"It was."

Vicky stood glaring at him. "I should get you breathalysed."

"Sorry, Sarge. Have I touched a nerve?"

"I had a dog from Brown Street when I was growing up. Sonic." Vicky felt a sting in her stomach. "*Never* joke about that sort of thing, especially on a case like this."

"Sorry." Considine bowed his head. "Was he from in there?"

Vicky shook her head. "No, we got *her* from the council one up the road."

"Look, I won't do that again."

"You might want to think about your rambling club, okay?" Vicky entered the corrugated iron building through the main door, flashing her warrant card at the receptionist. "We're looking for Alison McFarlane. Is she here?"

"She's in the middle of a meeting just now." The receptionist crossed her arms. She wore a set of green scrubs with darker epaulets on the shoulders.

"When will she be free? I need to speak to her."

"Can I ask what it's about?"

Vicky showed her a copy of the newspaper article. "We're looking into this case again. I wondered if she might be able to assist."

The receptionist got to her feet. "I'll see when she's free." She went through a door behind the desk.

Considine leaned against the counter. "I'm sorry about what I said there."

Vicky avoided eye contact. "Don't sweat it."

"I'm serious. It was out of order."

The receptionist reappeared. "She'll see you now." She lifted up a partition and led them through to an office. She knocked on the door and waited, looking through the window to the yard. Rows and rows of dog cages, with only one family looking around, a mum and dad with a surly teenager.

The office door opened and six females all left the office, dressed similarly to the receptionist.

The receptionist left them to it and Vicky led Considine inside.

Two women sat across a desk, the computer on one side surrounded by a selection of small pot plants, their leaves covering the beige monitor.

Vicky smiled, her gaze dancing between them. "Alison McFarlane?"

"That'll be me." The older of the two pushed her keyboard away as she stood. She was a good few inches taller than Vicky, her spiky blonde hair streaked with grey, skin aged from a working life clearly spent outdoors. She offered a hand.

Vicky shook it. "Thanks for seeing us."

"Not a problem." Alison gestured at her colleague. "This is Yvonne Welsh. She's really the brains behind the operation."

Yvonne blushed. Even sitting, she appeared taller than Alison. Her auburn hair was knotted into a ponytail, a chunk on the left braided. She waved her left arm around the room, her t-shirt sleeve lifting just enough to reveal a tattoo on her toned bicep, a cartoon cat raising its paw. "This is Alison's place, really. I just help out, that's all."

Vicky sat in one of the chairs, which was still warm from the meeting. "Nice place you've got here."

Alison grinned. "We try our best. We don't have as many dogs as the council one just up the road but we don't put them down if they're not rehomed. That's incredibly important."

"I didn't realise they did."

"It wasn't many, to be honest. Usually a result of age or temperament. We managed to get them to stop and give us the dogs at risk. We've managed to build up a network throughout Tayside which fosters any overspill we've got. Since we started in ninety-seven, no dog in Dundee's been put down as a result of not being able to be rehomed."

"That's quite some achievement." Vicky showed them the article. "Do you remember this?"

"Of course."

"We're investigating the abduction of the breeder in this article, Mrs Rachel Hay."

Alison put a hand to her mouth. "Oh my goodness. Is she okay?"

"She's in hospital."

"Good God."

"We're looking for anyone who may have a particular bone to pick with Mrs Hay. The comments you made in this article were quite inflammatory. You said, '*They should be strung up.*'"

Alison exchanged a look with Yvonne before coughing. "I was just making a wider point about dog breeding. There are more than enough animals to go around."

"Stringing someone up's quite similar to locking them naked in a cage, I'd say."

"I understand." Alison made a steeple with her fingers. "People making money out of the poor animals makes my blood boil. We were heavily involved with this particular case. That was the third or fourth case of NME we had from their kennel."

Vicky opened her notebook. "Why were they brought here?"

"We provide a service for dogs suffering from congenital defects. I'm not the expert on this, but I'd say NME is caused by inbreeding in pedigree dogs, especially pugs with their limited breeding stock." Alison looked away. "I hate that term."

"If it's not you, who would be the expert on this?"

"Yvonne here's certainly an expert on treating these animals. Most vets just put them down but she's developed a way of helping them manage the symptoms so the dogs' lives are extended by a few months, sometimes up to a year."

"I see." Vicky focused on Yvonne, whose eyes were locked on the window. "Ms Welsh?"

Yvonne swallowed as she made eye contact. "Sorry, I'm not good at speaking with people. I understand animals. People, I just don't get."

Alison smiled. "We've almost managed to domesticate Yvonne."

Yvonne glanced at Alison then Vicky. "Pugs are particularly prone to inbreeding. We see quite a lot of it, usually in the smaller dogs."

"Which dog species are we talking about?"

Yvonne scowled. "A dog *is* a species. I'm talking about *breeds*."

"Sorry. What breeds then?"

Yvonne took a deep breath. "Specialist breeds like pugs are really heavily bred."

"What do you mean by heavily bred?"

"It means there are so few of them they have to breed mothers with sons, brothers with sisters, stuff like that. As I said, we've had a fair few pugs in here."

Alison narrowed her eyes and let out a sigh. "People usually bring them in when they realise the cost of keeping the animals alive. They pretend to have found them. I've not done it yet but we could actually trace these dogs back to purchases."

"How would you prosecute the owners?"

"We've partnered with the SSPCA a few times. They've got a dedicated legal team. We're much more at the coal face of dog care."

Vicky tapped her pen on her notebook. "I've heard this NME condition mentioned a few times. What is it?"

Yvonne rubbed at her eye. "Basically, their brains get inflamed. We can't cure it but, as Alison says, we can help the dogs. Normally, they get put down within weeks of diagnosis but, with some medication, we can help them live a bit longer. And not in pain."

"How do they catch it?"

"It's hereditary."

"So if there was a — I don't know how to say this — dodgy breeding pair?"

Yvonne nodded. "Dodgy is putting it mildly. If one of the dogs has it, it's likely the pups will get it."

"This sounds like a very specific condition." Vicky scanned the article again. "You said all breeding is evil."

Alison sat back in her chair and fiddled with her necklace. "Particularly pugs, though."

"Why do you say that?"

Alison sat forward. "Do you know much about biology?"

"Very little."

Considine raised a hand. "I did it at uni."

Alison inched further forward. "Basically, all dogs are grey wolves that have been selected for morphological features present in a small part of their DNA."

Considine nodded. "How they look, basically. If loads of dog breeds were bred over and over again through generations, you'd end up with a kind of wolf thing."

Alison beamed. "Precisely. Dogs've been bred to be machines over the years, much like cattle and horses. Hunting dogs or Collies or Bull Mastiffs, for instance. They've been selectively bred for certain characteristics. A Jack Russell is small because it's bred to go down rabbit holes. They've just picked very small dogs over and over again."

Vicky frowned, close to losing the trail. "What about pugs?"

Alison slumped back in her chair. "Pugs are different entirely. They've been bred purely for size and looks."

"So, you find a dog that looks strange and mate it with another one that looks similar?"

"Yes. Do that enough times and eventually you'll get a pug."

Vicky scribbled a diagram in her notebook. "Did you rehome a dog to Gary Black's family?"

"I don't normally comment on such matters, but if it helps your case then so be it." Alison brushed some fluff off her shoulder. "They took one of our more needy dogs, a cross between a chocolate Lab and a Collie who only had one eye. They gave us a good donation, for which we're eternally grateful."

Vicky sat back and stared out of the window, across the pound—
the family from earlier had been joined by a couple walking a black
Alsatian. She turned back to Yvonne and Alison. "Do either of you
know anything about any domestic terror cells?"

Alison glowered at her. "We're not that sort of place."

"I asked if you knew anything about them, not if you were
involved."

"I think you should leave."

"And I'm quite tempted to take you to the station for further
questioning."

"That won't be necessary." Alison stared at her hands. "We've
surely given you more than enough of our time?"

"I'll be the judge of that. Can you account for your whereabouts between four p.m. on Wednesday and midnight yesterday?"

"I was working here. Yvonne can vouch for me."

"We were both here." Yvonne stood up, tugging at her braid.
"I don't know what you're trying to do. We're just helping animals."

"I understand." Vicky noted it. "I just want to make sure you're
not harming people at the same time."

"The less we have to do with people, the better, believe me."

Vicky licked her lips and got to her feet. "Very well." She put
a business card on the desk. "We may be back, but please give us a
call if anything comes to mind."

Chapter Twenty-Four

Considine held the door open. "What do you think?"

Vicky walked towards her desk. "I doubt they're involved."

"You seemed to think they were."

"I was just being grumpy. I thought we were getting somewhere, but it's not likely they're doing this."

"Their alibi's funny. Just the pair of them to vouch for each other's whereabouts. I never like that."

Vicky rolled her eyes. "Do you want to check up on it, then?"

"Aye, all right." Considine nodded towards Zoë, sitting at her desk, Beats headphones on, lost in a video playing on her laptop. "After I've finished briefing young Zoë. Better prospect than following you around all day."

Vicky folded her arms. "What are you saying?"

"You're too old for me."

"Sure she's not too young?" Vicky shook her head and sat at her desk, throwing her coat on the back of her chair. She scowled at Zoë. "I was looking for you earlier."

No response.

"Zoë, I was looking for you before lunch."

Nothing.

Vicky tugged at her t-shirt. "Zoë?"

She jumped. "Shit. Sorry." She tugged her headphones off, dumping them on the desk. She stabbed her finger in the direction of her laptop. "I found something." She pressed one of the laptop's media keys and the video went back to the start.

The screen went dark. A light switched on, revealing the cage in the industrial unit.

Vicky pressed a finger against the screen. "Is this Rachel and Paul?"

Zoë nodded. "Think so."

The camera focused on Paul as he staggered around in the cage, gagged and smeared with excrement.

Rachel lay on her front behind him, staring into space.

A black leather-gloved finger pointed in front of the camera at Paul. "There he goes. He's just about ready. You'll see why they call it doggy style." The distorted voice was deep — the laptop's speaker struggled to replicate the sound.

Another voice with the same effect but slightly higher. "Right."

"What's up?"

"Nothing."

The camera moved closer to the cage. The hand reached out and started rattling the frame. "Go on, boy, get it up her." The hand pointed at the cage. "What's he doing?"

"This is a bit too cruel."

"They're animals. There's nothing cruel about this." The gloved hand rattled the cage again.

Paul glowered and bared his teeth at the camera.

The video bleached white with a loud clicking sound then shot back to darkness before recovering the image of them in the cage. The clicking came again but the hand was by the cage now. There was a Taser at the bottom of the shot.

"Don't make me use this again."

Paul's gaze moved from the Taser to his sister as she lay prone in the cage. He started breathing faster, on the edge of hyperventilation.

"Christ's sake. We'll never get these two to breed at this rate." The Taser sparked again — the gloved hand held it jammed against the bars. The voice kept laughing throughout, the sound deep and unnatural.

The camera tracked Rachel crawling to the far corner of the cage, tucking herself into a foetal position.

"Want to be a good boy?"

Paul glared at the camera again, a primal moan coming from his chest.

The screen froze on Paul's wide eyes staring at the camera. Text appeared across the image.

Dog Breeding Is Evil.

Siblings don't have a choice whether they're bred with each other.

The 10,000 pugs in the UK have the genetic diversity of 50 individuals.

Meanwhile, 9,000 dogs a year are put down because homes can't be found.

The video ended.

Head spinning, Vicky turned to Zoë. "Where did you find this?"

"I was up in the Forensics area. Got speaking to one of the guys and he helped me with a few things. I got this on the dark net."

"Who posted it?"

"I'm not sure we'll find out." Zoë sniffed. "The dark net's all about hiding. It's designed for pirates and child pornographers avoiding people like us. While we're getting better at catching people, it's not as simple as some idiot tweeting racist shit at Stan Collymore. These are people who love to hide."

Vicky tapped the laptop screen. "Can you do anything with the voices?"

"They're scrambled, ma'am."

"Can you descramble them?"

"I'll try. Anything else?"

"Just find whoever posted it."

Chapter Twenty-Five

Forrester swallowed as the video finished on the screen in his office. His Adam's apple bobbed up and down. He looked over at Vicky. "You told us there was a camera, didn't you?"

"Paul thought there might have been one."

"This isn't good." Forrester stretched his back out before frowning at MacDonald. "You think this is terrorism, Mac?"

"Not sure, sir. Dark net, right?"

"Aye."

"Until about ten minutes ago, I doubt any of us knew it even existed."

"Vicky?"

"If they're posting it there, they're preaching to the converted. Terrorists don't tend to do that."

"Go on."

"I'm struggling to see why they'd go to the bother of doing this video, only to release it to a small group. I don't know how many people will see that but it's not exactly spreading their message, is it?"

"Nothing about this makes sense to me." Forrester leaned further back in his chair. "What was the flashing thing?"

"It's a Taser overloading the sensor on the camera." Vicky handed him a print Zoë had obtained. "If you remove the cartridge it doesn't send the spikes out, just acts like a cattle prod. Paul Joyce thought they were using a cattle prod."

"Unbelievable." Forrester took a deep breath. "Who did this?"

"We don't know, sir. I've got Zoë checking just now."

"Just as well we got her in." Forrester drummed on the desk. "Let's get back to the real world. Did the CCTV at Dryburgh show anything, Mac?"

"Nothing so far, sir. Likely be Monday before we get anywhere."

"And the street teams?"

"Nothing so far on that, either."

"So, we've got nothing?"

"Basically, yes."

"Bloody hell." Forrester sat up again. "How's the Fife case review going?"

MacDonald scowled. "Not well. This DC Reed guy documented everything, and I mean *everything*. Considering it was a relatively minor crime at the time, they really went to town."

"Nothing wrong with that, Sergeant. At least we won't have to open old wounds if we get a link." Forrester scratched the back of his head. "So we reckon it'll be Monday before we've got a decent picture of the case?"

MacDonald nodded. "And that's with most of our team working this weekend."

"Christ, as if my OT bill isn't high enough already."

There was a knock on the door.

Zoë stood there, clutching her laptop and tugging her hair round her ear. "I think I've got something useful."

Forrester motioned towards the third chair in front of his desk, between Vicky and MacDonald. "Have a seat. Zoë, is it?"

"It is, sir." She perched on the front of the chair, laptop resting on her knees. "I've found IP addresses of seven users of the forum the video was posted on."

Forrester leaned forward, arms folded. "So we can trace them?"

"Yes, sir. No messing about — this is genuine. I've had them double-checked by Edinburgh and the Met."

"So, one of these people posted the video?"

Zoë bit her lip. "No. These are users of the forum it was posted in. It's a message chain called *Animal Rites* — as in last rites — on a forum called xbeast. These are people who've posted comments."

"Right, right. Do you know who posted the video?"

Zoë shook her head. "No, sir. That's still masked. Can't get through it. Doubt I ever will."

"Go on, then. These seven people you've found?"

"I've got three in the Dundee area and four in Fife."

"At least they're local, I suppose. Mac, can you get the Fife boys on it?"

"Will do, sir."

Forrester leaned forward. "Tell me about the Dundee three."

Zoë checked her laptop. "Two users have the same IP. I've traced it to a location on the Perth Road. The other is matched to a flat in the Hilltown."

Forrester got to his feet, hands in pockets. "Vicky, can you do the Hilltown? Mac, can you do the Perth Road once you've told our Fife cousins what's what?"

"Will do, sir."

Forrester patted Zoë on the shoulder as he passed. "Thanks for this. This is so good I'm going to report it to Raven in person right now." He left them in the room.

Zoë closed her laptop, fingers tight around the case. "Does he touch everyone like that?"

Vicky laughed as she got up. "Believe me, it's a good sign."

Chapter Twenty-Six

Vicky waited in Considine's car, looking down the Hilltown. They were parked by a patch of waste ground across from a bookie's and two takeaways. "That it over there?"

Considine checked his notebook then nodded. "That's the address Zoë gave us."

"Sheltered housing?"

"Aye."

A panda car pulled in a couple of spaces over from them.

Vicky got out and walked over, crunching across the loose gravel.

"Vicky Dodds."

Vicky nodded recognition at PC Woods. "Afternoon, Colin."

"Afternoon." Woods thumbed in the car at his colleague. "This is PC Soutar." Then he gave her the up and down. "Lost my wife, have you?"

"Karen's back at the station. I've got a new monkey to dance when I grind the organ."

Considine scowled at her. "I resent that."

"Just keep your mouth shut and don't stop dancing, Stephen."

Woods got out of the car and took off his hat. "So what're you needing proper coppers for this time?"

"We've traced an IP address to a Brian Morton." Vicky got out her notebook, waving it in the direction of the flats. "We understand he lives in the ground floor flat there."

Woods grinned at his colleague. "This is the sort of muck detectives get up to while we're doing the proper work."

Soutar nodded. "So I see."

Vicky narrowed her eyes at them. "We need to bring him in for questioning, that's all. I just need you to help apprehend him."

Soutar frowned. "You got a warrant?"

"Just had it approved, aye."

Woods rubbed his hands together. "Lead the way then, Vicks."

Vicky walked back to the street and traced the line of the road down the hill. The flat entrance was on Ann Street, a dark wood door with a ramp leading up. She pressed the buzzer for flat two, holding it for a few seconds.

"Yo?"

Vicky raised an eyebrow at Considine, who glanced away. "This is the police. We need access to your property."

"Not without a warrant."

"We're in possession of a warrant to access this property. We're looking for a Brian Morton."

The line went quiet for a few seconds.

Vicky pressed the buzzer again. The door clicked open. She nodded at the door. "Come on."

Inside, a man stood in the doorway to flat two, muscular arms folded. Navy jeans with a shirt and jumper combo. He pushed his glasses up his nose. "How can I help?"

Vicky flashed her warrant card. "Can we come in?"

The man shook his head. "Not until I see that search warrant of yours."

Vicky handed it over. "Mr Morton, we've got reason to believe you're involved in a kidnapping."

He licked his lips. "This isn't me."

"Aren't you Brian Morton?"

"I'm just visiting. That's my brother."

"What's going on, John?" A buzzing came from the hall behind. A mobility scooter appeared with a morbidly obese man sitting on it, his jowls sagging, the fabric of his shell suit stretched tight.

"It's the police, Brian." John Morton lowered his head to his brother. "Have you been an idiot on the internet again?"

Chapter Twenty-Seven

Vicky sat in the interview room, staring at the lawyer. "Ms Nelson-Caird, your client needs to start co-operating with us."

Kelly Nelson-Caird looked to be in her mid-thirties, her mouth seeming to lag behind her brain. She tapped a finger on the table. "Mr Morton hasn't committed a crime, Sergeant."

Vicky glanced at Considine, who was still silent as instructed. "If you'll let him speak, I might be able to determine that for myself."

"Very well." Nelson-Caird snorted. "Can you please outline the offences you believe my client *may* have committed?"

Vicky laid her hands on the table and focused on Brian. He was heavily out of breath and sweat dripped from his lank hair, only adding to the stench. She didn't want him to keel over there and then but he clearly knew something. "Very well."

Nelson-Caird sat back and folded her arms. "Please continue."

Vicky leaned forward on both elbows. "Mr Morton, we've brought you in for questioning because your internet account was used to access a message board called xbeast. In particular, it accessed a user forum called *Animal Rites*. Are you following me?"

Brian nodded, his mouth twitching.

Vicky massaged her left temple. "The message board in question had a video posted on it. The footage related to a crime we're currently investigating. One of the users who posted a comment to the video was you."

Brian shifted his head around, not letting it settle in one position. "I don't know what you're talking about."

"Mr Morton, please look at me."

Brian angled his head slightly. "I said I don't know what you're talking about."

Vicky produced a sheet of paper. "This shows a trace on that account back to your IP address."

Brian picked it up. "This doesn't prove anything. You can mask IP addresses."

"So you do know a bit about computers?"

Brian swallowed. "A bit."

"You're quite correct." Vicky leaned back in her chair. "My analyst tells me this IP address was masked. That said, we're getting very good at defeating the masking, apparently — I'm not particularly technical, but she tells me they can work out the originating IP address. They can even work out if that's masked as well. Can you believe that?"

Nelson-Caird frowned. "Are you insisting my client is here as a result of a trace on an IP address?"

Vicky nodded. "That's correct."

"Which you yourself admit may have been tampered with."

"It was most definitely tampered with and we have a full audit trail, right back to the originating node."

"And you know it's completely accurate?"

"I don't follow you."

"Someone could be posting on there and making it point to my client. They could be putting a smokescreen up to implicate Mr Morton here. It's completely inconclusive that my client is behind either the masking or the account."

"We'll have to agree to disagree on that." Vicky felt sweat trickle down the back of her blouse. "Mr Morton, what were you doing on that forum?"

"I don't know what forum you're talking about."

"Fine." Vicky took a moment to consider her next step, the nerve in her neck stinging. "What were your movements on Wednesday evening?"

"I'm housebound." Brian tapped his wheelchair. "The only reason I'm here is because you removed me from my mobility scooter and put me in this."

"And yet here you are."

Brian's breathing quickened. "I was in hospital on Wednesday afternoon. Ask my brother."

"You do know that housebound means never leaving the house." Vicky ran her tongue along her teeth. "What were you doing in hospital?"

"I was having a check-up."

"What for?"

Brian looked at the lawyer, almost pleading with her. Nelson-Caird just shrugged. He focused his gaze on the table. "I'm getting a gastric band fitted. It was a check-up to make sure my body's still ready for it."

"And this accounts for your whereabouts?"

Brian nodded. "Yes. I was in all afternoon."

"Can I have the name of the surgeon?"

Brian gripped the handles of the wheelchair tight. "John will know."

"Fine." Vicky took a note to ask. "And what about this afternoon? I'm interested in the time between two and two thirty."

"I was at home, having lunch."

"Were you using your computer?"

Brian let out a sigh.

"Mr Morton, we can check with your internet provider."

Brian wiped his brow, now soaked with sweat. "Yes, I was."

Vicky picked up the sheet of paper and turned it over. "You didn't post a message saying *'They got what was coming 2 them LOL'*?"

"No."

"You didn't post a reply saying *'PMSL'* to a post saying *'Wouldn't take one of their pups!'*?"

Brian shook his head. "No."

"Mr Morton, you're under caution. This will be admissible in court."

Nelson-Caird licked her lips, smudging her lipstick. She leaned across and whispered in his ear.

Brian shook his head. "But I didn't do it."

"Could anyone else have access to your computer?"

"No."

"What about your brother?"

Brian laughed. "John doesn't even know how to turn it on, let alone put an HTTP tunnel in."

Nelson-Caird rubbed her forehead. "Sergeant, can we pause this interview, please?"

"Interview terminated at sixteen oh nine." Vicky reached forward and pressed the stop button on the tape recorder. "If that's how you want to play it, Mr Morton, then I'm not sure you're prepared for what's going to happen next."

Brian hit his hand on the desk. "This is persecution."

"Of what?"

"Of obese people."

"It's not a hate crime, Mr Morton. Besides, I'm not aware of persecuting you. I've asked you questions relating to your internet usage, which appears to link to a crime we're investigating." Vicky got to her feet and left the room. She led Considine down the corridor. "Any idea what PMSL stands for, Stephen?"

"Pissing Myself Laughing."

"Shouldn't it be PML?"

Considine shrugged. "Americans."

"Come on. Let's speak to his brother."

Chapter Twenty-Eight

Can I take Brian home now?" John Morton sat in the waiting area, arms clutched tight to his chest.

Vicky shook her head. "No, we'll need to take a statement from you regarding your brother's movements."

"Am I under arrest?"

"No."

John tightened his cheeks. "Is Brian under arrest?"

"He's under caution, yes."

"Christ." John gripped his knees. "If you've got him in a cell just now, his stomach will be eating itself. He needs to eat every couple of hours."

"Needs to, does he?"

"Well, there'll be a tantrum if he doesn't. I've had to look after him since Mum died. It's not been easy."

"I'm sorry to hear that."

"We're kind of over it now, but looking after him's almost a full-time job."

"That's very community-spirited of you."

John shrugged. "Brian's not a well man."

Vicky opened the door to an interview room adjacent to the one Brian was still in. "If you'll just join us in here, sir?"

John got to his feet and followed her in. Considine closed the door behind him.

Vicky produced a copy of the sheet she'd shown Brian. "We've got evidence pointing to your brother being active on an animal rights forum known as xbeast. He's commented on a threat relating to an active kidnapping case."

"Okay." John picked at the desk. "What proof have you got?"

"We've traced a user account back to his IP address."

"What's an IP address?"

Vicky stared at him — was he just playing dumb? "It means Internet Protocol, I believe. It's a unique code given to users when they log on. Some are random, some are fixed. Either way, the Internet Service Providers can point us to who was using one at a given point in time. There was some level of obfuscation going on but we've significant reason to believe your brother used an account to post messages in response to a video."

"What was this video?"

Vicky handed him a series of screen grabs of the footage. "It showed the victims of the abduction."

"So, what, this is some sort of ransom demand?"

Vicky shook her head. "No, it just shows these people being forced to . . . do things they didn't want to."

"Why?"

"What do you mean, why?"

John shrugged. "I mean, why post a video if you're not after money?"

"The victims were liberated yesterday afternoon."

"Right. So?"

"So, your brother was posting on this forum today."

John leaned forward on the table and took off his glasses before rubbing his eyes. "You're telling me you think he's involved?"

"We *know* your brother's involved, Mr Morton. He was using the computer at the time these messages were posted." Vicky pushed another sheet across the table. "Read them. Does that look like the sort of thing he'd post?"

John carefully inspected them. "Maybe."

"Is your brother into animal rights?"

"Animal welfare, certainly. He's not vegan or anything but he doesn't eat meat. He hates cruelty. All of his cheesecakes have free-range eggs and so on."

"His cheesecakes?"

John put his glasses on again. "Yeah. Brian pretty much lives off desserts. Cheesecakes, gateaux, that sort of thing. I can't stop him. If I don't fill a trolley with frozen cakes on a Saturday, it'll be a week of tantrums. It's worse than a child."

"Your brother posted some messages in support of this act. We'd like to understand if he knows who posted the video."

"I take it Brian's not been playing ball?"

"Would we be asking you if he had been?"

John chuckled. "Maybe."

"Do you think he could've been involved in this?"

John started cleaning his glasses on his jumper. "Look at him. He can't leave the house without me carrying out a military operation. That computer's all he's good at."

"How good is he?"

"I don't know. I'm next to useless myself. I can get on Facebook and the BBC, but that's pretty much it."

"Where was your brother between two and two thirty this afternoon."

"At home, I think."

123

"Were you there?"

"No. I was meeting a client. I popped in to see him after I finished. That's when you lot came blundering in."

"Where was your brother on Wednesday evening?"

John swallowed. "Ninewells. He's supposed to be getting a gastric band fitted. He was in hospital yesterday as well. Last hope for him. Did you see the guy in Livingston who died last week? Brian's now in the top five heaviest people in the UK."

"That must be pretty hard for you."

John put the glasses back on. "It is."

Vicky checked her notes — aside from getting Considine to verify the appointment at the hospital, she had little else. "Mr Morton, can you please detail your movements on Wednesday afternoon?"

John's gaze darted between Vicky and Considine. "Look, what is this? Do I need a lawyer or something?"

"We simply need to eliminate you from suspicion."

"You mean I'm under suspicion?"

"Mr Morton, everyone in Scotland and the north of England is until we rule them out."

"Fine." John took a few seconds before continuing. "I was with Brian at the hospital. Then I drove down to Armadale in West Lothian."

"What were you doing there?"

"I went to the Speedway, to see Edinburgh Monarchs. Edinburgh play there since they shut down the greyhound track in the city centre. I was with my mate, Steve. He can confirm it."

Vicky glanced at Considine, who started writing. "Please can you tell me what speedway is, Mr Morton?"

John pushed his glasses back up his face. "It's team motorbike racing. I got into it when I lived down south. Started going to the Rye House Rockets. When I moved back here after Mum died, I started going to Edinburgh and Glasgow."

"What did you do down south?"

"I was a journalist. I moved into PR afterwards. I've got a small company doing publicity now. That was the client I was meeting at lunchtime before I checked on Brian."

"Okay." Vicky inspected her notebook for anything not asked. "This is a serious crime we're investigating. Your brother may be involved. We'd appreciate if you'd let us know of anything that comes up."

Chapter Twenty-Nine

Vicky found Forrester in his office, the coffee machine spitting in the corner. She twisted a chair round and sat, pointing at the filter and tapping her watch. "I hope that's decaf."

"Decaf coffee? What's the bloody point?" Forrester leaned forward. "Have you got some good news for me?"

"Maybe." Vicky put the tape from Brian's interview on the table. "We spoke to Brian Morton and also his brother, John. They've given us solid-looking alibis, which I've got Considine validating." She tapped the tape. "Brian kind of slipped up, mentioning an 'HTTP tunnel'. He sounds like he knows what he's doing."

"Think they're our guys?"

"See, that's the thing, sir. He's probably thirty stone, maybe more. His brother reckons he's in the top five in the UK now. Unless he's wearing a fat suit like in that Gwyneth Paltrow film, he's clearly not abducted Rachel or her brother."

Forrester wiped his mug with a paper towel then poured in some coffee. "Do you think he's done anything?"

"Maybe. He could've posted the videos, though Zoë's not managed to prove it yet. I think he knows something but he's not giving anything up. If he's not involved, he'd surely just say he posted those comments and he doesn't know any more."

"Or he's not involved."

"Sorry?"

Forrester shrugged. "Could be the trace Zoë did was flawed. Wouldn't be the first time."

"You think she's unreliable?"

"She seems okay. I meant techies in general."

"Well, I think he posted them." Vicky slumped back in her chair. "Either way, if he's involved, he's not giving up any of his colleagues."

Forrester took a slurp of coffee as he sat. "So what about this brother?"

Vicky thought about it, the acrid tang of the coffee filling her nostrils. "He doesn't seem the sort."

"What does the sort look like?"

"Precisely. He's fit and healthy, unlike his brother, but I just can't see it."

"So what do you want to do, Vicky?"

"Brian's still in custody. We arrested him. There are a few things we can charge him with that mean we can keep him in."

"Or we can let him go?"

"I'd say we keep him in."

"Is this the man who had to get lugged in by Karen Woods' husband? Guy on the mobility scooter?"

"It is, yes."

Forrester wrinkled his nose. "Not sure keeping him in's going to be a great idea. What if he has a heart attack?" He put his feet up on the desk and stared into his mug for a few seconds. "Let them go and get surveillance put on both of them. Kirk and Considine just lost their weekends."

Vicky folded her arms. "Come on, sir."

"Other than one of them watching a dodgy film, what've they done?"

"Brian's into animal welfare."

Forrester laughed. "Shall we bring Jamie Oliver and his mates in?"

"I'm serious. We should consider Brian as a suspect."

"Noted. He's top of the list. We'll watch him and his brother over the weekend. Get Zoë monitoring his internet usage, okay?"

"Fine."

Forrester slammed his empty mug onto the desk. Beads of coffee flew out. "Look, Vicky, we could arrest the staff at the dog pounds between here and Glasgow. What good would it do?"

"Okay, sir." Vicky bunched up her ponytail, tightening her grip around it. "Where've we got with the others?"

Forrester checked his watch. "The Fifers should just be coming over the Tay Bridge right about now. Bunch of schoolgirls, would you believe? Their parents and teachers weren't impressed when half of Glenrothes CID pitched up at the school. I'm going to get Buchan and some uniform to lean on them and scare the holy crap out of them. Hopefully they'll blab."

Vicky nodded. "Are we speaking to their boyfriends? Reed seemed to think it might've been local youths egged on by their girlfriends."

"Good point." Forrester sat forward and noted it down. "I'll get onto his DI and see what we can do there."

"What about MacDonald's two, sir? The accounts linked to the same IP?"

Forrester cleared his throat. "Mac's not been able to get a hold of them yet."

"Them?"

He grinned. "We know who it is. Traced them with BT. It's a couple — Sandy and Polly Muirhead."

"But you can't find them?"

"Not yet. He's been at their workplaces and the house. Nada." Forrester leaned across his desk. "Vicky, can you and Considine head out to their house?"

Vicky scowled at him. "I need to get away, sir."

"And I need you to stay. I've got the OT approved from Raven."

Vicky leaned back, torn between maybe closing the case and spending time with her daughter. The money didn't really come into it. She bit her nail. "Okay."

Forrester put his feet on the table. "Good girl."

Chapter Thirty

Vicky parked behind a blue BMW. The daylight was just dying as the sun dipped below the hills beyond Perth to the west. The street was one of the better ones in Dundee, a short row of old stone houses. "That's MacDonald's car there."

"The 1-Series?" Considine laughed. "It's a hairdresser's car."

"Not as macho as a Subaru?"

"No way."

Vicky got out and headed over, sitting in the seat behind MacDonald, Considine sitting behind Karen Woods. "Evening." She grinned at MacDonald. "Stephen was just saying this is a hairdresser's car."

MacDonald twisted round to glare at Considine. "That right?"

"You're not disagreeing with me, are you?"

MacDonald chuckled. "I've seen your car, boy racer."

Karen looked out of the passenger window.

"I just like a fast car, that's all."

"A boy who likes a fast car. A boy racer."

Considine shook his head. "Whatever."

Karen turned back to glare at them. "Have you two finished comparing dick sizes?"

MacDonald shrugged. "Just about."

Vicky cleared her throat, regretting starting the whole thing. "Anything happened here?"

"No." MacDonald glanced at the time display on the dashboard. "We've been here half an hour and there's been no movement."

Vicky opened the door. "Back in a minute." She got out of the car and dialled her mother.

She answered this time. "That you, Victoria?"

"It is, Mum."

Out of breath. "What is it?"

"I'm going to have to work late tonight."

"I see."

"Come on, Mum, you know how it is."

"I thought I'd stopped all this when your father retired."

"Can you just look after Bella till I get back?"

"When's that going to be?"

"Late, I imagine."

"I'll put her to bed and wait at yours till you get back."

"Thanks, Mum. You're a lifesaver." Vicky closed the phone and got back in the car. Considine and MacDonald both had their arms folded.

Karen looked around. "Who was that?"

"Mum. Oh, I saw Colin earlier."

"So I gather. He texted me, said you were up to your psycho bitch stuff with some disabled guy."

"He wasn't disabled. He was just obese."

"You're not denying the psycho bitch stuff, though?"

Vicky laughed. "Too late now."

The Airwave on the dashboard crackled. "Control to DS MacDonald. Over."

MacDonald grabbed it, holding it up to his mouth. "Receiving."

"Car with plates matching your search pattern's heading your way."

"Thanks." MacDonald pocketed the Airwave and turned round. "Time to go."

At the junction with the Perth Road, a dark red Fiat slowed as it turned the corner into the street, headlights shining, before pulling in by the house.

"That's him." MacDonald opened his door and got out, leading them over to the car. He rapped on the passenger window as the engine switched off. It wound down. "Mr Muirhead?"

"Aye?"

MacDonald got out his warrant card. "Detective Sergeant Euan MacDonald of Police Scotland. Can we have a word?"

"What's this about?"

"Better discuss this inside, sir."

Muirhead got out of his car and locked the door. He was medium height, maybe late thirties with a slight paunch and a shaved head. "Look, what's this all about?"

"Is your wife home, Mr Muirhead?"

He shook his head. "She should be home soon."

"Right."

They were lit up by another set of headlights. A cream Fiat 500 stopped in the street at the entrance, the right indicator still flashing.

MacDonald grabbed Muirhead. "Is that your wife?"

"A-a-aye."

"I'm on it." Vicky jogged to the car, Considine following. She held out her own warrant card, waiting for the window to crawl down. "Polly Muirhead?"

The woman in the car nodded, eyes wide.

Vicky opened the door. "We need to speak to you."

"Okay."

"Move the car forward, please."

Polly stalled the car before eventually getting it to jerk forward, parking just behind her husband.

Vicky looked at Considine. "I could just see her making a run for it there."

"Aye, and I don't fancy our chances with your motor."

"I suppose yours would have been better, right?"

"Aye." Considine shrugged. "The Python can nail most cars in a dead heat."

Vicky rolled her eyes. "At least you've not got pet names for parts of your anatomy."

Considine paused and raised his eyebrows.

Chapter Thirty-One

Vicky sat at the interview room table, the smell of Brian Morton's stale sweat still lingering. She nodded at Considine to lead.

He cleared his threat. "For the record, please state your name and occupation."

"Fergus Duncan." Without looking up, Polly Muirhead's lawyer tapped at a high-end mobile phone. His face was covered in acne even though he looked late twenties. He wore a dark pinstripe suit with a bright orange tie. "I'm a lawyer, employed by Gray and Leech."

Considine cleared his throat. "Mrs Muirhead, for the purposes of the tape, can you state your full name and occupation?"

Supposedly in her mid-thirties, Polly Muirhead had a woman's face on a girl's body, her boyish figure not rounded with curves like Vicky's — no danger of those tiny breasts making her look fat. "Polly Morag Muirhead. I'm a solicitor at Gray and Leech in Dundee."

"Do you understand why you're here?"

"No."

"We're investigating a kidnapping perpetrated by a group who may or may not have an animal welfare agenda."

"And?"

"We believe you may be attached to that group." Vicky produced a similar document to the one she'd shown Brian Morton, this time tracing the accounts to the Muirheads' IP address. "We believe both you and your husband were active on this particular site and both commented on a video showing the kidnap victims." She handed them some stills from the video.

Polly's eyes shot up. "You think *I* did *this*?"

"Do you deny being a member of xbeast?"

Duncan glanced up from his mobile, a frown etched on his forehead. "What's xbeast supposed to be?"

"It's the message forum where this video was posted, entitled *Animal Rites*. Your client has a user account there."

"That's a strong accusation."

"We've got proof."

"I'm sure this sort of thing can be tampered with."

"This trace is sound."

"I'll take your word for it."

Vicky turned to Polly. "Do you deny having a user account?"

Polly exhaled. "Fine, I'm a member of the group."

Duncan leaned over and whispered to Polly, who stared into space for a few seconds before shaking her head. "My colleague — sorry, my *client* — wishes to make it clear that, while she does indeed have a user account on the website in question, she is categorically *not* affiliated with any terror groups."

"Very well." Vicky opened her notebook. "Mrs Muirhead, did you post the video?"

"No."

"Did you post a reply stating *'They didn't go far enough'*?"

Polly swallowed. "Yes."

Vicky leaned back in her chair. "Why did you post that?"

"It's a personal belief. I'm against animal cruelty. I'm a vegan." Polly shrugged. "I work in law, yes, but I give half of my time *pro bono* to animal welfare charities. This is supported by my employers. My husband pays our bills and I give most of my salary to charity."

Vicky pointed at her notebook. "You're saying you think these people should have been murdered?"

Polly stared at the ceiling. "I'm saying they got off lightly. Being filmed naked in a cage is nothing compared to the crimes committed by that woman."

"Which woman would that be?"

"Her name is Rachel Hay."

"How do you know her name?"

"It said so on the video file."

Considine tapped the table. "Did you do this at work?"

Polly shook her head. "At home. I was on my lunch break — it's a five-minute drive."

"At the back of two?"

"I had a client conference until then. I'm allowed a lunch break, after all."

Vicky flicked back through her notebook, unfolding a still from the video's metadata. "You said it was Rachel Hay who perpetrated the crimes and not her brother?"

Polly nodded. "That's correct."

"What makes you say that?"

"I already told you. It was on the file."

Vicky held up the screen grab. "It just says 'Rachel and Paul'."

Polly gripped her left shoulder. "I've never heard of her brother but I know about Rachel Hay."

"What do you know about her?"

"She's the pug breeder who was in the papers, isn't she? That's the real crime you should be investigating. I can't believe she's not rotting in prison for what she did to those poor animals."

"Have you ever spoken to Mrs Hay?"

"No."

"Do you know where she lives?"

"Dundee, I presume."

"Where were you between three p.m. and midnight on Wednesday?"

Polly glanced at Duncan. "I was at work until about six. Mr Duncan can confirm that."

He nodded. "That's correct."

"And after that?"

Polly bit her lip. "I met my husband and we went for dinner with some friends."

"And after dinner?"

"We went to the Rep."

"The theatre?"

Polly nodded. "Yes."

"What did you see there?"

"*And Then There Were None*. It's based on an Agatha Christie novel. It was very good."

Vicky scribbled it down. "And you were definitely there?"

"I've got the ticket stubs in my purse if you don't believe me."

"We'll need to take them in as evidence."

"I see." Polly sighed as she rummaged around in her handbag, retrieving her purse. She unclipped it and hand over two tickets, the paper torn at the edges.

Vicky checked the stubs — they looked genuine. "Who were the friends you were with?"

"Simon and Emma Hagger. They live in Barnhill."

Vicky made a note — another Considine task. "Do you know a Brian Morton?"

Polly narrowed her eyes. "Should I?"

"He's another user on there."

Polly coughed. "Well, other than my husband, I've no idea who anyone is on there. It's entirely anonymous."

Chapter Thirty-Two

S hut the door, Stephen." Forrester leaned against the edge of his desk and looked around at the team, all huddled in his office, getting warmer by the second. "It's Friday night, I'm knackered and I'm going to the pub for a pint after I've told Raven where we've got to." He glanced around the room. "So, where *have* we got to? Mac?"

"Finally got the NCA information in, sir. Nothing active relating to animal cruelty cells operating in Scotland or the north of England."

"Fantastic. What about this video?"

"Looking to find who posted it. Zoë's identified a set of users who posted comments in response to it and we've now spoken to all of them."

Zoë was almost hiding behind a filing cabinet. "I haven't matched any more users to IPs yet, sir."

Forrester rubbed his chin, his hand rasping against the stubble. "Let me get this clear. They kidnap Rachel and Paul and film them as they try to force them to have sex. Then they post it on some weird little website where only nine people can access it. Right?"

"Correct."

"Why?"

Zoë blushed. "I don't know, sir."

"Sorry." Forrester held up his hands, looking from officer to officer. "It was a general question."

"It's not clear." MacDonald smoothed out his blue tie. "We assume a terror group's behind this."

"Precisely, Mac. A terror group would shove it on YouTube and get the press and news all over it, wouldn't they?"

"Maybe."

"Who've you spoken to?"

"I've just come out of speaking to Sandy Muirhead. DS Dodds spoke to his wife, Polly. He gave us an alibi of being at the theatre. I've not managed to check it yet."

Vicky nodded. "His wife gave us the same one."

Considine raised his hand. "I'll check them both out, sir."

Forrester focused on Vicky and MacDonald. "Are these pair suspects?"

Vicky nodded. "Yes."

MacDonald shook his head. "No."

Forrester laughed. "Well, which is it?"

MacDonald gestured to Vicky. "You first."

Vicky smiled. "When I interviewed her, Polly Muirhead suggested Rachel was the target, not Paul."

Forrester screwed up his face. "Did she say why she thought they were targeting her?"

"The defective pugs she sold." Vicky read from her notebook. "Polly's aware of who Rachel is, plus she gives money and professional time to animal charities. I'd say she fits our profile."

Forrester nodded before looking at MacDonald. "So, Mac, tell us why not?"

"Two things. First, they've got an alibi. Second, this is a lawyer and an accountant, not tree-hugging hippies."

Vicky scowled. "Do they have to be?"

"It'd help." Forrester narrowed his eyes at Vicky. "I'll think about it. Anything more on these brothers of yours?"

"I think we should keep Brian in custody."

Forrester stared at the wall for a few seconds. "I've had his lawyer on the phone shouting the odds about human rights. I said we're letting him go. We're sticking to that."

"But, sir —"

Forrester held up a finger. "As I said, we've got surveillance in place." He glanced at Kirk and Considine before looking back at Vicky. "What about his brother?"

"We're putting surveillance on him, as well. It's not like Brian will run away anywhere."

Forrester leaned back in his chair. "Do we need surveillance on the Muirheads?"

Vicky raised her eyebrows. "You're not letting them go, are you?"

Forrester shrugged his shoulders. "We've got nothing to charge them with. If we charged everyone who'd been stupid on the internet, half of Dundee would be in the cells."

"There's a difference between stupidity and what these people have been up to, sir. They're all suspects."

"We've got nothing tying them to the Dryburgh Industrial Estate other than some vague comments on a video file."

"I still think we should keep Brian Morton in."

MacDonald put a hand in his pocket. "Brian needs an accomplice to carry out the crimes."

"What about his brother?"

MacDonald shrugged. "He's got an alibi."

"Had some uniform pop in to see his mate about it." Considine tilted his chin down. "Boy lives in Fintry. Looks like John *was* at the Speedway."

"Bloody Fintry." Forrester cracked his knuckles. "What about these Fife kids, then, Mac?"

"Buchan's in with them now, sir. Not had word since the second round of interviews. Doesn't look like they're involved — just a bunch of schoolgirls being daft on the internet." MacDonald winked. "Like half of Dundee."

Vicky folded her arms. "Zoë, did you get any joy unpicking that voice scrambler?"

"It's called a voice changer, ma'am. I spoke to one of the guys upstairs about it. It's next to impossible to descramble. That's why they use them. It's a complex series of Fourier transfo —"

Vicky held up a hand. "In English, please."

"Okay." Zoë licked her lips. "They're basically doing stuff to the voice, like changing the pitch, distorting it, adding phase and ring modulation and so on. To descramble it back to the original, we'd need to know exactly what they've applied to it. Unfortunately, the only way to know is to have the original recording."

"So it's chicken and egg?"

"Right. Without it, we'd just be guessing. It could be worse than nothing. It might sound like someone it's not. I doubt it'd be admissible as evidence."

Forrester got to his feet. "Right. Let's see how it goes with the surveillance over the weekend. Dismissed."

The others got up and left the room, Vicky staying behind.

Forrester was putting on his jacket when he noticed her. "What is it, Vicky?"

"Can I keep Zoë on?"

"Approved. I'll get her assigned for at least another week, okay?"

"Fine." Vicky got to her feet, not used to it being that easy. "Have a good weekend, sir."

"Aye, you too."

Vicky left the room, bumping into MacDonald outside. "Euan."

"Vicky." He grinned at her. "What a first week, eh?"

"Tell me about it."

"Fancy a drink?"

Vicky pursed her lips, sorely tempted. She checked her watch —
just about enough time to make it home to tuck Bella in. "Sorry,
I've got to head home, I'm afraid."

"Just so's you know, if you knock me back three times I'll take
it personally." MacDonald held her gaze for a few seconds before
looking away. "Anyway, I'll wait and see if Forrester fancies a pint.
See you on Monday, okay?"

"Have a good one."

Chapter Thirty-Three

Vicky sat on the edge of Bella's bed, the room illuminated by the small Cinderella lamp on the pine chest of drawers. Disney posters filled the walls. "Night-night, sweet pea."

Bella struggled to keep her eyes open as Vicky kissed her on the forehead. "Has Granny stopped shouting at you yet, Mummy?"

Vicky took a deep breath — Mum should've kept her voice down. "She wasn't shouting, Bells."

"She was cross with you, wasn't she?"

"She was. Mummy had to stay late at work."

"Were you catching baddies?"

"Maybe. I don't know yet."

"Why?"

"Bella, Mummy's not at work tomorrow. We'll do some fun stuff, okay?"

"Can we catch some baddies?"

"We'll see. Remember, if you're a good girl, you'll get to stay with Cameron and Ailish tomorrow night?"

"Yay!"

"Do you want me to read you a story?"

"Sleepy, Mummy. Night-night."

"Goodnight." Vicky left the room and stood outside Bella's door, listening to her breathing. She wiped the tears from her cheek and slowly walked down the stairs.

In the kitchen, she reached into the fridge for the bottle of wine. She went over to the sink and tipped it out. She leaned against the sink, her eyes filling with tears again.

Bella's life was just passing her by.

Her eyes moistened again. She remembered giving birth, Liz holding her hand tight, like it was yesterday. Where had the years gone? Before she knew it, Bella would be leaving home and she'd have nothing to show for it but memories of tucking her in.

There was a scratching at the back door. She blinked the tears away as she let Tinkle in, the cat shivering from the rain. Vicky picked her up and cuddled her for a few seconds before leaving her on the counter while she got the tin of cat food from the fridge and spooned it into her bowl.

She watched the cat eat, realising Tinkle was at the opposite end of the spectrum from the animals Rachel Hay was selling, a half-feral tabby who'd softened over the years to the point where she could be picked up and handled. When she was hungry.

Her mouth went dry. Rachel lying in the hospital bed, Paul almost catatonic. She'd no idea where this case was going. Whoever was doing it was beyond sick. What they'd tried to force Rachel and Paul to do . . . Christ.

She poured a glass of water, sipping as she stared out of the window into the dark night.

Saturday

29th March 2014

Chapter Thirty-Four

Vicky woke up, her mouth dry. She reached to the bedside table for her glass of water. Empty.

She squinted at the alarm clock. 7.04.

A banging noise came from downstairs. Her heart fluttered.

She got up and tugged her dressing gown around her, tying it as she raced downstairs, narrowly avoiding stepping on Tinkle as her little fat body raced up the stairs to the warmth of Vicky's bed.

There was someone at the door.

She opened it, blinking at the early morning light.

"Morning, Vicky."

"Dad?"

He held up his toolbox. "I've come to put those shelves up in Bella's room."

Vicky rested a hand on her face. "Dad, it's *seven* on a Saturday."

"Well, I was up anyway and your mother's baking scones for a coffee morning so I thought I'd get out and be useful."

"At least it's not Bella waking me up today." Vicky opened the door wide. "Come on in, then."

Dad lifted his head, his nostrils twitching. "Is that coffee I smell?"

"I don't drink coffee, Dad."

"Right. Of course you don't. Have you got any?"

Vicky tightened the belt of her gown. "Aye. Come on, I'll make you some."

"There's a good girl. I've had my porridge but a coffee would be smashing."

Vicky led into the kitchen and filled the kettle, clicking it on. "Milk and two still?"

Dad seated himself on a stool at the breakfast bar and produced a small white box. "Your mother's got me on these sweeteners. They taste horrible if you try to eat them but they're not too bad in a coffee."

"Okay." Vicky poured milk over the instant coffee granules and started making a paste as the water boiled, the sharp aroma hitting her nostrils. "Remember when me and Andrew were wee and we used to dunk biscuits in your coffee?"

"Like it was yesterday."

"That's the only time I'll have the stuff." The kettle clicked off and she filled the mug before stirring it. "There you go, Dad."

"Cheers." He clicked in four sweeteners before taking a drink, showing no reaction to the temperature. "How's work going?"

"So you still miss the force then, Dad?"

He shook his head. "Never retire, Vicky. It's a bloody nightmare."

"In what way?"

"I just keep thinking about old cases and people who'd want to get me. It's hard to switch off." Dad took another sip. "Tell me about this case. I've asked twice now."

Vicky laughed. "You're not really interested in the detail, are you?"

"Not really. Are you still enjoying it?"

"I am but I'm struggling with the stress."

"It gets to you in the end, my girl."

"The case we're working on just now, nothing seems to fit together."

"That's the bit I loved most about being a detective. Everything feels like chaos."

"So what would you do?"

"Threatening to kick the shit out of them usually helped."

"Dad!"

He laughed. "In all seriousness, it was always a case of just speaking to more and more people. Usually, they'd done something stupid somewhere along the line. What's this case you're working on?"

"A kidnapping. A brother and a sister were abducted and taken to an industrial estate."

"You find them?"

Vicky nodded. "We did, aye."

"Didn't see anything in the paper about it this morning."

"Yeah, think we're trying to keep it out of the press just now."

"But you've caught the kidnappers?"

Vicky shook her head. "No, we rescued the brother and sister but we didn't get whoever did it."

"I see."

Vicky reached into the fridge for the two-litre bottle of Diet Coke. She poured out a glass and took a sip — almost entirely flat. "I'll take Bella up Dundee Law today, I think."

"What, driving up?"

"No, I'll walk. It'll tire her out."

"That's what me and your mother did every weekend. Get you and Andrew to run around and exhaust yourselves."

Vicky stared into her glass, only a couple of bubbles dancing on the surface. "I'm worried I'm pissing Mum off."

"Why?"

"Dumping Bella on you guys all the time. I'm such a shit mother. Why can't I just look after her and do my job?" She started crying, images of Bella asleep in her bed creeping all over her.

Dad got up and held her in his arms. "Hey there, baby girl, that's no way to be."

"I'm ruining her life, Dad."

"She's a good girl." He stroked her back, slowly, just like when she was a child or a teenager, heart broken by an idiot boy. "And don't worry about your mother."

"You sure Mum's not getting pissed off at me?"

Dad stood back and held her out at arm's reach. "Don't worry about pissing your mum off. For one, you know she's always like that. Second, we love looking after the wee girl. Keeps us young, I think." He stared into space. "Takes your mother's mind off what's happened to your brother."

"How's Andrew doing? I mean really?"

"Not good. The boy's a chip off the old block but I can handle it, whereas he obviously can't. This ME or whatever it is, it's killing your mother seeing him like that. The silly bugger pushed himself far too hard and just didn't know when to stop."

"Quite a pair we turned out to be."

Dad stroked her arm. "We're proud of you both. Never forget that."

"Grandad!"

Dad spun round and lifted Bella up in his arms, twirling her around the small kitchen. "How's my girl?"

"Mummy says we're going to go catch baddies today, Grandad!"

Dad beamed at Vicky. "She's another chip off the old block."

Chapter Thirty-Five

Vicky leaned against the railings at the top of Dundee Law, bracing herself against the wind as she took in the view south across the sprawl of Dundee towards the Tay with its twin bridges leading into Fife. Dark clouds loomed overhead, a heavy curtain hanging all the way over to Perth in the west.

"Up, Mummy!"

Vicky looked down at Bella. "We are up."

"No, up! Up on the metal things!"

"It's not safe, Bella."

"My wee leggies are tired. That was a long walk."

Vicky lifted Bella up and rested her legs on the cold metal, careful to support her.

Bella pointed to the river. "Where's that?"

"That's the River Tay. The land behind it's Fife."

"Five?"

"No, Fife. It's where Auntie Karen and Uncle Colin come from."

"I thought Cameron was born in Fumdernland, not Five."

"Dunfermline. It's in Fife."

"Oh." Bella took in the panorama. "Where're the baddies?"

"There aren't any baddies up here."

"I thought there would be."

"Is that why you didn't want to come up?"

"Grandad said I wouldn't be able to get up the hill with my wee leggies. I did, though."

So that's where she'd got it from. "Why did you think there would be baddies up here?"

"It's called the Law Hill. Grandad said it's a prison."

"It's not been a jail for a long time."

Bella pointed at the war memorial. "Is that not it?"

"That's not the jail. That helps us remember people like Granny's uncle Jimmy who died in the War."

"Oh."

Vicky lifted her down from the railings. "How was playgroup this week?"

"I liked it. Caitlin and Jayden were my best pals. They gave me football stickers. I like Arsenal." Bella looked up at the memorial, legs crossed in the way she'd inherited from her mother. She stared up at Vicky. "Mummy, why haven't I got a daddy?"

Vicky gasped, the nerve in her neck starting to jangle. "You've got a mummy, Bells. Isn't that enough?"

"Stinky Simon doesn't have a daddy. Hayden has a daddy but not a mummy."

Vicky's phone rang — saved by the bell. She tucked Bella between her legs before getting out her phone and checking the display. Dad. "You haven't burnt the house down, have you?"

He laughed. "No, not yet, but that cat's not speaking to me. I only tried to stroke her."

"Why are you calling?"

"It's noisy where you are."

"I told you, we're up the Law, Dad."

"You couldn't pop into B&Q or the new place on the Kingsway for a bag of eight-mil screws, could you?"

Vicky rubbed at her face. "Couldn't you have done that before you came round this morning?"

"I wanted to get a head start. Besides, there's two short in the box. I'm not going to take it back down now."

"Right, fine. I'll get it. Bye." She pocketed her phone. She knelt, looking through the railings across the southern edge of Dundee, resting her head on Bella's. "Have you been a good girl?"

"No."

"Why not?"

"I've not helped Mummy catch any baddies yet."

Vicky laughed. "You've been a good girl so far. Come on, Toots. Let's get some hot chocolate before we do our shopping."

Chapter Thirty-Six

"No! Mummy! I want to see the owls!"

"Come on, Bella." Vicky lifted her up, her police training stretched almost to breaking as she tried to maintain calm amid the hostile stares from the other customers.

A collection of poor-looking birds of prey — owls, kites and a few others Vicky didn't recognise — sat in a stall to the side of the entrance to Fixit DIY. The rat-faced proprietor wandered over. "Can let your wee girl see the birds for half price if you keep her quiet."

"No, thank you."

"She doesn't seem to think so."

"*She* had a giant hot chocolate and her blood sugar level's collapsing." Vicky barged past him, carrying Bella inside the store. "Come on, Bella, that man's a real baddie."

Little fists pounded on her back. "Mummy! No!"

Vicky hurried around the store, getting lost as Bella screamed and hammered at her back. She ended up in the paint aisle then the kitchens. She doubled back and crossed the aisle. There they were.

Eight mil — was that the drill size or the screw size? She grabbed both bags before racing to the tills. The self-service was free so she scanned the bag as Bella clung tight, her tears slicking onto Vicky's shoulder. She put Bella down so she could pay, then led her out of the store.

Bella stopped by the bird display, tiny hands rubbing at her eyes. "Grandad would let me see them."

"Mummy will need to have words with Grandad, then."

"Why won't you let me see the birds?"

Vicky took a deep breath, the knot in her neck tightening. Rachel and Paul in their cage. "It's cruel, Bells. The birds don't want to be there."

"Are they sore?"

"Very sore. They're in agony." Vicky grabbed her hand. "Come on, let's go get our shopping."

Chapter Thirty-Seven

"Why's this called the Riverside, Mummy?"

Vicky stood by the chiller in Tesco, cold air blasting out, the smell of doughnuts wafting over from the bakery. She pointed past the tills. "That's the river we were looking at up on the Law. We're just beside it."

"Okay."

Vicky held out a packet of own-brand free-range chicken Kievs. "Shall we have these for tea next week?"

Bella folded her arms around her chest. "I like eating at Granny's. I get soup there."

"Just soup?"

Bella giggled. "Biscuits. And sausages. And chicken nuggets. And tablet!"

"Did Granny tell you to say soup?"

Bella pouted. "Maybe."

Vicky pushed the trolley towards the next aisle. Thank God the tantrum was over.

"Why do we do the fridge bit last, Mummy? Granny always does it first in the Co-op."

"The Co-op's a lot closer to Granny's house than the Tesco is to ours, so Mummy wants the cold stuff to stay as cold as it can."

"Oh. Are those the baddies?"

Vicky followed the line of her finger. "I don't know." Her phone rang. She got it out, expecting another fool's errand from Dad. Considine.

"You on today, Sarge?"

"Day off. What is it?"

"No need to be so clipped. Just thought I'd let you know John and Brian left the house and are at the Riverside Tesco."

"Right." Vicky pocketed the phone, eyes shut. "Shi — sugar." She opened them, looking around for Brian or John. She knelt down. "Bella, if you want to help Mummy catch the baddies, you'll be as quiet as a mouse."

"As quiet as Tinkle when I feed her?"

"Quieter." She picked Bella up, grabbed her empty bags for life and left the full trolley in the aisle, hurrying towards the tills and the exits.

"Where are we going, Mummy?"

"Monifieth."

"Why?"

"Mummy remembered she needs something from there."

"Are there baddies in here?"

"Maybe."

At the end, two middle-aged women stood chatting, arms waving in the air, heads craning back in laughter, their trolleys across the full width of the aisle.

Vicky barged past, shoving a trolley into one of them.

"Excuse me?"

"Sorry." Vicky started jogging, desperate to get out of the shop.

A mobility scooter came round the corner just ahead of her, Brian Morton's flab rolling over the sides. John Morton pushed a trolley loaded with cakes — artisan brands Vicky could never afford. She swapped Bella to the other hip and walked back down the aisle, the nerve throbbing. "Come on. We better go this way."

She raced as fast as she could, a shelf stacker already checking out her abandoned trolley, continually looking back the way she'd come.

John stood at the end of the aisle, gesticulating to his brother.

Vicky cleared the end and put Bella down. Racing past the bakery and its cloying fresh bread smells, they cut up through the fruit and veg section, dodging trolleys as they went. She made it out of the front of the store, Bella skipping alongside as they walked back to the car.

"Morning, Vicky."

She stopped dead, eyes shooting around.

"Over here." Considine sat in a dark grey Mondeo, eyes hidden behind shades, arm resting on the open window.

Vicky allowed herself to breathe, eyes on the front of the store. "Didn't fancy taking the Python out?"

"This blends in better."

"You're not being very inconspicuous, Stephen. You look like you're in *Reservoir Dogs*."

"Never mind. They'll be ages in there. Can't believe you were there as well."

"Me neither." Vicky stared up at the heavens. "John said he filled a trolley in Tesco."

"Aye. Probably the only thing he was telling the truth about."

Vicky put a hand on her hip, her heartbeat slowing. "Have they done anything today?"

"Nothing." Considine looked at Bella, who was in the middle of a little dance. "That your kid?"

"Aye. I'll see you on Monday." Vicky tugged Bella's hand, leading her towards their car, slamming the central locking on when they got in.

"Mummy, was that man a baddie?"

"No, but he's going to catch the baddies for us. Shall we go home and get some soup?"

"Can I have biscuits and crisps after?"

Vicky ruffled Bella's hair. "Just one biscuit, though."

Chapter Thirty-Eight

A car horn sounded outside. Vicky got up from the sofa and opened the curtains, looking out onto the dark street.

Karen sat in her Volvo estate, waving, the faces of Cameron and Ailish pressed up against the back window.

Bella was sitting against the back of the sofa, legs stretched out fully, eyes locked on the TV screen.

Vicky took her hand. "That's Auntie Karen for you, Bells."

Bella didn't look away. "Okay." She got to her feet and put her coat on, still entranced by the screen.

Vicky grabbed her backpack and led them out into the cold air.

Bella ran along the short drive into Karen's arms.

Karen opened the back door. "Come on, you. Let's get you buckled in."

Vicky knelt and cuddled Bella.

"I love you, Mummy."

"I love you, too." Vicky kissed her hair then waited, arms folded against the cold, while Karen put Bella in the car.

Karen shut the door and came over. "Busy today?"

"In a way." Vicky tightened her arms around herself. "I almost fucked up the surveillance on Brian and John Morton.

Considine was waiting outside the Riverside Tesco when we were there."

"And those brothers were in as well?"

"Aye."

"Nightmare. We always go to the Kingsway one or to Arbroath. Did they see you?"

"I don't think so."

"Typical day in the life of DS Vicky Dodds." Karen laughed. "How's she been today?"

"She had a tantrum about some bloody owls, of all things." Vicky caught Bella waving from between Cameron and Ailish. She returned it. "I think it was her being a grown-up like Mummy and having a deluxe hot chocolate."

Karen winked. "Like Mummy's a grown-up."

Vicky laughed. "I gave her some soup and an apple when we got home. She's had some pasta for tea and I let her watch *Charlie and the Chocolate Factory*. I think tonight'll be tantrum free."

"From Bella at least." Karen rolled her eyes, nodding at the car full of kids. "Right, I'll drop her off about eleven, Vicks, in case you get lucky tonight."

"Like that's going to happen."

"You okay?"

Vicky glanced round as the sodium lights switched on. "I've no idea what to wear."

"You'll be fine, Vicks, you always are. Jeans and a clingy top — show off your boobs."

"Yeah, maybe." Vicky stared at the light by her bedroom window, tiny dots of moths starting to congregate.

"It's not clothes, though, is it?"

Vicky looked back at Karen. "No, it's not."

Karen patted her arm. "You okay?"

"I don't know, Kaz. I just don't. Maybe I should cancel, pretend I've got a cold or something."

"You're going to be fine."

Vicky gripped her bottom lip between her canine teeth. "I just don't think I will. It's been so long since I've been on a date. What do I say? 'Oh, hi — I catch criminals and look after my daughter and that's it.'"

"That's not bad, is it?"

"Really?"

"Aye. You're quite something, Vicks. Not many people could cope with your life."

"Not sure I do."

"Of course you do. You, Bella and Tinkle are great."

"Maybe."

"You've got nothing to lose, okay? If the guy's an idiot, you've lost an evening — some nice wine and a curry will compensate for that. If he's a lovely guy . . ."

Vicky let herself chuckle. "That's what I'm worried about."

"Typical Vicky."

"You know me." Vicky looked over at the car again, three little faces pressing lips to the window and blowing, their cheeks billowing out. "Good luck with that lot."

"It's okay. I've got Colin to keep them in check. He's mostly useless but he *can* shout."

"She'll be okay, right?"

"Yes!" Karen gripped both of Vicky's shoulders. "She'll be fine. They'll be fine. We'll be fine. Now, off you go and make yourself beautiful. That's an order."

"Yes, boss."

Chapter Thirty-Nine

Yeah, come on, you'll love it. I'll get you some vodka." The kid in front of Vicky on the bus was sixteen at most, his head shaved and ears pierced, mobile blaring out some tuneless hip-hop.

The bus rolled round the corner and stopped at the lights in Broughty Ferry. Vicky realised how much of a pain in the arse the Gulistan was, being halfway between bus stops.

Another Eminem track started up.

Vicky got up and went downstairs, clocking the ned checking her out as she descended. She got off the bus and walked along Queen Street, the heels on her boots clicking as she walked past the library, catching herself in the reflection from the bus shelter.

The flouncy top was the right choice. Might live to regret the FM boots under her jeans, though. Should she have worn her hair up? Too much make-up?

Too late.

As she entered the curry house, her heart beat faster with every step, the knot tightening its grip on her. A dozen waiters milled around, though it seemed fairly quiet for a Saturday night.

She looked around, savouring the spices in the air, gentle sitar music coming out of the big speakers mounted to the ceiling.

She spotted Liz and Dave in the far corner, sitting on opposite sides of a table. "Evening."

Liz inspected her before glancing at Dave. "Robert'll be drooling when he sees you, Vicks."

Vicky sat between them, hanging her leather jacket on the back of the chair. "Have you guys been betting or something?"

Liz seemed hammered already. "Dave said you wouldn't even turn up."

Dave held up his hands. He was fresh-shaven for once, his large frame pressed into a tight shirt, the sort of pattern he'd never have chosen for himself. "She's twisting my words, Vicks."

"I'll bet." Vicky smoothed out her black jeans, her hands clammy. "Where's this fancy man, then?"

"Robert's just at the bar."

"Don't they have waiter service?"

Dave shrugged. "He wanted a proper pint instead of a Cobra or Tiger or whatever. What can I get you?"

"Bacardi and Coke."

Dave got up, tossing his napkin on the table. "Back in a sec."

Liz leaned back in her seat. "First time I've seen you have full-fat Coke in ages."

Vicky shrugged. "Thought I'd push the boat out a bit."

"You excited?"

"I'm not the world's biggest curry fan, but we'll see how it goes."

Liz rolled her eyes. "I meant about Robert."

"I know. I was being deliberately evasive."

"So, *are* you excited?"

Vicky blushed. "A bit."

Dave reappeared carrying two pints of red beer, placing them on the table. "Just off for a sla — to the toilet."

Robert appeared, carrying the ladies' drinks. Vicky examined him closely. He seemed middle-aged, maybe ten years older than her, but athletic. At least he still owned his own hair. He wore stone-washed blue jeans with a grey shirt open to the neck, wiry hair crawling out of the front.

He handed a glass of rosé to Liz and a Bacardi to Vicky, before offering a hand to her. "Robert Hamilton."

Vicky shook it. "Vicky Dodds."

Robert sat, almost spilling his pint as he jogged the table leg. "Whoops. I'm sure Lizzie will have told you everything about me."

Vicky nudged Liz. "What, when she's not talking about herself?"

Liz play-slapped her hand. "I'm not that bad, am I?"

"On a scale of one to ten, you're about a seven, maybe?"

"Shut up, Vicks."

Dave returned, drying his hands on his jeans. "Bit of a mission to the bo — to the toilets. Practically have to cross the Tay Road Bridge."

Robert bellowed with laughter. "I'll bear that in mind when I go."

"I've broken the seal now." Dave took a sip of beer and gasped. "Oh, that's nice. Cheers, Robert."

"You chose it."

"So I did." Dave gave a chuckle. "You been here before, Vicks?"

"Don't think so. Dad's family used to talk about it in the eighties when this was the big place to go."

Dave frowned. "They were out in India for a bit, aye?"

"Dad was born in Calcutta."

Robert took a gulp of beer. "Wow."

Vicky over-emphasised a wince. "I could've got you with my 'I'm half-Indian' wind-up there."

Robert smiled. "Maybe you can try it on later?"

"I'll do that." Vicky tapped her nose. "Hey, Robert, did you know my father's Indian?"

Robert chuckled. "Gosh, Vicky. You don't look half-Indian."

"His parents were both from Dundee. They worked in the jute business. Boom, boom." Vicky took another sip. "So. Anyone else been here before?"

Dave put his pint glass down, half-sunk already. "We come a lot. Good curry in here." He picked up a menu. "Who's for a starter?"

"Not for me." Vicky checked out the listing — under-eating when drinking was never a good idea. "I'm going for the chicken saagwala."

"Again?"

Vicky shot daggers at Liz. "What do you mean, again?"

Liz rested a hand on Robert's arm. "We've been for a curry with Miss Dodds twice now. Once to one up the Perth Road in Dundee and once to the one in Carnoustie. Both times Vicky had chicken saag."

"As I said, I'm not the biggest curry fan in the world."

Robert raised his eyebrows. "We can go get a burger or a steak if you'd rather?"

Vicky held up a hand. "It's fine." She took a drink of Bacardi, feeling it sit on top of the half-bottle of wine she'd drunk at home. "I can eat a saag or saagwala, whatever they call it."

"Nothing too hot for me, either." Robert checked his menu. "Which one's saagwala?"

"Lots of spinach."

"Right, I know it."

The waiter appeared. "Please?"

Dave ordered. "One chicken saagwala, a chicken tikka and a lamb phall. Robert?"

Robert held up his menu. "Is the chicken free-range, do you know?"

"It is, sir. I can show you the box, if you want?"

"No, it's fine. I'll go for a vegetable biryani."

The waiter scribbled it down. "Rice or naans, please?"

Dave leaned back in his chair, hands clasped behind his head. Alpha male. "Two naans, garlic and plain, and two portions of pilau rice?"

"Very good, sir." The waiter left them.

"I wanted a peshwari naan." Liz shook her head at Dave as she took a drink of wine. "You'll not be able to finish that phall. It's too hot for you. Remember the last time?"

"Who can finish a curry, though, Liz?"

Vicky glanced at Robert. "I didn't think to ask."

Liz frowned. "Ask what?"

"If the chicken was free-range."

Robert shrugged. "I try to avoid animal cruelty."

"Me too. I'm dealing with it at work just now."

"You're a police officer, aren't you?"

"Detective Sergeant." Vicky took another sip. "For my sins."

Dave held up his glass. "Here's to a great night."

Chapter Forty

"A top-up, Vicks?"

"Don't mind if I do." Vicky leaned forward on Liz's sofa and held out her glass, getting a waft of potpourri in the process.

Liz topped it up, eyebrows gesturing to Robert and Dave at the far end of the room as they fiddled around with a tablet, cueing up enough music to last a week of partying. "Well?"

Vicky looked around the room. "I like what you've done. Looks fresher."

Liz's hand shot to her mouth. "Tell me you've been here since we repainted it?"

"I don't think so."

Liz called over to her husband. "Dave, when did we paint this room?"

He stayed focused on the tablet. "Last May. Just before we went to Majorca."

Liz slumped on the sofa next to Vicky. "My God. That's shocking."

"You know how it is. I've been busy with Bella and work and everything."

"Nice try." Liz raised an eyebrow. "You know I meant what do you think of Robert?"

Vicky shrugged. "Seems okay."

"I don't get you, missus."

"What's to get? I'm too busy to get into anything right now."

"Is that *really* the case?"

"Maybe."

"Aye, and maybe not." Liz took a sip. "What's going on in that head of yours?"

Vicky played with her ponytail, feeling the hair loosen. "I just don't know if I can get into anything now."

"How long's it been?"

"Four and a half years."

"Isn't that enough time?"

"Maybe. It's just —"

"Vicks, quit it with the 'it's just'. I know. I get it. You've had enough time. More than enough time. You know that, right?"

"I do, it's just —"

Liz held up a finger. "No more 'it's just', okay?"

Vicky laughed, eyes shut. Then grimaced. "I worry about who I'm letting in."

"You're not going to know until you let them in, though, are you?"

"That's the problem. I don't want to let an arsehole in again."

Liz nodded over at the men. "Robert's nice."

"Yeah, but you've only known him five minutes. What do you really know about him?"

"Here we go, the police officer coming out again."

The music changed — a blast of staccato guitar-bass-drums followed by a sinister voice. Vicky frowned over to the stereo. "Is that Therapy?"

Dave held up the tablet, showing a man sticking his head down the toilet. "Aye."

"Christ, I've not heard them in years." Liz cackled. "Remember when we went to Lucifer's Mill to see Oasis? There were only a hundred people there. Mental."

"When was that?"

"Ninety-four, I think. You were really into them."

"So that's twenty years since I've had vodka."

"That's right! You were so pissed we were lucky we got in."

Vicky sat and took a sip of wine, her foot tapping to the music. "Did we see this lot?"

"T in the Park, I think." Liz tapped her nose. "Another nice diversion, though."

"Right. You got me bang to rights, guv." Vicky put her glass on the side table, almost missing the edge of the coaster before she righted it. "I see so many absolute animals each week, about eighty per cent of them male. It's hard to trust the gender."

"That's not what every bloke's like, though, Vicks."

"Yeah, but chances are I'll end up with one of the animals." The track changed and Vicky scowled. "Is that *Pearl Jam*?"

Dave glanced at them. "It is, Vicks."

Robert held up his hands. "I put it on. Don't hold it against me."

"I'll try not to."

Liz grinned. "What was it your brother called them?"

"A bad Red Hot Chili Peppers covers band fronted by that guy from Hootie and the Blowfish."

Robert winced. "That's a bit harsh."

Vicky shrugged. "Accurate, though." She picked up the wine glass and took a sip.

Nobody spoke. Robert shot a glance at Vicky, did it again before Dave showed him something on the tablet.

Liz leaned over. "How's Andrew doing?"

"Not great. Haven't seen him for a while. Supposed to be taking my wee princess round to Mum's for lunch tomorrow."

"Send him my regards."

"Will do."

Liz picked up the bottle and tipped the remaining dribble into her glass. "You did it again. Avoiding."

"Come on . . ."

"I'm serious. Robert's lovely — you should give him a go."

"He's over there hiding from me."

"Well, you're a frightening police officer. You've tucked yourself into your tight top to show off your boobs. Maybe he's intimidated."

"Is that all?"

Liz held up her glass. "One thing I should've said, maybe. He's a widower."

Vicky rubbed at her forehead, the vein in her neck pulsing faster than the music. "What?"

"Aye. His wife died last year." Liz drained her glass. "He's even more broken than you, is what I'm saying."

"Great. So I'm looking for broken biscuits in the reduced section of the Co-op?"

"Hardly. I'm just saying, he's not one of those bad guys."

"Unless he killed his wife."

"Killed her with cancer?"

"Ouch. Maybe not."

Liz looked over at the men again. "He's got a wee boy. Jamie. Sweet kid."

Vicky put her head in her hands and groaned. "This just gets worse."

"Look, I'll let you speak to him, okay?"

"Liz . . ."

"Enough." Liz held up her glass then inspected the empty wine bottle, clearing her throat just as the music switched track. "I'll need to get another bottle." She called over to Dave. "Come and help me with the cheese."

"I'm stuffed after that curry, Liz."

"Come on."

Dave scowled at his tablet then his gaze shifted to Liz. "Oh, right. Aye." He handed the tablet to Robert and followed her into their kitchen.

Robert rested the tablet on top of the stereo and turned the volume down before smiling at Vicky, deep ridges on his forehead.

Vicky returned the smile, the vein throbbing harder. "So you like Pearl Jam?"

"They were my favourite band when I was a teenager. I had the ripped jeans, the plaid shirt, the hair."

"Don't remind me. I was a grunge kid as well."

"This was a non-album single, I think, or maybe on a compilation."

"Wasn't it on that *Singles* film?"

"Oh, Christ aye. I forgot about that." Robert took a sip of beer. "I remember going to see them in London with my mates back in the day. We caught the coach down and hung around in the bus station overnight waiting for the first one back. My mate's genius plan was to stay at the YMCA."

"Oh my God."

"Gets worse. His plan was to hop in a taxi and get taken to the nearest one. Guy didn't know."

Vicky smiled. "I kind of liked them at school but they've not aged well."

"Not really, no." Robert came over, the sofa creaking as he sat on the arm. He nodded at the kitchen. "Not exactly subtle, are they?"

"Lizzie couldn't even spell it. S-U-T-I-L."

Robert chuckled. "That was a nice curry, though."

"I enjoyed it."

"Sorry, it was my suggestion. I didn't think you wouldn't like curry."

"It's fine. You can stop apologising."

"Okay." Robert leaned back and took a drink. "Are you working on anything interesting just now?"

"It's never that interesting. This case is as close as it comes, I suppose. Lots of internet stuff."

"Oh, I'm useless with computers."

"Me too." Vicky stared into her glass. "My brother used to work for the police doing that sort of thing before he got ill."

"I'm sorry to hear that."

"He was a silly bugger. Still is."

"What happened?"

"They don't really know. He got ME. One thing I do know is he used to absolutely destroy the energy drinks so he could pull really long shifts. I used to get texts from him at four in the morning still at work. Those guys are supposed to be nine to five. His bloodstream was ninety per cent caffeine. I can barely cope with Diet Coke. Could really do with him on this case."

"Why, what's it like?"

Vicky raised her eyebrows. "Why the sudden interest?"

"I wouldn't say it's sudden. More like Dave and Liz dominating conversation and me not getting to ask you about yourself."

"Before they left the room, I think the only words I've said to you were my name and I was hard pushed to get my surname in."

Robert laughed. "No, I'm an avid reader of detective books. James Ellroy, Ian Rankin, that sort of thing."

"Oh, right. I never get round to reading much."

"Don't suppose you do. It'll be like a busman's holiday, I imagine."

"The only thing I've read in the last ten years was *Twilight*."

"Right. Any good?"

"Didn't like the fourth book much. Vampire babies. It just weirded me out."

"That does seem a bit odd."

Vicky drained her glass. "So what do you do then, Robert?"

"I'm a PE teacher at Monifieth High."

"PE? I wasn't very good at PE at school. I played tennis a bit."

"It was one of the few things I was good at. I was diagnosed with dyslexia when I was sixteen. The damage had kind of been done by then. I didn't read a book until I was twenty. I just couldn't concentrate enough. Now I can't put them down."

"That must have been hard."

Robert nodded. "I managed to get through my exams okay in the end, well enough to get into Moray House in Edinburgh."

"That's pretty good."

"PE and secondary education aren't exactly rocket science." Robert pulled an ancient Nokia out of his pocket and placed it on the table. "It's getting stuck in my jeans pocket. I'm too used to wearing trackie bottoms all day."

Liz paced back through, a bottle of Prosecco in her hands. "Right, who's for some cheese?"

Chapter Forty-One

Vicky stopped outside her house, reaching into her handbag to retrieve her keys. "This is me."

Robert raised his eyebrows. "Oh."

"Thanks for walking me home. Even though you live next door to them."

Robert raised his shoulders as he pushed his hands into his pockets. "I wouldn't like to let you walk home alone."

"I'm a police officer." Vicky tried to steady herself on her feet. The bloody heels. Maybe the booze played a part. She reached over and pecked Robert on the cheek. "Very chivalrous of you, though."

"I'm not really being chivalrous. I'm just trying to be a nice guy."

"And you are."

He looked down Westfield Street, past Vicky's house towards the park at the end.

She folded her arms. Was he angling for something?

He blinked a few times. "Do you want to go for a drink sometime?"

"I'm a bit busy just now."

"Oh."

She tottered forward and patted his arm. "I'm not brushing you off, Robert, I'm just being honest. I'm not going to invite you in for coffee if that's what you're angling for."

"I don't drink coffee. I'm a tea man."

"Okay, I'm not inviting you in for a cup of tea, then."

"I'm not —"

Vicky touched his arm. "Relax."

"So, will I see you again?"

She reached into her purse and got out a business card. "Give me a call sometime."

He took it, lips pressed together. "Thanks."

She winked then whispered. "Don't tell Dave or Liz about it." She fumbled with her keys, eventually getting the lock to turn. She blew him a kiss. "Goodnight, Robert."

"Goodnight, Vicky."

She shut the door behind her and leaned against it. "What the hell am I doing?"

Sunday
30th March 2014

Chapter Forty-Two

Vicky walked along Bruce Drive, heels clicking on the pavement, coat tugged tight around her, breath misting in the late morning air.

A horn honked behind her. A green Volvo. Karen. It parked outside Vicky's parents' house. The lights were off in the front room. Andrew's bedroom curtains were still drawn.

Karen waved as she got out of the car before helping Bella out of the back seat, winking as she approached.

Bella hugged Vicky's leg, her backpack bobbing up and down. "I love you, Mummy."

Vicky knelt to kiss Bella on the forehead. "I love you too, Bells."

"Need a jobbie!" Bella wandered up the drive to the house, knocking on the glass. The front door opened and Dad lifted Bella up, waving at them.

Vicky held up her hand, signalling two minutes. She looked at Karen. "What's up with her?"

"She wouldn't go at ours this morning after Cameron told her about the jobbie monster."

"Oh no." Vicky huffed out into the cool air before nodding into the house. "How was she?"

"Good as gold. No tantrums." Karen checked her watch. "I'd better go. We're running late for swimming in Arbroath."

Vicky patted her arm, eyes still on the house. "I'll let you get on. Thanks for looking after her."

Karen got in her car and started the engine. "Any time. She's no bother."

"See you tomorrow."

"I want full details at lunch, okay?"

"Right." Vicky watched Karen's car drive off round the loop.

She took a deep breath and stared at the door. Get ready for another battering from Mum.

Vicky went inside, cooking smells coming from the kitchen — lamb, maybe? "I'm here!"

Bella wandered out of the bathroom, backpack still on. "Poo won't flush."

Vicky helped Bella take her backpack off — what the hell had Karen been feeding her? "I'll have a look in a minute." She checked Bella's clothes — not too bad given she'd had a sleepover. "Come on, let's see what Granny's been cooking."

"Good! I'm *really* hungry!" Bella skipped through to the kitchen, the room warm from the oven. "When's lunch, Granny?"

Mum beamed as she hunkered down to cuddle Bella. "It won't be long, poppet."

"I'm really hungry. Just had porridge for breakfast. Makes my wee tummy feel empty later."

Mum tapped the end of Bella's nose. "Well, it won't be long."

Bella squealed with laughter as she hugged Vicky's leg.

Vicky sniffed the air, still couldn't place the roasting meat. "What are we having, Mum?"

Mum leaned against the solid oak cabinet, letting her apron come free. "Roast pork."

"I love the way you say pork, like it rhymes with cork."

"What about the way she says oven?" Andrew leaned against the door frame, tightening the belt on his dressing gown.

"Uncle Andrew!"

He rubbed her hair. "Morning, Bella." He plodded into the room, sitting opposite Vicky at the kitchen table, bearded, purple bags under his eyes, his hair in a mess, looking heavier than she'd ever seen him. "Morning. Afternoon. Whatever."

Mum prodded her cooking fork towards him. "You're a cheeky so and so, Andrew Dodds, getting up at this time."

"What's a so and so, Granny?"

"Your uncle, for starters." Mum nudged Vicky's dad. "Does Grandad want to go and play with Bella?"

"Grandad's doing the Sudoku." Dad stayed focused on his paper, sitting to the left of Andrew.

Mum chuckled. "Grandad's been doing the Sudoku for over an hour now. Bella wants to play."

Dad folded up the newspaper and pointed at Andrew. "Don't you finish that when I'm away."

Andrew smirked. "Do you want me to tell you where you've gone wrong?"

"Hilarious." Dad picked Bella up and carried her through the conservatory into the garden.

Mum sighed at the window. "Somebody's full of beans today."

Vicky nodded. "I've no idea what Karen was feeding her last night. Haribo, no doubt."

Andrew looked up from the newspaper, pen in hand. "Wish I had that energy."

Vicky stroked his forearm. "How are you doing?"

"Okay, I suppose."

"What's the doctor saying about it?"

"Definitely ME. They call it CFS these days rather than Yuppie Flu. Chronic Fatigue Syndrome or something."

"Must be good to get confirmation, at least?"

"They're not going to do that."

"Why?"

Andrew shrugged. "Because they'll have to pay me off, I suppose. I'm so skint you wouldn't believe it. Why else do you think I'm back here?"

"Oh. How're you coping?"

"I'm not, really. The doctor's got me doing small incremental walks to try and build myself up. I can make it to Wallace Street without sweating."

"But that's just the end of the road."

"Small acorns, he reckons." Andrew waved at their mother. "Any chance of a coffee, Mum? Thought I smelt some."

"Drinking coffee is what got you into this state in the first place, Andrew Dodds."

"Mum, there's no link between coffee and ME."

"I know that, Andrew, but you pushed yourself too hard and you broke down. They shouldn't have let you do it. While you're under my roof, you'll look after yourself."

Andrew stared at the Sudoku. "The only time I feel normal's when I have a coffee."

"Just remember what it feels like the next day, son. And the day after that."

Andrew rubbed his beard. "You're probably right."

Seeing her older brother like that made Vicky's gut wrench. "Are you still on the books, then?"

Andrew nodded. "I'm still an employee of Police Scotland, if that's what you mean. Had a meeting with my manager last week. Turns out they've got some wee lassie from Strathclyde in to help out after they sacked that boy who was stalking you."

"He was hardly stalking me."

"Whatever."

"Do you mean Zoë Jones?"

"That's the one." Andrew grinned. "You're jealous."

"What?"

"Nice little lady like that. You must resent her getting all the attention in the office these days."

Vicky glowered at him, feeling like she was fifteen again. "Shut up, Andrew."

"Why do you ask?"

"She's working for me on this case. She managed to find some stuff on the dark internet. It's pretty much our only lead so far."

"I see. I take it you can't tell me more?"

"Not really, no."

Mum huffed by the cooker, taking a tray of spitting potatoes out of the oven. "Right, I'll go get Bella and George." She walked off through the conservatory.

Vicky nodded after her. "Still talking to herself, then?"

"Getting worse." Andrew leaned over the table. "They asked me if I was able to come back to work."

"And you haven't told Mum?"

Andrew shook his head. "No."

"What're they asking you to do?"

"I take it you've heard about this Tetra scanner someone's got in Dundee?"

Vicky frowned. "The Airwave scanner?"

"Aye, that. I was on the team that installed the system back in the day. I'm the only one left."

"But you're ill, Andrew."

He shrugged. "I'm feeling a bit better."

"Well, you know your own body. Have you talked to Dad about going back to work?"

"He says I should do it."

Mum reappeared, Dad and Bella trailing behind. Vicky couldn't tell who looked more disappointed to have their play ended.

"Can we go after baddies today, Mummy?"

Vicky reached over to kiss Bella. "After lunch maybe."

Bella tugged at Andrew's sleeve. "Will you help us catch baddies, Uncle Andrew? Grandad's going to help."

"If Grandad's helping then you don't need me or your Mummy."

Bella snuggled in close to Vicky. "I'll always need Mummy."

"Thank you." Vicky kissed her on the head. "Go and wash your hands before lunch. There's a good girl."

"Okay." Bella skipped off into the hall.

Andrew watched her go. "Like I say, bundle of energy."

"Tell me about it. I was thinking of taking her up to Crombie for a walk with Dad. Do you fancy it?"

"How far round?"

"All the way, probably."

"Better give it a miss." Andrew smiled.

Mum put the bowl of roast potatoes in the middle of the table. "Go and get dressed, Andrew. You're worse than Bella."

Chapter Forty-Three

Vicky collapsed back in the sofa and yawned, legs still sore from her afternoon with Bella. She hit the power button on the DVD player. Play from the start or the last memory? She pressed a button, hoping it was what she was after.

Her phone buzzed on the table. A text. She didn't recognise the number. *THSI IS MY NR. ROBERT X*

She grinned as she thought of the ancient Nokia Robert had placed on the table at Liz's. The X after it . . .

"Fuck it." She texted back. *Hey Robert. Fancy a drink *without* Liz and Dave? Vicky X*

She sat for a minute, heart pounding, as she waited for a response, eyes locked on the screen.

Buzz. *TOMOROW?*

Her fingers battered the keyboard of her phone. *Stag's Head @ 7? X*

Vicky stared at the wall opposite. Tomorrow? What was she getting herself into?

The phone buzzed again. *ITS A D8!!! R*

She paused before giving in and hammering out a text to Liz. *Seeing Robert again tomorrow.* The phone bounced as soon as she put it down.

SQUEEEEEE!

Vicky chuckled as she settled back, returning to the main menu on the DVD so she could watch the episode from the start.

Monday

31st March 2014

Chapter Forty-Four

"Granny!"

"Hey there, Bella. Are you ready?"

"Yes I am!"

Vicky shut the door behind Mum. She stared at her daughter. She'd miss her — another weekend spending nowhere near enough time together.

"You can get yourself to work, Victoria."

Vicky bit her lip, getting lipstick on her teeth already. "Can you look after her tonight?"

"Is this more police work?"

"A date."

Mum let out a deep sigh. "Finally."

Vicky smoothed down the hem of her skirt. "I'll be home around six-ish. Can you bring her here and babysit?"

"Fine. So long as you tell me how it goes with this mystery man."

Vicky hugged her. "I don't know what I'd do without you, Mum."

"I don't know what you do with me, either."

Vicky's phone rang in her bag. She fished it out and checked the display — Forrester. "Mum, when did the clocks go forward?"

"Last week, Victoria."

"Cheers." Vicky put the phone to her ear. "Good morning, sir."

"Morning, Vicky. Sorry about this but can you get out to Barry?"

"Barry?"

"Aye. It's the next village over from Carnoustie, isn't it? As in, really near where you live?"

"I can be there in about five minutes, sir."

"Good. Place called Hunter's Farm. I'll be at least half an hour getting out of Dundee."

"What's happened?"

"Not a hundred per cent yet, but I think there's been another one."

Chapter Forty-Five

Vicky pulled in off the main road, parking behind a long row of vehicles — two panda cars, an ambulance and the local Scenes of Crime van. She got out, recognising a few reporters standing smoking across the road. Following the sign for *Hunter's Farm,* she walked up the drive, noticing a male uniformed officer armed with a clipboard.

She produced her warrant card. "DS Dodds on behalf of DI Forrester."

"Why are the Dundee MIT here?"

"How do you know I'm not North CID?"

"Because I know them." He folded his arms, biceps bulging under his short-sleeved shirt. "Why're you here?"

"This might be linked to a case we're investigating. Going to tell me what's happened?"

"Don't you lot speak to each other?"

"DI Forrester was in a bit of a hurry when he passed on the instruction to get out here."

"Right." He held out a hand. "Ronnie Arbuthnott."

"You the Duty Officer?"

"For my sins."

"Okay, so are you going to tell me what's happened, given I've asked so nicely?"

Arbuthnott stuck his clipboard under his arm, narrowing his eyes as he appraised her. He stared at the dark farm buildings. "Got a call out at half seven this morning. Couple of my boys pitched up. Found the family trapped inside one of the sheds, crammed together in a cage. The kids have passed out. Supposed to be a fire engine on its way over from Carnoustie to cut them out but they had a fire on Carlogie Road."

"So the family are still in there?"

"Aye. The girls have had their hair shaved off."

"Christ."

"Aye, that's not the worst of it. Can't get close enough, but it looks like something's happened to the farmer."

"Is he still alive?"

"Aye. Just. He's lying in the corner of the cage."

"How long have they been in there?"

"Wish I knew. These Polish boys work here." He indicated two men giving statements to some other uniformed officers, skinheads and pointed cheekbones. "The farmer's daughters help out at the weekend, apparently, so the boys get the time off. There was nobody around when they pitched up this morning. Had a wee look around, heard screaming from one of the barns but they couldn't get in, so they called us."

"I take it they don't know anything?"

"Barely speak English. We're getting a Polish officer down from Brechin to help take their statements. They're both pretty spooked, wondering if they're being targeted by some racists or whatever. They've got mates in Dundee and Edinburgh that've got into fights with locals. We're lucky they called us out at all."

"Who did it?"

"No idea. Sounds like the farmer's quite security conscious — unlocks the building himself every morning and likes to keep an eye on his staff as they clock in and out."

"What happened when your men turned up?"

He held up a set of keys. "We managed to find these inside the house, which let us into the barn."

Vicky took a deep breath. "Can you show me them?"

Arbuthnott called over to another officer. "Here, Iain, can you cover for me?" He tossed him the clipboard.

Iain dropped it, sending it skittering across the ground. "Sorry, Sarge."

"Idiot." Arbuthnott shook his head at him. "Right, let's go." He led Vicky along a wide lane between stacks of wooden outbuildings with pitched roofs, the eerie sound of grouped hens sounding like howling wind. They entered the sixth building on the right, signed in at an Inner Locus and put crime scene suits over their clothes.

Vicky pulled on her second glove. "Nobody's died, right?"

"Not yet. We've just got the paramedics standing around smoking till that fire engine shows up. This way."

Vicky followed him through a security door into a long room. Thousands of hens were crammed tight in tiny wicker cages, rows of uncollected eggs underneath them. Two birds climbed to the top of the rest in one cage before falling back down. A blast of birdshit stung Vicky's nose, mixed with something meaty — bacon, maybe.

Arbuthnott shook his head. "Makes you want to get free-range eggs, you know?"

"I do already." Vicky followed him, the calls of the hens almost deafening.

"Help! Get us out!"

Girls' voices, coming from the end of the row they were ploughing down. All she could see were similarly suited figures at the end. They sped up.

Against the far wall, wedged next to a hen run, someone had added some metal cages. One contained two adults, the other two girls, not much older than Bella, their heads trimmed down to stubble. All naked. A man lay in the corner, barely moving, hands clamped to his face.

Vicky looked around, her desperate fingers trying to open the cages.

A SOCO smacked her hand. "Keep away from that. Might be some evidence there."

Arbuthnott stepped forward. "I told you they've welded the cages shut."

"They can barely move in there." Vicky was breathing heavily now, condensation forming in her face mask. "There's got to be something we can do."

"Ah, you bugger. This thing's still on." The SOCO by the cage stood back, waving his hand in the air.

Vicky stepped over. A large grey box sat on a table, a strip of metal mounted on two poles sticking out of the front, the whole strip glowing red. On the table was a bracket with three holes, a screw hanging out of the bottom. She looked at Arbuthnott. "Any idea what this is?"

He nodded. "Aye. It's a hot knife machine."

"What's that for?"

"Debeaking chickens. You can get hundreds of them done in an hour."

"Why is it still on?" Vicky spun round to the cage, focusing on the one containing the adults. "Have they done something to him?"

The mother put her face up to the bars of the cage. "They put Graeme's face up to that! He won't let me see what's happened!" She tugged at his arm, twisting him round.

He let his hands go — the tip of his nose was a blackened stump, at least a centimetre shorter than it should have been.

Vicky shut her eyes, swallowing hard. "They've debeaked him."

"Looks like it." Arbuthnott's Airwave crackled. He held it up. "Arbuthnott receiving, over."

"Fire engine's just turned up, Sarge."

"Finally." He strapped the device to his suit. "Should be able to get them out of there soon."

Vicky took another moment to inspect the place, her neck jangling. Graeme Hunter huddled back in a ball. Nothing to do but wait. "Jesus Christ." Her gaze settled on the kids and the surrounding chickens. "I need to get out of here."

Arbuthnott led her back outside.

Vicky tore off her mask. "What the hell happened?"

"We just don't know." Arbuthnott shoved his own mask onto the top of his head. "We're hoping there might be some sort of security system, CCTV maybe. Going to have to wait on them getting out till we find anything."

"Was there a note, do you know?"

"A note?" Arbuthnott scowled. "We did find something on the kitchen table."

"What did it say?"

"No idea."

"Show me."

As they walked back through the farmyard, Vicky tried to calculate how many birds were suffering inside the many buildings. Thousands, maybe. Justification for a burnt nose? Saliva filled her mouth. Her gut churned at the thought.

At the entrance, Arbuthnott retrieved an evidence bag from Iain.

Vicky snatched it off him — it was another note, matching the style of the three previous ones.

Not so comfy, is it? Hope that 24 hours or so in one of these doesn't damage you like one year does to the birds. Feathers = hair. Hope you start to respect them.

"There's another one." Arbuthnott handed her another bag.

*Whether it's from shock in front of the machine or starvation/ dehydration cos their beaks have been mutilated, **beak trimming kills**. Be thankful you're still alive.*

"I take it you recognise these?"

Vicky nodded. "We've got three of these already. Same style." Her phone rang — Forrester.

"Just got here, Vicky. Where are you?"

"I'm here. Just been inside. We've got two notes."

"Shite."

"It's worse than the other one, sir. He's had his nose burnt off."

"Christ." A pause. "Right, the press are here. Mac and I can deal with it. Can you get up to Ninewells and speak to the wife?"

Chapter Forty-Six

Vicky stood in the car park at Ninewells hospital, watching the ambulance carrying Graeme Hunter arrive, Considine's Subaru just behind. The rain started up, small droplets dotting the ground, the smell of ozone with it.

As Considine got out, Vicky started off away from the car. "You're late."

He jogged to catch up. "Sorry, Sarge. Got stuck with Buchan speaking to these schoolgirls from Fife. Daft wee lassies didn't really know what posting on that message board actually meant."

"I see. Bet you enjoyed speaking to young girls again."

"Not really." Considine caught up with her. "Heard you were first out at this farm."

"I wasn't First Attending Officer but I was the first of our lot out there."

"Sounds nasty."

"They burnt his nose off. It's no worse than what they do to those chickens."

Considine held open the hospital's front door for her. "Tell me you're not sympathising with them."

Vicky stared at him. "Seeing all those hens, even you'd start to think about it."

"You're not involved, are you?"

"Don't even joke about it."

Considine called the lift. "What's the wife's name?"

"Rhona Hunter. Her daughters are Amelie and Grace."

"Weird names."

"You know my daughter's called Bella. Is that weird?"

"Maybe." Considine entered the lift. "Which floor?"

"Three. Same ward as Rachel Hay and her brother."

Considine hammered the button. The lift shuddered as it started to climb. "It's like we're getting our own ward here."

Vicky nodded. "At this rate, we'll be filling the hospital soon."

The doors ground open and Dr Rankine was standing at the reception. "DS Dodds, I've been waiting for you."

"Sorry we're late." Vicky exhaled. "How's Mr Hunter doing?"

Rankine grimaced, her eyes shut. "He's in surgery now."

"He'll live?"

"Of course. There's no question of reattaching anything, more a case of seeing what rhinoplasty can do to make him look normal. A lot of the flesh and cartilage has been burnt away. The wound was cauterised with the heat."

Vicky nodded, torn between sympathy and anger at the way he was treating the birds. "Can we speak to Mrs Hunter yet?"

"I think so. She's mostly worried about her children. And her husband, of course. She's suffering from exhaustion and dehydration but she's capable of speaking to you. Just don't push her too hard."

"As if I would."

Rankine led them into the ward. Rhona's bed was stuck behind a wall of curtain.

Vicky pointed at it. "Isn't she getting her own room?"

"None free." Rankine opened the curtain and let them through. "Mrs Hunter? This is the police to speak to you."

Rhona lay on a bed, a drip entering her arm, eyes looking dead. A hand clasped to her scalp, tiny dots of stubble covering her cranium. "How're my girls?"

"They're fine. We're just keeping them in for observation until your husband gets the all-clear."

"How is he?"

"I'm not entirely sure. He's in surgery just now."

"Okay." Rhona wiped a tear from her face. "Thanks."

"I'll let you know as soon as I hear." Rankine smiled and left them.

Vicky sat next to the bed, Considine on the other side. "Mrs Hunter, I'm investigating what happened to you." She got out her notebook. "Can you describe what happened yesterday morning?"

"I was in the kitchen with the kids while Graeme was sorting out the ducks. I was cooking soup for our lunch. We do that every Sunday morning. He listens to *The Archers* on the radio as he mucks out the duck house — we've got about thirty Indian Runners and they get filthy." Rhona swallowed. "A car pulled up."

"Do you get that a lot?"

"Aye. People get lost out our way all the time. We're a bit off the main road, but people don't realise the dual carriageway to Dundee is a couple of miles up that road." Rhona's eyes widened as she took a breath. "Anyway, Graeme went over to this car."

"What kind was it?"

Rhona shrugged. "Black thing it was. I don't know much about vehicles without four-wheel drive and tyres weighing thirty stone, I'm afraid."

Vicky got out the sample photos of the car from Dryburgh Industrial Estate. "Was it like any of these?"

"That sort of thing. Could be any one of them, though. I'm sorry."

Vicky scribbled it down. "Did you see who was in the car?"

"I didn't get too close a look at who was behind the wheel."

"Why?"

"A man grabbed Graeme from behind. I couldn't see his face or anything. Next I know, the driver's out of the car, balaclava on and a knife in his hand. They came inside and threatened us."

"Were they both wearing balaclavas?"

"Aye."

"Did you see anything at all? Any features?"

"Just their eyes."

"What colour were they?"

"I can't remember. I'm sorry."

"Don't worry. What about a physical description?"

"Like what?"

"Well, were they male?"

"One was definitely a man. The other, I don't know." Rhona rubbed at her forehead with her palm, her fingers resting on the stubble. "It could've been a woman or maybe a —" She leaned forward with great effort and spoke in a whisper, "— a *homosexual*."

Vicky noted it down. "What makes you say that?"

"Just the way they walked."

"Could it've been a woman?"

"Well, maybe. I got the impression it was a man, though."

Vicky made a note. "And you were in the kitchen?"

"I was. I just stood there, couldn't do anything." Rhona rubbed at the tear sliding down her cheek. "If only I'd got Graeme shotgun . . ."

"Did they speak to you at all?"

"They barely said a word. Everything they did say sounded garbled. It was really deep and sounded rough."

"What happened next?"

"It happened so fast. They brought Graeme inside the house and shoved us in the kitchen. They got me and kids at knifepoint. The driver held us in the barn for half an hour."

"What were they doing?"

Rhona's hand started shaking. "The man got these cages out of the car and put them in one of our barns. Must've taken all that time to assemble them. The other one took us over there and shaved our heads."

"What did they do next?"

Tears welled in Rhona's eyes. "They shoved the girls inside a cage then welded the door shut."

"Did they look like professional welders?"

"I wouldn't know. Next, they put me in a different the cage. One of them held me at knifepoint, while the other —" She broke off, her red eyes screwed up, tears flowing down her face. "I'm sorry, I —"

"It's okay." Vicky smiled at her but kept her distance. "Take your time."

"They had Graeme hot knife on." Rhona clenched her jaw. "Stuck his head against it." She shut her eyes. "The sound of him screaming, the smell, it'll go with me to the grave."

"Did they say anything to you while this was happening?"

"Nothing. They just shoved Graeme in the cage with me and welded it shut. He'd passed out by then. They left us in the dark with the hens."

Vicky noted it down. "Did they video this, do you know?"

"I don't think so."

Vicky closed her notebook. "Thanks for your time. We'll be in touch."

"Get these bastards for me."

Chapter Forty-Seven

Cheers, Vicky. Thanks for the update. I appreciate how difficult it is." Forrester stood at the front of the gathering of officers. "This looks like another crime perpetrated by the same criminals behind the attack on Rachel Hay and Paul Joyce. I'll be honest, these people are impressive — two kidnappings in the space of four days."

DCI John Raven entered the room, standing off to the side and leaning against a laser printer. Not the tallest of men, he focused on personal image instead — shiny grey suit, striped shirt and black tie. He nodded at Forrester then focused on his BlackBerry, his stubby thumbs hammering the keys.

Forrester exhaled slowly. "Right, then. To summarise, we're looking at two cases, potentially linked by these notes. We need to dig deeper into the sightings of a black car. Mac, can you take lead on that?"

MacDonald slurped at a navy mug. "Will do, sir."

Forrester looked around the room. "This family were abducted and locked in cages. They look similar to the cages we found Rachel and Paul in. I want them looked into as well."

MacDonald noted it down. "DC Woods already has that on her work stack."

"Excellent."

Considine walked in, gaze darting between Forrester and Raven. "Sorry I'm late, sir."

"What's kept you, Constable?"

"I was just over at the Forensics lab." Considine held up photocopies of the notes retrieved from all four locations. "The notes match. Typography, paper stock, even the newspapers they were taken from, *The Sun* and the *Daily Mail*. Printer used was a Brother MFCJ4510DW with recycled ink cartridges."

"I thought this was a glue job?"

Considine leaned against a desk. "It is but there are some printed elements there. They reckon they printed the message out before sticking the letters on."

"Can we trace it to a sale?"

"PC World had the printer on special a few weeks ago. There'll be thousands of them across Tayside by now." Considine checked his dark grey notebook. "Some better news, though, sir — they reckon the paper was unbleached recycled. Quite unusual in these parts."

"That's useful, I suppose."

MacDonald set his mug down. A dribble of coffee slid down the outside, a black smear on the navy blue. "Do you think these people are terrorists, sir?"

Raven looked up from his mobile. "Aren't the NCA interested in taking it off us?"

MacDonald shook his head. "Tried and failed that, sir, though we just had the one case at the time."

"What was their justification, Sergeant?"

"They deem it a vigilante action targeted against specific individuals. We don't know who's behind it and their watch lists are all Irish and Islamic, no active animal rights cells at present. They reckoned there's not much of a threat to the general public unless you've been caught doing something bad to animals."

Raven scowled. "They said that?"

MacDonald blushed. "That's me paraphrasing, sir. More interested in people poisoning reservoirs, blowing up hotels, sending anthrax to abortion clinics, that kind of thing."

"Given this morning's events, Sergeant, it's worth picking up with them again. A man losing his nose is a tad more serious than what's happened previously."

"Will do, sir."

Forrester glowered at Raven. "I reckon we're capable of solving this."

"Prove it, then."

"Certainly." Forrester straightened his navy tie, adjusting his white tie pin in the process. "Additionally, we've got the case in Fife with the woman in the bin, which may or may not be linked. How's that going, Mac?"

"Still in the analysis phase, sir. The resources looking at it were on surveillance for the Muirheads and the Morton brothers over the weekend."

Forrester pursed his lips. "They're still doing that?"

"Yes."

"Let me think about it." Forrester stared at Considine. "Did you ever verify the Muirheads' alibi?"

"I did, sir. I spoke to the friends and they confirmed it. They went for dinner, then to the Rep to see some play. Think we've got the ticket stubs from the wife."

"Fine." Forrester licked his lips. "Last thing, DCI Raven and I are giving a news conference. Vicky, since you've led most of the investigation so far, can you be on hand?"

Vicky swallowed hard, butterflies flapping in her stomach. "Certainly, sir."

Forrester smiled at Raven. "Do you want to say anything, boss?"

Raven joined Forrester at the front, smirking as he nodded his head. "No, that just about covers it, David. I just need to be able to brief the Super and the Chief Super. That's the main thing at the moment. While they're comfortable with your approach so far, it's key to note we're not dealing with a murder here. This is a reasonably well-organised collection of individuals with an agenda as yet unknown. We progress as you've been doing so far until we obtain any intelligence that we're dealing with a known group."

"Thanks, boss." Forrester nodded around the group. "Dismissed."

Chapter Forty-Eight

Vicky sat in the canteen, playing with the last two leaves of her salad. Sticky dressing pooled in the centre of her plate.

Karen waved her hands in front of Vicky's face. "Feels like I'm having lunch on my own."

"Yeah, sorry. I'm just distracted. I hate doing news conferences."

Karen pointed at the screen in the corner. Vicky was talking to the camera, the sheet of paper in front of her shaking. "You look good on the TV, Vicks."

Vicky scowled at her. "Shut up. I look like I'm twenty stone."

Karen leaned forward. "You look good."

"For my age?"

"No, generally. Tying your hair up really suits you."

"Right." Vicky fiddled with her ponytail. "I hate doing those things. I doubt anything'll come from it, anyway." She rubbed at her neck. "My neck's killing me again."

"Did you try those bras I recommended?"

"Didn't make any difference at all. I think it's stress related."

Karen set her cutlery down on her plate. "This is the first time I've spoken to you today. Spill."

"I saw you yesterday when you dropped Bella off."

"And I was in a rush. Spill."

"Kaz, there's nothing to spill. We had a nice meal in the Ferry, then went back to Liz's house for some drinks. That's it."

"Did you . . . ?"

"No."

"No?"

"*No.*"

"Vicky . . ."

"What?"

"Come on, Vicks. Are you losing your juju?"

Vicky folded her arms. "Robert walked me home, if you must know."

"But he lives next door to them!" Karen laughed. "Did you ask him in for coffee?"

"I gave him my number."

"Oh good." Karen stretched out her tongue on the roof of her mouth. "You seriously didn't shag him?"

"No! I'm not that sort of girl." Vicky crossed her arms. "You know I'm not."

"Did he do anything with your number?"

"He texted me his."

"So are you seeing him again?"

"Going for a drink tonight in the Stag's Head."

Karen started waving her arms in the air. "Oh my God. I can't believe it."

Vicky clocked MacDonald approaching. She leaned forward. "Karen, stop shouting."

"Can't believe what?" MacDonald stood over them, frowning.

Vicky glared at Karen. "This case."

"Really?"

Karen screwed up her eyes. "Aye."

"It's a bugger, that's for sure." MacDonald gestured at one of the spare chairs. "Mind if I sit here, ladies?"

Karen shifted her tray to one side. "Not at all."

Vicky pulled her ponytail over one shoulder. "How do you think the news conference went?"

MacDonald shrugged as he chewed a mouthful of salmon and broccoli. "Seen worse."

Vicky glared at her can. "You mean my performance?"

"You were fine." MacDonald shook his head. "This is a nation of animal lovers. It's going to be hard to get them motivated to punish vigilantes tracking down animal cruelty."

"Tell me about it."

"This can be a tough job at times."

Karen leaned on one hand. "You got any pets, Sarge?"

"I'd love a dog one day, but it'd be cruel keeping it in a flat." MacDonald ate a mouthful of couscous. "Have you been busy this morning?"

Karen sat up. "Aye. Been looking into these cages."

Vicky slid her seat back as she stood up, noticing a few extra eyes on her, none looking away. "I've got to prep for the briefing at one. You coming?"

Karen nodded.

MacDonald rested his fork on the plate. "I'll be there after I finish this."

Vicky left him to his lunch.

Karen tapped her shoulder as she caught up. "Christ, Vicky, wait up."

"What?"

"Why don't you want him to know about your date?"

Vicky shrugged, biting at her bottom lip. "I wish I knew what went on in my head sometimes."

Chapter Forty-Nine

Forrester stormed into the office, clapping his hands as he headed to the whiteboard in the middle of the office space. "Come on, gather round."

The rest of the team congregated, with Vicky standing nearest.

"Sorry. Forty minutes late isn't acceptable — especially when I demand punctuality from you lot." Forrester put his hands in his pockets. "I've just had my nuts toasted by the Super and I've not eaten so I want this done quickly. Given the fun we had out in Barry, I want a full update on where we are. Mac?"

"The SOCOs still haven't finished their search yet. As tight-lipped as my ex-colleagues in the south, so I don't know if there's anything useful yet. DC Woods, where are we with these cages?"

Karen cleared her throat. "The bad news is loads of places sell them across Dundee. The good is I've got a guy coming down from Aberdeen to help me look at the ones in Barry. He's pretty much a UK expert on animal cages."

"Takes all sorts, I suppose." Forrester scratched at the hair on the back of his head. "What do you hope to get out of it?"

"Well, hopefully he can nail it down a bit more than us looking for a metal cage. He reckons he can get make, model, the works. Maybe even tie it back to a supplier."

MacDonald nodded. "Make sure he's reliable, yeah?"

"Will do."

"Sounds decent." Forrester scribbled on the whiteboard. "Are we anywhere on the car?"

MacDonald shook his head. "Woods and Buchan have been going through CCTV from the industrial estate. Nothing concrete. The number plate search using the ANPR system has come up blank, which means they didn't go through the Kingsway or the low road."

"The Riverside."

"Right. We're looking at other possibilities but the CCTV teams are now actively looking for anything that matches our description."

Vicky raised her hand. "Given we've just announced the fact we're looking for a car to the bits of Scotland who can bother with watching the news, I seriously doubt they'll use it again."

"Agreed." Forrester loosened his tie — the tie pin now hung vertically. "Those Fife schoolgirls are in the clear, by the way. They've admitted posting stuff on the message board but they were all on some sort of school trip when Rachel and Paul were done. If they know anything, they've not spilled anything so far." He stared at Vicky. "You next."

Vicky nodded. "Zoë, everything we've got is predicated on the links you've identified between these accounts on xbeast and real people. Have you managed to prove how reliable it is yet?"

"I've been working with a couple of colleagues in the Met." Zoë tugged at her bra strap through her t-shirt. "They've got dummy accounts set up on there for this sort of thing. They posted some stuff, I posted some stuff. We used police accounts, mobiles, home broadband, mobile broadband dongles, even dial-up. They were all traced back to the correct IP address. In two cases we put a couple of chains of IP address maskers in there, which we managed to unpick successfully."

"Good work." Vicky checked her notebook. "The alibis for John and Brian Morton both check out. Turns out Brian was in the hospital on Wednesday, under John's supervision."

"I meant to speak to you about this earlier." Forrester tucked his hands into his armpits. "Mac mentioned we're still running surveillance on them. Is that right?"

"We are. And the Muirheads."

"Have we actually got anything to show for it?"

Vicky shrugged. "John Morton took his brother out to Tesco on Saturday."

"That's it?"

"Afraid so." Vicky shook her head. "They were in when the battery hen farm attack was supposed to have happened."

"You think this is a red herring?"

"Looks that way."

Forrester rolled up a sleeve. "I'm cancelling the surveillance as of now. This fat boy in his scooter's an idiot but he's not involved. Get Kirk and Buchan back in."

"Will do."

"Where are we with the Muirheads, Mac?"

MacDonald grimaced. "Their lawyer's threatening to sue."

"What for?"

"Anything he can find. Guy called Fergus Duncan."

"Bloody hell. Look, I don't trust them. We've still got surveillance on them?"

"Yeah."

"Scale it back, but keep an eye on what they're up to."

"Will do."

Forrester rolled up the other sleeve. "If we can confirm the link, I'll be a bit more comfortable. I'll get the press release updated and get on the phone to a few contacts so it goes in the overnight editions." He scribbled a note on the board. "Mac, can you please pick up the NCA strand again? I'm feeling a bit exposed here, especially after both Raven and the Super just asked me about it."

"Got a few contacts I could use. Been thinking the National Wildlife Crime Unit in Livingston might be a better bet. They're nationwide and specialised in this sort of thing. Could drive down there this afternoon."

"I'll join you, Sergeant." Forrester adjusted the first sleeve, making it the same length as the other one. "You got anything else, Mac?"

"Still looking into the cat bin case in Fife. Nothing so far."

Summers held up his hand. "Sorry, sir. I just finished my review of the Fife case files. I found a note at the back of the file referencing a car speeding away. Matches the loose description of ours."

Forrester put his palm over his eyes. "Buggeration. We just went on the record with the media saying we're dealing with just the two cases."

"Sorry, sir. Should've caught you before."

Forrester scowled at him. "You'd forty minutes to brief Mac or Doddsy."

Summers blushed. "They were both busy, sir."

Forrester glared at him for a few seconds before turning to Vicky. "Can you pick up on this Fife case and see if there really are any ties to the other two?"

"Will do, sir."

"Really don't want to look like a bunch of idiots with this." Forrester looked around the room. "Dismissed."

Chapter Fifty

"... had this to say. 'On Thursday we, uh, received a call-out to Invergowrie to the west of the city. A woman ha —'"

Vicky reached over to snap off the radio.

Considine pulled up outside the sheltered housing, a sprawling complex of concrete blocks and mossed tiles. "Not like hearing your own voice, Sarge?"

"Does anyone?"

"DCI Raven certainly likes the sound of his own voice."

"And DCs looking to make DS shouldn't be saying that aloud."

"Right, aye." Considine looked around, pink blotches climbing his neck. "Doesn't look like Reed's here yet."

"We'll wait."

"Summers got himself right in the shit at briefing, didn't he?"

Vicky glanced at him. "That's a bit pottle."

"A bit what?"

"Pot calling the kettle black."

"Right, with you now." He frowned. "How?"

"You've a tendency to keep things to yourself, don't you? Early sharing of information is critical."

"Okay. I'll try harder next time."

"Don't you get on with Summers?"

Considine shrugged. "I'm not a fan of rugger buggers like him."

"And here was me thinking you DCs were thick as thieves."

"Thick as pig shit, more like."

Vicky laughed before spotting Reed trudging their way. "Speaking of rugger buggers." She got out, meeting him by the entrance. "Thanks for driving up from Glenrothes, Constable."

"Just want to make sure us Fifers get a fair hearing, that's all."

"DI's orders?"

"Something like that."

"Nothing to do with you not mentioning this car when we came out last week?"

Reed narrowed his eyes. "No need to be like that. One tiny part of this case might overlap with yours. Big deal."

"This woman lived round there, right?"

"Aye. Irene Henderson."

"And this guy saw a car speeding off?"

"That's about the size of it." Reed smirked. "Not sure what you want to get out of it."

"Come on." Vicky pressed the buzzer and nodded at Considine. "You lead."

Considine stood up taller and nodded. "Sure thing, Sarge."

The door was answered by a middle-aged woman, wisps of smoke from her cigarette misting the entranceway. "Can I help?"

"Looking for an Irene Henderson."

"Aye?"

"Is that you?"

"It is, aye."

"Can we ask you a few questions?"

Irene stared at Reed as she sucked on the cigarette, the tip glowing orange. "This about those wankers who put me in the bin?"

"It is, aye." Reed nodded, stepping in front of Considine. "These detectives are investigating crimes in Dundee that might be related to yours."

Irene leaned against her front door and exhaled through her nostrils, red lines of scar tissue tracing up her nose. "You still haven't caught who did that to me. Why should I care about anyone else?"

Vicky nudged Reed to the side. "Ms Henderson, I'm Detective Sergeant Vicky Dodds. I'll give you two choices. Talk to us here or at the police station in Dundee."

Irene stabbed a finger at her own chest, her pink t-shirt rippling as the flesh underneath wobbled. "I'm the victim in all of this. I don't want to speak to you, here or in bloody Dundee."

"Ms Henderson, the people who committed the crime against you haven't been apprehended. We believe we may have some leads in the case."

Irene folded her arms. "Like what?"

"Here or Dundee. Which is it?"

"Fine." Shaking her head, Irene pulled the door fully open. "In you come."

Vicky followed her down a tight corridor. The cream, textured wallpaper was marked in a few places. The lounge was at the end, the small room stinking of stale cigarette smoke, the air thick with it. A carriage clock ticked away on the marble mantelpiece beneath a landscape painting — men in straw hats tending to a boat on a river, the canvas dark and brooding.

Irene sat in her armchair in the window, reaching over to a bronze ashtray in the middle of a long coffee table covered in a brown and ivory checkerboard pattern. She picked up a cigarette that had been carefully stubbed out so as to be relit. "Do you mind?"

"We do, as it happens." Vicky perched on the front edge of a sofa, Considine slumping alongside. Reed remained standing. She got out her notebook. "Tell us what happened the night you were taken."

Irene sighed and put the cigarette back on the ashtray. She stared out of the window, eyes narrowing further, then glanced at her ashtray. "Sure I can't have a fag?"

"Once we leave."

"This is stressing me out just thinking about it."

Vicky held up a finger. "Once we leave."

"Right, right." Irene took a deep breath, eyes on the cigarette. "People ask me if I regret what I did. I don't. That cat had it coming to it. The little bugger used to walk right through my garden. I used to chase it off but it'd be back doing its business the next day. It knew what was coming to it."

Vicky exchanged a look with Considine. The woman was unrepentant, even with an entire country lambasting her for her behaviour. "Did you see a car that night?"

"Aye, right before it, a car pulled up outside the door."

"This is the black car you mentioned in the statement you gave to DC Reed?"

"Aye. I was feeling pretty edgy, as you can imagine. I'd had all this hate mail since it was all over the bloody papers. I went to the door and opened it on the safety chain thingy. Three people were standing there wearing balaclavas."

Vicky frowned. "You're sure there were three?"

"Aye. Three. One of them grabbed me, taped my mouth up and shoved me in the back of the car. They drove me to the other side of town and dumped me in the bloody bin outside a factory."

"Can you describe them?"

"Not really." Irene sniffed and rubbed at her nose. "There was definitely one woman in the group, though, I remember that."

"You're sure about that?"

"Definitely."

"What about the others?"

"I'd say there was a man, for certain. The third one, I don't know."

"Were they androgynous?"

"What does that mean?"

"It means they could pass for being either a man or a woman."

Irene scowled. "Like a trannie?"

"No. A *cross-dresser* is a man wearing the clothes normally associated with a woman, but I'm talking more in terms of build, you know, smaller, no obvious curves or bumps."

Irene shook her head. "I didn't get a good look at them."

"And nobody saw this happen to you?"

Irene laughed. "This is Fife, sweetheart. Nobody sees anything."

"This car you saw. What kind was it?"

"Just a black car driving very fast." Irene nodded at Reed. "That's what I said when the officers came round. Wasn't it?"

"It was."

Vicky showed her the sample photos of the cars from the other sites. "Was it like any of these?"

Irene looked long at them before shaking her head. "Sorry. Can't remember. It was dark. Didn't get that good a look at it, like I told him and his mates."

"But it was black?"

"Aye."

"And it was a saloon like these?"

"I think so."

Vicky held up the pages again. "But not like these?"

"These ones look too fancy."

"So it was a cheaper make?"

"Could've been, aye."

"Right." Vicky scribbled it down. "You said you got a lot of hate mail?"

"Aye, and cat shit through my letterbox."

"Was any of the mail particularly threatening?"

"It was all particularly threatening. That's why I gave it to the police."

Vicky reached into her bag, retrieving a copy of one of the poison pen notes. "Was there anything like this?"

Irene squinted at it. "Can't remember, sorry. I got a load of mail when the story was in the papers and again after what happened to me."

"Okay, that's helpful."

Irene picked up her ashtray. "Can you let me have my fag now?"

Chapter Fifty-One

Considine eased his Subaru onto the Tay Road Bridge, electronic dance music playing at a low volume.

Vicky watched the wide river foaming beneath them, a few small boats bobbing in the brown water beneath the dark clouds. The car juddered as it powered over the long bridge punctuated with tall lights, its sister rail bridge curving away to the left. Dundee sprawled on the hill at the end, the high-rises of her youth now replaced by dockside developments. On the hill to the left, the new Wellcome and uqTech buildings flanked the older university tower. "Seems like every year there are less multis."

"You mean fewer."

"Fewer?"

"Fewer multis. Less doesn't apply to numbers. It's like it's less cloudy, but not there are less sheep on the hills. There are fewer sheep. There are fewer multis."

Vicky raised an eyebrow. "Maybe I've misjudged you, Stephen."

Considine shrugged.

"So anyway, there are *fewer* multis every year in Dundee."

Considine nodded. "And that's a good thing. Pain in the arse having to climb the stairs to the top of one of them when the lifts are knackered — and they're *always* knackered — only to find whichever scumbag you're after isn't even in."

Vicky chuckled as she tugged at her ponytail. "I took Bella to see them get torn down last year."

"Felt good to see them demolished, didn't it?"

"Made me feel a bit better about Dundee. The number of times I did that in the arse end of the Hilltown when I was in uniform . . ."

The car stopped vibrating as they crossed to the Dundee end of the bridge and descended to street level.

Considine glanced over. "So, do you think these cases are linked, Sarge?"

"Almost certainly."

"I knew it when we went over last week."

Vicky scowled at him. "Why didn't you say?"

"Not my style. Besides, that Reed guy's a total fanny. You need hard evidence to use against a prick like him."

"And you've got this evidence now, have you?"

"Feels like we've got more evidence in the last two hours than he's stuffed in that big case file of his." Considine shook his head as he stopped at the lights outside the train station. "Useless wanker."

Vicky's phone rang — Karen. "Hi, Kaz."

"Hey, Vicks. You seen MacDonald?"

"You were at the briefing, weren't you?"

"Aye."

"Well, if you'd been listening, he and Forrester have gone to Livingston to speak to some farming cops or something."

Karen tutted. "Right, that's where they've gone."

"Anything I can help with?"

"It's these cages. That guy's just left. Reckons there's only one supplier in the UK. I've called them and got a credit card number. No joy with it, I'm afraid. Card was stolen. Happens all the time."

Vicky swapped the phone to the other hand. "Go on."

"Turns out they delivered the cages to the building on Dryburgh Industrial Estate, though."

"When?"

"Last Monday morning."

"Did they use a courier firm?"

"Aye. A local one."

"Thank God. I was expecting someplace in Edinburgh or bloody Glasgow. Where are they based?"

"West Pitkerro Industrial Estate."

"Just behind Sainsbury's, right?"

"Right. Will I meet you there?"

Vicky stared through the window at the familiar mill buildings of the Marketgait to her left. "I'll see you in the car park. We're just about back at the station now." She glanced at Considine and spoke louder. "I'll get DC Considine to drop me off. He's got a fair amount to write up after our visit to Fife." She ended the call and noticed a text from Forrester. *Can u stay on tonite? Back@5ish. DF* Not a mention of the five missed calls from her. She put her phone away, glad she could actually stay late-ish for once.

"Can't I come to the courier firm, Sarge?"

"You're getting good at listening to half a conversation."

"It can help."

"No. I want that statement written up and I want you to go through the file in detail. I don't trust what Summers has done with it."

Chapter Fifty-Two

Scott Keillor?"

The man in a brown and orange uniform stopped loading stuff into his van and looked Karen up and down. His goatee was streaked with white hairs. "Aye. Who's asking?"

She showed her warrant card. "Police Scotland. DC Karen Woods and this is DS Vicky Dodds. Your manager said we'd find you here."

Keillor's lip turned up. "Right, so this is why I got called back in from my round?"

"I did offer to meet you elsewhere."

"Did you, now?" Keillor flashed a smile. "Okay. How can I help, ladies?"

"We prefer 'Officers', if it's all the same." Karen put her card away as her face tightened. "We're investigating a kidnapping and we understand you delivered an animal cage to unit seventeen at the Dryburgh Industrial Estate. Is that correct?"

Keillor frowned. "When would this've been?"

"Last Monday. The twenty-fourth."

"Right. Give me a sec." Keillor reached into his van and retrieved his PDA, stabbing the stylus against the screen. "Bloody thing." He stabbed harder. "Right, here we go. Aye. Delivered it in the afternoon."

"Was it signed for?"

Keillor stabbed at the PDA again. "Aye." He handed it to Karen.

She inspected the device. "This is just a squiggle."

"That's one of the better ones, believe me." Keillor prodded the screen with the stylus. "You recognise that name?"

Karen returned the device to Keillor, eyes on Vicky. "It's sent to Paul Joyce."

Vicky groaned. She nodded at Keillor. "Can you remember who signed for it?"

He took a deep breath, arms folded and staring at the ground, kicking at the loose grit. "Can't remember much, no."

"Mr Keillor, this is a serious case we're investigating. Anything you can remember would be helpful."

Keillor rubbed at his goatee for a few seconds. "I *think* it was some bloke in a hoodie. Had a scarf on, too. One of those Take That ones, you know, all tied back?"

"So you didn't see much?"

He shook his head. "Nope."

"You didn't think it odd you couldn't see his face?"

"It was cold. Dundee in March is like that. I didn't think much about it, no."

"What about height and weight?"

"Sorry. You wouldn't believe how many people I see every day."

"Was it definitely a man?"

Keillor shrugged. "Could have been a big lassie, I suppose."

"So they were tall?"

"Aye, five eleven, maybe six foot."

Karen handed him a card. "Thanks for your help, Mr Keillor. Should you remember anything, please give me a call on either of those numbers."

Vicky led them back to Karen's car. "Think you're in there, Kaz."

"Shut up."

"You should make it harder to get your number."

"I'm a married woman."

"I'm just saying."

"Says the woman who's meeting Mr PE Teacher tonight." Karen turned the key as she did up her seatbelt.

Vicky bit her lip. "Aye. I'm having another crisis of confidence about it."

"You mean you've not thought about it all day?"

"Except for when you remind me, no." Vicky sighed. "Do you honestly think he's interested in me?"

"He's called you, hasn't he? Well, texted."

"Yeah, does that mean something, though? Surely if he was interested he'd have called?"

"You're quite intimidating."

"Am I?"

"Aye."

"Bloody hell." Vicky's phone rang. Forrester. She tugged her seatbelt on before answering it. "Afternoon, sir."

"Can you do me a favour? Been stuck in bloody Livingston all afternoon. Just got back in the car and my phone's filled up with messages. There's a journalist in the station needs speaking to. She's been there a few hours."

Chapter Fifty-Three

I've been here for over two hours. You do know that, right?" Anita Skinner folded her arms, her wristwatch sliding up to the middle of her forearm. She was mid-thirties, tall and athletic. Her green eyes seemed to shimmer in the lighting of the interview room. "Can you just get on with it?"

"Okay. That shouldn't have happened. I can only apologise." Vicky smiled, trying to disarm her. "I need you to take us through your story from the start, please?"

"Okay." Anita took a deep breath, eyes closed. "I'm a freelance journalist. I've done work for all the nationals. I was at your press conference this morning, doing work for the *Record*. Just after that, I received an email linking to some video footage relating to the case you briefed us on."

"It just fell into your hands? That's very convenient."

Anita reached across the table, pawing at her laptop in front of Considine. "Are you implying I'm involved in this?"

"Are you?"

"I swear I'm not. Look, why would I come in here voluntarily if I was involved in this?"

"A diversion?"

"Come on." Anita rubbed at her forehead. "If you'd just look at my laptop . . ."

Vicky leaned back in her chair, scowling at Anita. "What I want to know is how a journalist managed to come by footage from the darkest corner of the internet."

Anita grabbed a fistful of her hair and tugged at it. There were streaks of silver in the dark brown. "I've *told* you, I was sent the links in an email."

Vicky folded her arms. "Anita, I don't know you from Eve, but you're really in trouble with this, okay? We're investigating anyone who's accessed those videos or been active on that forum. The fact you've volunteered yourself is immaterial. It might hold some sway with a jury, but not me."

"And I've told you. Someone just sent me the links. If you look at my laptop, you'll see."

"Would you click on anything you received?"

"Of course not."

"The site you were on is a haven for child pornography. If you'd clicked on anything else, we'd be charging you with some pretty serious crimes."

"I didn't know."

"Really?"

"I swear. I shouldn't have clicked on the link."

Vicky stared at her before glancing at Considine. "Constable, can you power up the laptop, please?"

"Sure." Considine snapped on a pair of nitrile gloves. He opened the evidence bag and took out the laptop, a black machine looking a good few years old. He pressed the power button, eyes locked on the screen as the machine whirred. "What's the password?"

"It's 'Anita two thousand' with a four at the start instead of the *A* and an exclamation mark instead of the *i*. The two thousand is letters — zed, oh, oh, oh."

Considine tapped at the keys. "We're in." He drummed his fingers on the case. The plastic near the spacebar was rubbed smooth. "Which email is it?"

"I got it yesterday afternoon at the back of five."

Considine worked at the machine for a few seconds. "Right, got it."

Vicky swivelled the machine round and checked the email. She frowned. "There's no sender."

"I know." Anita rubbed at her left shoulder. "That's one of the things that made me suspicious."

"Not enough to stop you clicking on it." Vicky scowled at Anita. "Did you send it to yourself?"

"No."

"Get Zoë on it." Vicky handed the machine back to Considine. "Why did you open an email that wasn't from anyone?"

"Look at the subject." Anita leaned forward, forehead almost kissing the desk. "'*Rachel Hay's crimes*'. Are you telling me *you* wouldn't open that?"

Vicky stared up at the ceiling. A couple of the beige tiles were missing in one corner. She looked back at Anita, who was squirming in her chair. "Ms Skinner, clicking on the link is one thing. That would've put you right on our radar anyway. My IT analyst is looking into this. She'll trace your IP address to the site's access logs. If you've been up to anything else on there, you need to tell us now. And I mean *everything*."

"I just clicked that link."

"We will find out." Vicky took a breath. Move on. "Now, have you done anything with this?"

"Maybe."

Vicky shut her eyes. Great. She opened them again, glowered at Anita. "What have you done with it?"

"I published the story on my blog."

"Your blog?"

"Aye, it's a Dundee news site. My take on news stories."

"What did you publish?"

"The truth." Anita pointed at her laptop. "That video and what was in it. You've been hiding that video from people — it happened last Thursday, for crying out loud."

Vicky rubbed her tongue across her teeth. "How many people read your blog?"

"A couple."

"So two?"

"Maybe more. Not more than ten, anyway." Anita rubbed at the sleeve of her t-shirt. "They're all journalists and editors, though. And it publishes onto Twitter and Facebook automatically."

"Christ." Vicky looked back at the ceiling, noticing a flicker from the dull strip light. "So you decided to publish the video despite the clear message at the press conference this morning not to disseminate any information?"

"Yes."

"Why would someone not involved in the crimes do that?"

Anita stabbed a finger in the air at Vicky. "Because you lot are hiding something."

"What are we hiding?"

"The messages. You're trying to deny any animal cruelty angle to this. You're treating it as a kidnapping."

"We are, are we?"

"Look, I'm a journalist. I'm just looking for the story here. If you're burying something, that's a story."

"We're not burying anything, Anita. We're protecting people."

"I need to be sure of that."

"Seems to me if someone was involved, publishing the message would be exactly what they'd do."

Anita held her gaze. "I'm not involved."

"So why publish the story?"

Anita held her head in her hands. "I'm trying to make a name for myself. It's really hard out there these days. Papers are sacking people left, right and centre. My blog's the only thing I've got since I got made redundant. My hits went through the roof when I posted it. My phone's ringing constantly."

"Thought you said you only had ten people reading it?"

"Normally. My hits were over fifty when I last checked." Anita looked up at them again. "Listen, I thought if I got myself known to other journalists, maybe on the TV, it might have —" She shrugged. "I don't know."

"Sounds a bit like a fairy story to me."

"I swear it's the truth. I'm going to get chucked out of my flat. I can't afford my rent."

"So why come in here?"

"One of the people I spoke to was a guy from your press office. He advised me to speak to you. Reckoned I'd not made myself popular with you lot."

"You know what you've done here, don't you? You've let the world know about these videos."

Chapter Fifty-Four

As he marched across the office, Forrester pointed at Vicky then at the whiteboard before going into his room.

"Gather round. Briefing time." Vicky went over to the whiteboard, waited as the others assembled.

Forrester joined her, one hand stuck in a packet of Quavers, the other clutching a white mug, the odour of burnt coffee wafting up from it. "I'm bloody starving."

"Don't they have shops in Livingston?"

"Not so's you'd notice. Mac managed to get us totally lost there and back. Bloody nightmare, that place. It's like Glenrothes without the Fifers."

Vicky laughed. "Did you get anything out of them?"

Forrester lifted the bag up and tapped his nose. "All in good time, Sergeant."

The rest of the team had assembled around the area, with MacDonald perched by the printer, arms folded.

Forrester cleared his throat. "Right. Thanks for staying late. I've got an update with Raven in fifteen minutes, so we'll get through this sharpish, okay?" He nodded at MacDonald. "Mac, do you want to give an update on what we did in Livingston?"

"The National Wildlife Crime Unit were actually pretty helpful. Got a couple of officers on secondment from the Met's National Domestic Extremism and Disorder Intelligence Unit." A grin flickered across MacDonald's lips. "That's a mouthful. Few possibles they're going to email through to us but I've not checked my inbox yet."

Vicky tapped at *Terror?* on the whiteboard. "Are they going to treat this as terrorism?"

Forrester shook his head. "They're happy with the arm's-reach approach. They've seen what we've got and they reckon this is small beer. Until we get evidence of a wider group, or a deeper plot comes out, they're happy for it to be a 'CID crime', like that means something."

"Any idea why?"

MacDonald smirked. "The fact nobody's dead yet."

"We've got to keep in touch with them over the next couple of weeks. Hopefully this'll just die out." Forrester folded his arms. "Anything been happening here?"

Vicky got out her notebook. "A few things. Considine and I went to Cupar to investigate what happened to Irene Henderson, who everyone seems to call 'Cat Bin Woman'. The sighting of the car is as confirmed as we'll get it. Looks like it pulled up on her street, some people in balaclavas got out and nabbed her. That's pretty much it."

Forrester peered at the whiteboard. "Is there anything else we can get from her?"

Vicky shrugged. "We'll see. Summers and Kirk've been through the case file and I've got DC Considine going through it again. That's pretty much it, as far as I can work it out."

"Fine."

Vicky nodded at Karen. "DC Woods, do you want to give an update on the cages?"

"I confirmed that the cage used for Rachel and Paul was from the same manufacturer as the one at the hen farm. There's only one supplier in the UK. Bad news is there's no joy with tracing the transaction. It was reported fraudulent by the cardholder in Derby. He doesn't look like he's involved."

"Bugger." Forrester shoved a few more Quavers in his mouth.

"The good news, sir, is the cages were delivered to the unit at Dryburgh last Monday. That means we know when they started occupying the building and can widen our CCTV search."

Forrester crumpled up his crisp packet. "Good. What else?"

"We spoke to the delivery driver." Karen did her tongue thing. "Didn't get a good look at the person he dropped it to as he was wearing a hoodie and a scarf. Reckons they were about five eleven, maybe six foot. Most likely male."

"But not definitely?"

Karen shook her head. "Could've been female."

Vicky tapped on the whiteboard above *Male*. "We've updated the description and I've got some uniform going round the industrial estate again."

Forrester glared. "Do *any* of the people we've interviewed so far meet that description?"

"Not off the top of my head." Vicky nodded at Considine. "Can you look into that?"

"Will do." Considine raised an evidence bag. "Just hot off the press — I've been through the hate mail she got. Reed had them couriered up from Glenrothes. Ms Henderson got a poison pen letter matching the other four."

Vicky glowered at him — why not mention it while they waited for Forrester? "Are you serious?"

Considine nodded, looking pleased with himself. "Just sent it off to get analysed but I'm confident it'll match. Doubt we'll get anything from it, though."

"Good work, Constable." Forrester picked at his teeth for a few seconds. "So these are linked cases, then?"

Considine rolled his shoulders. "Looks that way, sir."

"So, when was this?"

"Fifteenth of November, sir."

Forrester's eyes widened. "So, they've been at this six months?"

"Could be."

"Reckon this cat bin woman's a trial run, Vicky?"

"Probably. One thing that sticks out for me is there were three people in Cupar. Definitely one female. The most we've got at the others is a male and an androgynous person."

Forrester nodded slowly. "Is there nothing else from the chicken farm?"

Vicky shook her head. "Sadly not. It's so remote it just doesn't get a lot of passing traffic. The news conference hasn't yielded anything yet and the Forensic report isn't complete."

"Disappointing. I got a call from that doctor — Rankine, is it?"

"Aye."

"She says they doubt they'll be able to repair Hunter's nose. It'll take years to make it look human again."

Vicky swallowed down the sour taste in her mouth. "Jesus."

"Tell me about it. Did you speak to that journalist?"

Vicky nodded. "Anita Skinner. I did, sir. Wasn't best pleased with being kept waiting. I doubt she's involved but we should keep her in until Zoë's finished with her laptop."

"Well, Raven's just let her go."

"You're happy with that?"

"Aye. Reckons she's just a greedy idiot." Forrester shook his head. "Half of Scotland seems to have got that bloody email. She was the only one daft enough to publish it. That Media Officer boy, can't mind his name, he's been going spare trying to keep a lid on it. Had to get the Chief Constable involved, get him speaking to our friends in the fourth estate."

"So they're not getting their message out there?"

"Not quite. It's like bloody Whac-A-Mole — hit one and another pops up."

"Nice." Vicky looked at Zoë. "Did you get anywhere with the email she got?"

"I was just about to have a look at it, ma'am. I'll have an update tomorrow."

Forrester took a deep breath before checking his watch. "Right, I think we've made some good progress today, considering what we're up against. Dismissed."

As the team broke up, Forrester cornered Vicky at the white-board. "Have you got any food in your desk? I'm starving."

"Sorry, sir."

"Right. Hell of a business this." Forrester did up his tie. "Off to get the other bollock toasted by Raven."

"He's not that bad, is he?"

Forrester raised his eyebrows. "You heard him after the news conference." He left the room, slamming the door behind him.

Vicky went back to her desk and put her coat on.

Karen winked at her. "Good luck tonight, Vicks."

MacDonald frowned. "What's tonight?"

"Nothing." Vicky scowled at Karen as she picked up her bag. "Goodnight."

Chapter Fifty-Five

Vicky stopped outside the Stag's Head and checked her watch — five to seven and no sign of him. She decided to wait for Robert outside what used to be the video shop.

The daylight was just starting to die, the stream of traffic on Carnoustie's long High Street navigating the single-file parking system that so infuriated her dad. There was a crane a couple of hundred metres away, involved in the demolition of her old primary school.

Vicky looked at the *Evening Telegraph* she'd bought on her way along. The cover featured her face, looking fat, bored and out of her depth at the news conference. The column at the side had head shots of the victims in the case so far — Rachel Hay, Paul Joyce and Graeme and Rhona Hunter. This late edition even had Irene Henderson.

A Volvo pulled in and flashed its lights.

"Bloody hell." Vicky leaned into the driver's side. "Karen, what're you doing here?"

"Driving home."

"This isn't the way to East Haven."

"Okay. I just wanted to meet this man of yours."

"He's not mine."

"Not yet." Karen checked her out. "You're looking smoking hot."

Vicky held up the paper. "I don't think so."

"Forget about that. You look ravishing." Karen licked a finger and smoothed down Vicky's hair at the side. "You're nervous, aren't you?"

"Aye, I am." Vicky looked at the ground. A ball of chewing gum was flattened out at the edge of the pavement. "I can't handle any more rejection."

"You've had one date with the guy and you're thinking of when he'll dump you?"

"I can't help how my brain works."

"Sure you can. Just stop thinking things like that." Karen gripped Vicky's cheek between thumb and forefinger. "You poor thing. Most men would kill to have you, you know that?"

Vicky laughed. "You're such a bad liar."

"I'm not lying. You're a good person."

"Maybe." Vicky spotted Robert across the street as he entered the pub, his black leather jacket matching her own. "I'd better go."

"Was that him?"

"It was."

"Nice bum."

"Christ, Kaz, don't you ever stop?"

"Never." Karen flicked the indicator. "I'll see you tomorrow."

Vicky stepped back and watched her drive off, mouth dry. She waited for a break in traffic to cross the road and entered the pub.

Robert was standing at the bar, phone in hand. He waved when he saw her. "Was just about to call you."

Vicky leaned against the bar, unsure whether to offer a hand, peck his cheek or what. She kissed him, lips rasping on his stubble. "I was waiting for you outside, as it happens."

"Oh, really? I didn't see you."

"I spotted someone I knew across the street."

"Okay." Robert put his phone away. "You look nice."

Vicky smiled. "Thanks. You don't look too shabby yourself."

He laughed. "What do you want to drink?"

"I'd say a glass of white wine but Carnoustie doesn't do wine. Bacardi and Coke."

Robert turned to the barman, who was midway through pouring a pint of IPA. "Bacardi and Coke as well, please."

"I'll bring them over, pal."

Across the empty bar, Vicky spotted a huddle of men her age, all beer bellies and bald spots, as they watched the preamble to some football match on the large TV. She sat diagonally opposite, making sure neither she nor Robert could be distracted by the screen.

Robert perched on a stool and thumbed behind him. "Do you know that lot?"

She shrugged. "I think I recognise a couple of them from school. They've filled out a bit."

"I don't imagine you have."

"Hardly." Vicky looked around the room, frowning. "They've done this place up. We used to call it the Slag's Bed when I was growing up." She raised her hand in panic. "Not that I was the slag."

"Wasn't thinking anything of the sort."

The barman appeared with their drinks.

"Thanks." Robert raised his glass before taking a gulp. "So, you grew up in Car-snooty?"

"Not you as well. I hate it when people call it that."

"It's what we called it in Arbroath."

She smirked. "I suppose everything's relative."

"So did you?"

"What, have a slag's bed?"

"No." He laughed. "Grow up in Carnoustie."

"Aye. Kinloch Primary then the high school. I went to uni in Aberdeen."

"And you came back?"

Vicky stared into her glass. "Aye, I did. Lived in Dundee for a bit. Got a job with Tayside Police as was, working up the Hilltown. My boyfriend at the time worked at *The Courier*."

Robert nodded before taking a drink, eyes locked on Vicky. "I've always liked the town."

"Even though we're all toffs in Car-snooty?"

"Even though."

"Is that why you moved here?"

Robert took a drink, staring at the tabletop for a few seconds. "I moved to Carnoustie to get a new start. Aye. His wife died last year."

Vicky nodded, the nerve in her neck twanging. "I'm sorry to hear that."

"It was mercifully quick, to be honest. Cancer." Robert stared into space. "With my uncle, it took years. It felt like we were keeping him alive for my aunt's sake more than his. He was like a dog that couldn't stop pissing on the carpet." He took another drink. "With Moira, it was quick. There was no option of chemo. Died a month after she was diagnosed."

"That must've been hard."

"Christ, it was." Tears welled in his eyes. "The hardest part was all the bloody admin I had to do after she'd gone. I just wanted to lie in bed for a month, thinking about the good times and getting used to her being gone. Instead, I had so much crap to do. In the end, I went walking in the Cairngorms for a week. That's when I decided to sell up and move."

Vicky really didn't know how to respond. "Corbie Drive's a nice street."

Robert nodded. "I feel lucky. Liz and Dave are really nice. Seems to be a real community there."

"I wish I could afford to live there."

Robert finished his pint. "Your house isn't so bad."

"Really? I'm a police officer and I live in the worst bit of Carnoustie."

"Not like it's Arbroath."

"That's true." Vicky checked the bar was free then put her hand round his empty glass, still cold. "Another?"

He nodded. "Get me the Ossian this time."

"Sure." Vicky took his glass to the bar, finishing hers as she waited for their drinks.

She watched Robert read her paper. Now she was pretty much sober, she revised his age down. Maybe not even forty. He seemed less nervous than on Saturday. Maybe the text messages and letting him walk her home had helped.

She was a bit freaked out about how serious the conversation had got so quickly. Her instinct was to run away. She stared at the door — she could just leave.

No way could she do that.

The barman put the drinks in front of her. She paid and returned to the table.

Robert held up his glass of ale, almost clear. "Cheers."

They clinked glasses.

Vicky took a decent sip. "Billy Connolly's first gig was supposed to be in here."

"Really?"

"Aye. He was in the Territorial Army, staying at the camp at Barry."

"Never knew that." Robert picked up her *Tele*. "I saw you on TV. Impressive."

"You think so? I kept stumbling over my words. My boss's boss has made me book a media training course. A whole week."

"You didn't look like you needed it."

"Thanks, but that course will cost hundreds and, with the cost-cutting going on, it wouldn't have been agreed if I hadn't made a complete mess of things." She took a drink. "I don't know what happens to me. When I've got my warrant card, I'm really confident, but outside of work, I'm a total mess. Talking to the press kind of blurred the lines. I become a wreck in front of a camera."

"It's never easy talking to a camera."

"Have you had training?"

Robert nodded. "I was involved in a community outreach thing Arbroath Football Club did with the schools in Arbroath and Carnoustie. We did a video. I *hated* it. Absolutely detested it."

"Sounds like a good thing to do, though."

"It was. I'm more into animal welfare, though."

"Really?"

He held up the paper. "I'm not involved in this case, before you ask."

Vicky laughed. "Wasn't going to suggest it."

"How's that going?"

"Well, I'm not really supposed to talk about it but that's three cases we've got now."

"Three? It was just two on the telly."

Vicky rested a finger on the photo of Irene Henderson in the *Tele*. "We found one in Fife. The woman who got stuck in a bin last year?"

Robert took a drink. "I read about that." He shook his head. "What she did made me really angry."

"Me too. And that was before I met her. We think it might be vigilantes."

"Wouldn't blame them if it was." Robert flipped the paper back to the sport pages. "Have you got any pets?"

"Just a scraggly little cat."

"What's he called?"

"Tinkle. It's a she." Vicky took a big drink. "How about you?"

"Two dogs. Retired greyhounds. They're lovely but I have to come home to walk them every lunchtime. That's all the exercise they need but one of them doesn't like being left alone." He laughed. "That's why we got the other one."

"Have you had them long?"

"A few years. Moira loved the dogs." He sat back and held up his hands. "Sorry, I keep going on about her. I swear I'm over it. As over as I can be . . ."

"I wasn't saying anything."

He smiled. "I don't want to give the wrong impression. Dave and Liz kind of forced us into this blind date business."

"They did."

Robert stared at the tabletop. "I didn't feel forced is what I'm trying to say. It's why I texted you. It's why I'm here."

"That's why I texted you back. It's why I gave you my card in the first place."

Robert finished his pint, still avoiding eye contact. He tapped her half-full glass, touching her finger. "Another?"

Vicky bit her lip. "Sorry, I've to go back to see Bella, my daughter."

"Oh. I didn't know."

"Is she a problem?"

"No, not at all." Robert shook his head, his lip out. "Did you get her name from *Twilight*?"

Vicky pointed a finger at him. "No, and before you start, I hadn't even heard of that bloody book when I had her."

"What's she like?"

"She's good." Vicky tugged her ponytail tight, the knot in her neck now a dull ache. "She's a bit too much like me. Prone to tantrums, shall we say. She's really friendly, though, so she'll be okay." She finished her glass. "I do worry I'm fucking her up, though."

Robert frowned. "Why on Earth? You seem like you'd be a good mother."

"You hardly know me."

"Even so."

Vicky sighed. "It's just the amount I have to rely on my own parents to look after her."

"I know the feeling. I've got a boy myself. Jamie."

Vicky nodded. "I like that name."

"His mother did, too." Robert cleared his throat. "This was good. Let's do it again soon."

"Definitely."

"Absolutely. Let's do dinner sometime."

Vicky thought quickly. "Wednesday. My place."

Robert grinned. "Wednesday's good for me."

"You can bring Jamie if you want."

"He's with his gran on a Wednesday."

Vicky leaned across the table and pecked him on the cheek. "I'll see you then. You know where I live."

Chapter Fifty-Six

She walked along Barry Road, past a long row of terraced houses, most with some form of dormer upstairs, all hiding behind a brick wall. Two cats were having a hissing fight in the middle. The streetlights opposite lit up the row of beech, casting long shadows across the waste ground next to the roundabout. "So, yeah, Liz, that's what happened."

"Sounds like it went well?"

"I think so." Vicky turned down her street, saw the light in her front room burning away. "All the stuff about his wife was a bit doom and gloom, mind."

"Oh. Has that put you off him?"

"Not sure." Vicky swapped her phone to her other ear, stopping outside her house and leaning against her car. "I think I wasn't my cold bitch self for once. It felt . . . okay."

"You two were like a pair of teenagers on Saturday night, Vicks. I'd be surprised if he didn't like you."

"He's not interested in me, is he?"

"What makes you say that?"

"Well, I'm worried he's only seeing me because you're forcing this on us."

"Have you asked him?"

"I did."

"And?"

"He said he's not."

"Vicks, I'm sorry if you feel this is being forced on you. Stop being so hard on yourself, girl. You're fine."

"I'm not so sure."

"Are you seeing him again?"

"Dinner on Wednesday."

"Squeeee!"

"Liz, I swear if you make that noise one more time, I'll never speak to you again."

"Sorry." Liz laughed, the phone distorting the sound.

"Look, I better go. Got to check on the devil girl and let Mum get back."

"She's not that bad."

"Mum is. Just be thankful you've not got kids, Liz."

"Just be thankful we've *chosen* not to have kids."

"Goodnight." Vicky pocketed the phone before opening the door.

Mum stood in the sitting room doorway, coat already on. "Well?"

"Well what?" Vicky hung up her coat. "Is Bella asleep?"

"She is. Poor wee thing fell asleep watching the TV." Mum beamed. "We saw you on the news. Bella was so happy."

"I'm glad I've managed to avoid it so far. It was horrible."

"You came across well, Victoria. I'm very proud of you. So's your father."

"He's at least done press conferences without every second word being *um* or *ah*."

Mum screwed up her eyes. "How was your date?"

"It was fine."

"Are you seeing him again?"

"Maybe. I just had two Bacardis with him, Mum, that's all."

"Just allow me to be happy for you."

"For once, maybe I'll let it pass."

She hugged Vicky tight. "I'm pleased for you."

Vicky put her arms around her. "Is the only good thing about my life the fact I've been on a date?"

"No!" Mum stood back, looking her in the eye. "Why would you think that?"

"You just go on about how bad I am, Mum. The only time you're happy's when I've got a man on the scene."

"Victoria, I know how hard it is for you and Bella on your own. You're doing a brilliant job of raising my wee girl. Me and your father aren't going to be around forever, though."

Vicky rubbed a hand across her face, trying to cover the tear before it slid down. "Don't say that, Mum."

"I just want you to be happy, Victoria, okay?"

"Okay, Mum." Vicky coughed, her voice thick with the tears.

"I'll need to collect your father from the station. God knows what sort of a state he's got himself into."

"You go. I'll drop Bella off at eight tomorrow, okay?"

"That's fine."

"Cheers." Vicky pecked her on the cheek.

Mum let herself out, grinning as she shut the door behind her.

Vicky climbed the stairs, making for Bella's room. She nudged the door open, the shaft of light creeping across the floor towards the bed covered in toys with barely enough room for Bella.

Vicky knelt and gently kissed her daughter on the top of her head.

Bella's eyes flickered open. "Mummy catched baddies on telly."

Tuesday
1st April 2014

Chapter Fifty-Seven

Forrester started the morning briefing with a smile. "Got some slightly good news this morning. The SOCOs found a couple of human hairs in the farmhouse near to where the first note was found. The colours didn't match any of the family. Dark brown versus blonde. The hair on the wife and kids was shaved in the barn, so we think this could be a lead. They're off getting deep analysis in Glasgow."

He held up two newspapers. "*The Courier* and the *Press and Journal* have it on their front pages. It was in last night's *Tele*, too. All of the Scottish nationals have gone with it, plus *The Guardian*, *Mail*, *Star* and *The Daily Telegraph*. Luckily, nobody's gone with the notes or video in any great detail."

Vicky stared at Zoë. "Keeping on topic, how are you doing with the email Anita Skinner received?"

"I had a good look. It had links to the notes used as well as the video. I don't think we'll get anything from it but I've sent it to a few contacts to verify. I think she's innocent. Since last night, I've got hold of a few other copies of this email, which suggests she's not involved."

"Good work. Sorry, sir."

Forrester shrugged. "The phones have started going mental and we've had to divert some of the calls to Edinburgh. Nothing of note so far. I want the DCs going through call logs as a priority, reporting to Mac or Vicky on an hourly basis." He smiled at MacDonald. "How's the street team doing?"

"Uniform still going around the industrial estate. Not got much, I'm afraid. Don't expect anything at this point but it's worth a shot." MacDonald waved a sheet of paper around. "Just received a copy of the statements from the two Polish farm workers. Uniform reckon they've checked out but I want to go through them with a fine-tooth comb after this."

"Good work." Forrester leaned back against the wall. "Did you get a chance to look at the Wildlife Crime Unit leads?"

"Yes, sir. Was in till ten last night going through the stuff then in at six to finish off."

Vicky rolled her eyes at Karen. How many Brownie points was that?

Forrester folded his arms. "And did you get anywhere?"

MacDonald checked a notepad. "Gave me two key leads they reckon are possibly relevant. Both have undercover operatives so we're treading on eggshells." He licked his lips. "First, commune near Redford called Phorever Love, spelled with a Ph."

Vicky smirked. "Sounds like a Shamen song."

Forrester winked. "Showing your age there, Vicky."

"Wildlife guys gave us permission to speak to them about our cases." MacDonald sniffed. "Group's got a public profile, usually picket places. Did Hunter's Farm a few years ago, stopped the delivery lorries getting in for a week before they were turfed out."

Forrester stood up straight. "Are you serious?"

"Yes, sir."

"Do they reckon they're involved?"

MacDonald shrugged. "Why they gave us the lead, I suppose."

"What's the other one?"

MacDonald checked his notepad again. "Other lead is a group of cyberterrorists, thought to be located in Scotland. Haven't got an exact location — they could be anywhere, but there's a suspicion they may be in rural Angus. An off-grid kind of deal."

"Why do they think this lot might be involved?"

"Took down a few company websites, including a GMO company in Midlothian and a cattle feed company in Paisley. Sites were down for over two weeks. Hacked a few meat companies' Twitter accounts and so on. Made them look like idiots."

Forrester rubbed his chin. "Right, Vicky, I want you to focus on this camp."

"Will do, sir."

"You've been dealing with this 'dark web' stuff I won't even begin to pretend to understand, so can you take lead on the cyber-terrorists as well? Be careful no cover's blown. These are people's lives we're dealing with, all right?"

"Certainly."

"Fine. Mac, please focus on the door-to-door investigation. That'll need a lot more attention given the news conference yesterday."

"Sure thing."

"Okay. Dismissed."

Karen grabbed Vicky's arm as everyone got to their feet. "How did it go last night, then?"

Vicky spotted Zoë making a beeline for her. "Got to go. Chat at lunchtime, yeah?"

"Fine." Karen stomped off.

Zoë tugged her hair, avoiding eye contact. "Do you want to go through that dark net stuff just now?"

Vicky shrugged. "You know what you're doing more than me. I'm going to head out to Redford once I've read the report, so if you can let me know where you've got to by lunchtime?"

"Sure." Zoë blinked a few times. "That's fine."

Vicky took a deep breath. "Speak to DC Considine if you need anything else."

"I'll try not to need anything."

Chapter Fifty-Eight

Considine turned right just before the road to Crombie Park, heading deeper into the Angus wilderness.

Vicky glanced at him. "Did Zoë speak to you about the cyber-terrorists, Stephen?"

"Aye, she did. I briefed her. Poor thing was lost in that case file MacDonald gave her."

"I see." Vicky smirked. "And you helped her, of course?"

Considine blushed as he powered through Carmyllie, passing a farm shop Vicky had been to a few times with her parents. "Of course I helped her. It's a useful lead."

"Do you have a thing for her?"

"No comment."

Vicky had to look out of the window to stop from laughing.

Considine turned down a country lane, passing entrances to two large farms on opposite sides of the road, before taking a right along a single track. "It's down here, I think." He trundled on for a few minutes, the car's suspension rocking. "Thank God we took the Python."

"Don't call your car that. Seriously."

"I was thinking of getting a sticker above the windscreen."

"If you do that, don't even think of driving it on police business."

"I'm joking."

"Of course you were."

Considine slowed as they came to a set of large walls, barbed wire along the top, a steel gate blocking the entrance, 'Phorever Love' graffitied in pink and red. "Doesn't look like much love's going on in there. It's like something out of that *Walking Dead* thing on the telly."

"I seriously hope there are no zombies in there."

"Can't beat zombies."

"Zombies or not, it's not exactly what I was expecting from a hippie commune." Vicky pointed to a passing space on the left. "Pull in here."

Considine slowed to a halt, leaving the car running.

"Doesn't the Python know to turn itself off?"

Considine twisted the key in the ignition, killing the engine. "I'm regretting telling you."

"You do know you should really regret calling it that, don't you?"

"Whatever."

They got out of the car and walked over to the gates.

Considine knocked on the corrugated iron then shook his hand in the air. "That was bloody sore."

The gate slid open. Two men stood there, both dressed in army surplus clothes. The older of the two had blond dreadlocks tugged back into a ponytail, while the younger one's shaved head had the look of a soldier rather than a Buddhist. Both had dark rings around their eyes.

Vicky held out her warrant card. "We're looking to speak to the leader."

Dreadlocks nodded. "That'll be me, then. Kevin Simmers. I run this place."

"We're investigating two vigilante actions in Dundee, sir. They appear to have been committed against people with a public record of animal cruelty. Can you help us?"

Simmers laughed. "With what?"

"Do you know anything about it?"

"No, we don't. Goodbye."

The skinhead edged closer. "Are you implying we're up to something?"

Vicky narrowed her eyes at him. "And who are you?"

"Andy Salewicz. Not that it's any business of yours."

Vicky folded her arms. "We've got intelligence linking your group to these crimes."

"Where did you get this from?"

"I'm not going to name our sources. We believe you picketed Hunter's Farm in Barry. Is that correct?"

Salewicz shrugged. "Might've done."

"I wonder if you'd any idea who might wish to trap the whole family in a cage in the farm?"

Salewicz glanced at the leader. "Want me to get rid of them, Kevin?"

Simmers shook his head before taking a deep breath. "Officers, we're a strictly pacifist group. When were these crimes supposed to have been committed?"

"Wednesday and Sunday, for starters."

Simmers chuckled. "We've just had a week-long rave."

"A week-long rave?"

"We had a police presence throughout. Nobody got in or out. Whoever gave you this intelligence isn't very intelligent, are they?"

Chapter Fifty-Nine

"You got a minute, Euan?" Vicky drummed a finger on the back of MacDonald's desk.

MacDonald put down the report he was reading. "Sure."

"Is Forrester in?"

"Up with Raven."

"Let's go to his office." Vicky led him across the room, shutting the door behind them. "Who gave you the intel on those crusties?"

"Not a very nice way of putting it."

"Who gave you it?"

MacDonald shrugged. "Wildlife Crime boys. Why?"

"It was shite."

"In what way?"

Vicky rested a hand on her hip. "For starters, they've just had a week-long rave with police presence. Gives them a pretty robust alibi."

"Right." MacDonald took a deep breath. "You ask about the picket at Hunter's Farm?"

"I did. They admitted it."

"So?"

"So the problem is, nobody at that place left in the last week. I checked on the drive back down — there were no fewer than four officers stationed by it *all week*."

"Fairly solid, I suppose."

"It is." Vicky put her other hand to her hip. "It was a bit of a waste of time heading out there. Me and Considine in the Python."

"The Python?"

"It's what he calls that Subaru he drives."

MacDonald smirked. "Boy racer, I told you."

"What can we do about this?"

"I'll get back to my contact, see what he's got to say about it."

"Do you want me to speak to them?"

He shook his head. "I'll deal with it."

"Fine."

MacDonald rubbed his chin. "Getting anywhere with the cyberterrorists?"

"I haven't caught up with Zoë yet."

"Right."

Vicky sat on the edge of the desk and sighed. "We're chasing our tails."

"Tell me about it. Gave the street teams a rocket up their arses but I doubt it'll do any good. Nothing there we don't already have."

"What about the phones?"

"Usual nonsense. Lots of people taking credit for it, none of them did it. Put them in a room with a twenty-stone constable and they change their minds pretty quickly."

"I'm not getting a warm fuzzy feeling about this."

"These cases can be like that. Can take a while."

"I guess you're right." Vicky got up again. "Have you seen Zoë?"

"She's not been at her desk all morning."

"She has been working, though, right?"

MacDonald held up his hands. "No idea. If I see her I'll point her in your direction."

"You do that."

"You had your lunch?"

Vicky nodded. "Just had a sit-down with Karen."

"Oh, okay." MacDonald nodded and left her in the room.

She slumped back in the seat — how had she gone from giving him a doing to being coached?

She stood up, smoothing down her skirt before leaving Forrester's office.

Zoë stood by their desks, MacDonald pointing at Vicky. "She's just there."

Vicky smiled at her as she sat. "I've been looking for you."

Zoë remained standing. "Stephen said you were looking for me. Sorry, I've been up with the Forensic guys."

Considine sat opposite them, perching on a chair the wrong way round. "Zoë's done a search on the known activities of your cyberterrorist group."

Vicky leaned back in her chair, eyes drilling into Zoë. "What have you found?"

"I managed to match some stuff together."

"That sounds technical."

Considine raised his eyebrows. "Zoë's managed to tie the IP addresses from the cyberterrorists to this group out in Redford."

Vicky sat back for a few seconds, trying to process it. "Why didn't this come up before?"

Zoë kicked her heels. "The search hadn't come back. Some things take time, you know?"

"Okay. Do you have people we can bring in for interviews?"

"I've got IP addresses linking back to Phorever Love but I've not got real people, no."

'Zoë, can you work on linking the Muirheads and Brian Morton to these crimes? See if one of them posted that video?'

'Will do.'

'Cheers.'

Vicky folded her arms and glanced at MacDonald. His eyes darted up from her legs. "Euan, has your Wildlife squad guy got back to you yet?"

MacDonald shook his head. "Not yet."

"Reckon we should bring them in?"

MacDonald inspected his nails. "Not too happy about it. Got a deep undercover operative at risk there."

"I'm not sure we've got anything concrete on them yet." Vicky tossed her ponytail. "Are there any links to xbeast?"

Zoë nodded. "Yes, ma'am. Active posters on there, but I can't trace them back. Sorry."

"Should we bring the Muirheads and those two brothers back in?"

"What I'm thinking." MacDonald got to his feet. "Let's ask them about the group and about the hen farm attack."

Vicky stood up. "I'll take Brian Morton."

MacDonald glanced at Karen. "See you in the car park in five, okay?"

Vicky let him go.

Karen leaned over the desk and winked. "Physical contact, Vicks."

"Stop it."

"He's getting on well with Zoë."

"She's welcome to him."

Chapter Sixty

Vicky sat in Brian Morton's living room. The magnolia walls were bare, the curtains drawn, a naked light bulb hanging from the ceiling the only source of light. "Mr Morton, do you know anything about a group near Redford called Phorever Love?"

"I don't know what that is." Brian shook his head. "John!"

His brother stayed looking at the TV.

Considine loitered in the window overlooking the street. "You sure about that, Brian?"

Brian's breathing quickened. "I've no idea what you're talking about."

"You sure?"

Brian's face reddened. "I'm sure. I've never heard of Redmond."

"Redford."

"Where is it?"

"Near Forfar."

Brian slammed a fist against his scooter. "Do I look like I can get there?"

Considine shrugged. "You get a decent battery life on those things, don't you?"

"I know absolutely nothing about this Love Forever group."

"Phorever Love."

Brian ran a hand through his hair, now soaking with sweat. "I still don't know anything about them."

Vicky crossed her legs and smoothed down her skirt. "See, members of the group posted on the same forum you did — xbeast."

"So?"

"They'd a campaign against a place near Barry called Hunter's Farm."

"And?"

"Do you watch the news, Brian?"

Brian shook his head. "The only time the telly's on in here is when he's around."

Vicky glanced at John, still watching the news. "Well, Hunter's Farm just happened to have a similar attack to that perpetrated against Rachel Hay and Paul Joyce. If you'll recall, you took great delight in what happened to them."

Brian tightened his grip on the arm supports. "Whoever did this hasn't done anything wrong."

"We beg to differ. Kidnapping's against the law."

Brian pounded the scooter again. "I don't know anything about it!"

Vicky uncrossed her legs and got to her feet. "Come on, Constable, we'll need to get Mr Morton here down to the station."

John looked over from the TV. "This isn't good for Brian's heart."

Vicky smiled at him. "Then it's in his interests to answer the questions."

"If he says he doesn't know, he doesn't know."

"I'm not saying your brother did anything."

"Seems like it."

"We just want to know if he's got any leads on that message board."

"Why?"

"He's an active participant on there. I can quite happily believe he's not involved in this, but I want to know if there's any help he can give us to find these people."

Brian slammed his fist on the scooter again. "I'm not going to help you. Whoever's doing this is a hero."

John held up his hands. "He doesn't mean that. Brian's heart's in the right place. He's just interested in helping the animals. That's right, isn't it, Brian?"

"I just want people to stop being nasty to animals."

Vicky nodded. "We all do."

"I don't believe you."

"Why not? I buy free-range chicken and eggs."

Brian glowered at her. "You're not doing anything about it, though, are you?"

Considine crouched in front of the scooter. "Brian, we're looking into this forum in a lot of detail. We've got an IT analyst working full-time on this. If you've been a naughty boy on there, it's in your interest to tell us now. Okay?"

John tilted his head at Vicky. "Can I have a private word, please?"

She nodded and followed him into the kitchen. Ten empty cheesecake and gateaux boxes sat on the counter, giving off a sickly sweet aroma. "Tell me he doesn't eat these."

"It's like I told you the other day. He lives off them. That lot's just this morning." John started putting the boxes in the recycling. "It's all he'll eat since Mum died. She used to look after him and managed to feed him decent stuff. I had to move back up from Essex but I've just not got the patience she had, or the time. Does that make me a bad person?"

Vicky leaned back against the counter, the chipped wood digging into the palms of her hands. "I'm not sure."

"He has tantrums like he's a kid."

"I can relate to that." Vicky frowned. "There's nothing wrong with him, is there?"

"It's just obesity." John held up the last cheesecake box. "You should see him destroy one of these. It's like that *Man Vs Food* programme."

Vicky folded her arms. "I assume you didn't call me in here to tell me about your brother's eating habits?"

"No." John stuffed the last box in the recycling bin, the lid not quite shutting. "See, the other thing is his stress. He gets really bad. You saw what he was like in there. His heart isn't great. Our old man died from a heart attack."

"I'm sorry to hear that."

"He was an arsehole. It's no great loss." John pushed his glasses up his nose. "To save us both hassle, is there anything I can do to help? I don't want my brother dying. As much of a nightmare as he is, he's all I've got left."

Vicky stood up straight. "This is a serious matter, Mr Morton, as I'm sure you can imagine. People have been abducted and tortured in some cases. There are now three cases."

John's forehead creased. "Said two on the TV."

"We've found another."

John threw his arms in the air. "Look, I don't give a shit about all this animal crap. I *do* give a shit about my brother. I almost had to take him into the hospital on Friday night after you let him go. I managed to get his breathing and heart rate back under control."

"I wouldn't be doing this if I didn't think he knows something."

"I get that." John licked his lips as he stared at the door back to the living room. "How about I speak to him for you?"

"How about I just take him down the station?"

"I told you, it's not going to be good for his heart."

"I think your brother knows something."

"If it'll get you lot out of his face, I'll ask him."

Raised voices came from the living room, sounding like Brian screaming at Considine.

John waved his hand at the door. "See, this is what I have to put up with. His blood sugar level's always collapsing because of the bloody cakes he eats."

"You could stop feeding him them."

John raised his shoulders. "You're welcome to look after him."

"I'll pass, thanks."

"Thought so."

Vicky rested her hands against the countertop — the last thing she needed was a coronary on her hands. "Right, fine. You speak to him and see what he can help us with."

John nodded. "Sorry about this but it's just not good for him."

Vicky handed him her business card. "In case you've lost the last one."

Chapter Sixty-One

Vicky held open the front door to the station. "What did you ask him to make him scream like that?"

Considine shrugged as he entered the station. "Nothing. I swear."

"Didn't sound like nothing."

"He was just rambling at me." Considine swiped through the security door, the lock clunking as it released. "Just kept talking to himself, like I wasn't even there. Mad stuff about not going back to the police station. He was just building himself up into a froth."

"Great."

"Thought he was going to keel over there and then."

Vicky opened the door to the stairwell and started climbing the stairs, her fingers kneading her neck as their words echoed around the tight space. "I can't figure out how he fits into this."

"From the witness statements, all we've got is three people at most." Considine accelerated the last few steps to hold the door open. "One bloke, one woman and someone of indiscriminate gender. Brian doesn't fit the profile of any of them."

Vicky waited in the corridor outside their office space — two male detectives from another team were chatting further down. "So you think he's not linked to this?"

"IT support is all I can think."

"He's a terror group's helpdesk?"

Considine laughed. "No. He's doing all this stuff online for them. It's a big part of what they're up to, isn't it?"

Vicky peered through the open door, clocking Zoë tapping at her laptop. "Let's see what young Zoë's got so far." She went and stood over her, hand on hip. "What progress have you made with Brian Morton?"

Zoë swallowed. "Been flat out, ma'am. Not had a chance to look into it too much."

"What have you been flat out on?"

Zoë flicked her eyebrow up at Considine before focusing on her laptop again. "First, I was just confirming I could get nothing from the emails to the journalists."

"And?"

"Well, I can't. Anita Skinner's site got taken down. The Met are trying to purge it from Google's search results, but they're not exactly playing ball."

Vicky looked around, the nerve in her neck tightening. "Has anyone else published the email?"

"I'm afraid so. I just found this." Zoë tapped her screen, flicking through the poison pen letters and a screen grab from the video. "Some WikiLeaks clone published the notes."

"Who posted them there?"

"I'm just getting onto that."

"Was it Anita Skinner?"

"Definitely not. I installed some friendly malware on her laptop. If she so much as goes near the dark net or the files she got sent, I'll know about it."

"Is that legal?"

"It's not strictly illegal."

"I'm getting more impressed with you by the day." Vicky craned round to look at Considine, massaging down the knot in her neck, now reduced to a dull ache. "Tell Forrester about this, please."

"Me?"

"Please." Vicky crouched alongside Zoë. "What was the second thing?"

"Right. Well, I've been doing some more digging into the user names on xbeast. It's the first step in trying to prove who's posted that video."

"And?"

"I've got another user who posted some comments in support of the actions. They were posted last night so I didn't spot them till now."

"Show me."

"Here." Zoë flipped to another screen and turned her laptop to show a page of indented text. "For the video, they've posted *'why are the police looking into us? we've not committed a crime. dog breeding is a crime.'*"

"They said 'us'."

"I spotted that, too." Zoë switched to another document. "For that battery hen farm attack, they've posted *'we should have firebombed it with them inside.'*"

"Is this someone taking credit for it?"

"Doesn't really look like it to me." Zoë shrugged.

Vicky nodded. "I'd expect them to be more overt. Publishing somewhere a bit more public."

"Could be like in football." Considine lifted up his coffee mug, dark grey with orange lines, the black Dundee United lion rampant in front of an orange and white harlequin diamond. "When I'm talking about watching United, I'd say 'we played well today', even though I'm nowhere near the pitch. The royal 'we'."

Vicky shook her head. "The royal 'we' means referring to a single person as a plural, like the Queen does. It's shorthand for 'God and I'. The divine right of kings and all that. I did it at uni."

"And to think I had to pick you up on the correct use of 'fewer'." Considine smirked. "Whatever. You still get my point, though, right?"

Vicky tugged at her ponytail — it made sense. "Anything else?"

Zoë stared at the screen. "I've been through their post history. The same user posted in October, when that cat bin woman got done — *'shame she got found'*."

"Who is it?"

Zoë shrugged. "I'll be a couple of hours getting an IP address, if we're lucky."

"Is it Brian Morton?"

"I don't know."

Vicky stood up, knees creaking. "This is your highest priority."

"Understood." Zoë nodded. "Oh, Mac was looking for you. Wanted you to help interview someone."

Chapter Sixty-Two

We have no connections to that group." Muirhead let his arms go, his cufflinks rattling off the interview room table. "I do wish you'd stop hounding my wife and me."

"And I wish you'd stop posting things on parts of the internet we're monitoring for terrorist activity." MacDonald left the room, storming off down the corridor.

Vicky had to jog to catch up, weaving between a couple of uniforms coming the other way. "Did you get what you wanted, Euan?"

"Maybe." MacDonald shrugged. "Thanks for stepping in, by the way. DC Woods got called home."

"Oh. I hadn't heard. Nothing serious, I hope?"

"Son was coughing. Got sent home from nursery."

Vicky grimaced — Bella better not have caught anything from Cameron at the weekend. "Do you think the Muirheads are involved?"

"An hour each with them and we've got nothing. Deny, deny, deny." MacDonald stopped by the door to their office space, his blue eyes darting about. "Whether they're involved? Not sure. Sandy Muirhead fits the profile of the male perpetrator."

"Isn't he a bit short?"

"Maybe, but we've got really flaky descriptions. They could be anyone."

"His hands are quite small. Nobody's mentioned that."

"They've not seen the hands, as far as I can tell. They've been wearing gloves. Easy to pad out."

"Did you get anything from the interview with his wife before?"

"Nothing. Again it was just denial." MacDonald drummed his fingers on the doorframe. "How did it go with Brian Morton?"

"We got nowhere. He was going ballistic at Considine. Looked like he was going to have a heart attack."

"Where have you left it?"

"His brother's going to have a word with him."

"You think he's trustworthy?"

Vicky gave a half-smile. "I have problems with trust at the best of times."

"And at the worst?"

"Let's just wait and see what he comes back with."

MacDonald frowned, leaning against the door. "What's that Brian boy's story, anyway? He's huge."

"He's morbidly obese. He just lives off frozen desserts."

"Christ."

"I honestly don't know where he fits in." Vicky nibbled at her lip before stepping forward to avoid an officer hurtling down the corridor, getting within a foot of MacDonald. "Did you get anywhere with the Wildlife guys?"

MacDonald shook his head. "Called them between interviews. Going to be tomorrow before the lad on the inside speaks to his handler to confirm the tale."

"Right. I'll wait till he gets back to you, then."

"All we can do." MacDonald led them back to their desks.

"Ma'am." Zoë pulled out an earphone. "I've got an IP address back on that new profile."

"Who is it?"

Zoë held up her notepad. "Woman called Marianne Smith?"

Vicky gritted her teeth. "The gardener at the James Hutton Institute."

Chapter Sixty-Three

MacDonald pulled his BMW into the car park to the James Hutton Institute, slotting in behind a panda car. "This the place?"

Vicky nodded. "It is, aye."

"How do you want to play this, Vicky?"

"Let's just get her to come voluntarily. We need to watch when we caution her."

"Clock starts ticking, right?"

"Right. Did you and Forrester speak to the Wildlife guys about using terror powers?"

"Didn't really discuss it. David was going to chat to their DCI today."

"Given how hard it is to get any evidence, we'll need every second with her."

MacDonald rubbed his chin. "Not happy cautioning her without Forrester's say-so."

"Really?"

"It's the DI's case, Vicky. He's SIO."

"True." Vicky watched the two uniformed officers approach. "Come on, then. I'll lead."

"No problems with that."

Vicky got out of the car and nodded recognition at the two uniforms, her grin lingering on Colin Woods. "Afternoon, Colin. I heard Cameron's not well?"

"Aye." Woods nodded. "Nightmare. Parenthood affects even police officers."

Vicky patted MacDonald on the arm. "This is Karen's sergeant, DS Euan MacDonald. Euan, this is PC Colin Woods."

MacDonald smiled at him. "I'm not as bad as your wife will tell you."

"We'll see." Woods laughed. "What's the play here, Vicks?"

"Hopefully, there won't be one. We just need to speak to her. You're here to help us out."

"In case you fuck it up?"

"In case *we* fuck it up." Vicky shrugged before nodding at the front of the building. "Come on, then."

As they approached the Living Garden, Vicky could see Marianne Smith giving a talk to a group of schoolchildren — teenagers by the looks of things. "Great. That's all we need."

Marianne stopped talking as they neared, putting on a smile for her audience. "Can you all take a five-minute break?" She checked her watch. "Back here at three thirty?"

The group dispersed, three of the kids nearest retrieving smartphones from their bags, faces lit up by the screens.

Marianne nodded at Vicky, clenching her jaw as she looked at the flanking uniformed officers. "How can I help today?"

"We'd like to ask you a few questions, Ms Smith."

"I'm in the middle of something." Marianne folded her arms, looking at the children. "As you'll have no doubt heard, you've got five minutes."

"We'll need longer than that, I'm afraid."

Marianne settled her gaze on Vicky. "What's this about?"

"We found some messages posted on the internet in support of certain actions perpetrated over the last few days. We've tracked them back to your internet account."

"I'm sorry?"

Vicky showed her a print. "Do you deny you posted these messages?"

"Of course I deny it." Marianne shook her head. "You can see I'm in the middle of giving a talk. Perhaps you can come back later?"

"Ms Smith, can you please accompany us to the station?"

"And if I refuse?"

"I'll arrest you."

Marianne remained silent as her gaze bounced between the two uniformed officers.

Woods stepped forward. "Ms Smith, can you accompany us to the station, please?"

Marianne took a deep breath. "I'll need to arrange for a colleague to finish the talk."

Chapter Sixty-Four

Forrester loosened off his tie and put his feet up on the desk. "Think she's the criminal genius behind all this?"

"Maybe." Vicky flicked back through her notebook, glancing at MacDonald as he tapped his pen off his own. "Rachel Hay's dogs wrecked the garden she runs."

"I remember. Think that's a motive?"

"I do."

Forrester frowned. "See this Cupar case — think Smith could be the woman Irene Henderson saw?"

Vicky shrugged. "It'd be worthwhile getting a photo of Marianne Smith to her."

"Mac — thoughts?"

MacDonald clasped his hands behind his head. "Got three people directly involved in these cases. Marianne fits the very loose description we've got for one of the assailants, in that she's a woman."

"Wasn't there another woman?"

"Descriptions are ambiguous at best, sir. Won't stand up anywhere."

"Right, right. So, could it be her?"

Vicky nodded. "It's possible."

"Have we got any suspects?"

"The Muirheads." MacDonald rocked forward in his chair. "Sandy caused a right hullabaloo when we picked him up from his work this morning."

"Doesn't imply guilt."

"Pretty much all we've got, sir."

Vicky pointed her pen at Forrester. "Did you speak to the Domestic Extremism guys about using terror laws against these people?"

"I have done, aye."

"Do you want us to use them?"

"If you need to."

Considine rapped on the door. "Sorry to interrupt, sir, but DS MacDonald asked me to do some background checks on Marianne Smith."

Forrester beckoned him in. "Go on."

Considine shut the door behind him. "This is just preliminary stuff, sir, but she's known to be a bit of an agitator. Been moved on from protesting down the Murraygate on a Saturday afternoon a couple of times. Handing out flyers, collecting signatures, shouting on a megaphone." He held up a sheet of paper. "Plus, she lives in Cupar."

"Where this Henderson woman was chucked in a bin?"

"Aye, sir."

Forrester tapped his desk for a few seconds. "Mac, can you speak to your contacts at the NCA and see if they've got her on file? From what young Considine says, she's got to be known to them."

"Will do."

"Vicky, get her under caution and bring a lawyer in. You know better than me which sections of the laws to use. See what she knows."

Chapter Sixty-Five

Kelly Nelson-Caird sat back in her chair, a hand moving in front of Marianne Smith. "My client has answered the question."

Vicky cleared her throat and glanced at Considine, who was sitting next to her, writing everything in his grey notebook. "I need to ask again, Ms Smith. We found some messages in support of three crimes we're currently investigating. Do you deny posting them?"

"Of course I do. I've no idea what you're talking about."

Vicky pushed a sheet across the desk, visible to both Marianne and Nelson-Caird. "This is a message posted by the user tree_lady on the *Animal Rites* thread on the xbeast forum." She pushed a second sheet over. "This is the output of some software we have. It traces a user on that forum through to an IP address, which led us to a Virgin Media account." She gave them another sheet. "Can you confirm this is your address?"

Marianne swallowed. "Yes, it is."

Vicky pushed another two sheets over. "These are other messages posted by the user. They were traced to the same IP address and the same user at Virgin Media. This was you, wasn't it?"

"No comment."

Vicky leaned back in her chair. "Ms Smith, can you confirm your movements on Sunday the thirtieth of March?"

"What times?"

"The whole day."

Marianne glanced at Nelson-Caird, who motioned for her to continue. She scratched at the desk with a fingernail, her breathing fast. "It was raining, so I just stayed in."

"And what did you do?"

"I read a book, I think."

"Can anyone confirm this?"

Marianne shook her head. "I live alone."

"What about the fifteenth of November last year?"

"I've no idea."

"It was a Friday."

"I'll have been at work, most probably."

"We need to know for sure. Can anyone else confirm your whereabouts?"

"My manager at the Hutton Institute would be able to."

Vicky nodded to Considine, who scribbled it down. She turned back to Marianne. "Was there a lot of work to do in a garden in Dundee in the middle of November?"

"It's one of the busiest times, believe it or not. We're preparing the soil for the next season. We've a tight schedule, so when it comes round to planting in late February, everything must be ready."

"And in the evening?"

Marianne laughed, eyes burning. "You're asking me to recall what I did on a Friday night in November?"

Vicky nodded. "We are."

"I can't answer that."

"Can't or won't?"

Nelson-Caird bobbed forward on her chair, elbow clattering off the table. "Sergeant, I don't appreciate your insinuation. My client's been more than helpful."

"Then please confirm what you did on the fifteenth of November."

"I don't know."

Vicky pointed to the sheets in front of them. "Do you deny making those comments?"

"No comment."

Vicky took a deep breath before checking the Post-It she'd stuck to her notebook. "Marianne Smith, I'm arresting you under sections one and two of the Terrorist Act 2006, namely 'Encouragement of terrorism' and 'Disseminating terrorist publications'. You are not obliged to say anything but anything you do say will be noted down and may be used in evidence. Do you understand?"

Marianne shook her head. "No, I don't."

"Ms Smith, do you understand the fact you're being cautioned?"

"I do."

"Do you have anything to say?"

Marianne slumped in her chair. "I made those comments."

"Why?"

Marianne shrugged. "I'm involved in animal rights groups. So what? It's not a crime."

"People have been harmed in the execution of these acts."

"Are these people innocent?"

"Did Rachel Hay being a dog breeder have anything to do with it?"

Marianne licked her lips. "They're infernal dogs but, believe me, I had absolutely nothing to do with what happened to her."

"You're denying your involvement in the abduction of Rachel Hay?"

"My client is."

Vicky kept her gaze locked on Marianne. "And at Hunter's Farm?"

"Where?"

"It's near Barry in Angus."

"I have no idea where that is."

"Do you have any connections to the Phorever Love commune near Redford in Angus?"

"No."

"Do you deny being involved in the abduction and entrapment of Irene Henderson in Cupar, Fife on the fifteenth of November last year?"

"No comment."

Vicky sat back and fiddled with her pen — lots of denials but only one 'no comment'. "Do you deny involvement in Ms Henderson's abduction?"

"No comment."

Vicky dropped the pen — two now.

Nelson-Caird puckered her lips. "Sergeant, as you yourself stated, my client has the right to remain silent."

Vicky leaned across to the recorder. "Interview terminated at five thirty p.m." She got up and led Considine out into the corridor.

Forrester held open the door to the observation suite, next door to the interview room. "In here."

Vicky followed him. "I'll see you tomorrow, Stephen."

"Oh, okay." Considine frowned as he nodded before slouching off down the corridor.

Vicky leaned against the far wall, watching Marianne and Nelson-Caird whisper in each other's ears as the PCSO hovered by them. "I take it you two watched that?"

"Aye." Forrester creaked back in his chair, drumming his fingers on the table, eyes on MacDonald. "I'm trying not to read too much into her having the same lawyer as Brian Morton."

MacDonald frowned. "Think there's something in that?"

"Maybe. Let's keep an eye on it." Forrester stopped the drumming, cracking his knuckles instead. "We've got her under prevention of terrorism powers so we're not going to get caught in any thirty-six-hour nonsense with that lawyer of hers. Now she's under arrest, we can search her property. I expect we'll find sufficient evidence to convict."

MacDonald frowned. "Think she's the one emailing these journalists?"

"We'll soon find out. The Media Office's been working double time trying to stop anyone publishing it all over again." Forrester looked over at Vicky. "I'm going to catch up with the NCA guys just now."

MacDonald creased his brow. "Thought I was doing that, sir?"

"I need you focusing on operational matters, Mac. I've rustled up twenty officers to go round her house, even though half of them are Fifers."

"I'll forgive you."

Forrester laughed. "Fine. I just hope we find something."

Vicky raised a hand. "Do you need me in Cupar?"

"No. Off you scoot. My morning's now going to be filled with a two-hour conference with Raven and people more important than us so I want you back here at eight tomorrow, fresh as a daisy."

Wednesday
2nd April 2014

Chapter Sixty-Six

"oming up later on *Good Morning Scotland*, we'll have a
Scottish writer who moved to Australia fifteen years ago in
search of his long-lost cousin. The time's approaching five minutes
to eight."

Vicky snapped the radio off. Five minutes of chill time. She
looked around the car park, the tarmac patchy with drying rain.
The sky was clear, a dark orange to the south. Edinburgh. A thud
in her neck.

MacDonald's blue 1-Series pulled into its own reserved space.
Quick work. MacDonald got out of the car, tearing off a pair of
sunglasses, then headed away from the station. The café.

She let her seatbelt slide up, tempted to join him. Her phone
rang. She checked the display. Didn't recognise the number but
answered it anyway. "Hello?"

"Is that DS Dodds?"

"It is."

"Hi. It's John Morton."

"Good morning."

"So, I'm just calling about my brother, Brian. I spoke to him
like we discussed."

"And?"

"I didn't get anything from him. He refused to even speak to me."

"Relax — we've got a suspect."

"Oh. That's good. Does that mean you'll leave Brian alone?"

"If he keeps himself off the internet, yes."

"I'll see what I can do."

"It'd be appreciated." Vicky ended the call, stuffing her phone back in her handbag. She spotted MacDonald striding past, clutching a dark blue beaker of coffee.

Vicky waved as she got out of the car. "What's wrong with Forrester's machine?"

MacDonald stared at his cup. "Found out he reuses the coffee grounds. Gets pretty minging by the end of the day."

She laughed. "You look tired."

"I am tired. That's the last time I volunteer for searching a house after a full day shift."

"You volunteered? Thought Forrester asked you?"

He shrugged. "Volunteered just before last night's briefing. Regret it now."

"Did you get anything?"

"A couple of bits and pieces." He checked his watch. "Come on, we're late."

"Don't want people talking about us turning up together, do we?"

Chapter Sixty-Seven

MacDonald stopped outside their office space. "Warning you now — Forrester's in a grump today. Two-hour meeting just became four, apparently."

"Why?"

"Raven's been having kittens about the case. DCS in charge of the MITs got wind of what was happening, gave our Super a doing. Pask, is it?"

"Aye, Pask."

"Pask gave Raven a doing, so Raven gave Forrester a doing."

"Great."

Vicky led into the office.

Forrester was already perched by the whiteboard, tapping a pen against his hand and staring into space.

MacDonald went over to the window, leaned against the frame a few feet from the whiteboard. Took a sip of coffee through the lid.

Vicky sat on the edge of a desk, the corner needling her thigh through her skirt.

Karen joined her, smirking. "Interesting you two entering at the same time."

"Don't." Vicky shifted her gaze from MacDonald. "How's Cameron?"

"He's fine. Bloody nursery sending kids home is the bane of my life. Half of my bloody pay goes to them as it is."

"Good morning all." Forrester clapped his hands together. "Okay, let's get stuck into it. As you all know, I'm briefing Pask and Raven straight after this. Be thankful it's not you." He took a breath. "First, the good news. We have a suspect. Marianne Smith. The bad news is she's not talking and she's got two accomplices. DC Reed in Glenrothes put her photo in front of Irene Henderson. She couldn't say either way." He nodded at MacDonald then at Vicky. "Can you pair interview her again this morning?"

Vicky nodded, eyes locked on MacDonald. "Will do, sir."

Forrester grimaced. "I spoke to the NCA guys this morning on my way in. They've got Smith on record as an animal rights activist, active since the mid-nineties. Seems to have never committed a crime or been suspected of any."

He folded his arms. "The bad news. A very helpful news website decided to publish the notes and the messages from the videos in full. The Police Scotland Media Office's been trying to keep them out of the papers, but we've failed." He tilted his chin down as he held up the morning's *Scotsman*. "The cat's out of the bag, if you'll excuse the joke. Whatever message they're trying to spread, well, it's being spread." He waved a hand at MacDonald. "Mac, do you want to go over the search of her house?"

"Sure. First, found paper matching all five notes. Smith doesn't appear to own a printer, though." MacDonald took a drink of coffee. "Next, found books on domestic terror in the US. Anti-abortion lobbyists, animal rights groups. Real nasty stuff about modus operandi and methodology."

Forrester nodded at Vicky. "We might be able to charge her under section six of the Terror Act as well. Those books are tantamount to 'Training for terrorism'."

Vicky made a note. "I'll get Tommy Davies to add it to the charge sheet, sir."

MacDonald held up a blue folder. "Starting to acquire a wealth of evidence against her."

"It feels very circumstantial, though." Vicky folded her arms. "Have you proved her links to the user name on that forum?"

MacDonald narrowed his eyes at Zoë. "You're looking at her computer, right?"

"Not had a chance to look into it much, sir, but I did connect the dots. It proved what I'd been doing with the Met guys." She blushed. "I'll do a full check later on."

Forrester wiped the whiteboard clean. "Let's start again from scratch and do some work here." He wrote three crimes on the board — *Dog Breeder*, *Battery Hens* and *Cat Bin*. "What are the links between them?"

MacDonald tilted his cup towards the whiteboard. "Notes, for starters."

"Right. The notes are definitely a keeper. All five crime scenes so far have a note." Forrester added connections to *Note*. "What else?"

Vicky held up a hand. "The car was spotted at all three."

"Good." Forrester wrote up *Car*, drawing lines between them all. "Vicky, take us through everything we know about all three cases."

Vicky nodded. "Okay. First, on the fifteenth of November last year, three people abducted Irene Henderson and put her in a bin. Unbeknownst to the investigating officers at the time, our guys left a note, which we've subsequently matched to the others."

Forrester added three stick figures at the top. "What descriptions have we got?"

"One male, between five ten and six foot. One female, no description, and another person of indeterminate gender."

Forrester added notes to the board. "Okay, next?"

"Next, last Wednesday, Rachel Hay was abducted in Invergowrie. Her brother, Paul Joyce, had already been abducted in Dundee at the Dryburgh Industrial Estate. They were locked in a cage there and an attempt was made to coerce them into having sex. It failed. We found them on Thursday. Another note was left behind. The loose descriptions we have are of a man and another individual."

Forrester connected the male stick figure to the other crimes. "Do we know if it was the woman or the other one?"

"No."

"Right. Go on."

"On Saturday, a family were trapped in their battery hen farm in Barry. They were welded inside animal cages and the husband —" She swallowed hard before taking a deep breath. "The husband had part of his nose burnt off. They weren't found until Monday morning. Another note was left at the scene. Descriptions from Mrs Hunter match the male and the third suspect."

"So no female this time?"

"No."

Forrester connected the lines. "What else have we got then, Vicky?"

"The Phorever Love group DS MacDonald got from the NCA have been linked to the battery farm. I'm waiting on a further update from the undercover contact."

Forrester noted *For. Love* down. "Mac?"

"Proving difficult, sir, but I'll keep on top of them."

"Do it by the time I get back from my meeting, okay? What else have we got?"

"The kids in Fife posting on that board." MacDonald took a drink. "Live in Cupar, seem motivated. Worthwhile checking to see if they know Marianne Smith."

Forrester added it to the board. "Go on."

"Marianne Smith and Rachel have previous history. Maybe knew her dog walking route."

Forrester wrote *Smith* and linked it with the *Dog Breeder* box. "Is she the woman in the Cupar case?"

Considine scowled. "Could be, sir. Given what Zoë and DS MacDonald have said, there might be a link."

Forrester tapped at the stick figures. "So, one of them could be Smith, right?"

"Right." MacDonald rubbed his chin. "Could the Muirheads be the other two?"

Karen did her tongue thing. "They've got alibis, though."

MacDonald set his cup down on the window sill. "People can lie."

Forrester nodded. "Mac's right. Do they fit the description?"

Vicky pointed to the *Assumptions* box. "Assuming the androgynous person is Polly Muirhead. She's tall and not particularly curvy."

"Or it could just be a rubbish description." Forrester noted down their names. "Anyone else?"

"Brian Morton." Vicky tugged her hair behind an ear. "His brother called me this morning. He said he's not speaking to us."

"Do we need to get him back in?"

"Not sure, sir. I'd suggest we prove his connection to the case before we get him back in. According to his surgeon, he's a high heart attack risk. Plus he's nothing like any of the three sightings we've got."

"Christ, that's all we need." Forrester turned back to the board, writing *Working Hypothesis* in a box above *Assumptions*. "I'm going with Marianne and at least one accomplice. She's got no alibis, right? It's got to be her and, most likely, the Muirheads."

Zoë held up a hand. "Sorry, sir. I've been speaking to some of my contacts in the Met. I've managed to get access to some private messages sent by Marianne Smith."

"And?"

"Among many others, it looks like she received a message from Polly Muirhead on the twelfth of November last year."

"You're kidding."

"No, sir. It said *'How is Cupar this time of year?'*"

"Excellent." Forrester clapped his hands. "Just around the time of the cat bin attack." He made another section, titled *Actions*. "Right-o. Vicky, can you and MacDonald get in a room with Marianne Smith and ask her about these books, the paper and this message?"

"Will do, sir."

"We need to do something about these bloody schoolkids. I think they're just messing about, but you never know. I might just get some big Fifers to lean on them. Allan Reed in Glenrothes is big enough and ugly enough to frighten them." Forrester wrote the last action below it. "Last, bring the Muirheads back in. Vicky, Mac — get on top of them."

MacDonald picked up his coffee cup. "Absolutely, sir."

Forrester looked around the rest of the room. "These are the core activities. DS Dodds and DS MacDonald are leading this until our two o'clock briefing today, okay? Take direction from them. Dismissed."

Chapter Sixty-Eight

Marianne Smith cowered next to her lawyer, eyes red raw, deep bags underneath them. "When are you letting me go?"

"It's not up to DS MacDonald or myself when you'll be let go." Vicky started the machine recording. "Interview commenced at nine oh three on Wednesday the second of April twenty-fourteen. Present are myself, DS Victoria Dodds, and DS Euan MacDonald. Also present are the suspect, Marianne Smith, and her lawyer, Kelly Nelson-Caird." She caught her breath, eyes on Marianne. "Ms Smith, since your arrest yesterday, officers have completed a search of your house."

"My house?" Marianne stared at her lawyer. "Can they do this?"

Nelson-Caird nodded. "They can. I'll have to check their warrants are compliant."

"They are." MacDonald produced a ream of paper in a large evidence bag. "Found some interesting items in your residence." He tapped the paper. "The paper stock matches that used on the notes found at each of the crime scenes we're investigating."

Marianne blinked. "But that's just paper."

MacDonald nodded. "Quite rare paper, though. Found just a single supplier in the Tayside area and it's not available for general sale on the internet."

Nelson-Caird wagged a finger at him. "This is inadmissible as direct evidence against my client unless you can demonstrate these notes came from *her* supply of paper."

MacDonald produced a stack of books, all bound in evidence bags. "These textbooks all concern domestic terror. Care to explain?"

Marianne swallowed. "I did my thesis at university on domestic terror in Ireland, Spain and Germany in the seventies. I like to keep up to date on the topic."

"Don't look like anything to do with the IRA or Baader-Meinhof, though." MacDonald picked up a book and inspected the cover. "These detail methods used in issue-specific terrorism, such as actions made against abortion clinics or vivisectionists in America. Completely unrelated to the nationalist or communist groups you say you did your thesis on."

"No comment."

MacDonald glanced at Vicky. "DS Dodds?"

Vicky pushed a sheet of paper across the table, the yellow indexing sticker at the top right. "This pertains to a private message sent via the xbeast forum."

Nelson-Caird examined the sheet before folding it in half. "How does this relate to my client?"

"Ms Smith received a message from Polly Muirhead, a fellow member of the forum. As you'll see, the message read, *'How is Cupar this time of year?'*"

"And?"

"The message was sent three days before Irene Henderson of Cupar was locked in an industrial bin in the town."

Nelson-Caird folded her arms. "You do actually have evidence linking my client to this case, don't you?"

"These all link your client to this case."

"I beg to differ."

Vicky gestured at the sheet in front of them. "Do you have anything you wish to say about this message?"

Marianne shrugged. "I don't recall receiving it."

"That's very convenient. Do you know Mrs Polly Muirhead?"

"The name doesn't ring a bell."

"Ms Smith, I will remind you of the fact you're under police caution. This is admissible as evidence. We've obtained a number of messages being sent from Mrs Muirhead's account to yours. If you know her, you should state so clearly."

"No comment."

"You're on record as saying her name 'doesn't ring a bell'. Is that how you wish it to be noted?"

Marianne glanced at Nelson-Caird before nodding. "Yes."

"Very well."

MacDonald leaned forward, resting on his forearms. "Ms Smith, did you trap Ms Irene Henderson in an industrial bin on the fifteenth of November twenty-thirteen?"

Marianne shook her head. "No comment."

"Did you use Mr Alexander Muirhead, known as Sandy, and Mrs Polly Muirhead as accomplices?"

"No comment."

"Did you and Mr Muirhead abduct Mrs Rachel Hay from near your place of work and entrap her in a steel cage in a unit in the Dryburgh Industrial Estate in Dundee?"

"No comment."

"Did you and Mr Muirhead abduct Mr Paul Joyce and entrap him in a steel cage in a unit in the Dryburgh Industrial Estate in Dundee?"

"No comment."

"Did you and Mr Muirhead attempt to force Mrs Hay and Mr Joyce to have sexual intercourse while trapped in the cage?"

Nelson-Caird's nostrils twitched as her gaze shifted to her client.

Marianne rubbed at her eyes, tears welling up. "No comment."

"Did you record this act with a video camera and subsequently post the video online?"

Marianne stared at the ceiling. "No comment."

"Ms Smith, did you break into Hunter's Farm in Barry and forcibly entrap Mr Graeme Hunter, Mrs Rhona Hunter, Miss Amelie Hunter and Miss Grace Hunter in a steel cage?"

Tears slid down Marianne's face. "No comment."

"Ms Smith, did you forcibly apply a hot knife machine to Mr Hunter's nose?"

"My God." Marianne tugged at the collar of her t-shirt, eyes wide. "No comment."

Vicky checked her notebook. Only one avenue of questioning remained. "Ms Smith, do you know one Brian Morton of Ann Street, Hilltown, Dundee?"

"No comment."

Nelson-Caird tapped her thumb on the tabletop three times. "Mr Morton's my client."

"I'm aware of that. I haven't made any comment on the fact you represent two suspects in the same case."

"Do you really wish to have this on the record, Sergeant?"

Vicky folded her arms. "Do you?"

"My firm has a wide range of clients. Some are fee-paying, like Ms Smith here, while others are legal aid, like Mr Morton. My client base isn't pertinent to your investigation."

"Very well." Vicky leaned over the machine. "Interview terminated at nine sixteen." She got to her feet and stormed out of the room, waiting in the corridor for MacDonald with his evidence. "She's definitely involved in this."

"Agreed." MacDonald nodded at the paper, shifting the weight in his arms. "Any chance you could take a couple of books for me?"

Vicky picked up the topmost three. "I still don't like how Nelson-Caird is representing multiple suspects."

Chapter Sixty-Nine

Vicky stared at her email inbox — over two hundred unread. A quick glance showed nothing particularly pertinent to the case. She clicked on the first one, a calendar invite to her media training course. Her mobile rang. "Hello?"

"Is that Vicky Dodds?" Male. English accent, maybe London.

"Speaking."

"This is Andy Salewicz."

Vicky frowned as she tried to recall the name. "I met you yesterday at Phorever Love, didn't I?"

"Correct."

Vicky switched her mobile to her right hand so she could log the call in her notebook. "Are you going to threaten me on behalf of Mr Simmers again?"

"This isn't about that."

"Then what is it about?"

"My boss asked me to call you or DS Euan MacDonald. I work for the Domestic Extremist Team in the Met."

"You're working undercover?"

"I am. DI Andy Salewicz."

"You use your real name?"

"Saves hassle with the cover. My cover story's got military service in it — I was in Iraq for three tours. Besides, I don't want Someone I know in Tesco's saying 'Hello, Jock Wilson', do I?"

"Suppose not. Well, that was an impressive display yesterday. I had you tagged as hired muscle."

"It's tough, don't get me wrong. Thanks for not blowing my cover."

"I didn't know you were on my side."

"Good."

"Are you free to talk, then?"

"I just gave my rank, didn't I? I'm sitting in a garden centre in Brechin. Supposed to be collecting ten wheelbarrows but I've got peckish and have gone for some soup, if you know what I mean. I spoke to my DCI and I got a message to call you guys."

"Okay. Basically, I want to check the intel we've received is sound. We were told Phorever Love might be linked to these abductions or to the xbeast forum. Based on what you said yesterday, it looks like a load of bollocks."

Salewicz sighed down the line. "What, because local police were monitoring us during that week-long rave we had?"

"Yes, that."

"It's sound. Nobody here is directly involved with your cases."

"Indirectly would help."

A pause. "They're up to something here — drugs, though, not terror. I've been in deep cover just over six months. Simmers is only just starting to trust me now."

"Why are the Domestic Extremist Squad interested?"

"We got wind of a plot to poison a reservoir near Edinburgh, which made us think there was some environmental terror angle here, hence me being shoved up here. This lot aren't involved in that sort of thing." Salewicz sniffed. "They *are* involved in drugs, though. I think they know someone who's got a meth lab up in the Highlands."

"Like in *Breaking Bad*?"

"Exactly." Salewicz laughed. "I was halfway through the fifth series before I got put on this so *please* don't spoil the end for me."

"I'm just at the one where the fly gets stuck in the lab myself."

"That's a classic." Salewicz chuckled. "Anyway, the bottom line is they seem to be more into drugs than terrorism. My handler wants me to stay here and help the NCA. It's like a double secondment."

"So, it's a dead end for us?"

"Not quite. I keep hearing they've got a Tetra scanner but I've not seen anything with my own eyes."

"You mean an Airwave scanner?"

"Yeah. Supposed to be speaking to some guy in Dundee about it after I'm off with you. Same surname as you, as it happens."

"That'll be my brother, Andrew." Vicky stared at her blank notebook for a few seconds — it might just fit. "Do you have any idea why they'd want one?"

"It's a bit heavy duty for a load of drugs smugglers, to be honest."

"Really?"

"Well, maybe just a bit stupid. You'd use one for a broad brush search of what's going on in a city. It's labour intensive. Drugs guys tend to rely on paying people off, not on scanning the airwaves."

"Do you have a list of known affiliates to this group?"

Salewicz exhaled. "I need to check with my superiors about whether I can get you that. It's ultra-sensitive and it'll be a bit of a bugger to get access to it."

"When will you be contactable again?"

"I might need to come buy a load of dung tomorrow morning."

"Okay, thanks." Vicky was on her feet before she ended the call.

Considine leaned against the wall in Forrester's office, phone clamped to his head. He made a winding motion with his finger. "Sorry, I'll need to call you back. Yeah, we should." He smiled at her. "Landlord. Forrester's still upstairs with Raven and Pask, if you're looking for him."

"It's you I need to speak to." Vicky shut the door behind her. "I just got off the phone with your undercover guy in Phorever Love."

"Phoned you, did he? Interesting." MacDonald folded his arms. "What did he have to say for himself?"

"There might be something in it. It's not as good as you were initially led to believe but he's going to get back to me tomorrow with a list of known associates."

"Right. What do you reckon he'll come up with?"

"Phorever Love are linked to this Airwave scanner. That makes him think it's not exclusively drugs they're up to."

"Okay." MacDonald frowned. "While you're here, did we speak to the Rep about the Muirheads' alibi?"

"No, I think Considine just checked with the friends and got the ticket stubs."

MacDonald got to his feet. "We need to get someone out there."

Vicky looked up at him. "You think they're lying?"

"We're just doing a bit of due diligence, shall we say."

An Airwave buzzed on Forrester's desk. "Control to DS Euan MacDonald. Over."

He grabbed it, scowling at the machine as he stabbed a finger at it. "Receiving."

"Sarge, we've got another possible case for you. A greyhound trainer in Montrose has been murdered."

Chapter Seventy

Considine pulled a left off the main road through Montrose, heading away from the town along the northern shore of the tidal basin they'd just crossed, trees to the right opposite a new housing estate. "So you reckon it's another one for us?"

Vicky shook her head. "Control pushed it to MacDonald. Whether it's connected remains to be seen, but all animal-related crimes are being shoved to us now."

"It's a greyhound trainer, right?"

"It is."

"My granda used to take me to Dens Park to see the dogs."

"You've been to greyhound racing?"

"Aye, Sarge. It's magic."

"It's barbaric."

"I loved it. Been down to Newcastle a few times with my mates." Considine chuckled. "The trick is to watch for the one doing a big jobbie before they go in the traps then fire a load of cash on that."

"You said you went to Dens Park? That's where Dundee FC play, right?"

"Aye. They shut it when I was still at school. Late nineties? Granda died not long after." Considine turned his Subaru up a long farm lane.

The greyhound traps were visible as they approached — twelve long strips of grass surrounded by chicken wire, a small kennel at the end of each one. A couple of dogs paced around one in the middle, but the rest seemed empty. The house behind the kennels was typical of the area — multiple extensions quadrupling the size of an old stone cottage, now all a uniform white.

Vicky felt the twang in her neck — Robert and his retired greyhounds, taking the dogs away from the cruelty and exploitation. She got out of the car, meeting MacDonald and Karen in front.

Forrester appeared at the same time, jaw clenched and eyes narrowed. "Raven's brought Greig over."

MacDonald sniffed. "He's the other DI, right?"

"Aye. Keith Greig." Forrester squinted into the distance — Raven and Greig were chatting casually at the far side of the house. "This is *our* bloody case."

"Least it gets you out of that four-hour meeting, sir."

"True. But I fear it's merely postponed."

"What do you want us to do, sir?"

"I don't know, Mac. Try and find out what's happened." Forrester marched off towards Raven.

MacDonald watched him go for a few seconds. "Think we'll lose his case?"

"No idea." Vicky led them over to the house. "Morning, Johnny."

DS Johnny Laing stood at the entrance, manning access to the crime scene. Big, like he worked on a farm, his suit stretched at the buttons. He tugged at his curly locks, which were almost resting on his eyebrows. He nodded. "Vicks."

"What's happened here?"

"This is my gaffer's case. Better take it up with him."

"Come on, Johnny. We've been told to get out here and help. Let's leave that to them to discuss."

Laing nodded off away from the house to where Forrester and Greig were getting in each other's face. Raven was speaking into an Airwave. "That'll be them coming to an amicable agreement now, I suppose?"

"Most likely. Come on, what's happened?"

Laing sighed. "Right. Bloke called Micky Scott was found dead by his son, handcuffed to a treadmill."

"Does it look like anything sexual?"

"I know your love life's a bit racier than mine, Vicks, but handcuffed to a *treadmill*? Really?"

"I meant, does it look like a sex game gone wrong?"

Laing shrugged. "They don't think so. The pathologist's already left, reckons it looks like he died of a heart attack sometime last night. He's not confirming anything till he's got the body on the slab in Dundee."

Vicky looked up at the house, at the eaves hanging over their heads. Handcuffed to a treadmill implied premeditation. "Control said it was murder."

"Aye. That's how the gaffer's treating it."

"Who called it in?"

"The boy's son, Alec Scott. Local plod got out here first. Place was deserted. Supposed to be playing snooker with his old boy. PC Dickson entered the house and found the body."

"Any chance we can speak to the son, Johnny?"

"FLO's with him just now."

"Not inside, surely?"

"Took him up to his house." Laing shrugged. "Long as I don't get blamed for you pitching up there, I don't really care."

MacDonald nodded over at the two inspectors, who were now nodding at whatever Raven was telling them, then focused on Vicky. "I'll see what's going on over there. You go speak to the son."

Chapter Seventy-One

Considine swerved out into oncoming traffic before cutting back in, stuck behind the tractor. The sort of angry driving Vicky's dad used to practise as soon as anything went slightly wrong with the car or his children. "It's got to be around here somewhere, Sarge."

Vicky held up the road atlas. "I told you to take a left about a mile back."

"I should be able to get through the back way, though."

"If only you had a satnav."

Considine glared at her as he pulled in. "I don't need a satnav. I know where I'm going."

"Doesn't feel like it."

Considine did a three-point turn on the main road, making a Range Rover brake sharply, before shooting back the way they'd come. "Left up here?"

"No, right."

Considine turned down a country lane, its single track leading deep into the emerging spring green, passing a farm on the right, a monolithic granite farmhouse sitting beside giant steel silos. "This it?"

"Next one."

Considine ploughed on. The lane lost its tarmac and the car bumped up and down on the wild farm path. A stone cottage sat behind a thick beech hedge, maybe two rooms at most. "This it here?"

"Think so."

Considine pulled into the long drive beside the house. The garden was raised up with a retaining wall placed between the lawn and the pebbles he parked on.

Vicky got out first, crunched up the path towards the house. She rang the doorbell, an electronic buzz just audible through the door.

A female uniformed officer pulled open the door. "Yes?"

"DS Dodds, DC Considine." Vicky held up her warrant card. "We've just come from the crime scene."

"Okay." The officer stepped outside, holding out a hand. "PC Nora Armstrong. I'm the Family Liaison allocated."

"Okay. We'd like to speak to PC Dickson."

"He's inside. I'll warn you now, he's more shaken up than Mr Scott."

"I see."

"Come on." Nora led them inside the house. The door opened into a dark sitting room with thick curtains covering the windows, a couple of sidelights shining up the stone walls.

A police officer wearing full uniform sat on a sofa, rubbing at his thinning hairline and staring into space. There was a kitchen space behind him, a man in jeans and shirt standing beside another suited figure.

Vicky stopped at the sofa. "PC Dickson?"

He nodded, still staring into space. He was young, barely even twenty in her estimation, even though he'd lost almost half of his hair.

Vicky knelt in front of him, knees straining. "Are you okay?"

301

Dickson glanced up. "I found the body."

"Haven't you seen one before?"

"First time." Dickson blinked a few times, pupils dilated. "I tried to feel a pulse. I've never felt anything so cold in my life."

Vicky nodded over to the kitchen space. "Is that the son?"

"It is, aye. Alec Scott." Dickson rubbed at his eye. "Seems to be okay, considering."

Vicky got up. "I'll maybe need to speak to you again." She tugged her warrant card out of her jacket as she walked over, flashing it at the police officer, who looked more seasoned and heavy than Dickson. "DS Dodds and DC Considine. We've been assigned this case."

"I'll see how young Stuart's doing." The officer went over to the sofa.

Vicky smiled at Alec Scott. "Are you in a position to answer our questions, Mr Scott?"

Alec nodded. "Aye. I want you to find whoever did this to Dad."

Vicky leaned against the counter and got out her notebook, Considine echoing the motion. "Can you go through what happened at his house this morning?"

Alec sucked in some air. "I play Dad at snooker every Wednesday. We usually do a best of five then go for something to eat at the Corn Exchange in town."

"Where do you work?"

"I train greyhounds as well."

"Here?"

"Aye. Got a much smaller operation than my old man. Six dogs, two bitches."

"Are your father's dogs safe just now?"

"I spoke to the stable girl who does the horses at the farm next door. She's going to head over there."

"And longer term?"

Alec shrugged. "Have to see what's in the old boy's will, won't I?"

"You don't stand to inherit?"

"I don't know."

"Okay, so going back to this morning, then. You were due to play snooker with your father?"

"Aye. He didn't show up. I played a frame on my own against myself. If you take it seriously it's a good laugh." Alec bit his lip, colour draining from his face. "I called him. No response. I thought it was odd how he'd not pitched up. I drove out there and tried to see what's what. No answer, so I called the police."

"You don't have a key?"

"Not since I left home."

"So entry was forced?"

"It was, aye. Lucky we did." Alec waved at Dickson on the sofa. "Me and the constable there checked a few rooms on the ground floor. No sign of him. We went upstairs and the door to the gym was open." He took a few seconds to himself, eyes filling with tears. "Dad was lying on the treadmill. Well, just off it, like he'd fallen over. It was still running. We checked to see if he'd just knocked himself out." He shut his eyes. "He was dead."

"Was there anything unusual about how you found him?"

"He'd been *handcuffed* to the treadmill. Isn't that unusual enough?"

"Did your father possess any?"

Alec's eyes widened. "Not that I know of."

"Was your father into exercise?"

"Aye. He used to play for Dundee in the eighties. Played with Gordon Strachan and Bobby Connor, you know? Opened up his knee playing Rangers so he had to give it up. Took up greyhound training. Couldn't play topflight football again but he kept in at the running, tried to keep in shape, not like some of these old pros you see on the telly."

Vicky turned the page in her notebook. "Can you think of anyone who'd have cause to harm your father?"

Alec shook his head, almost too quickly. "No."

"What about your mother?"

Alec bit a fingernail. "She died when I was ten. Cancer. Dad didn't remarry."

"Any other family in the area? Brothers or sisters?"

"My sister emigrated to Australia a few years ago. My uncle Bobby — Dad's brother — died of a heart attack two years back."

"Does he have many friends in the area?"

"None that spring to mind."

"Did your father drink in town?"

"He was teetotal."

"No other family?"

"He loved my wee boy, Michael."

Vicky noted it down. "Is he at school?"

"Aye, he is. We're supposed to be going to a caravan up by Grantown-on-Spey next week when the schools are off for Easter. That's not going to happen now."

"Is that with your wife?"

Alec shook his head. "Julie didn't like it up here. She moved back to Carlisle a couple of years ago."

"How was her relationship with your father?"

"They didn't see eye to eye. Dad used to spoil Michael something rotten."

"Why didn't she take custody of your son?"

"She didn't want him. I did." Alec shrugged. "Simple."

"What about professionally? Were there any people in the greyhound business your father had any run-ins with?"

"Not that I can think of."

"Are you sure?"

Alec let out a held breath. "There were a couple of guys in the Newcastle area he'd had a few arguments with."

"What about?"

"Race fees, prize money, stuff like that."

"You don't know who?"

"I try to keep away from the business side. I like working with the dogs and I like to keep a distance from the gangsters who run the meets."

"Do you have any names of people in the Newcastle area?"

"I don't, sorry."

Considine's mobile rang. He walked off to take the call, stopping by the door.

Vicky made a note to get a search done for contact books and 0191 numbers in particular. "We're looking into this case in conjunction with a few others we're investigating."

"I thought I recognised you. You were on the telly the other day, right?"

"Correct."

"You think someone's killed my old boy because he raced dogs?"

Vicky folded her arms. "Do you think it's likely?"

"It's possible."

"Were there ever any protestors at his house or any hate mail, anything like that?"

"Never."

Vicky checked her notebook, lifting out a tattered photocopy of the first note. "When you found your father, did you also find a note like this?"

Alec scowled at the page. "No."

"Would it be possible his newspaper lay on top of it, maybe?"

"Dad doesn't get a paper. Gets all his news on his iPad these days."

Considine returned, tapping his mobile against his hand. Leaning in close, he whispered in Vicky's ear. "That was Mac. Raven wants us back in Dundee for a briefing."

Chapter Seventy-Two

Forrester stood outside the incident room, thumbs prodding his BlackBerry, the keys clicking. "Bloody hell."

Vicky stopped next to him, waiting for the corridor to quieten down. "Why are we in there?"

Forrester sighed. "Raven's booked it. Largest bloody room in West Bell Street."

"Is it just for a briefing or an incident room?"

"No idea." Forrester held the door open for her. "Come on."

They were the last in. Vicky leaned against the far wall, Forrester next to her.

Raven's gaze swept over the assembled officers as he waited for silence to fall. "We've now got a murder to deal with. Michael Scott was handcuffed to a treadmill in his home gym. We've no reason to believe he was in possession of any handcuffs and we don't believe he handcuffed himself to the treadmill. The machine was still running and the safety cord hadn't been tugged."

He crossed his arms, his suit jacket riding up. "We have a potential connection to David Forrester's three cases, all seemingly involving vigilante action against animal cruelty. The Super has appointed me as SIO for both of DI Forrester's cases and for this new murder. I want three plans of attack. First, David, I want you and your team to continue investigating these as if they were separate because we didn't find a note at this crime scene. I want this greyhound case kept completely separate from your three."

"Are you sure?"

Raven nodded. "Of course I'm sure. Next, I've asked DI Keith Greig and his team to focus solely on the murder of Mr Scott."

Greig sucked in his gut as he looked around at Laing and the rest of his team, a hand reaching up to scratch his moustache, almost as grey as his thick hair. "Thank you, boss."

"Lastly, I want David's team to also focus on the links between the crimes. You'll have full access to all case files but I want a Chinese Wall around these, okay? No cross-contamination of evidence. I want clear audit trails in all cases. If they're one and the same — and I seriously hope they aren't — then we'll get together and review integrating them. From bitter experience, I know it's easier to merge than to split. Is that clear?"

Forrester stared at Greig for a few seconds before nodding, Greig following his lead.

"Right. David, Keith, in the event this is escalating, I want us to get on the front foot, okay? I've scheduled a meeting with the NCA later. Dismissed."

MacDonald wandered over, sucking at the lid of a coffee cup. "What do you make of that, sir?"

Forrester scowled at Greig as he led his team to the opposite corner. "Right, you pair. Let's get a coffee."

"In your office?"

"No, Mac. Across the road. I want to get out of this bloody place."

Chapter Seventy-Three

Vicky sat in the window seat of the Old Mill Café, looking at the spring rain as she waited for them.

MacDonald screeched a chair across the floor and sat. Forrester was still at the counter. "Feels like we've lost something."

"Didn't know we were fighting."

Forrester dumped the full tray on the table, handing her a Diet Coke and sliding off two coffees. "There you are." He chucked some pre-packed sandwiches and bags of crisps on the table before leaning the tray against the leg. "Might not get another chance to eat today." He tore open a sachet of brown sugar and poured the contents into his mug, stabbing a knife at the dark liquid. "Right. Thoughts?"

Vicky poured her Diet Coke in the glass, watching the bubbles burst inches above the surface. "I can't fault Raven's logic in keeping the two investigations separate but I'm just not sure about the personnel being asked to lead the murder inquiry."

"In what way?"

"Laing? Seriously?"

"Noted." Forrester blew on his coffee. "Mac?"

MacDonald blew on his coffee. "Honestly?"

"Shoot. Both barrels."

"I'm pissed off, sir."

"Why?"

"We can do this better than them."

Forrester took a sip of coffee, eyes narrowing as he inspected MacDonald over the rim of the mug. "What makes you think that?"

"How many murders has Greig investigated?"

"Medals on the table time, is it?"

"I did twenty murders in a *year* in Strathclyde. Raven's got it the wrong way round. *We* should be leading on the greyhound case, not Greig."

"I've worked with Keith for years. He's a decent officer."

"Decent, maybe, but not great. Unless the SOCOs play a blinder, we're relying on him to solve the case."

"I need to know now if you've got previous with him."

"Before today, sir, I'd never even heard of him." MacDonald opened one of the sandwich packs, resting half on the lid.

"So you're basing his inadequacy on one meeting?"

"Just saying, sir. I *know* we can solve this. Don't know DI Greig from Adam but I know *I* can do this."

Forrester finished stirring his coffee and laid his spoon on the table, the metal clanking. "Remember why you're here, Sergeant."

"What's that supposed to mean?"

"You're here as my second DS, not as another DI." Forrester took a drink. "Besides, it's not definitely the same case as ours."

"Probably is, though. Greyhound trainer killed in mysterious circumstances. Doesn't seem like a coincidence, does it?" MacDonald waved across the table at Vicky. "DS Dodds did the initial interview with the victim's son. We should've been given time to investigate, sir."

"John Raven likes to move quickly and decisively."

"So I see." MacDonald shook his head. "John Raven's Newsround."

"More like Countryfile." Grinning, Forrester took another gulp of coffee. "Vicky, you've been quiet."

She tugged at the ring pull on her can. "I'm with Euan, sir. I don't think this is the best use of resources. By all means, give us more DCs, but let *us* investigate, not them."

"Listen to the pair of you." Forrester opened a sandwich packet and took a bite. "There's going to have to be a street team out in bloody Montrose. Are either of you raising your hands to manage that along with the one we've still got in Dundee and whatever else we need to do in Fife?"

Vicky took a drink. "No, sir."

"Didn't think so." Forrester finished his coffee. A tall trail of grounds stuck to the inside of the cup. "Right. Let's get our heads together, assuming your egos are now sufficiently repaired?"

Vicky gripped her can, dimpling the sides. "It's not mine that was damaged."

MacDonald grimaced. "Let's just get on with it."

Vicky raised an eyebrow — sense of humour bypass.

"I'm not sure how I want to divvy this up." Forrester chewed at another bite. "What have we got open just now, Mac?"

"Looks like Raven has taken the NCA liaison from me."

"Certainly looks that way."

MacDonald took a drink of his coffee. "Other than the street team in Dryburgh, I've got nothing, then."

"Vicky?"

"The Cupar stuff's dead. We've both been looking at the Muirheads and Marianne Smith. There's a few things I need to catch up on with them but that's pretty much it."

"Okay. Mac, can you pick up the links between the cases? I want you to assume they're linked. Prove they're the same case. Do some digging into this boy. Be a dick about it, okay?"

MacDonald raised his eyebrows. "Sure I can manage that, sir."

"Vicky, you assume they're separate, okay?"

"Am I to be a fanny about it?"

Forrester laughed. "If Marianne Smith's behind this, she's clearly not working alone. Can you get in a room with her and ask about this greyhound stuff?"

"Will do, sir."

Forrester put the tray on the table and started piling it up with their cups and Vicky's can.

Vicky took the last sandwich from the table. "Tuna? Some pair of gentlemen you are."

Chapter Seventy-Four

Vicky paid for her cheese and tomato sandwich, slapping the change on her tray. *Tuna*. She looked around the canteen, hoping for a seat on her own. Was that Andrew?

She walked over with a smirk on her face and gripped his shoulder with her free hand. "Andrew Dodds, come with me."

He pulled his hands up to his chest, letting go of his tablet. The device clattered off the table. He looked around and let out a deep breath. "Jesus, Vicks."

"Should've seen your face." She looked at the pile of stuff next to him — a plastic sandwich tub, folded-up crisp packet, squashed can of Red Bull. "Mind if I join you?"

"No, that's cool." He pushed his stuff to the side. "Mum made my lunch."

Vicky sat opposite, tearing open her sandwich wrapper. "Classic. Even packs Red Bull for you."

"Keep quiet about that."

"Maybe." Vicky pointed at the shirt and tie he was wearing. "You been in court today or something?"

"No. I'm working. This Tetra scanner stuff."

"Right. Seems to have gone all quiet at our end."

"Not at mine."

"You look tired."

"I am tired. I've forgotten half of what I knew about it."

Vicky took a bite and chewed. "Lucky I saw you. Wanted to ask you about something."

"I'm shattered, Vicks, and I need a break."

"Just a little thing?"

"Fine. What?"

"You know this Zoë girl, right?"

"Aye, I spoke to her today. She was up with the team for once. You've really got her under lock and key downstairs, haven't you?"

"Did she say that?"

Andrew chuckled. "Hardly, but I know you."

"Right." Vicky swallowed down her mouthful. "She reckons she's traced these users back to IP addresses."

"I know. I showed her how to do it."

"Did you?"

"Aye."

"So, how accurate is it?"

"These days? Close to a hundred per cent. The stuff she's been doing, that's nailed down. I can get you twenty experts in a room if you need it validated."

"So the work's solid?"

"Almost as good as if she had the originating machine in front of her."

"Almost? So it's not totally solid?"

"Christ, Vicky, everything's got to be perfect for you, hasn't it?"

"You know how it is. I'm the one who has to stand up in court with this or deal with the Procurator Fiscal's office." Vicky started on the second half of the sandwich. "Your name came up this morning."

"What have I done now?"

"Andy Salewicz?"

"Undercover guy, right?"

"Aye." Vicky laughed. "He better watch out — he's not going to be undercover for long at this rate."

Andrew grinned. "He was asking me about the Tetra scanner. Reckons this commune up in the glens are using it."

"And are they?"

"Don't think so. I've managed to get a ping back from rogue devices in the area. There're two at most and they've both been inside Dundee for the last few days."

"Where?"

"It's not that accurate. These guys just don't want to be found."

"How are they doing it?"

Andrew shrugged. "Bent coppers selling their codes? Don't know."

"Should I take him at his word?"

"There aren't many men you'll trust, sis, but Salewicz seems like he's on the level."

"Thanks." Vicky tapped at the Red Bull can. "You know what Mum'll say, don't you?"

"Yeah, 'You'll be back to square one, Andrew Dodds, just you mark my words,' or something like that."

Vicky grinned. "Glad she can focus on someone else's failings."

"You get off pretty lightly."

"Not sure about that." Vicky took another bite. "How're you coping?"

"Like I said, I'm absolutely knackered, Vicks, but it's good to be working again."

"I can imagine. We should get lunch one day."

"This *is* lunch."

"No, a proper lunch. With forks and knives and stuff."

"Right. Aye, let's do that."

Vicky finished her sandwich and checked the clock on the wall. "Got to dash."

Chapter Seventy-Five

Kelly Nelson-Caird gripped the edge of the table. "I've told you to stop asking the same questions repeatedly. My client has answered to the best of her knowledge. I shouldn't be the one telling you this but this will look fairly poor for your side in court if they constantly see the same questions being asked of my client in the interview transcripts. I'll be forced to point it out."

"Forced to?" Vicky held Nelson-Caird's gaze for a few seconds, glancing at MacDonald. "Can I just point out we haven't actually asked the question yet?"

"Excuse me?"

"We've been in here for fifteen minutes and you've prevented me and my colleague from successfully asking it."

Nelson-Caird licked her lips. "Very well."

Vicky leaned across the table, staring at Marianne. "Ms Smith, given you've been in custody, we know you clearly weren't directly involved, but I'd appreciate any assistance you can give us into the death of Michael Scott."

"I'm sorry?"

"Mr Scott lived near Montrose in Angus. He was a greyhound trainer."

"I see."

"Do you know anything about him?"

"Nothing whatsoever."

"He was a greyhound trainer."

"My client heard you the first time."

"Were you involved in what happened to him?"

"I've no idea what you're talking about. I've never even been to Montrose."

"Do you know people who'd like to cause harm to a greyhound trainer?"

"Lots of people. It's beyond barbaric. I don't know anyone who'd actually carry it out, though."

Vicky exhaled slowly, thinking through her options. "We can potentially offer you a deal."

MacDonald raised an eyebrow.

Nelson-Caird sat back in her seat. "What sort of deal are we talking about?"

"I can speak to the Procurator Fiscal. If Ms Smith can supply information leading to a successful prosecution, it may reflect well on her case."

The corners of Marianne's lips curled up. "Much as I'd dearly love to assist you in your investigations, I'm afraid I just don't have any information to offer."

Vicky held her gaze for a few seconds before leaning across the desk. "Interview terminated at twelve twenty-seven."

Chapter Seventy-Six

Vicky glanced at MacDonald as they made their way to Forrester's office. "What is it?"

MacDonald smirked. "Brave."

"What, offering her the deal?"

"Aye, that."

"Didn't exactly go for the carrot, did she?"

"You think the PF would go for it?"

"Who knows? It's been known to happen." Vicky crossed the office space and shut Forrester's door behind MacDonald. She sat next to him.

Forrester scowled at them. "I've only just seen the pair of you."

"Need to update you, sir." Vicky dropped the interview tapes on the desk, the pair skittering across the wooden surface. "We've just been in with Marianne Smith again. She's denying any knowledge of Micky Scott or the attack."

"Figures. She's denied everything else so far."

Vicky brushed back her hair with her hand. "Her lawyer's getting shirty with us."

"It's the young female one with the teeth, isn't it?"

"It is."

"That's all I need." Forrester rubbed the back of his neck before pushing a report across the desk. "The DNA check came back. It wasn't Marianne Smith's hair at Hunter's Farm."

"Interesting." Vicky crossed her legs. "I'm worried about how long we're keeping her, sir."

"Vicky, *you* arrested her. Are you saying she's not involved?"

"I'm just saying we need to start charging her."

"Give it another day or two. We're gathering evidence. It's all above board."

"Fine. I'm just concerned we don't really have anything on her."

Forrester's eyes narrowed and he shook his head. "Have you got any good news for me, Mac?"

"Before we were in with Marianne again, I was digging into Mr Scott's background." MacDonald held up a hand, pre-empting Forrester's interruption. "Passed my findings onto DI Greig's team already, sir."

"Good, good."

"Not that I've had anything back, mind."

"Have you found anything?"

"SSPCA were investigating him for animal cruelty."

Forrester frowned. "Are you serious?"

"Absolutely."

Vicky stared at the picture over Forrester's head, a photo of the Tay Rail Bridge in the fog. "The perpetrators seemed to pick their victims based on the media splashing a story. Was it in the press?"

MacDonald flicked through a report. "I don't think so. Why?"

"Well, unless it's someone on the inside at the SSPCA, the MOs for the other three seem to be based on public knowledge of the crimes. Irene Henderson was on the TV news, Rachel Hay was in the press for the dog with PDE and *The Courier* featured the campaign Phorever Love group instigated against Graeme Hunter."

Forrester leaned forward, elbows on the desk. "Assuming this greyhound death is done by our guy, right?"

"Aye."

MacDonald wrote something down. "Might be something the Media Office can help with. I'll get on to them."

Forrester rested his head on his hands. "What about getting young Zoë to look into it as well?"

"Will do, sir."

"Right, come on. Let's see what this latest news conference is going to give us."

Vicky scowled. "Do you need us both there?"

"Aye. Show of face and all that."

"Right. At least I won't be umming and ahing over this one."

"Don't worry, Vicky, now we've got a murder, Raven won't let anyone else anywhere near this."

Chapter Seventy-Seven

Vicky shivered in the early April wind, waiting for the news conference, rubbing at her arms. "Wish I'd brought my jacket."

MacDonald stood next to her tapping on his phone.

Forrester scowled on the other side. "Never leave the office without it, Vicky."

"Can I have your attention, please?" The North division's lead Media Officer, a fat man in his mid-forties with designer glasses and haircut, cupped his hands around his mouth. "DCI Raven is ready to start."

Raven joined him in front of the station. "Good afternoon and thanks for joining us here in Dundee. I'm joined by Detective Superintendent Gregor Pask, head of the Specialised Crime Division's MIT North, and Assistant Chief Constable Helen Queensberry, head of Local Policing North."

The other two senior officers, both in full uniform, smiled as their names were announced.

Pask held up a sheet of paper and cleared his throat, hat clutched between arm and torso. He wore a more formal uniform than Queensberry, tassels and buttons gleaming. "This morning, detectives were called out to an address in Montrose in Angus.

Upon entering the premises, we discovered the body of one Michael Scott, better known as Micky. While a post mortem has not yet been performed, Mr Scott was declared dead at the scene. Our initial analysis means we believe cause of death was a heart attack sometime yesterday evening. The circumstances surrounding it are highly suspicious. John?"

Raven looked around the audience, focusing on Vicky and Forrester in turn. "We're appealing to witnesses in the area who may have seen anyone in the vicinity of Mr Scott's home between the hours of noon yesterday and eleven o'clock this morning. Additionally, we are looking to speak to anyone acquainted with Mr Scott's daughter-in-law, one Julie Scott, believed to now reside in the Carlisle area. Finally, we're investigating leads in the vicinity of Newcastle-upon-Tyne with colleagues in Northumbria Police. Helen?"

Queensberry smiled at their audience, taking a few seconds before she started, running a hand through her curly red locks. Her black short-sleeved shirt made her look like she'd just been round Fintry or the Hilltown. A fluorescent yellow jacket was tucked under one arm. "As the head of Local Policing in the North division of Police Scotland, I'd like to stress the importance of tracking down Mr Scott's killer or killers. This is an unusual crime and we believe attempts have been made to mask it. I'd echo DCI Raven's request for information. A safer Scotland is greatly helped by people coming forward with information, no matter how insignificant it may appear." She paused for a few seconds. "Any questions?"

MacDonald whispered in Vicky's ear. "Looks like they're nowhere."

She nodded, noticing Considine heading their way. "Here he comes. Better keep himself off the TV." She frowned at another face in the crowd — Anita Skinner.

Skinner raised her hand. "Is this linked to the other cases we were briefed on the other day?"

Pask grinned, patting Raven on the back. "I've appointed DCI Raven Senior Investigating Officer on both cases, so he's best placed to answer. John?"

Raven nodded. "I'd say it's a possibility. I've asked DI Forrester and his team to continue to investigate those cases for me. We're following best practice and treating this as a separate investigation, sharing intelligence where appropriate on a regular basis. Two officers are fully allocated to proving or disproving any links between the cases."

"When you spoke to us on Monday morning, you said it was two cases."

"That's correct."

"It's three, though, isn't it? Four if you count this one."

Raven screwed up his eyes at her. "We're investigating whether this is connected to the other three."

Another journalist raised his hand, looking lost in his thick wool jacket. "You've got a body on your hands now. First you had a kidnapping then a farmer had his nose burnt off. A murder surely represents an escalation, does it not?"

Raven held out his hands. "It may or may not be related. As it stands, we've no further leads or links between them. That's all I'll say on the matter with the information I've been given."

Queensberry smiled at the journalist. "We're asking those living in the north of Scotland, particularly Tayside, Fife and Angus, to be extra vigilant over the coming days."

Raven held up his hands. "That's all we have time for. Thank you."

Considine went straight for Forrester. "Excuse me, sir. I've got something you need to see."

"Go on."

"It's about the Muirheads' alibi. Kirk checked with the Rep."

"And?"

"Doesn't look like they were there, sir. He got the CCTV. It shows their friends getting there but they were on their own. No sign of either Sandy or Polly."

Forrester glared at Vicky. "Get them back in here. I don't care whatever malarkey their lawyer's up to. And get the buggers under arrest."

Chapter Seventy-Eight

I still can't believe Tommy Davies allowed that slimy creep to take his client into a private conference before speaking to us." Vicky checked her watch as she waited in the interview room. "I'll give them a minute, then they're getting dragged in here."

MacDonald looked up from his notebook. "Think they're actually involved?"

"Having their alibis shot to bits isn't looking good for them."

MacDonald rubbed his forehead. "No, it's not."

The door opened and Sandy Muirhead traipsed in, sitting opposite.

Fergus Duncan wagged a finger at Vicky. "A word in private, Sergeant?"

Vicky sighed as she got to her feet. She joined the lawyer in the corridor, leaving the door wide open. "What?"

"I assume you're comfortable interviewing just one of my clients today?"

"Where's Mrs Muirhead?"

"In court."

"And if I'm not happy?"

"I'll need to arrange for cover." Duncan checked his own watch. "I'm due in court myself in an hour."

"Didn't stop you having a fairly lengthy meeting with your client."

Duncan produced his mobile phone, an expensive-looking Samsung in a bright orange case. "I've got your Chief Constable's number on this little baby. Don't make me phone him."

"We've given you a fair amount of latitude so far, Mr Duncan. What were you discussing in the meeting room?"

"My fee structure. My clients have been relying on Mrs Muirhead's status as an employee of Gray and Leech to cover my costs thus far. We've a fairly generous allowance — all taxed, of course — but they've exceeded it. I wanted to keep Mr Muirhead apprised of the situation."

"Nothing to do with why your clients have been brought here?"

Duncan smirked. "I'm still in the dark."

"Are you really?"

"Of course." Duncan's finger hovered over the touchscreen of the phone. "Remember — one press and I'm through to your Chief Constable."

"Are you threatening me?"

"I'm trying to ensure the course of justice is allowed to flow freely."

"Is that right?"

Duncan tapped his watch. "Clock's ticking."

"Cancel whatever appointment you have and get Mrs Muirhead in here *immediately*, otherwise I'm sending some uniform to pick her up from the court."

Duncan stared at her for a few seconds before looking away. He pressed a button on his phone and put it to his ear, gaze locked on Vicky. "Hello? Yeah. Two things. Yeah, sorry to have to do this. Aye, I know."

Vicky folded her arms, her mouth now dry.

"First, can you get down here? I know, Polly, but I need you to come down as soon as you can."

Vicky exhaled before pushing past him into the interview room. She leaned over and whispered into MacDonald's ear. "He's threatening to call the Chief."

"Wanker."

Vicky sat down and straightened her clothes, vaguely aware of Muirhead looking down her low-cut black top. Should've worn the blouse.

Duncan sat opposite, placing his mobile in front of him. "She's on her way here and you've got the pleasure of my company for the next two hours, should it be required."

"Nice to see justice being able to flow a bit more freely." Vicky started the interview. "Mr Muirhead, can you confirm your whereabouts on the evening of Wednesday the twenty-sixth of March?"

"We've already been through this." Muirhead frowned. "My wife and I were at the Rep with friends."

"You're sticking to that, are you?"

Muirhead scowled. "Are you accusing us of lying?"

Vicky handed an A4-sized photo over the table, tagged as evidence. It was a freeze-frame of CCTV footage from the Rep theatre, showing a large crowd of people either queuing at the bar or chatting, a middle-aged couple in the centre of the shot staring straight at the camera. "We've evidence suggesting you weren't at the theatre that night, Mr Muirhead. Please can you confirm Mr Simon Hagger and Mrs Emma Hagger are present in these photographs. For the record, I've presented evidence items P01 through to P04."

"That's correct. They're in the middle, looking at the camera."

"Mr Muirhead, can you confirm neither you nor your wife is present in these photos?"

"We're not."

"Why would that be?"

Muirhead swallowed. "Camera angle?"

Vicky fanned out another three shots. "In summary, these are from four cameras placed around the foyer of the theatre, taken over a fifteen-minute interval."

"Maybe we went to the toilet."

Vicky handed over a printed document with a passage highlighted in orange. "Mr Muirhead, on Friday evening you stated you went for dinner with Mr and Mrs Hagger. This is from the transcript of your wife's statement, an exact match of yours, except for providing more detail about what show you went to."

"We went to see that play." Muirhead placed the sheet on the table. "I assume you've still got the ticket stubs Polly gave you?"

Vicky nodded. "We do. But you weren't there, were you?"

"No comment."

"Mr Muirhead, you may wish to consult with your solicitor on this matter. You're being formally interviewed. Your friends can be charged with providing a false alibi."

Muirhead swallowed hard, eyes bulging as he stared at the table. He leaned in close and whispered to his lawyer.

Duncan peered at Vicky. "DS Dodds, may I have a word with my client in private?"

"I'd appreciate it if your client answered my question first."

"It pertains to that matter." Duncan placed his mobile on the table, finger poised over the screen. "Please confirm that's how you wish to progress."

"Mr Muirhead, why did you lie about your whereabouts?"

Muirhead licked his lips. "My wife and I are having . . . marital difficulties, shall we say. We had a raging argument last Wednesday. We were supposed to meet Simon and Emma for dinner but we never made it."

"So why did you lie?"

Muirhead placed his hands on his bald head. "We wanted cover from the argument. We didn't want any of that dredged up by the police or for any of our friends to know about it."

"This is a murder case."

Duncan moved his finger away from his phone. "Murder?"

Vicky nodded. "Mr Muirhead, can you confirm your actual whereabouts last Wednesday evening?"

Muirhead shut his eyes. "My wife and I were at home, arguing."

"What about, say, Sunday morning?"

"No comment."

"No comment?"

Muirhead nodded.

"What about yesterday afternoon?"

Muirhead opened his eyes. "Yesterday?"

"Yes."

"I was at work."

"And after?"

"I went home. We'd been in here and I was quite stressed by it, as was my wife."

"And this morning?"

"I was back at work, trying to catch up."

"And what do you do, Mr Muirhead?"

"I'm an accountant."

"Where do you work?"

"Whitehall Crescent."

"Were you in the office this morning?"

"I was."

"Can anyone vouch for that?"

"My secretary, I suppose. I had some client meetings."

"You do realise the seriousness of this, don't you?"

Muirhead nodded. "I understand. But we haven't done anything."

Chapter Seventy-Nine

Vicky stood outside the interview room next to the one they'd just left, scowling at the door. Her gaze flicked to MacDonald. "What's he up to?"

"Duncan? No idea. Give him the benefit of the doubt — maybe he's looking after his clients' interests?"

"And you think we'll have better luck with Polly?"

He nodded. "She's the weak link. Meeting her in the worst of the rooms is all part of the plan."

"When did you work out there was a worst room?"

MacDonald shrugged. "First day. I went for a wee wander round the station, trying to get my bearings and discover the lay of the land."

Duncan opened the door, waving his phone at them. "We're ready." He turned around and entered the room.

Vicky sat across from Polly and started the tape recorder, waiting for the entry beep to finish. "Interview commenced at fourteen thirty-one on Wednesday the second of April twenty-fourteen. Present are myself, DS Victoria Dodds, and DS Euan MacDonald. Also present are Polly Muirhead and her lawyer, Fergus Duncan. Mrs Muirhead, can you please detail your movements on Sunday afternoon from eleven in the morning until six at night?"

Polly took a deep breath. "We went for a drive to Dunfermline. My sister lives there."

"Can she vouch for your whereabouts?"

Polly nodded. "I'd certainly hope so."

"Hope so?"

"My client means yes."

"We will of course check with her, so you may wish to revise that."

Duncan's finger hovered over the screen of his mobile, now sitting on a folded sheet of paper. "Why would Mrs Muirhead wish to do that?"

Vicky glared at Duncan. "Mrs Muirhead, your husband gave a 'no comment' response to the question of where you were on Sunday. Why do you think that would be?"

Polly shrugged. "I think my husband doesn't trust the police."

"Why?"

"You're clearly trying to pin something on us." Polly hugged her shoulders tight. "Fergus, I'm feeling quite stressed by this."

Duncan tapped at his phone's plastic case. "Noted."

MacDonald stared at Polly then her lawyer. "If you feel stressed, imagine what Graeme Hunter and his family are going through. They were trapped inside a pair of tiny cages for over twenty hours. Mr Hunter lost most of his nose."

"So?"

"Mrs Muirhead, do you deny any involvement in their abduction?"

"Of course I do."

MacDonald pulled out a sheet of paper. "Do you know a Marianne Smith of Cupar?"

Polly swallowed. "Maybe."

MacDonald pushed the sheet across the table. "We believe you sent her a message on the xbeast forum. The message read, *'How is*

Cupar this time of year?' This was sent three days before a Ms Irene Henderson was found trapped in an industrial bin in Cupar, of all places. There were several messages of support for the actions posted by a user account seemingly owned by Ms Smith."

"And what's this got to do with me?"

MacDonald gave them another sheet. "A witness gave us descriptions of her assailants. There was a woman, a man and someone else. Was this Ms Smith, your husband and yourself?"

"What proof have you got?"

"Ms Smith lives in Cupar. She posted a message in support of the attack and she sent you this message."

Polly clasped the collar of her cream blouse. "I saw this story in the papers. That woman got what was coming to her. I don't think anyone can disagree with that. I tell you one thing, though — the papers gave her air space. The stuff she was saying about cats turned my stomach."

"And you deny any involvement?"

"Listen, Sergeant, I've got sympathies with PETA. It doesn't mean I'll blow up a vivisection laboratory."

"So you deny it?"

Polly shook her head at him before nodding at Vicky. "I've already spoken to your colleague here. My professional time is divided between client work and *pro bono* work with certain charities. While being personally rewarding, it also yields far more positive results for any causes I believe in than shoving some daft woman in a bin. I'm trying to educate the wider public, not trap them."

"So you deny your involvement in the abduction of Ms Irene Henderson and her subsequent entrapment on the fifteenth of November twenty-thirteen?"

"I wasn't involved."

"Were you and your husband accomplices in this action?"

"I wasn't. My husband wasn't, to the best of my knowledge."

"What do you mean by 'to the best of your knowledge'?"

Polly narrowed her eyes. "What do you think I mean?"

Duncan tapped his phone. "Can you please clarify your questioning, Sergeant?"

Vicky sighed. "The alibis covering both of your clients are either absolute or they're not. The fact you're putting a caveat around it surely puts the veracity into doubt?"

Duncan smiled at MacDonald, his eyes thin. "Sergeant, please move on with your questioning."

MacDonald cleared his throat. "Did you and Mr Muirhead abduct Mrs Rachel Hay from Invergowrie and entrap her in a steel cage in a unit in the Dryburgh Industrial Estate in Dundee?"

"No, we did not."

"Did Mr Muirhead and Marianne Smith commit the crime?"

"To the best of my knowledge, my husband wasn't involved."

"And Ms Smith?"

"I couldn't comment either way. She's an acquaintance at best."

"Did you and Mr Muirhead abduct Mr Paul Joyce and entrap him in a steel cage in a unit in the Dryburgh Industrial Estate in Dundee?"

Polly rolled her eyes. "No, we didn't." She waved a finger in the air. "And I've no knowledge of whether my husband or Ms Smith were involved."

"Did you and Mr Muirhead attempt to force Mrs Hay and Mr Joyce to have sexual intercourse while trapped in the cage?"

"I most certainly did not."

"Did you post a video of this act online?"

"No. The only knowledge I have is from the TV news last night."

"Did you and your husband break into Hunter's Farm in Barry, abducting Mr Graeme Hunter, Mrs Rhona Hunter, Miss Amelie

Hunter and Miss Grace Hunter, subsequently trapping them in steel cages?"

Polly smiled. "No, I did not."

"Did you force Mr Hunter's nose against a hot knife machine?"

"Of course not."

"Did you witness the act?"

"No. I wasn't there."

"Do you know Brian Morton?"

"No. Who is he?"

"He's another member of the xbeast forum."

"Well, I don't know him."

"Are you in any way affiliated with the Phorever Love commune near Redford?"

Polly glanced away.

Duncan checked his watch, cleared his throat and pushed a document across the table. "I wish to place it on record that my clients are lodging a formal complaint with Police Scotland as to their treatment here."

Vicky inspected the first sheet, full of arcane legalese. "On what grounds?"

"One, corporate sensitivity and two, violation of human rights."

MacDonald scratched the top of his head. "Mr Duncan, your clients are suspects in three abductions and possibly a murder."

"My clients have provided alibis for two of them and yet you persist in bringing them back in for questioning. This is harassment and I would appreciate it if you'd please terminate this interview."

Vicky complied, her stare burrowing into Duncan's skull as she did so. "This isn't the end of the matter."

Duncan smirked. "You probably want to check with your bosses before you make such brash statements."

Chapter Eighty

Vicky slammed Forrester's office door. "You got a minute?"

"Come on in." Forrester put his phone on the desk. "What's going on?"

"We've just been in with the Muirheads. They backed up each other's story." MacDonald gave him Duncan's letter before sitting. "Copies have supposedly been sent to the Chief Constable and to Pask."

"I've heard about this." Forrester looked up at the ceiling, then back to MacDonald. "We need to let the pair of them go."

"You sure?"

"I am, Mac."

"We can't let them get away with this." Vicky ground her teeth. "He's playing games with us."

"Vicky, believe me, I know where you're coming from. Have we got *anything* on them?"

"Supplying a false alibi?"

"Have they actually done anything with the case, though?"

"At the moment, their movements while these crimes were being carried out — *including* Micky Scott's murder — are completely unaccounted for."

"I've just come out of an hour and a half of political nonsense and arse-covering with Pask, Raven and Greig. This comes from the top and I mean the very top. Until we've got hardcore evidence against these people, we're to lay off them."

Vicky folded her arms and leaned back against the door. "And you're happy with this?"

Forrester blew air up his face, shrugging. "What can we do? Unless we get some direct evidence implicating them in these crimes then we've been told to let them go."

"We're getting somewhere with Marianne, sir, and that's the same evidence."

"I know, Vicky, I know, but an email or whatever isn't enough."

"Come on, sir. You told me to arrest them. If we do that, we can search their home. That's where we got all the evidence against Marianne Smith."

"Look, Marianne's idiot lawyer isn't the one making official complaints to the Chief Constable's office. Fergus Duncan is." Forrester scratched the back of his head. "We need to let them go. They've got alibis."

"*False* alibis. They've *lied* about their whereabouts."

Forrester took a deep breath. "Let them go."

Vicky hit the desk. "Come on, sir."

"Mac, can you put surveillance on them? Buchan and Kirk. One on each, okay?"

"Get on it right now, sir." MacDonald left the room, shaking his head.

Vicky folded her arms. "What about the couple who provide the other half of the alibi?"

"The Haggers? I was thinking of getting some uniform to scare the shit out of them."

"This is bollocks, sir." Vicky looked around for a bin to kick. "Corporate sensitivity? Really?"

"One of the alibis for the Muirheads concerns a Gray and Leech client, I'm afraid."

"Jesus Christ. Is the client Marianne Smith?"

"No, it's someone a bit more high profile than her, apparently." Forrester smiled at Vicky. "You might think I'm a useless bureaucrat but I did push back a fair amount on this. Even you've got to admit we're fishing a bit with them. We've got to prove they're dodgy, and not the old-fashioned way, either. No-one can push back on solid evidence, corporate sensitivity or not."

"For what it's worth, sir, I never said you were a *useless* bureaucrat."

"But I'm still a bureaucrat, right?"

Vicky shrugged. "Someone's got to do my admin, I suppose." She got to her feet.

MacDonald appeared at the door. "Just got a call through from Control, sir. The Fixit DIY shop on the Kingsway has just got a poison pen note."

Chapter Eighty-One

"Colin, I'm starting to think you're involved in this somehow."
PC Woods shook his head as he leaned against the panda car. "I might have to log you as suspicious as well, Vicks."

Resting against the car, Vicky nodded across the car park at the looming DIY store, corrugated steel painted grey and orange, wind battering the row of trees shielding it from the road. "What's happened here?"

Woods held up an evidence bag containing the poison pen letter. "Turned up in their mail this morning."

Vicky took it off him and read it. *Yr Birds of Prey display is immoral. Stop it. Now. Or else.*

"Pretty weird, eh?"

"The 'or else' bit worries me." Vicky folded her arms. "Bella had a tantrum here at the weekend. She wanted to see the owls."

"Kaz told me." Woods nodded. "Cameron did a similar trick a few weeks ago. Little bugger. I was just wanting to get some nails and Karen had taken Ailish out to her pal's. 'I want to see the owls, Daddy!' Christ."

Vicky handed the note to Considine. "Get this verified by Forensics, would you?"

Snared

"Will do." He put the sheet in his charcoal-grey document holder and did up the zip. "Why have they switched to warning people all of a sudden?"

"I don't know. Did anyone see anything?"

Woods shook his head. "Got Soutar going through their mail room looking for an envelope. I doubt this has been franked and put through the Royal Mail."

"Agreed. Have you spoken to the guy who runs the display?"

"Had a wee word, aye. He's a total scumbag. Not budging."

"And the manager?"

"Wee gadgie from Monifieth. Done well for himself, mind. Reckon he knows how to handle himself in a fight."

"Come on." Vicky set off towards the birds display, stopping to let a white van past. The display was quiet, just a pair of kids in school uniform staring wide-eyed at the birds chained to their cage, their grandfather holding out a fiver.

The proprietor swaggered over, shoulders jerking with the exaggerated movement. His leather coat almost touched the ground, covering his sky-blue Manchester City top and beige cargo pants. Greasy hair long at the sides, a straight fringe at the front. He sniffed, eyes on the grandfather's money. "You the police? The detective ones?"

"That's us." Vicky showed her warrant card. "And you are?"

"Kyle Ramsay."

"Have you had any threats before?"

"Why would I?" Ramsay flapped open his long coat, arms wide to take in the full extent of his empire. "Perfectly respectable business I run here."

"Not everyone might agree with what you're doing."

"Listen, I paid a small fortune for these birds. I own them, all right? Nobody tells me what to do with them. *Nobody*."

PC Soutar appeared with a man in a suit, both frowning at Ramsay's rant.

"I pay my way, okay? Me and my birds aren't harming any-one's kids."

"I don't think that's the issue, Mr Ramsay."

"What is?"

"People might deem your display to be cruel."

"Cruel?" Ramsay snorted. "I'd like to see them threaten me, I tell you."

"What would you do if someone threatened you with your life to stop you doing this?"

Ramsay gave a 'come on' gesture — arms held out, fingers flap-ping towards him. "I'd like to see them have a go."

Vicky realised they'd get nowhere with him, but persisted. "Has anyone threatened you, Mr Ramsay?"

"No."

"Really?"

"Aye." Ramsay glanced at the grandfather. The fiver was now folded in half. "I better go and speak to these people, all right? They're the ones paying for my time, after all."

"Fine." Vicky turned to the manager and led them away from the display. "Do you run his place?"

"Graeme Christie." Tall, skinny, face full of acne even though he looked late twenties. He held out a hand.

Vicky shook it. "DS Vicky Dodds. I believe you found a note?"

"Aye. Been over it with your colleagues here. Didn't see who delivered it."

"Was there an envelope?"

Woods grimaced. "Not that I saw. Just checked with the mail room but they've not got it. Must've been binned. Bit of a long shot, I suppose."

"No problem." Vicky focused on Christie. "What's your com-pany's view on this threat?"

He shrugged. "The display stays."

"Is that your view or the corporate view?"

"Came down from the Chief Exec. He's the one who came up with the idea in the first place." Christie held up a hand. "Before you ask, our headquarters are over by Camperdown Park."

Chapter Eighty-Two

Considine kept the Python right up the tail of the lorry as they skirted round the Kingsway, the old ring road now deeply ensconced in the heart of Dundee. "I hate it when lorries overtake. Slows the rest of us down."

"It happens, Stephen. We're not exactly in a hurry."

"Really? Why are your hands drumming on the dashboard?"

Vicky stopped, unaware she'd been doing it. "Right."

"Who knows what's going to happen next, Sarge? Sticking people in cages is one thing, but they've chopped someone's nose off and killed someone now."

"We don't know if it was them who killed Micky Scott."

"All the same, they might blow that place up." He turned off the dual carriageway, straight into an industrial estate.

Vicky glanced back over the road at the cinema, the one she'd taken Bella to a few times. "You think that's likely?"

"I'm just saying, that's all. If that place gets blown up, we need to cover our arses."

"We are, Stephen. Believe me, we are."

Considine pulled up on the double yellows in front of the Fixit headquarters, a galvanised steel construction just off Dunsinane Road. "This it here?"

"Think so."

A dark SUV in the car park held Considine's interest. "Porsche Cayenne. Nice. Know how much that's worth?"

"No."

"Best part of fifty grand."

"Great. Come on." Vicky got out and entered the reception, holding up her warrant card to the middle-aged woman at the desk. "We're looking for a Willis Stewart."

The receptionist kept staring at the card. "I'll just see if he's available." She faced away from them and spoke quietly into a telephone extension.

Vicky took in the office space, the sort of grey that had been popular for a week or two in the mid-eighties and had largely died out, save for a few isolated pockets.

The receptionist smiled. "Mr Stewart can see you now. I'll just show you through."

Vicky followed her into the depths of the building. At the end of the long corridor, light streamed through a clear glass door. *Willis Stewart, Group CEO* was etched on it, aligned to the right.

The receptionist knocked before popping her head round the door. "That's the police for you now, sir."

"Send them in." Stewart's voice was deep and loud. Skinny, glasses, wearing the sort of suit a Savile Row tailor would charge a couple of grand for. His watch looked heavier than he did.

She showed him her warrant card before pocketing it and taking a seat in front of his desk. "It's quite some building you've got."

Stewart shrugged. "It's nothing, really. We're rapidly expanding just now. The store I believe you've just left is our flagship. It used to be a B&Q but I took over the lease when they opened their Warehouse on the Kingsway. Over the last few years, I've managed to swing deals for a few of their leases in Edinburgh, Dunfermline and Aberdeen."

Vicky nodded, clocking the moody photos of stores similar to the one they'd just visited — night shots with cars and lights blurring in front of the buildings. "You're growing a rival chain?"

"I'm trying to." Stewart smiled. "How can I help?"

"I understand you're aware of what happened at your 'flagship store'?"

"Ah, the letter." Stewart swung round in his chair to look out of the window running the full width of the room. "I plan to ignore it."

"I'd advise against doing that, sir."

"Why?"

Vicky produced a copy of the note from Hunter's Farm. "This was obtained on Monday at a battery hen farm near Carnoustie. The family had been trapped inside a cage overnight. The farmer has lost most of his nose."

"So?"

Vicky felt the throb in her neck. "So, Mr Stewart, this threat needs to be taken seriously."

Stewart leaned over his desk. "Sergeant, my family has a long history of falconry. I refuse to listen to some cranks and throw it all away just like that." He clicked his fingers.

"We're not asking for you to cease indefinitely. You can surely stop the display for a week or so, can't you?"

"No."

"No?"

"*No.*"

Vicky got to her feet, the nerve thumping. Arrest him. She clenched her jaw. "I'm sorry you see it that way, Mr Stewart. I'll have to escalate this matter to my superior officers. Your actions are potentially endangering members of the public."

"And they're potentially *not*. As a corporate policy, we do *not* negotiate with terrorists." Stewart looked at a laptop on his desk. "Shut the door behind you, please."

Vicky almost knocked it off its hinges as they left.

Chapter Eighty-Three

Considine pulled into the space next to Vicky's car and turned off the engine. West Bell Street station loomed over them. "That trip was completely pointless."

"Agreed. I'm going to have to speak to Forrester about escalating it."

"Reckon he'll go for it?"

"Here's hoping." Vicky shrugged. "I'd half a mind to arrest him there and then."

"Why didn't you?"

"Way things've been going today, I'd probably get my ovaries kicked for it."

Considine laughed. "It's a load of nonsense, this case."

"In what way?"

"Animal cruelty. Complete bollocks."

Vicky glowered at him. "People are being kidnapped, disfigured and possibly murdered, Stephen."

"I know. Don't get me wrong — I want to catch these fuckers. I just don't get why they're doing it. Animals are just food."

"Just food?"

Considine patted the steering wheel. "We haven't exactly needed carthorses since the invention of the internal combustion engine, have we?"

The nerve in Vicky's neck tightened its knot. "Don't you want the animal in your sandwich to have had a nice life?"

"It's just a beast."

"Aren't we beasts?"

"We're better than animals, Sarge. Come on."

"What about that taxi driver you went all hero cop on?"

"Now he *was* an animal. Nothing more than a beast. The way you're talking, sounds like you might be involved."

"That's not even funny."

"Christ, Sarge, I'm just pulling your leg." Considine waved at a passing car as it headed for a vacant space. "What do you want me to do?"

"I need the alibis on the Muirheads verified, okay?"

"Sure thing. Who do I get to accompany me?"

"Whoever's least busy." Vicky got out and crossed the car park, her pace quick enough to keep Considine at a distance. Her nerve was agony — ibuprofen level.

Sergeant Tommy Davies nodded recognition as she passed through reception. "Afternoon. Seen Charlie?"

"Who's Charlie?" Vicky swiped through the security door.

"Never mind."

Vicky headed down the hallway.

MacDonald thumped a vending machine halfway down the corridor, his fingers rattling the change door. He locked eyes with her. "You got any idea how to fix this? I just want a can of juice."

"What're you after?" Vicky stepped forward to let Considine pass behind them, a smirk on his face.

MacDonald pointed at a can at a diagonal on the second bottom row. "Red Bull."

Vicky checked the usual pitfalls — bags of crisps blocking the fall of a can, an errant empty space in the shelf. Nothing. She looked around. The corridor was now empty. "You didn't see this." She gripped the edges of the machine and gave it a shake, the metal rattling. The can popped down into the funnel in the middle. "There you go."

"Cheers." MacDonald knelt down to retrieve it, bending at the knees. He cracked it open as he rose and took a slurp. "How did you manage that?"

"When you drink as much Diet Coke as I do, you get used to this machine." She tapped at it with her foot then started off down the corridor.

MacDonald held open the door to the stairwell, grinning over the lid of the small can as he sipped. "How did it go out at that DIY store?"

Vicky sighed as she climbed the stairs. "It's the sort of nightmare I want to burden on Forrester."

"That bad?"

"Oh aye." Vicky pushed open the door and entered their office space.

Forrester was halfway across the quiet room, carrying the jug of his coffee machine, water swilling over the sides. He clenched his jaw. "Afternoon."

"You got a minute, sir?"

"Aye, go on."

MacDonald crumpled his can. "Need me there, sir?"

"Aye, the more the merrier." Forrester dumped the jug on the table by his coffee machine and started fiddling with his filter papers. "How did it go, Vicky?"

"Got nowhere with it, sir." Vicky rested against the back of the chair she usually sat in, fingers tight against the fabric. "I had to visit the CEO."

Forrester let his head drop. "The CEO?"

"Aye. The manager wasn't going to do anything about it. Company policy, apparently. So I headed up to head office just by Camperdown. He's a belligerent sod, sir."

"Great." Forrester tipped ground coffee into the filter paper. "Did you get him to budge?"

"Afraid not. I need you to escalate it, sir. We need someone senior to go there and have a word with him. Stewart's being pigheaded — some nonsense about falconry being in his family since the Domesday Book, if they even had that up here. At the moment, they've received a warning. We don't want it to become something worse."

"Right, right. I'll speak to Raven about it. Helen Queensberry loves this sort of thing."

"That sounds like the right course of action. If someone detonates a bomb near the shop, who knows who it could harm?"

Forrester started pouring water into the machine. "They've not mentioned a bomb, though, have they?"

Vicky got the note out of her bag and held it up. "Not on this, sir. Just an 'or else'."

"Still, it's a valid point." Forrester stared into space for a few seconds before looking back at MacDonald. "Got something for you, Mac. It's probably nothing, but young Summers found an old case going back to last summer. Might be linked, might not."

"What is it?"

"Some farmer up Edzell way got stuck in a snare last summer. Our lot could've been at it a while."

"Think this could link all of the cases together?"

"Aye."

"I'll get out there, sir." MacDonald pocketed his notebook and got to his feet. He nodded at Vicky, then left.

Forrester stared at the closing door and then glanced at Vicky. "He doesn't seem too bad, you know?"

"He seems okay." Vicky tried to click her jaw to ease the pressure on her neck. "What do you want me to do, sir?"

"Raven's been badgering me. 'There's a whole heap of paperwork needed here, David. Where's yours?' I know Mac's on top of his because I've seen it."

"And you're saying I'm not on top of mine?"

"I'm saying nothing of the sort, Vicky." Forrester went over to the spitting coffee machine, poured a fresh cup from the steaming jug. "I need you to use that giant brain of yours to think who the hell is behind all of this."

Chapter Eighty-Four

Considine joined Vicky at the window. "That's me just back from Mr Muirhead's place of work, Sarge."

Vicky put two capsules in her hand, swallowing them back with a glug of Diet Coke. She took in the evening skyline, streetlights and taillights pointing west to the sun setting just over Perth and its surrounding hills. "Did you get anything?"

"Nothing that made me think they're behind it."

"What about anything that made you think they're not?"

"Well, the boy was there. His secretary showed me his diary." He held up a sheet of prints from a calendar. "I was a bit of an arse and got to see the CCTV — all time-stamped, of course."

"Get it in the case file."

"Will do." Considine leaned back against the glass, arms folded. "What are you doing?"

"I'm thinking. Got a briefing with Forrester and MacDonald in five minutes."

"This how a DS works?"

"It is, yes."

Considine pointed back into the office space. "What's that wanker's name again?"

Vicky followed his gesture and groaned. "DS Johnny Laing. And you're right — he is a wanker. Never play pool with him." She smiled at Laing's approach. "Johnny Laing, we meet again."

"We do, indeed." Laing nodded. "You guys seen Big Time Charlie? Supposed to have a meeting with him."

Vicky frowned. "Excuse me?"

"New boy who's looking into the links between the crimes?"

"DS MacDonald?"

Laing shrugged. "Aye, that's just what we call him. That boy fancies himself."

"I like it." Vicky laughed. "Last I heard, he was out in rural Angus. What were you wanting to speak to him about?"

"This sighting he was looking at in Montrose."

"Thought he was in Edzell?"

"Aye, well, Raven got him to head over to Montrose after. Supposed to be updating me as soon as he's back."

"Right. I'll tell him."

"Cheers." Laing sighed as he stared out of the window.

Vicky grinned. "Take it the dream team are getting nowhere with this?"

"Kind of. Other than the vaguest of all sightings, we've got nothing. Forensics are taking forever to wave their magic wand. Still got a couple of people to speak to, mind." Laing looked around the room. "Being stuck here isn't helping."

"I'll let him know you're looking for him."

"You do that." Laing nodded at Considine before sauntering off.

Vicky smirked. "Big Time Charlie?"

"Cracking, eh?" Considine drummed at the windowsill. "Boy's a bit of a wanker."

"Keep that to yourself." Vicky spotted Forrester crossing the office space. He pointed at her then his office. "Duty calls." She crossed the office, shutting the door behind her.

Forrester hung his jacket on his coat rack and flicked on the coffee machine before slumping in his seat. "What a bloody day."

Vicky rested her elbows on the chair's armrests. "Having fun, sir?"

"Something like that." Forrester switched his focus to the door. "Evening, Mac."

MacDonald sat next to Vicky, crossing his ankles and slouching back. "Sorry I'm late, sir. DCI Raven had me out in Montrose."

"So I gather."

"Just got collared by that Laing guy. What a charmer."

"He's the least worst, trust me." Forrester let out a breath. His eyes danced over to the coffee machine in the corner before settling on Vicky. "Anyway, DI Greig and I have just had an enjoyable hour going through our strategy for the cases with Raven and Superintendent Pask. They don't seem to be getting anywhere out in Montrose."

MacDonald scowled. "More chance of getting blood out of a stone than info out of that lot. Thick as thieves."

Vicky frowned at him. "Have they really got nothing?"

MacDonald shrugged. "Nothing more than the news conference fallout."

"The post mortem on Micky Scott's being done this evening. They'll hopefully get a report back first thing tomorrow morning." Forrester checked the inside of his mug. "Look, Mac, just play a waiting game with this, okay? We've been told to focus on this, so we'll focus on this."

MacDonald folded his arms. "Fine."

Forrester got up and messed about with the coffee machine, shaking some part of it, hitting another. "You sure you don't want one, Mac?"

"I've had plenty today, sir."

Forrester went to his machine and poured a coffee before returning to his seat. "Can never get enough of this stuff."

The bitter smell of the coffee made Vicky's stomach churn. She nodded at MacDonald. "How did it go in Edzell?"

"This Cameron Lethnot character got stuck in one of his own snare traps. Showed us his injury — a deep gash just below his left knee. Still got the marks."

"Out in the woods?"

"Right by his house. Someone chucked a stone through the front window. He gave chase but got trapped in the snare. Didn't see it. Reckons he was lying there for hours until his wife got back from her sister's."

Forrester blew on his coffee before taking a sip and grimacing. "Any conclusions?"

"Got another one, sir. Saw a black car, obviously didn't get a good look at it. Reckons it could've been a Lexus or a Mercedes. Maybe a BMW or an Audi. Three people in it — two in the front, one in the back. Man and a woman. Wasn't sure who was driving."

Forrester took a slurp then dumped the mug on the desk. Coffee swilled over the edge. "Sounds like our lot."

"Plus, he received a note."

"Shite."

MacDonald held up an evidence bag. There was a note inside, weather-beaten and creased. "*Snares are death. You were lucky.*"

Vicky snatched it off him. "Where was it?"

"Lying on the mat by his front door. Reckons it must've been put through just before they tanned his window in. Didn't notice it when he ran after them. Wife spotted it the next morning, kept it in a book."

Forrester finished his coffee. "And he never gave it to us?"

"Checked with the investigating officers." MacDonald stared down at his notebook, flicking through the pages. "Reckon the questioning was done in the hospital, sir. Didn't hear from him again, didn't find any leads."

"So, has he put snares out?"

"Aye. Reckons they were 'fully compliant'. Used them for the deer eating his lettuces in the summer."

Vicky licked her dry lips, her throat suddenly tight. She coughed. "Was this in the papers?"

MacDonald nodded. "Someone wrote a letter to *The Courier* a while back. Lethnot sent one back and they exchanged a few more. Why?"

Vicky took a deep breath and set the note on the desk. "This is related, right? The note, the car with three people in it. Also, this Cameron Lethnot guy was in the papers." She nodded at Forrester. "Fits like a glove, sir."

"When was this?"

MacDonald nodded. "Nineteenth of February this year."

"So, three months after Irene Henderson." Forrester went back over to the coffee machine and set his mug in front of it. "So if it was them, it shows they were trialling their approach for a few months. And they're getting worse — snaring someone is worse than trapping someone in a bin, right?"

"Agreed." Vicky twisted round to look at Forrester. "So they chucked a stone through his window and relied on him, what, running into a snare they'd placed in his drive? Seems a bit hopeful."

"Agreed. The other attacks have relied less on luck and a lot more on planning." Forrester finished refilling his mug and took a slurp of coffee, eyes on MacDonald. "Did you speak to that woman in Montrose?"

"Nothing much to report. Got a description of a woman walking down the country lane last night." MacDonald shrugged. "Probably someone out walking."

"That doesn't add up for me." Vicky scowled. "Why walk there? It's at least three or four miles from Montrose train station to Micky Scott's farm. Why not just drive?"

Forrester lifted his mug up for a drink. Stopped just short of his mouth. "You gave a press conference asking for a black car." He took a slurp. "We've asked for information about their car, okay? They'll be shit-scared of driving it around now, that's for sure."

Vicky nodded. "Has anything else come up in the search for the car?"

"Mac?"

"Nothing at all so far."

Vicky sighed. "Maybe it is just someone out walking."

"In Montrose? In April? I'm starting to think it's our lot." Forrester grinned. "Anything else, Mac?"

"Nothing back on the media search and Zoë's drawn a blank so far."

"Anything else at all?"

"Street teams have nothing." MacDonald rubbed his chin. "Marianne Smith's the only one we've got anything on and she's not speaking."

"Raven was asking what searching we've done for this car."

"Had Kirk looking into it, sir." MacDonald rummaged through his navy notebook. "Got a list of everyone with a black Lexus, Mercedes, Audi or BMW saloon in Tayside, cross-referenced against being in the vicinity of Dryburgh Industrial Estate between delivery of those cages and us rescuing Rachel and Paul."

"I'm going to regret asking this, but can you speak to all of them?"

"Over a hundred cars, sir. OT bill will be colossal"

"I know, but it needs to be done." Forrester swigged at his coffee. "What about the surveillance on the Muirheads?"

"What about them? Both gone to work, sir. That's it."

Forrester peered over the edge of his mug as he drank. "We're to knock that on the head, by the way."

Vicky frowned. "Really?"

Forrester nodded. "Pask's orders. I tried to argue the case but I'm not exactly popular."

"Why?"

"Cost grounds, mostly. We can use Kirk and Buchan to speak to these car owners."

MacDonald shook his head, scowling. "Nothing to do with the threats Fergus Duncan's been making?"

"Not completely. He'd rather spend the money tracking down the cars."

"Bloody hell." MacDonald leaned forward. "What if this DIY store warning comes to something and we've not kept an eye on them? Their alibis haven't been remotely credible."

"I've raised it with the Super, Mac. That's all I can do. My hands are tied."

Vicky massaged her neck — it felt like the ibuprofen was doing some good. "Did you speak to Raven about getting Fixit to stop the birds display?"

"I raised it just then." Forrester glanced away. "Raven's going to speak to ACC Queensberry. Again, my hands are tied."

Vicky shook her head. "Do they actually want us to solve this case?"

"We've got very few leads, Vicky."

"We don't seem to want to try, though."

Forrester pushed his mug to the far side of the desk. "You've both done really well on this, okay? Pask might think I'm a fanny but he knows how good my team is."

Vicky got to her feet, fists clenched, nerve jangling a bit more. "I'll see you tomorrow, sir." She shut the door hard behind her before walking over to her desk and stuffing her possessions into her bag.

Karen took off her headphones. "You heading off?"

"Yes."

"Good luck tonight."

"The only thing that'll touch my bad mood will be at least three bottles of wine."

"Text me later, okay?"

"Maybe." Vicky left her to it. A glass or two, that'd have to do. "Shit, shit, shit." She had Robert coming round. She stopped by the door and texted him. *Sorry — running late. Can you get some wine? White or rose. X*

MacDonald appeared beside her. "What's going on here, Vicky?"

She snapped her phone shut, realising she was blushing. "You mean with Forrester and Raven?"

"Aye?"

"Politics, I guess. I've half a mind to go and slash Fergus Duncan's tyres."

"Not a bad idea. Halfers on the knife?" MacDonald scratched at the stubble on his chin. "Fancy a pint?"

Vicky smiled, feeling sliced in two. "Maybe tomorrow."

MacDonald made his hand into a gun, shooting it at her. "*Definitely* tomorrow."

Chapter Eighty-Five

Hope these are what you were after." Robert held up the Majestic bag, the contents clinking together. "I had to make a special trip up there, but I was running low anyway."

Vicky pecked him on the cheek and took the bag, glancing at the three bottles of wine. "I'll have to inspect them closely."

Bella lurked behind Vicky, hugging her leg and keeping a distance.

"Bella, this is Mummy's friend, Robert."

Bella stuck out a lip and hugged tighter. "Hello."

Robert laughed. "Don't worry, my Jamie's just the same with new people."

Vicky held open the door. "In you come."

Robert walked in, patting Bella on the head as he passed. She squeezed back against her mother.

Vicky led them into the kitchen. "Shuffle. I haven't put the oven on."

"Don't worry." Robert got out the wine bottles — all had matte black labels, beads of perspiration on the clear glass. "What do you fancy first?"

Vicky set the dial on the cooker. "You choose."

"Rosé it is."

Bella stood by the door, peeking into the kitchen. "Are you my Uncle Robert?"

Robert knelt as he shared a look with Vicky. "Not yet, anyway."

"Robert's just Mummy's friend, Bella."

"Is he a baddie?"

Vicky laughed. "Are you?"

"I'm not sure." Robert sat back on his heels. "Bella, what does your mummy do?"

"Catches baddies."

"Has she caught me?"

Bella pouted. "Don't know."

"Well, if she hasn't, am I not a goodie?"

"Don't know."

Robert smiled at Vicky. "What do you think?"

"The jury's still out."

"Why's jewellery out, Mummy?"

Vicky picked Bella up. "Jury. It's people who decide whether a baddie is actually a baddie or not."

"Do we need a jewellery for Robert?"

Vicky smiled. "What do you think, Robert?"

"I'm sure you and Bella would make a good jury."

"Bells, one thing a jury does is it deliberates."

"What's that mean?"

"It means they go to a special place and think about things for a few hours."

Bella pouted again. "Does that mean I have to go to bed?"

"It does."

"But, Mummy —"

"But *nothing*. It's time for your bed, young lady." Vicky held up Bella's arm. "Say goodnight to Robert."

Bella wiggled her fingers. "Night-night."

Chapter Eighty-Six

It's bloody ruined." Vicky gritted her teeth as she stared at the charred mess on her plate. Disaster.

"Looks okay to me." Robert picked at his food, holding up a lettuce leaf. "At least you can't burn salad."

"Oh, I could, believe me." Vicky stabbed her fork at the pasta before taking a bite. The food was still boiling hot. "Actually, it's not too bad."

Robert followed suit. "What cheese did you put on the top? Mozzarella?"

"No. It was a hard one. Parmesan, I think."

"That's what's burnt. You need a bit of moisture in the cheese. Otherwise it'll basically just go on fire." He took another mouthful. "Still, it's pretty good."

Vicky went through to the kitchen and found a block of Cheddar in the fridge. She grated it onto a plate, dumped the used grater in the sink then took the cheese through. "Try this."

Robert sprinkled the Cheddar on his pasta, which was still steaming. "Looks like it's going to melt." He took a forkful and ate it. "Right, that's the stuff."

Vicky tried some of her pasta, now heaped with orange cheese. "This is good, actually. I didn't know that about cheese."

"I used to work in a kitchen when I was a student. I learnt a lot, mainly how to make an arse of most dishes and then how to save them. But I generally only arsed them up once."

Vicky took a sip of wine — her glass was almost empty. "Ready for a top-up?"

Robert nudged his over. "Aye, go on."

Vicky poured. "Have you got school tomorrow?"

"I do, but Thursdays are pretty light for me. Lots of marking at this time of year, even in PE. Full afternoon, mind — First and Second Years are playing softball."

"Fills the time, I suppose."

"It does." Robert frowned as he ate some salad. "Does this taste burnt to you?"

"Very funny." Vicky took another drink. "Do you enjoy teaching?"

"I do, aye. PE's a pretty weird subject. There's nothing quite like it. All the kids get PE in First and Second Year. Bit of a nightmare as you've got the fat kids forced to do cross country and half the girls in the class having their period every week in swimming. What are the chances of that?"

"Don't." Vicky prodded her fork at him. "The boys in my class were practically wanking themselves off at the girls in the pool. It was *horrible*."

Robert laughed. "Aye. I tried to get them to split the sexes in swimming classes. The two jobsworths who do the timetable knocked it back." He took another drink of wine. "Anyway, the point is most kids doing PE learn to hate exercise. If we taught them to do what they enjoyed, then we wouldn't have such a problem with obesity in this country."

"I can understand that."

"For me, it only gets interesting when I get my Standard Grade and Higher pupils. They're the ones who're really into it. They can run and they play football because they're good at it, not because their dad wants the next David Beckham to pay off his mortgage or whatever."

"Is Jamie going to pay off your mortgage?"

Robert chuckled. "Not by playing football. He's a maths prodigy. He'll be an accountant or an actuary or something." His smile thinned. "That's Moira's genes."

Vicky felt the nerve spike at her. "But you enjoy your job?"

"Of course. Wouldn't do it if I didn't, even with the holidays."

"Were you any good at football?"

"Dundee had me on their books when I was a teenager. Never made it, obviously. Went to uni instead."

"When was this?"

"You're trying to calculate my age, aren't you?"

She shrugged. "I might be."

"I'm forty-one."

"Well, I'm thirty-five." Vicky took a sip of wine before frowning. "Did you say you played for Dundee?"

"Tell me you're not United."

"My dad is. I can't stand it." She frowned. "No, I was wondering if you knew a Micky Scott."

"Name rings a bell. Why?"

"He was a greyhound trainer. Played for Dundee in the eighties according to his son. Got an injury and had to retire."

"Is this the new murder case?"

"It is."

"Mummy!"

Vicky set down her cutlery. "I could have sworn I put you to bed, young lady."

"I want to stay up with you."

"Mummy's having her dinner. You had yours at Granny's. It's bedtime."

"Okay."

"I'll put you back to bed."

"But, Mummy!"

"No buts, Bella." Vicky reached down to pick up her daughter before smiling at Robert. "Back in a minute." She carried Bella upstairs, the child's feet catching on the banister. She put her in bed and tucked the sheets around her, putting a couple of teddies on the floor.

"Think the jewellery's back in, Mummy."

"Oh, is it?"

"Is Robert a baddie?"

"No, he's not."

"Is he a goodie?"

"Mummy thinks he might be."

"Am I a goodie, Mummy?"

"Yes, if you go to sleep." Vicky tickled her sides. "Otherwise you'll be a baddie!"

Bella giggled. "Okay." She scrunched her eyes closed. "Night-night, Mummy."

Vicky kissed her on the top of her head. "Night-night, Bells." She raced down the stairs, almost skipping into the living room. "Sorry about that." She sat down, noticed that Robert had topped up her glass. "Are you trying to get me drunk here?"

"You're doing a very good job of it yourself."

Vicky took a sip. "I think Bella likes you."

"She's certainly much more personable than my Jamie."

"How old is he?"

"Six." Robert took a long drink. "Where's her father?"

Vicky looked away. "Alan lives in Edinburgh now."

"And he's not on the scene?"

"Never has been, really."

"I see. Must be hard raising her on your own all this time."

Vicky shrugged. "Mum and Dad help out way more than they should."

"That's the advantage of still living here, I suppose. That's how I cope, myself." Robert stared into his glass for a few seconds. "Bella's father doesn't help out, then?"

"Bella's father doesn't want to know about her."

Robert raised his eyebrows. "I didn't realise."

Vicky sipped her wine. "It's better for all concerned, trust me. We'd known each other for years and just got together one night. We'd only been going out for a few months when he got a job offer in Edinburgh. I found out I was pregnant but I was kind of settled here. He didn't want to stay in Dundee. I took that as meaning he didn't want to stay with me."

"He doesn't want her in his life?"

"No. It's fine. I'd much rather bring up Bella on my own than have to deal with him and his nonsense."

"Did you ever . . . You know?"

"Think about abortion?"

Robert scratched at his neck. "Aye."

"Every day at about this time." Vicky smiled. "Only joking. I did think about it but I couldn't bring myself to do it. I've not regretted it." She noticed that their plates were both empty and took a big dent out of her glass. "Shall we have a comfy seat?"

"Go on."

Vicky stood up, almost toppling over. She held out her arm for Robert to take. Instead, he put his hand on her arm and kissed her gently on the lips.

Chapter Eighty-Seven

Vicky got out of bed and crossed the room, tugging the dressing gown around her naked body.

"Not bad for your age." Robert grinned across the darkened room at her. Just the one sidelight was on.

She blushed. "I'll be back in a minute." She went into the bathroom, locking the door behind her, and sat down. She looked at the condom, the teat filled with semen, millions of half-Roberts swimming around. It stank. She dumped it in the bin, lifted the toilet lid and sat on the seat, head in her hands. "Shit, shit, shit."

What the hell was she doing?

Was it fair on Bella?

Bottom line, could she really commit to anyone other than herself or her daughter? And taking on a son?

Her breath came in short bursts as she felt the weight of the relationship crushing her lungs. She peed and flushed the toilet before splashing cold water on her face. In the mirror, her face was pink and blotchy, her make-up still underneath. She went back through and sat on the bed.

Robert snuggled up to her, kissing her neck. "I enjoyed that."

Vicky stayed still, letting him do the work. "You know you can't stay, right?"

"Wouldn't expect it any other way."

"Really?"

"What's that supposed to mean?"

Vicky shrugged. "I just feel like such a shit mother at times."

"You seem great with Bella."

"You think so?"

"I do. She loves you but you're not letting her take the piss." Robert brushed her hair aside and started stroking her neck, not far from that nerve. "Do you want to come to mine for dinner tomorrow night?"

"It's quite soon."

Robert gave her a puppy-dog face, lip out, eyes wide. "Don't you want to see me?"

Vicky laughed. "Okay, it's a date." She turned back to face him, tempted to kiss him back. "I'll get Mum to look after Bella."

"You could bring her, if you want."

"Two kids under the age of ten isn't going to be a great idea."

"Agreed."

Vicky glanced at the clock. 12.03. "I need to get some sleep."

"Okay." Robert got up. He slid his boxers on, then the first leg of his trousers, hopping as he put the second one on. He was much more athletic than she'd initially thought — his abs were tight, his shoulders firm.

Vicky looked down at her stomach spilling out of the gown. Not so good.

"Well, that's me." Robert put his shirt on, pulled his belt tight. "I take it you want me to slip out like a thief in the night?"

"You can tell you're a nineties boy."

"Eh? That's a Rolling Stones song."

"I thought it was Take That."

"All this talk of grunge is just a cover, isn't it? You're really a pop girl."

"No comment." Vicky led him downstairs, creeping so as not to wake Bella. She leaned against the open door. Tinkle milled around her ankles, rubbing hard.

Robert kissed her on the lips. "I like you, Vicky."

"Okay." Vicky pecked him back on the cheek. "See you tonight, okay?"

"Looking forward to it." He patted her arm and walked off into the night.

She watched him go, her heart jolting. That night, she'd be in his house, eating with his son, digging a deeper hole for herself. He seemed to have his heart in the right place, but was it?

Did she even like him?

Thursday
3rd April 2014

Chapter Eighty-Eight

The clock radio blared out REM's *Shiny Happy People*.

Vicky slammed her hand down on it, her boob falling free with the movement. She looked down, wondering where her vest top was. She was naked.

Robert.

She turned back over. What the hell was she doing?

The clock radio read 7.02. Her mobile lay beside it.

She spotted her dressing gown on the floor. She reached down to get it, tugged it on then sat up, trying to clear her head.

"Mummy!"

Vicky reached out to grab Bella as she jumped on the bed. "Somebody's full of beans today."

"Had good sleeps, Mummy. Can I catch baddies with you today?"

"Maybe." Vicky's phone buzzed on the table. She reached over and picked it up. Forrester. Bella hugged her tight. She put the phone to her ear. "Hello?"

"Vicky, thank God. All hell's broken loose here. Raven's got us in a 'power breakfast', would you believe? Mac and I can contain it but I need you to get out to the Fixit DIY store on the Kingsway."

Vicky jolted awake, nudging Bella to the side. "What's happened?"

"The store manager's been found outside."

"Is he dead?"

"No idea. Just get there as soon as you can."

Chapter Eighty-Nine

Hungry, Mummy!" Bella bounced in the back, her car seat rattling. "My wee tummy's empty!"

Vicky turned to grin at her daughter. "Come on, let's get you round to Granny's."

She pulled off and turned right onto Barry Road, drove down the long straight against the flow of traffic, listening to Bella singing. She wound through the corner bend then drove up past her first police station, now closed to the public. Bella stopped singing.

As she turned into Bruce Drive, Bella punched the door beside her. "Where's my daddy?"

Vicky turned around to see another tantrum forming, Bella's face twisted, her eyes narrow slits. "What do you mean, Bella?"

"I want my daddy!"

Vicky turned left towards her parents' house then sped on down the street, angling her rearview to keep an eye on her. "Bella, you don't have a daddy. It's just you, me and Tinkle. And Granny and Grandad."

"I want my daddy!" Bella punched her fist against the door again. "I want my daddy!"

Vicky parked outside her old house. She got out and pulled Bella out of the car, hugging her tight, and kissed her forehead. "It's okay, baby."

"Why do I not have a daddy?"

"You're a special girl, Bells."

"Catriona said everyone has a daddy."

Vicky pulled her tighter. "Well, Bella, you don't have a daddy, okay? You're a very special girl, Bells. Bells and whistles. Remember?"

"Why don't I have a daddy?"

"You just don't. Not everyone has to have a daddy." Vicky stood there for a few seconds, smelling Bella's clean hair. "Shall we get Granny to fill up your wee tummy?"

"Okay."

Vicky walked up the drive and knocked on the front door.

Mum came out in her dressing gown, milky eyes squinting into the light. "Is that you, Victoria?"

"Sorry, Mum. I need to get in to work early."

Mum shook her head as she laughed. "Just like your father . . ." She helped Bella up the steps. "How's my wee girl?"

"My wee tummy's empty, Granny."

"Well go inside, Bella. Grandad's just making some porridge."

"Yay!" Bella skipped past her into the dark house.

Vicky let out a breath. "I'm giving you a tantrum warning today."

"Is it her daddy again?"

"It is."

Mum shrugged. "You've made your bed, Victoria. I'll follow the party line but you know how I feel about it."

Vicky bit her lip. "Can Bella stay here tonight?"

"What's the occasion?"

"I've got a date."

"Same man as last night?"

"Yes."

"Of course she can stay." Mum looked to the heavens, her eyes losing their milkiness. "Thank God."

"Mum, I'm not even sure God can help sort out my love life."

Chapter Ninety

Vicky pulled into the car park at the Fixit DIY store. She parked by a police car just by the entrance — its blue lights were still flashing. She sat there, thankful she'd only got through one bottle with Robert. She got out and crossed the car park.

Colin Woods snipped the end of the crime tape as she approached. "This is getting beyond the joke, Vicks."

"I'm not *that* late. I think I broke most of the speed limits on the way here."

"No, I meant you and me being at the same crime scene again."

"Tell me about it."

Woods frowned as he inspected her. "You look a bit different today."

Vicky blushed. "Just tired." She nodded at the building. "Do you want to get me up to speed?"

"I just came on my shift when we got the call-out." Woods waved behind the tape. "The store manager was chained to the front of the shop. Some boy at the Asda round the back spotted him. I've sent him on his way but I'll follow up with him later just to make sure there's no funny business."

"What about the manager?"

"Poor boy's naked and it was a cold night. Some doctor from Ninewells is with him."

"He's still alive?"

"Of course he is." Woods laughed. "Christ, Vicks, do you think it'd just be you on your lonesome if there was a body? This place would be swarming with C&A suits if it was a murder."

"What was he tied up with?"

"The chains that bird gadgie uses. Soutar's just freeing him now."

Vicky put a hand on her hip, trying to focus. "Let's see him."

A four-by-four pulled up alongside them. Willis Stewart got out and ran towards them, eyes bulging. "Where's Graeme? Is he okay?"

Woods held him back. "Please, sir, this is a crime scene. I need you to vacate the area."

"Don't you know who I am?"

"I don't, sir. Now, I'm going to need you to calm down."

Stewart pushed Woods' arms away. "I'm the Chief Executive of this company!"

Woods raised his eyebrows at Vicky. "What do you think?"

Vicky clenched her fists as she scowled at Stewart. He'd ignored the warning and this is what'd happened. "He needs to stay back here."

"But —"

Vicky put a finger to her lip. "No buts, Mr Stewart. I'll be back in two minutes to give you an update. Okay?"

"Very well."

"Do I need to suit up, Colin?"

"Should be okay, Vicks. It's been raining since we got here."

Vicky pushed through the tape to inspect the locus.

PC Soutar was slicing at some chains with a hacksaw, torn Fixit packaging at his feet.

Vicky picked up the bag. "Did you get this from inside?"

Soutar nodded. "Aye, the shop was open. Found the keys by the door."

Dr Rankine was kneeling beside Graeme Christie, the store manager, who was shaking as he lay there. She got to her feet and nodded at Vicky. "Good morning, Sergeant."

"What's good about it?"

"Well, at least you're not tied up naked."

"Chance would be a fine thing."

Rankine smiled before a glance at Christie wiped it from her face. "Poor man's in a terrible state."

"How is he?"

"Not good. It was four degrees last night with no cloud cover until the rain started just after six. He's suffering from mild hypothermia. I need to get him inside once he's free."

Vicky snapped her fingers at Rankine. "Come with me." She jogged over to where Stewart was still hassling Woods. "Will the store office be warm?"

"Should be." Stewart frowned, eyes still on Woods. "Why?"

"I need to get Mr Christie inside."

"Why?"

Rankine folded her arms. "To help with his passive external rewarming."

"What's that?"

"Do you need to know?"

"Yes. It's my shop."

Rankine rolled her eyes. "To help his body generate its own heat. I've got some special clothes in my car that'll help. We need to get him somewhere warm. He might die if we don't. An ambulance will be too long."

Stewart nodded. "The office has a heater." He opened the front door to the shop and entered. "I'll just get it fired up."

Vicky glanced at Rankine. "That man will be the death of me."

"Just make sure he's not the death of Mr Christie." Rankine patted Vicky on the arm. "Back in a sec. Can you get him inside?"

"Will do." Vicky looked back the way they'd come.

Woods and Soutar half-carried Christie over, his shaking arms draped round their shoulders. Christie was naked except for his underpants.

"Follow me." Vicky led them inside, following the trail of lights triggered by Stewart's tramp to the far end of the store. She spotted him by a door, putting his keys back in his pocket, and jogged up to meet him.

Stewart thrust out his chest, clearly pleased with himself. "I've got the fire on full blast in there."

"Good." Vicky led him through the door. The room was tiny, with only four desks, green-screen terminals perched on top.

Woods and Soutar helped Christie through the door. His body was shaking hard, his teeth chattering together. They put him on a seat.

Rankine appeared, clutching a shell suit, and began to help Christie into it.

Vicky looked around for something to do. She shut the door before wheeling the fire over. "Will I be able to ask him some questions?"

Rankine zipped up the front of the jacket and fastened the Velcro. "You can. He's out of the woods now, I think."

Vicky knelt in front of Christie. "I'm going to need to ask you some questions, okay?"

Christie nodded through his shivering. "Th-th-th-that's f-f-f-fine."

"Mr Christie. What's the last thing you remember?"

"L-l-l-locking up."

"What time was this?"

"E-e-eight. J-j-j-just affffffffter."

"What happened?"

Christie struggled for breath. "H-h-h-hit on head."

Rankine started rubbing his shoulders through the fabric. She raised her eyebrows.

Vicky ignored her. "Did you see who attacked you?"

"M-m-m-m-m-man."

"Was he tall?"

Christie nodded.

"What was he wearing?"

"B-b-b-b-b-b-balac-c-c-c-c-clava."

"Was there anyone else?"

Christie hugged his body tighter as he shook his head.

Vicky exhaled slowly. "Thanks. My colleagues will take a full statement from you later."

Christie gave a slight nod.

Vicky looked at Rankine. "There's an ambulance on its way to take you to hospital." She joined Stewart by the window.

He avoided her gaze. "How's he doing?"

"He's not going to die, Mr Stewart."

"That's good."

"That's *lucky*."

"I've told you bef —"

"Is there active CCTV here?"

Stewart pinched the point of his chin. "There's a camera round the back. The one at the front is out of action."

Vicky rubbed her forehead. "Is this public knowledge?"

"Shouldn't be."

"You're very lucky he's still alive. You know that, right?"

"I'm very lucky my shop hasn't been raided." Stewart avoided her look as he held up a letter, his hand shaking. "I just found this."

Vicky snatched it off him. *"Listen to us. Lose the birds, set them free. Otherwise we're not responsible for what we do next. You've got till lunchtime. You've seen what we can do."* She scowled at Stewart. "I normally hate to say I told you so."

"Your Assistant Chief Constable told me so as well. I've told you before — I refuse to negotiate with these people."

"You need to get rid of the birds."

"I refuse to do anything of the sort."

"This is your fault, Mr Stewart." Vicky got in his face.

Stewart stared her down. "The birds stay."

Chapter Ninety-One

Forrester held the station's front door open for Vicky. "Raven's having just the one briefing today — wants to get us all together. He's worried about what's happening here."

Vicky entered through the security door and started off along the corridor. "So why was it just me at the DIY store?"

"I told you, all hell was breaking loose."

"That sounds like someone forgot to order paperclips."

"It was bulldog clips, if you must know." Forrester exhaled. "The Chief Constable was after an update so we had to run around pulling it together. I try to keep you away from all that nonsense, Vicky."

"I appreciate it, sir. Was it anything to do with Fergus Duncan calling him?"

"Probably."

Vicky followed him into the incident room, which was packed with the officers from both teams. She spotted reps from Scenes of Crime and the various forensic analysis teams, including Zoë.

Her mobile chirruped in her bag. She retrieved it and set it to mute. A text from Robert — *Hd nice n8. R* She put it back, deciding texting wasn't one of Robert's skills.

Raven went to the whiteboard, which was neater than Forrester's. "Good morning all. I want to thank you for attending so promptly. Format for today is as follows. Keith and DS Laing will give an overview of where we've got to with the murder case, before handing over to David and DS Dodds for an update on where they're at with their cases. Finally, I'll ask DS MacDonald to update on his work linking the cases together."

"Cheers, boss." Greig leaned against the pillar nearest the whiteboard. "This is in no particular order. As ever, stop me if you've got any questions. First, the post mortem of Michael Scott has confirmed he died from a heart attack, most likely from the running he'd been doing on his treadmill. Time of death was between nine p.m. and ten p.m. on Tuesday night. Now, this is where it gets interesting."

He picked up a sheet of paper and read from it. "This is from the draft report. 'The muscle spasms present on the subject's back indicate the use of a Taser in Drive Stun mode, applied with some force.' For those of you who don't know — and I didn't until twenty minutes ago — that means the Taser is used without the cartridge being present and the electrodes therefore don't fire. Apparently, it's just like a cattle prod. What appears to have happened is it was held up to the body and repeatedly sparked. We can therefore deduce that Mr Scott had been running under some duress, to the point where he suffered a coronary."

MacDonald held up his hand. "So it's linked to our cases?"

Greig frowned. "Why would that be?"

"Our first case involved a Taser in Drive Stun mode."

Greig glanced at Raven. "We'll need to review that."

"We'll cover that in Mac's update, okay?" Raven clapped his hands together. "I was fairly clear in the steer I gave yesterday — separate until proven otherwise. We've no solid proof to the contrary yet. On you go, Keith."

"Right." Greig cast the sheet of paper aside. "Next is the street investigation in Montrose. Given where Mr Scott's house is located, the information received has been somewhat sketchy so far."

MacDonald raised his hand again. "I investigated a potential sighting yesterday. Have you found her?"

"Listen, the information we received was ambiguous at best. There's not a lot to go on here."

MacDonald crumpled his coffee cup. "Right."

"Okay?" Raven nodded. "DS Laing, can you give us an update on the son's ex-wife?"

Laing shrugged. "Looks like she checks out, sir. She's been in Majorca this week and last. Won the holiday through a golf club raffle or something. Local Cumbria Police are doing secondary checks on the story but it looks sound."

"Could she have paid for a hit?"

Laing shook his head. "No way, sir — she's skint. She's not pay-ing for a killing without selling a kidney. We're sifting through her bank statements this morning and early indications are no funny business."

"You heard back from Mr Scott's daughter?"

"Aye, sir. Went into a police station in Melbourne last night with her passport. She's not involved."

Greig looked around the room. "That's where we're at just now. Any questions?"

The room remained silent.

Raven glowered at Forrester. "David, do you want to give us an update on your case?"

Forrester nodded. "There were a couple of areas where we made some solid progress yesterday. First, we've made some inroads in interviewing the owners of black saloons spotted near Dryburgh Industrial Estate. We've spoken to over forty people, obtaining alibis in every case so far. We've also discovered what appears to be a first crime perpetrated by this group in August last year. A farmer out by Edzell in deepest, darkest Angus was trapped in a snare. He spotted a black car with three people inside."

Raven sniffed. "I thought Pask told you to stop finding new cases, David."

"It's an unsolved, sir, so it'll tick another crime off the list." Forrester shrugged. "Anyway, it fits. The guy had a bit of 'flame war' in *The Courier* ten years ago with a lecturer at Abertay. She died not long after."

"What about the other stuff, David?"

"The alibis of Sandy and Polly Muirhead collapsed." Forrester licked his lips, eyes focused on Raven. "We've let them go and were instructed to cease all surveillance activities. Marianne Smith remains in custody, however." He checked a sheet of paper, snapping it in the air. "We've got the forensics back from Hunter's Farm. We'd found a hair in the particular barn in the battery hen farm where the family were trapped. Unfortunately, the DNA doesn't match anything we've got on record, including Marianne Smith."

"What about Polly Muirhead?"

"As we haven't arrested her, sir, we don't have her DNA on record."

Raven scowled. "Anything else, David?"

"No, sir."

Raven stared at MacDonald. "Mac, how's your investigation into the links going?"

"Neither proved nor disproved a link, sir. Only thing linking them is the Taser. Got a call-out with a ballistics expert in Glasgow. She'll hopefully assist in identifying whether we're dealing with the same weapon. Should point out that in the other cases there's no possibility of the device being used to harm the victim. Appears to be the secondary cause of death with Mr Scott, but I've not read the post mortem yet."

"Cheers, Mac." Raven folded his arms. "You should all know we've received a further warning from the group yesterday. DS Dodds discovered a note at the Fixit store on the Kingsway, warning of further reprisals if the birds of prey aren't removed from display." He sniffed. "Well, we've had the reprisals. Vicky?"

"I attended the crime scene at the store this morning. The manager, one Graeme Christie, was chained up in the birds display and left overnight." She cleared her throat, conscious of how cracked her voice sounded. "His condition has stabilised and he's been taken to Ninewells. We're pretty much filling a ward there now." She flashed a photocopy of the latest note across the room. "We received this — it's another warning. '*You've got till lunchtime. You've seen what we can do.*'"

Raven took a deep breath. "We've no idea what this threat is. Were it not for a shelf stacker at Asda, we could've had another death on our hands with Mr Christie."

MacDonald raised a hand. "Why didn't we stop this? Surely we could've shut the stall yesterday?"

Vicky folded her arms, winked at MacDonald. "When I spoke to the CEO, he point-blank refused to. I raised the matter to DI Forrester."

Raven nodded. "And we discussed the matter with ACC Queensberry yesterday evening. It's part of her remit."

"A lot seems to be getting discussed with ACC Queensberry." Vicky rested a hand on her hip. "We should've got a couple of big uniforms over there yesterday to close it down."

Raven held up a hand. "We're not crying over spilt milk here. Our priority now is this warning. We need to do everything we can to maintain public order, including stopping this display being set up as DS Dodds mentions."

MacDonald frowned. "And you still want us to keep the Montrose case separate from these?"

"I've been perfectly clear on that." Raven took a step back and tapped Forrester on the arm. "David, can you bring those idiots you've had back in? The Muirheads and the boy in the scooter? We need to get alibis from each of them covering last night."

"Will do."

Vicky put a hand on her other hip. "They were released under your instructions, sir. We wouldn't need alibis if you hadn't cancelled the surveillance."

Raven glared at her. "We've got no concrete evidence against anyone except Marianne Smith. Mucking about on message boards isn't sufficient to charge anyone else, especially when that idiot Fergus Duncan is threatening us with legal action. Let's do this by the book."

"Mucking about on message boards was all we had on Smith until I arrested her, *sir*."

Raven rubbed at his forehead. "Just get them in here and clear them or charge the buggers, okay?"

Vicky stared at him till he looked away. "Fine. I'll get them brought in, sir."

Raven cleared his throat. "Right. I want us to cast the net wide. I've already asked David to go to town on checking for this black car. On top of this, I want to look into anyone in the Tayside area with sympathies to animal charities or other welfare groups. Large donations, activities on marches, that sort of thing. DS Dodds, your actions list is the lightest. Can you take lead on that?"

"Will do, sir."

"I've managed to secure the Met Domestic Extremism resource supporting the Wildlife Squad. DS MacDonald, can you work with them?"

"Yes, sir."

"Thanks. Anyone got anything else before I finish up? No? Excellent. Dismissed."

Forrester looked round at Vicky as the crowd broke up. "See what I'm dealing with here?"

Chapter Ninety-Two

Vicky sat in the corner of the Old Mill Café, which was breakfast-time busy.

Forrester smiled at MacDonald as he laid their drinks down. "Cheers, Mac."

"No bother." MacDonald sat next to Vicky, almost brushing his leg against hers.

Forrester took his coffee. "What did you make of that, Vicky?"

"Why's Raven so adamant about keeping the cases separate?"

"He keeps going on about best practice. You know what they're like with the buzzwords."

"Even with the sighting and the Taser?"

Forrester stirred sugar into his mug. "The good thing is it's up to us to prove the cases are linked." He shrugged. "Let's just let Raven manage up the way."

"We'll show him." MacDonald blew on his coffee.

"Don't." Forrester shook his head. "You two were pretty far over the mark there. Mac's already been mauled by Raven this morning."

MacDonald narrowed his eyes. "Should've kept up the surveillance on the Muirheads. This might not've happened."

"You heard him, though. Fergus bloody Duncan's been at the bloody Chief with this. We've got an official complaint to deal with."

"Sir, with all due respect, the Muirheads are solid suspects. They've already lied about their alibis."

"Aye and we'll get them for it in due course." Forrester sipped his coffee. "I've been thinking about something John Raven said at the briefing." He held up a hand. "I know, I know — always dangerous when I think, but humour me. The crimes have been escalating so far, right? Chucking a woman in a bin, trapping a crofter in his own snare, forced incest, chopping a farmer's nose off, killing a greyhound trainer. Tying a bloke up in a car park's a bit of a step down."

"So what are you saying, sir?" Vicky took a drink of Diet Coke.

"I'm saying this could just be a warning. Something worse might be on its way."

Vicky's phone rang — Salewicz. "Do you mind if I take this?"

"Go for it." Forrester waved her away.

Vicky turned away from them. "Hello?"

"Good morning, DS Dodds."

"Thanks for calling me back."

"You were after lists of visitors, right?"

"Have you got it?"

"I have. I'll send it over but I need to warn you about something first — I gather you've had Polly and Sandy Muirhead in for questioning?"

"How the hell do you know that?"

"I had to run this list past my handler. He said there's a flashing red flag next to their names."

"They're potentially involved in this group perpetrating the crimes we're investigating." Vicky swapped hands. "Are they on the list?"

"They're frequent visitors here. Anyway, my handler got warned off by the NHTU."

"That's Vice, isn't it? Why are they looking into them?"

"No idea. We collaborate with them a lot. It's a fairly murky world, as I'm sure you can imagine. At the end of the day, it's your battle to fight."

"Any chance you could ask your handler?"

"Given how deep I am here, it was one-way info from him to me. I'm not going to press it."

"Okay, thanks for passing it on. Do you lot have any active interest in them?"

"Well, they were known to my handler."

"Can you send the list over?"

"It's in your inbox now."

"Thanks." Vicky turned back and put her phone on the table, adjusting her skirt.

"Look, Mac, that's the end of the matter, okay? We've got a job to do, let's do it." Forrester took a slurp of coffee and glanced at Vicky's mobile. "Who was that?"

"Salewicz, the undercover guy at Phorever Love. Reckons the Muirheads were frequent visitors."

"Shite."

"That's not all. His handler was warned off them by the NHTU."

MacDonald frowned. "The National Human Trafficking Unit are interested in the Muirheads?"

"That's what he said."

MacDonald looked over his mug at Forrester. "Used to work in the predecessor in Strathclyde a few years ago, the old Vice and Trafficking Unit. Could check it out, if you'd like?"

"Do it." Forrester tapped his fist against his lips. "How does this relate to human trafficking?"

"Might not, sir."

Vicky cleared her throat, feeling like something was stuck in it. "Have we been told to kill the surveillance because Vice are interested in them?"

"Probably." MacDonald finished his coffee. "Vice investigations usually push everyone else to arm's reach."

Forrester shook his head. "Christ's sake."

"Let me pick up with the NCA guys." MacDonald pushed his mug away. "Might be something in this."

Forrester nodded. "Vicky, I don't care what Raven's telling us to do and I don't care about Fergus bloody Duncan. This is solid intel. Give the Muirheads hell when they get here."

Chapter Ninety-Three

Vicky tugged at her blouse collar. "Thanks for coming here voluntarily again. We appreciate your co-operation."

Fergus Duncan sat between Polly and Sandy Muirhead, a grin on his face as he fiddled with his mobile. He scowled as he looked up. "Please cut the preamble. My clients are very busy people."

"First, we're looking to establish your whereabouts between seven p.m. and nine p.m. last night."

Muirhead looked up from Vicky's chest, flicking his tongue over his lips. "We were at a dinner party with friends."

"I hope for your sakes it's not Simon and Emma Hagger."

Duncan raised his eyebrows. "Excuse me?"

"We've been led down the garden path by your clients in relation to the previous alibi from them."

"I assure you this is the truth." Muirhead stared at her, eyelids flickering. "We were with friends last night."

Vicky sighed. "What are their names?"

"There were eight of us. I can give you the names of the hosts."

"That'll suffice for starters."

"Connor and Jennifer Ewing." Muirhead took a sheet of paper from Duncan and wrote on it before passing it to Vicky. "This is their address."

Vicky checked it — the arse end of Broughty Ferry. She stared at Muirhead again. "Were your friends Simon and Emma Hagger there?"

Muirhead nodded. "They were, aye." She nodded at Considine. "We will, of course, verify the story."

Muirhead unclenched his fists. "By all means."

Vicky sat back in her chair and smoothed down her skirt. "This is your chance to change your mind if this is made up."

"It's the truth."

"You're definitely sure about that?"

"Aye!"

Duncan tossed his phone on the table. "Sergeant, please desist from this until you've bothered to validate the story."

Vicky glanced at Polly. "Anything else to add, Mrs Muirhead?"

Polly shook her head, still staring at the tabletop. "No."

Vicky looked at her for a few seconds. Something was being hidden here. She stared at Muirhead. "We want to understand your whereabouts on the nineteenth of August last year."

Muirhead creased his forehead, the wrinkles smoothing out as he smiled. "That's easy. We were on holiday in Riga."

Considine frowned. "In Latvia?"

"Aye." Muirhead kept smiling. "My wife and I are making an effort to visit every single country in Europe. That's the fourteenth country on our list."

Vicky made a note. "Again, we'll check that out. Flight reservations, hotel bookings, that sort of thing. We'll need to speak to the airlines and hotels to make sure you were actually there."

"We were!"

"I'm not comfortable just taking your word for it, Mr Muirhead." Vicky drilled a stare into Polly. "We've reason to believe you were frequent visitors to the Phorever Love commune out by Redford."

Neither responded.

Vicky raised her hands up, then let them drop back to the table-top. Both looked up. "Is that correct?"

Polly drummed her thumb on the tabletop, the frequency and velocity quickening. "We were there as part of the *pro bono* work I do at Gray and Leech."

"What work is this?"

"I've mentioned it before. The work we're doing is helping a small operation deal with complex contracts."

Vicky looked at Duncan. "Is that true?"

"It's confidential."

"Is it true, though?"

Duncan spun his phone on the desk. "My clients have stated the reason for their visit. The action now rests with you to verify that, should you wish."

"We will." Vicky resisted throwing Duncan's phone against the wall. "You said this was work related and yet both of you went?"

"My wife and I decided to combine business with pleasure."

"What's that supposed to mean?"

Polly shrugged. "We had a day out in the countryside after-wards. Cup of tea, spot of lunch."

"We'll have to check with your employers."

Duncan rolled his eyes. "I can confirm it's true. The details are confidential, but they are clients of ours."

"We'll need to obtain that from the partners in the firm, not just a lowly member of staff."

"I beg you —"

"Does this matter pertain to your complaint of corporate sensitivity?"

Duncan put his hand over the tape recorder's microphone. "Of course it does."

Vicky held his gaze till he looked away.

Muirhead held up his watch. "Is that it? Are we free to go?"

Vicky sat back, thinking what else she could do. Raven just wanted them cleared. Until the latest alibi fell apart, they had to keep them on that side of the line. "For now."

Chapter Ninety-Four

"Got an update on the Muirheads, sir." Vicky sat in the chair in front of Forrester's desk, stamping her feet on the carpet.

"Glad to hear it."

MacDonald burst in the room. "I've got something, sir."

"Sorry, Mac, Vicky's first."

"But, sir, thi —"

"Mac. Vicky's first, okay?" Forrester shook his head. "Worse than bloody children."

MacDonald slumped in the other chair, his foot tapping. "Right."

Vicky crossed her legs. "Just been in with the Muirheads as per Raven's instructions. The latest spurious alibi is they were at a dinner party. Considine's checking it out. Polly reckons she was doing *pro bono* work at Phorever Love — that seems to be the corporate sensitivity angle Duncan was banging on about."

Forrester rubbed his eyes. "What do you want to do, Vicky?"

"I want to arrest them. I think they're involved in this."

"Good old policeman's hunch like your old man?"

"Police*woman*'s hunch."

Forrester stared at the window in his office. The blinds were drawn to block the mid-morning sun. "Get a team doing traces into them."

"That's it?"

"This Duncan boy's threats aren't something Raven's taking lightly. Leech, of Gray and Leech fame, goes back a long way with the Chief."

Vicky leaned back in the chair and stared at the ceiling. "So it's an old boys' network thing?"

"We just need to be careful, Vicky, that's all."

"I'll get Considine speaking to her employers about this *pro bono* work."

"Fine." Forrester got up to open the blinds. "What about this snare attack?"

"Turns out they were on holiday in Riga, Latvia."

"You believe them?"

"I doubt it like everything that comes out of their mouths. I'll get Considine to check it out. We need solid evidence they weren't in the country on the nineteenth of August."

MacDonald flipped his hands up. "Are you done now?"

"Suppose so." Forrester sat. "Go on, Mac."

MacDonald rubbed his hands together as his foot stopped tapping. "I had DC Reed's boys interview those Fife schoolgirls to see if they were involved."

"I told you to interview them *with* his help."

"There were far too many for just me and DC Woods, sir." MacDonald couldn't stop himself grinning. "One of the schoolgirls reckons Marianne Smith tried to recruit her to some group."

Chapter Ninety-Five

Vicky waited with Forrester in the room adjacent to the interview suite, gaze flicking between the clock on the wall and the two-way mirror. "Are they just about done?"

"Doesn't look like it."

DCI Raven and DI Greig sat opposite Marianne Smith and Kelly Nelson-Caird, whose voices came from speakers mounted above the view screen.

Raven adjusted his tie. "Ms Smith, you really need to start co-operating with us. We've had two threats made now by your group relating to these birds. One crime's already been committed. Does it have to be mass murder before you'll help us?"

Marianne glanced at Nelson-Caird. "No comment."

Vicky folded her arms and sat back. "They're getting nothing out of her."

Forrester smirked. "Nice to see it's not just us."

"Marianne's become seasoned to this."

Forrester shook his head. "We'll need to get her shifted to Cornton Vale soon."

Vicky watched Marianne Smith, who sat hunched and shrunken. She felt almost sick with guilt — she'd cautioned her and put her there. "I can't help but sympathise with her, sir."

Forrester laughed. "And people say you're a cold bitch."

"I thaw out occasionally."

"I take pity on your poor daughter."

"She gets the good side of me, believe me."

"If Marianne's not involved in this, she knows who is. I'm happy to convict her for what we've got so far. Reckon we should ask her about the snares while we're in there."

"Might be worth a shot." She tapped the glass. "Those two haven't."

They waited a few minutes for Raven to get to his feet. Greig leaned across the desk. "Interview paused at ten oh six. We'll be back."

MacDonald opened the door and popped his head in. "That's us."

Vicky followed Forrester into the corridor.

Raven nodded at them before waiting on Greig to shut the door. "How do you think that went, David? Nice to see a master at work?"

"About as well as could be expected, I suppose."

Raven clenched his fists. "I take it you're not sitting eating popcorn in there, right?"

"No, sir." Forrester tilted his head towards the room. "We've just discovered she's been trying to recruit schoolgirls for some group."

"Christ on a bike. Where?"

"Fife."

"Bloody Fife."

"We're also thinking the Edzell one was a trial run."

MacDonald held up a file. "Got a fair amount on Ms Smith from the NCA."

Raven stabbed a finger at the interview room. "On you go. We'll observe through the glass."

"Fine." Vicky went in and waited for MacDonald and Forrester. She got the tape machine going again. "Interview recommenced at ten eleven. DCI Raven and DI Greig have left the room, replaced by myself, DS Victoria Dodds, DI David Forrester and DS Euan MacDonald." She tossed her ponytail to the side. "Ms Smith, we have a few supplementary questions to ask."

Nelson-Caird scribbled something in her pad. "Please ask them."

"Ms Smith, can you tell us your whereabouts on the nineteenth of August last year?"

Marianne stayed looking at the table. "I don't know."

"Are you sure?"

"I'd need to check."

"Are you acquainted with a Cameron Lethnot?"

Marianne didn't look up. "The name doesn't ring a bell."

"On that date, Mr Lethnot had his leg caught in a snare trap just outside his house near Edzell. Do you have any opinions on snares?"

"The law doesn't go far enough. They still get away with murder."

"We've grounds to believe the same people who did this committed the other four crimes."

"It wasn't me, if that's what you're getting at."

Forrester stepped in front of the mirror, eyes locked on Marianne. "Ms Smith, we're investigating your involvement in these crimes."

"I don't doubt it."

MacDonald passed Nelson-Caird the statement Reed had obtained. "This is from a Gemma Platt of Cupar. Do you know Gemma, Ms Smith?"

The remaining energy drained out of Marianne, whose eyes went dead and her skin turned pallid. She nodded. "I do. Nice girl."

"I refer you to the statement she gave to our colleagues in Glenrothes earlier this morning. *'I like Marianne. She's really cool. She tried to include me in her group.'* When asked what group, she replied, *'It was something to do with animal welfare. She didn't say the name.'* She was asked if she joined, to which she replied, *'No. I didn't want to get into any trouble. Marianne's cool but I've got my Highers coming up.'*" MacDonald put his copy down on the table. "What group's this?"

"I don't know what she's talking about."

"Really?"

"I've absolutely no idea."

"Sounds like you tried to recruit her into an animal rights group."

"You know what children are like. They get fantasies in their heads."

MacDonald rubbed his hands together. "Fantasies about marrying that bloke from One Direction? Maybe." He scowled. "Fantasies about being recruited to terrorist groups in Fife? Bit more difficult to make up."

"I swear. She's making it up. It's not true."

"There's a terrorist group perpetrating acts against known animal welfare abusers. Wouldn't be the same group, would it?"

"No comment."

"You're under caution. This is your chance to clear yourself. Gone are the days when silence showed innocence."

"Do you know what I'm going through? I'm still detained without charge."

"You've been cautioned."

"With some spurious charges relating to some books you found in my house. You'll be lucky to get a fine for those."

"Wouldn't be so sure about that. Those books, well, not the sort you can buy with One-Click on Amazon, are they?"

Marianne lowered her gaze. "I've spoken to Gemma at numerous events in Cupar. She's a lovely girl but I swear I never tried to recruit her."

"Meaning you've tried to recruit other people?"

"No! There's no group!"

MacDonald leaned back in his chair. "Not sure of that. We've got five, maybe six occasions when related crimes have been committed against people with public record of animal cruelty. August and November last year, three people were involved. The three in the last nine days, down to two. You've been in here for most of that time. Bit of a coincidence the group went from three to two with you being in custody, isn't it?"

"I wasn't in custody last Wednesday or on Sunday." Marianne snorted. "I know nothing of this group. You're clutching at straws."

"This possible sixth crime involved a fatality."

Nelson-Caird leaned across the desk. "I suggest you alter your line of inquiry, Sergeant."

MacDonald opened the file in front of him, casually flicking through the pages. "You involved in any groups at all?"

"No."

"Think you might be." MacDonald pushed a sheet across the table. "From the file held on you by our colleagues in the NCA. It's heavily redacted, of course, but it clearly shows your membership in several groups."

"It's not a crime, is it?"

"Not exclusively, no." MacDonald dropped the file on the table. "You wouldn't be trying to recruit for these groups, would you?"

"No!"

"What about the group making threats against Fixit DIY stores?"

Marianne frowned. "I'm sorry?"

"Same group as did the others has threatened the Fixit DIY store on the Kingsway. You recruiting for them?"

Nelson-Caird put a hand over the microphone. "Your superiors were just asking about this."

"I know." MacDonald pushed her hand away and showed a copy of the poison pen letter from that morning. "What does '*You've got till lunchtime*' mean?"

Marianne shook her head. "No idea."

Vicky cleared her throat. "This is a serious crime, Ms Smith. You're in over your head, aren't you?"

Marianne smacked her fist on the table. "I've got no sympathy with any of the victims. I stand by my comments on the message board."

Vicky grinned. "You denied making them the other day."

Marianne's eyes bulged.

"So it *was* you, Ms Smith?"

Marianne glanced at Nelson-Caird. "No comment."

Chapter Ninety-Six

Forrester leaned against the back of Vicky's chair, now vacant. "Good result back there, Vicky. More charges we can level at her."

Vicky, standing behind him, nodded. "Still not that much further forward, though."

MacDonald perched against Vicky's desk. "Need a bad cop with inexperienced people like her. Poor thing's way out of her depth." He shook his head. "Honestly think she's close to confessing."

Vicky nodded. "She looks like shit."

"You have sympathy for her?"

"I've got a certain amount."

"Didn't seem like that in there."

"So I'm a cold bitch." Vicky shrugged.

MacDonald laughed as he held up his file from the NCA. "This has got the known MOs of each group she's a member of, none of which matches ours."

Forrester tightened his fingers around Vicky's chair. "What about the press side of things? Can we link them using that?"

"What, how they seem to have picked their targets from newspapers?"

"Aye."

"Don't know."

Considine looked round. "Sorry, sir, I couldn't help but over-hear. I just got the media search back. Turns out the SSPCA took out a court action against a company called Red Mountain Racing."

Vicky nodded. "Montrose. *Monte Rose*. Red Mountain, right?"

"French. Get you."

"It's Italian, Stephen. Rose is pink in French. I take it Micky Scott owned the company?"

"He did, aye. Supposed to be getting his retired dogs put down instead of rehoming them."

"Oh, good Christ."

"Micky Scott isn't mentioned in the news reports. But if you do a quick Google . . ." Considine nudged Zoë.

Zoë pulled headphones out of her ear. "What is it?"

MacDonald tapped her laptop. "Google Red Mountain Racing for me."

Zoë's hands were a blur on the keyboard and the trackpad. "There you go."

Her screen showed an amateur-looking page, the left side filled with an aggressive shot of a muzzled greyhound mid-race, the right with a panting dog being walked around on a lead by a small boy.

Considine tapped at the bottom of the screen. "Name and address there, see?"

Zoë's phone rang. She looked at it before answering it.

MacDonald exhaled. "What does that tell us?"

Considine scratched at his scalp. "They haven't broken the MO? They're still targeting people from the press. The sighting by

Montrose was of a woman on foot. As I pointed out yesterday, us going public with the car sighting means they've stopped using it. That's why we've had no more sightings of it."

"I'll check it now." Zoë ended her call. One hand toyed with her headphones, while the other fiddled with her laptop. "You guys might want to look at this." She dragged a window from her laptop screen to the monitor on her desk.

Vicky wheeled her chair over, snatching it from Forrester's reach, and sat down. "What's this?"

Zoë clicked play on a video file. "My guy in the Met's been monitoring the account that posted the earlier video. It's just posted this."

The screen lightened, revealing a figure running on a treadmill. A man, thin and athletic, his gait crooked on the left.

Vicky looked at Forrester. Half of the team was now crowded around Zoë's machine. "Is that Micky Scott?"

MacDonald nodded. "Looks like it."

A male voice called out from behind the camera, deep and distorted. "Go faster!"

Scott didn't, just kept to the same slow pace.

A spark of light flashed in front of the camera before something reached over to Scott. He ran faster, trying to put distance between himself and the device. "Come on — faster, boy, faster!"

Vicky tapped at the screen. "That's a Taser."

The act was repeated three further times — slow down, buzz with the Taser, speed up. The final time, Scott fell to his knees, clutching his chest. The running machine pushed him off the back. His left hand stayed stuck in place by the handcuffs as the belt kept turning round.

"Come on, you prick. Get up!" The hand reached over and pressed the Taser into Scott's back. No reaction. Held it against him for almost a minute. "Shit, I think we killed him."

Another arm crept into view. "This is going too —"

The sound cut and the camera moved to Scott's body lying prostrate on the floor. The image froze and text bounced in.

Dog Racing Is Murder.
Officially, 9,000 greyhounds a year retire from racing.
Unofficially, 40,000 are drowned, shot or beaten to death when they don't make the grade.

Forrester smacked his fist off the back of Vicky's chair. "So these cases *are* bloody connected."

Chapter Ninety-Seven

Raven leaned back against one of the posts at the front of the incident room, Greig's and Forrester's teams scattered around him. "Let me be clear — these cases are now combined." He thumbed at the screen behind him, the video locked on the final message. "This video is proof of the relationship. Whoever killed Michael Scott is involved in the abductions of Irene Henderson, Rachel Hay and Paul Joyce and the barbaric crime they perpetrated on Graeme Hunter and his family, namely Rhona, Amelie and Grace." He gestured at MacDonald. "DS MacDonald was central to establishing the relationships among the many cases we have under investigation. Solid work, Sergeant."

MacDonald nodded. "Thanks."

Zoë raised her eyebrows at Vicky then stared at her fingernails.

"As of now, DI Greig's in charge of the inquiry teams, supported by DI Forrester. Can I ask David's team to move everything pertaining to this investigation into the incident room and report directly to my Office Manager, DS Kelly, for actions?"

He straightened his tie. "We're actively investigating the use of a Taser as an MO. Anyone in the UK who's ever used one in anger's going to get brought in over the next couple of days to explain their actions and the current whereabouts of their weapon. Any questions?"

MacDonald raised a hand. "Already got a suspect in custody, sir. Marianne Smith."

"And?"

"Ms Smith can't have committed the last four crimes. Had sightings of three people in the first two cases but only two in the Hay and Hunter cases."

"Okay. I want her kept in. We're still well within our rights to keep her here given what she's done, regardless of whether she's involved. She might lead us to the others." Raven looked around the room. "Right, dismissed."

Vicky grinned at MacDonald as he turned to leave. "That you rocking the boat a bit there?"

"Made a valid point." He shrugged. "John told me he likes officers who express an opinion."

"That the case?"

"Aye."

"I'll catch you later." Vicky walked off, stopping in the middle of the room to speak to Laing. "Looks like we're working together again, Johnny."

Laing sniffed. "We'll all be working for Big Time Charlie soon enough."

"You reckon?"

"Fiver says he's a DI by Christmas."

Vicky nodded in Raven's direction. "Any idea what Kelly's got me down for?"

"Leading six DCs is what I've heard, Vicky. Street teams out in Montrose."

"Bloody hell." Vicky's phone rang. Unknown caller. "Better take this."

Ed James

"Vicky, it's Tommy Davies at the front desk here. I've got someone here for you."

"Who?"

"A Robert Hamilton."

Chapter Ninety-Eight

Vicky entered the Old Mill Café and looked for a table. One in the window, covered in junk. She made her way towards it. "You can't just show up like this."

Robert scratched at his temple. "Sorry, Vicky. I wanted to surprise you. I've got a few free periods today."

"I'm coming to yours for dinner tonight." She sat down, arms folded. "Sure you won't get fed up of me?"

"No way. I'm looking forward to it." Robert smiled. "How's your head?"

"Needing something to eat."

"What can I get you?"

She stared at the board above the counter. "Lentil soup, thanks."

"Back in a sec." Robert got up and went over to the counter. His black tracksuit was more casual than anything she'd seen him wear so far.

She put her head in her hands, catching her sleeve in a puddle of tea. What the hell was she getting herself into? The case had just gone mental and Bella was playing up.

Why had she slept with Robert? He was probably still grieving. Had she led him on? Was it her fault?

She piled up the empty plates on the table, pushed them to the side, the spoons chinking in the cups.

Where was the relationship heading? Nowhere, if her track record was anything to go by.

Robert carried the tray over — two cans of full-fat Coke alongside two bowls of soup with a large hunk of white bread on the side. He sat and passed her lunch across, leaving his on the tray. "This smells good."

Vicky tried not to smile as she picked up her spoon and stirred. "Thanks."

"It's good seeing you." Robert dunked his bread in the soup. "I enjoyed last night."

"Me too." Vicky slurped at the soup. It was just the right temperature to let her blast through it.

"You seem a bit distant, Vicky."

"I get like this."

"Is it something I've done?"

She reached across the table, touching his hand. "I like you, Robert. I really do."

"This is an 'it's just', isn't it?"

"It's just I'm really busy today."

"I knew it was an 'it's just'."

Vicky laughed. "I'm serious." She pulled her ponytail over her shoulder. "Just bear with me, okay?"

"I'm not going anywhere."

"Thanks."

"So." Robert leaned back. "Have you had a fun-filled morning?"

"Like you wouldn't believe. Politics, mostly. Christ knows what's happening with this case. Always feels like second fiddle when the big boys and girls get involved."

"And here was me thinking the police wouldn't have any politics."

"Are you serious?"

"I thought you'd all be too busy catching baddies."

Vicky laughed. "I wish." Vicky pushed her empty bowl to the side just as her mobile buzzed in her bag. "Sorry, Robert." She rummaged around and found it. Forrester. "DS Dodds."

"Vicky, where did you go?"

"I'm meeting a friend for lunch."

A pause. "Right."

"What's up, sir?"

"Some kid's been abducted from school. We're on our way there. Need you to go to the house and speak to his parents."

"Think it's another one?"

"Well, his father's Gordon Urquhart. Owns uqTech."

Vicky slapped a hand to her forehead. "The vivisectionists?"

Chapter Ninety-Nine

Considine parked just off Claypotts Road in Broughty Ferry. The Urquhart mansion was surrounded by ten-foot stone walls with jagged glass on the top. He led up the drive and rang the bell. "I heard the boy's at Dundee High?"

Vicky nodded. "Only private school for miles around. That's where Forrester's gone just now."

Considine scowled. "There's a decent school just down the road from here, though."

"The sort of people who live in a house with walls like that aren't going to send their kids just anywhere, are they?"

A man answered the door, his eyes moist. Quiff sculpted from grey hair, black designer specs, grey suit trousers and matching waistcoat, dress shirt rolled up at the sleeves. "Can I help?"

Vicky frowned. "Gordon Urquhart?"

"Yes."

She flashed her warrant card. "DS Dodds. This is DC Considine."

"Oh, thank God you're here." Urquhart led them into the living room, a colossal space looking out to the front. Heavy antique furniture filled the place. A few tall pot plants sat in the window. "This is my wife, Heather."

She sat on an armchair clutching a hankie, her face red with tears. Wide hips gave way to a narrow chest, spiky hair poked out at oblique angles. She got to her feet, letting the tissue fall to the floor. "Have you found Calum?"

Vicky shook her head as she sat. "Not yet. There's a team in the centre of Dundee searching for him. We're here to ask you a few questions."

Heather nodded before perching on the arm of the chair. "Go on."

"Is it possible Calum could've run away?"

"I don't think so."

"What makes you think he's not just run away?"

Urquhart scowled before nodding. "Just a second." He retrieved a sheet from a table at the back of the room. "Heather got this earlier this morning."

Vicky read it. *"We've got your chick. We're moving to clinical trials."*

Heather pressed at her temples. "Does this mean he's been kidnapped?"

"We don't know yet." Vicky got out her notebook. "Let's start with the basics. How old is Calum?"

"How's this supposed to be helping?"

"We need to understand the boy and his likely movements. How old is he?"

"Thirteen. He's at Dundee High." Heather kneaded her forehead with her left hand. "He's supposed to be going to the dentist up at Panmuirefield village this afternoon. He was coming home for lunch. I was going to drive him up before taking him back to school. He didn't turn up."

"What time did he leave?"

"Twelve."

"Twelve exactly?"

417

"The school said he left the main building two minutes before, by their clock."

"How far would he have to walk for the nearest bus stop?"

"There's one just across the road."

"When should he have got here?"

"About half twelve?"

Vicky checked her watch. "That's over an hour ago. I take it nobody at the school has seen him since he left?"

"No."

"Thanks." Vicky nodded at Considine, making sure he noted it down. "No answer on his mobile?"

"None."

"What bus would he be getting?"

"A twelve or a seventy-three, I think. He should get off just at the end of the road."

Considine nodded before leaving the room. "I'll get on it."

"Is there anyone you can think of who would have taken Calum as a way of getting at either of you?"

Urquhart took a deep breath. "No, there's not."

Vicky held his gaze, waiting for him to look away. "I know what you do for a living."

Urquhart let out a deep breath. "I run uqTech, yes. We're a biosciences business with strong links to Dundee University and St Andrews. Nothing sinister."

Vicky squinted at him. "Not vivisection?"

"We do *not* do vivisection."

"So what do you do?"

"We're leading the way in a whole new world of transplants."

"And you don't perform animal experiments?"

"We . . . may do."

"Does anyone have any grievances against you?"

"No."

"No ex-employees who left under a cloud?"

"No."

"No animal rights groups sending you packages?"

Urquhart let out a deep breath. "We've had our fair share of aggro from those freaks over the years but, believe me, nobody who would have done this."

"I need you to think carefully."

"I've told you, there's nobody."

"Please. Think about it, *sir*."

"I've told you, there's nobody."

Vicky noted it down.

Considine reappeared. "Just spoke to the bus company, Sarge. They checked the cameras on the bus for me. There's a five he could have got on as well but the roadworks on Ward Road are slowing down the buses getting up there. Only one stopped within ten minutes of when Calum was supposed to have' been waiting there. He didn't get on."

Heather got to her feet. "So someone's taken him?"

"Maybe." Vicky held up the note. "Have you seen anything like this before?"

Urquhart stared at his wife, then looked away.

Vicky inched forward in her seat. "Have you?"

Urquhart nodded. "I got one yesterday."

"Where is it?"

"I threw it away."

Vicky exhaled. "You should've called us. Did you see the news?"

Heather tugged at Urquhart's waistcoat. "Gordon, is this like that farmer without the nose?"

"It can't be."

Vicky sighed. "We believe it is."

"Oh my God." Heather clasped a hand to her mouth, eyes clamped shut.

"What did it say?"

"I don't remember."

"Did it warn you?"

"It said something like, '*What you do is wrong. Stop it or we'll see what happens.*'"

"And you ignored it?"

"Of course I bloody did."

There was a knock at the front door. Urquhart clenched his jaw as he headed off to answer it.

Heather collapsed into the chair, letting the arm slowly regain its shape. "I can't believe this is happening."

"I can understand."

Urquhart appeared, leading Forrester towards them. "Is that so? My son's been abducted and you've got officers here standing around chatting? I expect you to have *all* of your officers out searching for him!"

"Mr Urquhart, I've got over twenty officers on the case." Forrester folded his arms, his thick winter coat puckering at the sleeves. "We believe we'll find him."

Urquhart stabbed his finger in the middle of Forrester's chest. "I sincerely hope you're trying to figure out what you can charge Willis Stewart with."

Forrester pushed his hand away. "What's Mr Stewart got to do with this?"

"This is all his fault."

"That's a fairly serious accusation."

"Look, I know Willis from the Chamber of Commerce." Urquhart scowled at Vicky. "I believe he received a note warning of reprisals if he didn't remove a display at one of his stores."

"How the hell did you find that out?"

"I know people, David. This is all his fault. Willis wilfully ignored the note and this is what happened. It's his fault my boy's been taken!"

"Mr Urquhart, if you cou —"

Vicky muscled in between them. "Mr Urquhart, you just told me you received a note yesterday."

Urquhart flared his nostrils. "I want Willis charged with something."

"You both received notes. If we charge him, we'll have to charge you. You understand that, right?"

"Do you want me to phone Helen Queensberry? I believe she's the Assistant Chief Constable? We go back a long way."

"I'm not sure I understand your threat, sir." Vicky licked her lips. "Neither I nor DI Forrester report to her."

"I'll bloody do it, I'm warning you."

"Phoning her isn't going to find your son, Mr Urquhart. I suggest you try to think of someone who could've done this. Someone who maybe disliked you cutting up animals."

"I'm not a vivisectionist!" Urquhart glowered at her as he folded his arms. "I suggest you focus your efforts on finding Calum and not on insulting me!"

"Very well." Vicky left the room and stomped down the hall to the front door before holding it open for Forrester.

Looking back the way they'd come, Forrester made a sucking sound with his teeth. "That's a guilty man if ever I saw one."

"Tell me about it. I bet that note said something a bit stronger." Vicky followed him outside. "I take it there's been no progress?"

"None. I've lost MacDonald to the street team. Last I heard, he was in the Wellgate asking questions like he's selling satellite telly. I've got to head back. Raven's leading another news conference at half three."

"What do you want me to do?"

"The bird of prey guy might've disappeared from Fixit."

"Kyle Ramsay?"

"Aye. Having the manager in hospital seems to have knackered the entire company. Ramsay didn't show up there this morning."

Chapter One Hundred

Considine tapped at the windscreen. "Which one's Kyle Ramsay's flat?"

"Let's find out." She got out onto Baldovan Terrace and looked down the long row of tenements pockmarked with satellite dishes, the parking bays now mostly filled with work vans. She crossed the road, running her finger down the list of flats in the first of the two possibilities. *K. Ramsay.* Bingo. "Here we go."

She tried the flat buzzer. No answer.

"Do you hear that, Sarge?"

Vicky frowned. Bird noises, squawking and cooing. Muffled and distant. "Yeah, I do." She cupped her hands round her eyes, peering into the window of the dark ground-floor flat. Just an unmade bed. The other window showed a settee. An Xbox lay on the floor in front of a TV. "Don't think it's coming from inside."

"Where is it coming from?"

"No idea." She took a step back and looked up and down the street. Didn't spot any likely flats, couldn't hear the noises any more clearly. She pressed the buzzer again and waited.

No answer.

She tried the buzzer next to it, *G. Scrimgeour.*

"Who's that?"

"It's the police." Vicky leaned against the wall, tipping her head towards the microphone. "I'm looking for Kyle Ramsay."

"Never heard of him."

"He's your neighbour. Can we have a word?"

The door buzzed open.

Vicky entered the stairwell, illuminated by shafts of light descending from a roof window.

"Gordon Scrimgeour." A wiry, grey-haired man wearing a track-suit and Dundee FC shirt stood across the corridor, arms folded, guarding his flat door. "I've not seen him today."

"Okay. Did you hear anything this morning?"

Scrimgeour frowned. "If I remember rightly, there was a bit of a commotion at about eight o'clock. Got me out of my pit."

"Did you see anything?"

"Not really."

"But you heard something?"

"Well, aye. Actually, now you mentioned, might've been a van driving off."

"What kind of van?"

Scrimgeour shrugged. "Dunno. I just heard it. Street's dark that time of the morning, you know? Could have been one of them cars the kids have buggered about with, I suppose. Loud exhaust on it, anyway."

"Okay."

"Mind you, Kyle's birds have been going mental all morning."

"Excuse me?"

Scrimgeour waved out to the street. "The laddie keeps them in his van overnight."

Vicky clenched her jaw. "Show me."

Scrimgeour shut his door and led out onto the street. A few spaces over from Vicky's car was an unmarked white van, ventilation equipment sticking out of the back. "Lad keeps the birds in there overnight, I think."

Vicky peered in the small back window. Rows of tiny cages inside, full of the birds from the display at Fixit DIY, the ones Bella wanted to see. She smiled at Scrimgeour. "Thanks for your time, sir."

"Is he going to get into trouble, miss?"

"I seriously hope so." She handed Scrimgeour her card. "Call me if he turns up."

Scrimgeour wandered inside, scratching at his bottom through the tracksuit.

Considine tapped at the glass. "You see that in there?"

"It's barbaric."

"You know, I actually agree with you."

"Good." Vicky scowled. "See when we find Ramsay, I'm going to nail his arse to the wall for this."

"Assuming he's still alive, Sarge."

Chapter One Hundred and One

Zoë pulled the headphones down to rest on her shoulder. The sun was just starting to appear through the window behind her. "I'm struggling to get this list of charity donors, ma'am. Sorry."

Vicky clicked her tongue a few times. "I'll sort it out." She got out her mobile and the business card she'd taken, and dialled Alison McFarlane's number.

"Tayside Animals! Alison speaking. How can I help?"

"Ms McFarlane, it's DS Vicky Dodds here. We spoke the other day?"

A pause. "How can I help?"

"One of my colleagues has been tasked with obtaining a list of donors from you and she called you. We've requested it from all animal charities in Tayside. Yours is the only one we've still not received it from."

"I can only apologise."

"When can we expect it?"

"Our accountant's on holiday just now. It's not something we organise ourselves, I'm afraid. I've got Yvonne running off the copy we just received. It shouldn't be too much longer. I'll send it through once we've got it. Zoë Jones, is it?"

"It is. Thanks for that." Vicky ended the call and looked over at Zoë. "Should be through soon. I should've got a DC to do it. Sorry."

Zoë nodded. "Thanks." She stuck her headphones on again.

Vicky looked across the almost-empty office at Considine, who was poring through a file, his thumb sticking out. "How are you getting on, Stephen?"

"Getting there, Sarge." Considine closed the file then got up and stretched his back. "Back in a minute. I need to do some chasing."

"Okay." Vicky watched him leave, sighing as he closed the door. Time to focus. She shuffled the papers on her desk, the transcripts of the witness statements and interviews. Christ.

She leaned back in her chair. It gave a squeak as she spun round to look through the smudges of the window, the jute mill opposite now lit up.

If Marianne Smith was involved, the evidence had to be in the files.

She had to be working with the Muirheads. The number of times Sandy and Polly Muirhead kept popping up . . .

She got up and unhooked the printer's drawer, nabbed a couple of sheets of A3. She knelt on the chair and started drawing a timeline of the case, focusing on the Muirheads' involvement.

15/Nov. Irene Henderson stuck in bin by three people driving black car. Note lost amongst hate mail.

19/Feb. Cameron Lethnot trapped in snare by three people driving black car. Note posted through letterbox.

Then, what? It paused for five weeks and someone dropped out.

26/Mar. Rachel Hay and Paul Joyce trapped in cage in industrial unit by only two people. Black car. Notes delivered with newspapers and pinned to cage. Tried to force them to have sex. Filmed and posted online.

30/Mar. Graeme Hunter and family trapped in small cages in battery hen farm. Black car. Note in kitchen.

1/Apr. Micky Scott handcuffed to treadmill. Forced to run. Death — heart attack. No car but sighting of woman, who might have nothing to do with it. No note but video posted by the same account as Rachel and Paul's.

2/Apr. Graeme Christie abducted outside store and chained up like birds of prey. No car. Note inside the store. Sighting of man.

3/Apr. Today. Kyle Ramsay abducted from home, most likely at 8 a.m. Warning delivered 2/Apr, ignored.

3/Apr. Today. Calum Urquhart abducted from school just before 12. Note delivered to parents. Warning delivered 2/Apr, ignored.

She sat back in the chair, rubbing at her thigh through the tights, trying to ease out the pins and needles.

Whoever it was had balls.

Despite a major police investigation being underway, they were still committing crimes, and getting quicker too — months between incidents had become weeks and then days, until two had been done that morning.

There was an intelligence to it, almost an art — inflicting cruelty back on people who themselves inflicted cruelty.

Victims were being chosen based on public information. The press had been sent links to the letters and videos. Only thin slivers of the case had been featured by the mainstream press, as the files were hidden in the dark net.

In all cases, the victims had been featured in the news. Except for Fixit DIY. They hadn't been in the press. Had uqTech?

Considine sat on the corner of the desk, holding up the latest note. "Jenny Morgan confirmed these are from the same printer and paper stock."

"Feels like we're past that now, Stephen." Vicky took the note, focused on each letter. Nothing there. She looked up at Considine. "Did you look into uqTech?"

"I did, aye." Considine nodded at her computer. "Go and get their website up."

Vicky found the uqTech website. The theme was grey with transparent images — a black man and an Asian woman in white lab coats, a white man between them resting arms on their shoulders, all showing white teeth in their smiles. "What's this supposed to show me?"

"Exactly. Pretty generic site. From that you'd get no idea what they actually did."

"Why are they being targeted?"

"I did a quick Google and I got some news stories."

"Go on."

"Heard of xenotransplantation?"

"What do you think?"

Considine grinned. "It's pretty grim, Sarge. They've been taking livers from pigs and sticking them in baboons."

"Christ."

"Aye. Supposed to show they can grow pig livers in another species so they can give them to people who need transplants."

"Fuck." Vicky swallowed hard. "Tell me that's not what's in store for Calum Urquhart?"

"Wish I could."

Vicky held her head in her hands. "Is this the escalation?"

"Maybe."

She picked up her phone and dialled the Urquhart house.

Heather answered. "Hello?"

"Mrs Urquhart, it's DS Vicky Dodds."

"Has something happened?"

"I'm sorry, we've got no update on your son's whereabouts."

A sigh. "I see."

"Can I speak to your husband, please?"

Pause. "Gordon's out, I'm afraid."

"When will he be back?"

"I don't know. I'm sorry."

Vicky ended the call. "He's not there. That's the end of that, I suppose."

"What next?"

"I'm still not buying the Fixit DIY angle. There's just some —"

"Ma'am, you need to see this." Zoë dropped her headphones to her desk. "The video's been posted on YouTube."

Vicky shut her eyes for a few seconds. "What?"

"Aye, just got an IM from one of the Met guys. They've taken down about ten in the last half an hour."

Vicky pinched the bridge of her nose, the nerve digging at her neck. "The greyhound one's technically a snuff movie."

"Aye. You should see the hits they're getting, though. Every time one goes up, thousands are watching it within minutes."

Vicky rubbed her forehead. "So the message is finally getting out there now."

Considine raised an eyebrow. "Can't believe people want to watch a greyhound trainer die on a treadmill."

"Who's posting them, Zoë?"

"That's the thing — we just don't know. The audit trails are totally masked. I think they're getting better at it. They're clearly learning from what we're doing."

"Right." Vicky looked over to see Sergeant Tommy Davies heading her way. She straightened herself up. "I thought you were umbilically connected to your desk."

Tommy smirked. "Wish that were the case. The boss has asked for your presence upstairs."

"Pask's based in Aberdeen?"

Tommy shook his head. "Not your boss. My boss. ACC Queensberry."

Chapter One Hundred and Two

A secretary guarded the entrance to Queensberry's office.
Vicky flashed her ID to him, her mouth dry. "I've got an appointment with ACC Queensberry."

He nudged the office door open with his foot. "Please wait in here for her."

"Do you know what it's about?"

He shrugged. "I know even less than you."

Vicky went inside the large room. Forrester sat at the meeting table, head in his hands. "Sir?"

Forrester looked up. "Vicky. Right."

"What's going on?"

"No idea."

"Have you seen Queensberry?"

"No."

Vicky looked out of the window across the car park. Two over from her own car, she spotted a Bentley, licence plate UQT1. "Gordon Urquhart, right?"

"Aye. Must be related to the threat he made against us."

"Like we've got time for this." Vicky slumped in the seat next to him, catching her knee on the underside of the table. "I take it there's no news?"

"None."

The door opened. Helen Queensberry showed Urquhart into the room. Both held coffee mugs in their hands. "Please, have a seat." She took off her uniform jacket, rested it on the back of the chair behind her desk. She sat in the meeting room chair between Vicky and Urquhart. "Thanks for joining us, David. DS Dodds, I don't believe we've had the pleasure?"

"I don't believe so, either." Vicky offered her hand, tensing her wrist to control the trembling.

Queensberry shook it before leaning on her elbows, her hands clasped. "Okay, let's get started. I received a call from Gordon about an hour ago regarding your investigation into the disappearance of his son, Calum." She smiled before taking a sip of coffee. "How are you getting on, David?"

Forrester leaned back in his chair, arms folded. "DCI Raven is the SIO on this case, ma'am, I'm not sure why —"

Queensberry held up a hand. "John's sent you along to deputise. You've been running this case longer than he has, I believe?"

"That's true."

"So, have you got anywhere?"

"It's early days, ma'am. We're making some progress."

Urquhart sighed, eyes pleading with Queensberry. "See, I told you, Helen, these officers just aren't up to it."

"You've raised a concern, Gordon, and I'm trying to assure you of the steps being taken to safeguard your son."

"These officers are spreading vile innuendo about my company."

"What sort of thing?"

Vicky raised her hand, smiling. "Ma'am, if I may?"

Queensberry shook her head. "Gordon, please continue."

"They're trying to imply Calum's been taken as some sort of vigilante action against my company. I take such slander very seriously."

"I see." Queensberry nodded at Vicky. "DS Dodds?"

"This is related to the crimes DCI Raven is investigating. You gave the news conference the other day, so you should know that the perpetrators of these crimes are targeting people with a history of animal cruelty."

Urquhart looked away. "My company doesn't commit crimes against animals."

Vicky leaned across the desk. "Regardless, there's a public perception of certain animal experiments being undertaken by your company and that seems to be enough for these criminals."

Urquhart shook his head vigorously. "Helen, this is *poppycock*. My company's listed on the FTSE 250. I can't just sit here and listen to this!"

"Gordon, do you conduct any trials involving animals?"

Urquhart looked away. "That's sensitive information."

"I'll rephrase that. Are you aware of anyone making allegations of your company conducting trials involving animals?"

"One or two." Fire burned in Urquhart's eyes, locked onto Vicky. "My legal division take regular action against websites who make such slander, believe you me."

"Mr Urquhart, you were warned." Vicky licked her dry lips. "Why did you do nothing about it?"

"This whole thing is *nothing* to do with my company. Willis Stewart is entirely to blame for this."

"Willis Stewart?" Queensberry frowned. "What's he got to do with this?"

"It's his fault Calum's missing. *His* fault!"

"I'm not sure I follow."

"It was in the paper this morning. He received a note warning something like this was going to happen."

Queensberry raised an eyebrow.

Vicky gripped the edge of the table. "Mr Stewart's company has been attacked again. Twice. One of his employees was chained up outside the store and another's gone missing."

Urquhart laughed as he turned his head to Queensberry. "So you see, Helen? My company's not the target here."

"But Calum went missing after you received a note." Queensberry inspected her nails before smiling at him. "I'm afraid I agree with my colleagues. These crimes are perpetrated by people who believe animal cruelty has taken place at your company. Innuendo seems to be enough for them."

Urquhart got to his feet. "So you're joining in with this?"

Queensberry put a hand on his arm. "Gordon, have a seat."

Urquhart shook his head before complying.

Queensberry narrowed her eyes at him. "Willis Stewart received a warning, which he ignored. Is what DS Dodds saying true? That you received one yourself?"

Urquhart nodded, nostrils flared. "Yes."

"And you did nothing with it."

"I don't have the time to deal with meaningless notes, Helen. We get one or two *every day*."

"Gordon, our time's going to be better spent looking for Calum than sitting here."

"I want Willis Stewart charged."

"Gordon, if I charge Willis, I'll have to charge you. You both ignored notes from these people. Willis at least had the decency to get in touch with us about it."

"It's not *his* son out there." Urquhart stabbed a finger against his chest, eyes filling with tears. "These people have got my Calum."

"Mr Urquhart —"

"No, just you listen to me, Helen. You told me when we were getting coffee that Willis ignored the advice you *personally* gave him. He's culpable here."

Queensberry raised her chin. "Mr Urquhart, the reason I was able to advise Mr Stewart is because we knew he'd received a note. You never told us."

Urquhart got to his feet, adjusting his waistcoat as he stood. "This isn't the end of the matter. If anything's happened to Calum, you'll —"

Queensberry waved a hand to the door. "My secretary will show you out, Mr Urquhart."

Urquhart shook his head then left the room, slamming the door behind him.

Queensberry folded her arms. "Well, that didn't go as planned."

Forrester tugged at his shirt collar. "We can charge him, if you want."

"I'm not sure what that would solve, David." Queensberry finished her own coffee. "Just find his boy and we'll deal with the fallout afterwards."

Vicky was out of the room first. "What an idiot."

Her Airwave sounded. "Control to DS Dodds. Over."

Vicky held it up. "Receiving."

"You're looking for a Kyle Ramsay, right?"

"Correct."

"He's been found in Dudhope Park."

Chapter One Hundred and Three

Considine pulled into the virtually empty car park by Dudhope Castle, less than a three-minute drive from the station. "Where is it again?"

"Just to the side there." Vicky opened her door and jogged across the car park. The medieval castle towered over them, its white walls in an L shape.

A group of people surrounded an object beside a patch of lavender making a vain attempt at growth, two police officers among the number.

Vicky flashed her warrant card. "DS Dodds. What's happened here?"

The nearest uniformed officer took off his hat and straightened down his hair. "PC Dean Fleming, Sarge. Think we've found your missing person."

Vicky's nose twitched. She smelt something, couldn't quite place it. Shit? "What's that smell?"

"Better show you." Fleming barged in and the group parted.

A giant bird cage stood on the cobbles.

Vicky sighed. "This looks similar to the cages in Barry and Dryburgh."

Considine nodded. "It does."

There was movement. Kyle Ramsay groaned as he sat up in the middle of it, naked. He was covered in human excrement. Underneath, his flesh was heavily bruised, dark purple blotches all over his chest and face. Deep gouges had been taken out of his legs and arms. Dried blood had mixed with the faeces. His hands and feet were tied up in chains, his mouth covered in tape.

A note was stuck to his chest.

Considine squinted at it, reading it aloud. *"Has the egg hatched?"*

Vicky covered her eyes with her hands then stared at Fleming. "Are the fire service on their way?"

"Aye." Fleming sniffed. "Should be here any minute."

"What happened?"

"Nobody saw anything." Fleming took a step back and motioned to one of the other men. "Jimmy here's the caretaker. He's the one who called us out."

Jimmy gurned at them, revealing his remaining three teeth. "Turn my back for a second and there's a bloody great bird cage with a man in it."

Vicky got out her notebook. "I assume it was longer than a second?"

"Aye, maybe ten minutes."

"When was this?"

"Back of three?"

Vicky checked her watch. Half an hour ago. Three hours after Calum Urquhart was abducted. "What is this place?"

Jimmy looked up at the white-harled walls of the castle. "Council offices. The staff are on an away day. I think that's what they call it."

"So there's nobody here?"

Jimmy gestured around the small group. "Just me and my boys. We look after the park and the offices."

Fleming's Airwave buzzed. "Control to PC Fleming." He walked off. "Receiving."

Vicky raised her voice. "Did anyone else see anything?"

One of the young lads folded his arms. "We were having our lunch."

"At three?"

"Aye. Got a problem with that?"

Jimmy scowled at the young man. "I wanted us to blitz the place this morning, so I bought doughnuts and cakes in for when we finished."

"And that was at three?"

"Aye. We were in our office in the basement. Came out to empty our industrial vacuum. Next thing I know, some bugger's parked this thing here."

Fleming reappeared. "The firies are just about here. They'll help get the poor bugger out. Why've they done this to the boy?"

"We think it's because he runs a birds of prey display at Fixit DIY." Vicky struggled to look at the cage, her stomach curdling from the smell. "Someone's taken a bit of a dislike to it."

"Like this stuff in Barry and Montrose?"

"Amongst others." Vicky looked around the space. Mature beech and oak surrounded the car park. A silver Audi pulled up near them. "Other than proximity to West Bell Street, it doesn't mean anything. Why here?"

"You're kidding, right?" Jimmy laughed. "Place used to have a menagerie. Birds and animals in cages. My grandpa used to bring us here."

"That makes sense." Vicky spotted Forrester, Raven and Greig heading over. She leaned close to Considine. "Can you and Fleming start getting statements from these men?"

He nodded. "Will do."

Vicky headed them off by the small picket fence. "Our bird man's turned up. He's covered in faeces and it looks like he's been severely beaten. Someone's been cutting his arms and legs, too."

Forrester shook his head. "Christ."

"There's a note, too."

Raven's face pinched tight. "What about Calum?"

"No sign here, sir. I've asked DC Considine and PC Fleming to start taking statements. There's nobody in the building today."

"Could Calum be inside?"

"I doubt it." Vicky shielded her eyes from the sun. "They've done a spring clean while the office workers are away at some function."

"So nobody's seen anything?"

"No, sir."

"How the bloody hell could nobody see anything?" Raven folded his arms. "This is the middle of the town!"

"I'll get my team down here, sir." Greig nodded at Raven. "We need people going door-to-door."

Raven rubbed at his eyes. "We're still nowhere with Calum. I don't want to have to call Pask and get some of his Aberdeen lads down here."

Greig glowered at Forrester. "I'll need all your DCs, David."

Forrester shrugged. "You've already got them, haven't you?"

Chapter One Hundred and Four

MacDonald sat next to Vicky and passed her a can of Diet Coke. "Here you go."

"Cheers." Vicky opened it and took a sip, looking around the near-empty office. There was just Zoë nodding her head to music, Beats headphones clamped to her skull. "It's very quiet having the children away, isn't it?"

He laughed. "Tell me about it. Covered virtually every shop in the city centre and nobody saw anything. Calum's just disappeared."

"Think he's dead?"

He paused before taking a sip of coffee. "Hope not. They killed Micky Scott."

"I know that." Vicky frowned. "On that video, though, it sounds like an accident."

"Putting a man in his fifties on a treadmill and forcing him to run is hardly an accidental death."

"Agreed, but it's not like Willis Stewart's received a finger in the post, is it?"

"True." He took a drink of coffee. "Pain in the arse. Lost our DCs and now we're sidelined while Greig and Laing run off with the case."

"It's Friday afternoon. Think of it that way."

"Don't like not being at the centre of things." MacDonald raised an eyebrow. "Don't think you do, either."

"You're right." Vicky finished the can and crushed it. "Heard back from Vice yet?"

"Not yet."

"Thanks for the drink." Vicky got up and wandered over to Zoë's desk. "How's that list of donors going?"

"Just got them through now, ma'am."

"Zoë, you don't have to call me 'ma'am', okay?"

"I know, it's just . . ." Zoë shrugged. "Force of habit."

"Never mind."

"Shall I just email you the list?"

"Can't you print it?"

"That's pretty old-fashioned."

Vicky shrugged. "Old dog, new tricks."

Zoë clicked her mouse. "That's it."

"Cheers." Vicky stood over the printer as it worked through the sheets, the stench of ozone rising up. She picked up the first page — it was still hot. Her tired eyes scanned the list. She spotted a healthy donation from Polly Muirhead just above Gary Black's two grand — the refund from Rachel Hay. The next name made her stop. "Shit."

Robert Hamilton.

Chapter One Hundred and Five

Vicky sat on the toilet seat lid, elbows on her knees. "Shit, shit, shit."

She clutched the sheet in front of her. The more she looked at it, the more it stayed there.

Robert Hamilton, Corbie Drive, Carnoustie.

She made it past the name and address for the first time — the donation was for ten grand.

She tried to keep her breathing under control. Robert was a good bloke, wasn't he? A goodie?

Asking the waiter in the Gulistan for free-range chicken then ordering a vegetable curry.

His retired greyhounds, rescued from the likes of Micky Scott. He knew Scott from his youth — they both played for Dundee.

Asking all those questions about the case . . .

Meeting her for lunch just before Calum was taken.

Was all that enough?

She bit her lip. What the hell was she going to do with this?

"Sorry, sir, my sort-of boyfriend might be behind this."
"Why, Vicky?"

"He gave a load of cash to the animal rescue place down the road."
"That's less than we've got on the Muirheads."

She laughed. Playing the conversation out like that helped.

Her watch told her she'd two hours before she went round to his house. What the hell was she going to do? "Shit, shit, shit."

"Are you all right in there?"

Vicky sighed, recognising the voice. "I'm fine, Zoë."

"You don't sound it."

"Too much Diet Coke, I think."

"Okay. Too much information."

The door shut.

Had Zoë heard her conversation with herself? She didn't even know if she'd spoken it aloud or not.

She got to her feet and straightened her skirt, pulling it back above her hips, and tugged her blouse down. Need to be professional. Go through the rest of the list, see if there's anything else on there.

Chapter One Hundred and Six

Forrester leaned back in his chair. Sunlight streamed through his office window and the open door. "It's just us three again. I kind of miss all those DCs. Poor buggers are out in Dudhope Castle and the Park, or still in the city centre." He cleared his throat. "Anyway, just out of Greig's briefing. The latest news conference is getting broadcast everywhere. It's going to be on the BBC and Channel Four, I think. Sky have already run it."

MacDonald sniffed. "Promising."

"Here's hoping. They put out a new information request for the car, looking for any black cars parked off road since Tuesday."

"Think they'll get anything?"

"It'll be a mountain of admin." Forrester nodded at Vicky. "The boy you found at the castle's doing better in hospital now. Not likely to be released for a while, though. He's got an infection in his legs and arms — can't remember the name."

Vicky clenched her jaw. "Is Raven going to charge Stewart or Urquhart?"

Forrester shrugged. "Hard to work out what to charge them with, I'm afraid. In Stewart's case, the boy didn't pitch up this morning, so he didn't *technically* disobey our advice."

"Come on. Of course he did. He was a complete nightmare about it."

"Anyway, Queensberry's not going to even think about charging Urquhart until his son shows up." Forrester checked his watch. "Last thing from the briefing. Raven's pushed us three off early. We're supposed to be back in early doors tomorrow. If there's still a case, we're to pick it up from Laing and Greig."

MacDonald sat there, open-mouthed. "Seriously?"

"Boss's orders, Mac. What've you been up to?"

"Mostly been going through the background checks on the Muirheads. Considine got them for me before he got nabbed. Not got much, I'm afraid — give me back the DCs and I'll see what I can do."

"Vice got back to you?"

"Not yet."

"This isn't good, is it, Mac?"

"Not really." MacDonald rubbed his chin. "Karen Woods spoke to Gray and Leech about the *pro bono* work. Backed up what Duncan told us. Need a warrant if we want specific case details."

Vicky raised an eyebrow. "Corporate sensitivity?"

"Aye."

"I'll have to get onto Raven for that." Forrester finished his coffee. "What have you been doing, Vicky?"

"Zoë got me that list of donors Raven was after. There are pages of it. It validates stories we've had from Polly Muirhead and Gary Black, the man who bought a pug from Rachel Hay. I need Zoë to do some more checks."

"Right." Forrester leaned back in his chair, staring up at the ceiling. "I've bloody lost her, too. Raven's got her checking the IP address of whoever's posting these videos."

Vicky frowned. "See this press angle we've been thinking about? Doesn't seem to be part of the MO for Fixit DIY."

"Explain?"

"Well, I haven't seen anything in the press about Kyle Ramsay's display."

MacDonald scowled. "Fixit's logo's a red kite."

"Can't be that, surely?"

MacDonald shrugged. "Ramsay's employed by Stewart. All their stores have birds of prey."

Forrester leaned forward on the desk, spinning his mug around. "He took a pretty severe beating, didn't he? Has he been done for violence to his birds or anything?"

"I'll check it out, sir." MacDonald made a note.

"Aye, good." Forrester sniffed. "Raven reckoned two of the birds have gone missing from the boy's van. Pair of owls. Supposed to have twenty, but we only found eighteen."

"The wounds on his legs and arms . . ." Vicky clenched her fists. "He's been pecked by his own birds, hasn't he?"

"Aye. And covered in his own shite, too. Smeared all over him." Forrester got to his feet. "Right, come on. It's time for a beer."

MacDonald hopped up. "Excellent."

"Vicky?"

She stared into space. "I can only stay for the one."

Forrester winked. "Aye, we'll see."

Chapter One Hundred and Seven

Vicky leaned back in the booth in the Old Bank Bar, watching MacDonald ease through the crowded bar area to the toilet. "I'm sure Euan's been buying me doubles."

"No doubt." Forrester fiddled with his mobile. "Oh, bloody hell."

"What's the matter?"

"Gordon Urquhart's just lamped Willis Stewart."

"You're kidding?"

"Wish I was. Raven's asking me to head out to Broughty Ferry." He started tapping at his phone. "*Sorry, sir. Gillian's at swimming.*"

"Are you telling me you're taking your daughter swimming when you get home?"

Forrester shrugged. "I'm not lying. She is at swimming. Just because I'm not there doesn't mean I'm lying."

Vicky laughed. "I'm sure Raven will love that when he finds out, sir."

"He's not going to, though, is he?" Forrester pocketed the phone. "And quit it with the 'sir', Vicky. I told Mac when you were in the toilet. We're out of the office. I like to have a clear hierarchy at work, but in the pub, forget it."

"I'll try and remember." Vicky took a sip of Bacardi, trying to suss out whether it was double-strength. "Why are we being pushed to the side?"

"Too many chiefs, I reckon." Forrester looked around the bar before speaking in an undertone. "Greig's achieved the square root of bugger all with this. You might think I'm a jobsworth but, Christ, you saw what it was like in Queensberry's office earlier? That shit will stick with me, just you watch it."

"I can't imagine it will, sir."

Forrester shook his head. "You know I had to pull MacDonald and Laing apart earlier?"

"No?"

"Aye. I hope we've not got another cowboy on our hands."

"I doubt he's as bad as Ennis."

"Maybe. Him going off on the sick meant we didn't have to sack him. Raven and I'd had a few meetings about it."

"Sure you should be telling me this, si — David?"

"Aye, I know I can trust you."

Vicky glanced over the pub. MacDonald was snaking his way to the bar. The clock on the wall read quarter to eight. "Shite, is that the time?"

Forrester grinned at her. "Told you it wouldn't be just the one."

Vicky grabbed her phone and stormed out of the front of the pub, joining the throng of dolled-up smokers. She dialled Robert's number.

"Hello?"

"Robert, it's Vicky. Look, something's come up at work. Sorry to have to bail out on you like this."

"Oh, I understand." He left a long pause. "I saw something on the news. Are you involved in that?"

Vicky locked eyes with a woman roughly her age, tarted up for a Thursday night out on the town. "Yeah. I thought I'd still be able to make it, but I've got to interview a suspect."

"I understand. Give me a call later when it's all died down."

"It'll probably be tomorrow, I reckon. These things have a habit of drawing out."

"Oh, okay. Good luck."

Vicky closed her phone and looked through the window at their seats, where MacDonald was putting more drinks on the table. What the hell was she doing?

The smoker next to her, her chubby face encased in make-up, nudged her elbow into Vicky's arm. "You've got some style, honey."

Vicky vaguely recognised her from an adjacent table. "Excuse me?"

"Lying like that." She exhaled a cloud of smoke and nodded at the window. MacDonald was laughing at some joke as Forrester got to his feet. "You trying to let that one over there get in your knickers?"

Vicky gave her a polite smile. "Something like that."

"Damn. Had my eyes on him. Nice arse."

Vicky chuckled then went back inside. She dumped her phone in her handbag as she sat.

MacDonald nodded at her bag. "Who was that?"

"Just a friend."

"Right."

"Where's Forrester?"

"Toilet."

MacDonald pushed over a glass filled with dark liquid. "Here you go."

Vicky finished her previous Bacardi and wrapped her hands around the new one. "I *was* going to head."

"Come on — night's still young."

"We do have to work tomorrow."

"Yeah, I know. Just out of interest, where's the best club in Dundee?"

Vicky shrugged. "You're asking the wrong girl."

"Thought you'd be into dancing?"

"No, it's nothing like that. It's just I'm a bit old for that now."

MacDonald licked his lips. "You're what, thirty, thirty-one?"

Vicky chuckled. "You've been trying to guess my age, haven't you?"

"What makes you say that?"

"You missed out the fact I went to university."

"Got me." MacDonald finished his pint of lager, pushed the empty glass over to touch Vicky's previous one. "Where's the cool place these days? Dundee usually has one or two decent clubs, right?"

"Right. I think it's Liquid or Fat Sam's just now. In my day, it would have been the Mardi, but that's long gone."

"Mardi Gras." MacDonald laughed as he wrapped his fingers around the new pint glass. "Been there a few times."

Vicky crossed her legs. "I forgot you were from around these parts."

"The accent, right?"

"Right. Where do you come from?"

"Coupar Angus."

Forrester bumped down on the bench, sending vibrations along it. "Bloody carnage in there. Some boy was snorting coke. Can you believe it?"

"Dundee on a Thursday." Vicky took a sip. Definitely a double.

Forrester took a drink of whisky, swilling it around his mouth. "So, Mac, you're pissed off at getting booted to the side, right?"

451

MacDonald knocked back some of his lager. "Could wipe the floor with Greig's lads. Laing's a useless prick."

"You burned out in Strathclyde, Mac. That's why you're here."

"*Burned out?*" MacDonald scowled at him. "I'm trying to progress my career by other means, David."

"I see." Forrester picked up a menu on the table. "Should we get some food? I'm bloody starving."

Chapter One Hundred and Eight

Forrester staggered to his feet, got his suit jacket on at the third attempt. "Right, I'm heading home, no doubt to a doing from the missus. You pair better get off home. In at eight tomorrow, okay?"

"Right." MacDonald helped him to the front of the bar then returned, grinning. "Absolutely hammered."

Vicky exhaled slowly. "I'm not much better."

MacDonald took a sip from his pint. "Quiet in here now, isn't it?"

"Everyone's left for the clubs. That or the coke's run out."

He smirked. "Still can't tempt you?"

"At my age?"

"At your age nothing."

Vicky glanced at the food menu on the table. "The boss didn't get round to getting food in. I'm starving."

"Me too."

Vicky finished her bottle of WKD then bounced to her feet. "Come on. Let's get some food then maybe I'll find my dancing shoes somewhere on the way." She sashayed out of the bar ahead of MacDonald into the cool air.

The smoker from earlier was back out, lips around another cigarette. She winked as they passed.

Vicky looked up and down Reform Street — it was dark, but the McDonald's near the Caird Hall end was open. She did a 180 and stared at the pillars of Dundee High lit up at the end of the street. Near the clubs. "Come on, this way." She led MacDonald up Reform Street towards the school.

He pulled on his suit jacket. "Where we headed?"

"Don't know."

"Fancy a curry?"

Vicky laughed. "Let's get something a bit more Dundee."

"Like what?"

"Chips, cheese and coleslaw. There's a good place on Panmure Street."

He laughed. "The most Dundee thing I've ever heard of."

Vicky glanced over at the back of the McManus Galleries to their right. "I saw someone eating a mince roll last week."

"A *mince roll*?"

"My dad used to have a Scotch pie on a roll."

"Seriously?"

"Aye. He ate the pastry off the top and the bottom first, then put it on a buttered morning roll and smeared tomato ketchup all over it."

MacDonald nodded slowly. "Sounds like a father —daughter bonding thing, right?"

"Maybe." Her heart jumped. "Shit, are any of our lot still out?"

MacDonald shrugged as he stopped in the street. "Shouldn't be. Why? You ashamed of being seen in public with me?"

Vicky wrapped her arms around her waist, guarding against the cold. "No. I just don't like how people talk."

"They do, don't they?" He smirked. "Zoë thinks you're a bitch."

Vicky shrugged. "I kind of am."

454

He laughed. "Wonder what they think of me."

"They call you Big Time Charlie."

"Doesn't surprise me." MacDonald licked his lips. "What's wrong with two single people going for a drink?"

"Nothing."

MacDonald stepped forward and kissed her gently on the lips.

She locked her eyes on his then tilted her head to the side and leaned forward, eyes closed, her mouth connecting with his.

His arms snaked around her, one hand cradling her neck, his tongue exploring.

"Get stuck in there, son!"

They broke off, Vicky taking a step back. A group of lads in rugby shirts walked along the street opposite, clapping and waving at them.

Vicky stared at the pavement. This wasn't in the plan. What the hell was she doing now? She put a hand to her face. "Look, I'm sorry, Euan, I really need to go." She flagged down a passing taxi, a silver Skoda.

MacDonald frowned at her, his mouth twitching. "Okay. See you tomorrow?"

"Aye." Vicky got in the taxi, shutting the door behind her. "Carnoustie."

The driver rubbed his hands together. "Tonight's my lucky night."

Vicky slumped back in the seat, not feeling so lucky.

Chapter One Hundred and Nine

Vicky woke up bleary-eyed, the rumble of the taxi going right up her spine. Took her a few seconds to recognise Monifieth passing through the window.

"You're awake again then, princess?"

"I'm not sure." She sat up and rubbed the sleep from her eyes. The cheeky bastard had taken the low road — must've seen her fall asleep when they were still in Dundee and decided to get a few extra quid out of his lucky night.

Her tongue stuck to the roof of her mouth. She swallowed. At least she hadn't gone to a club with MacDonald.

Did she really kiss him?

She should've gone to Robert's.

Only he was involved in the case, wasn't he?

"Shit, shit, shit."

"You all right back there, princess? Fifty quid if you chuck up."

"I'm fine." Vicky took a deep breath, massaging her churning gut. "Can you drop me at Corbie Drive instead?"

"Sure. It'll not save you anything, mind."

"I know that."

The taxi took a left at the new roundabout towards the old main road through Barry, then took the next right into Corbie Drive. Squat, boxy grey houses and their triangular roofs.

"Here'll do."

"That's twenty quid, love."

Vicky handed him the money. "Have a good night." She got out and the cold air hit her. She started shivering, goose bumps crawling up her arms. Rubbing at her arms, she started walking deeper into the cul-de-sac, tottered up the first left into Liz's street.

She tried to think through what to say. "Sorry, I got held back but here I am. Oh yeah, and I'm drunk. And I got off with my colleague."

Liz's house was at the end. Barry Church lurked in the street behind it. Robert lived next door but she didn't know which side. The bungalow on the right was surely out of the price range of a teacher.

She clicked her fingers — he'd said it was on the left. Shared a drive with Liz's — that's how he'd got talking to Dave. She stopped in the middle of the road. "Shit, shit, shit."

In front of Robert's house was a black Audi saloon.

Friday
4th April 2014

Chapter One Hundred and Ten

Vicky entered the incident room to find Raven's briefing was already underway. She skulked around the back of the room, hoping not to be noticed, and settled for a spot by Considine.

She texted her Mum. Her head was thudding, her mouth dry. *Thanks for lift. You're a lifesaver.*

Considine whispered in her ear. "Thought Forrester didn't like us being late?"

She glared at him. "Do as I say, not as I do."

Raven glanced their way before continuing. "The Newcastle lead in the Micky Scott death took an interesting turn yesterday. Mr Scott's son is, how shall I say this, causing mischief. He's recanted his statement given to DS Dodds relating to the suspicion of some person or persons involved in greyhound racing down there. We've been liaising with Northumbria constabulary and they've given us a list of suspects in Newcastle and Sunderland, all of whom have been under investigation for corruption. Sadly, we've nothing at present but we do expect to progress matters today."

He prodded at *Birds* on the whiteboard. "Yesterday's first big event, of course, was what happened at Fixit DIY. Graeme Christie's still in hospital. He'll be there for a while." He tapped on *Dudhope Castle*. "The street team around Dudhope have a sighting of a man and a woman driving away in a van near to where Mr Ramsay was found. We've just had word of a similar sighting at the Fixit store. Details remain sketchy but we're looking to get a concrete ID progressed this morning. We've got a revised information request out there."

He moved his hand to *Vivisection/UQTECH*. "Our highest priority is finding Calum Urquhart. His father remains in custody after his altercation with Willis Stewart last night. Street teams in the town have thus far yielded very little, I'm afraid. We believe he might've got in a car or van parked alongside the bus stop, potentially the same one as at Dudhope. This isn't an opportunistic abduction. This has been planned out, carefully. The CCTV around Dundee High is sketchy at best. We've got some possible sightings of this vehicle but nothing concrete."

Considine raised his hand. "Just had word back from Forensics, sir. All notes received so far definitely match."

Raven raised an eyebrow, briefly locking eyes with Forrester. "That's useful, Constable." He checked a sheet of paper on the desk in front of him. "On that topic, Scenes of Crime have found some hair trapped in the cage Mr Ramsay was found in. While it matches the hair found at Hunter's Farm, we're still no further forward in identifying whose it is."

Vicky cleared her throat. "Sorry, sir, but have we checked out if Ramsay's got any animal cruelty charges against him?" Shite — her voice sounded rough.

"No idea. Anyone?"

Karen nodded at him. "I ran a search this morning, sir. Nothing on the PNC but I found some stuff on the internet. Looks like he's been investigated for beating up his birds. There was a video of him punching them."

"Bloody hell." Raven pinched his nose. "Zoë, can you get on that? Find out who's posted it?"

"Will do, sir."

Raven reached down and retrieved a sheet of paper. "We don't know if this is genuine or not, but *The Courier* received a note warning against an attack on the zoo at Camperdown Park. DI Greig, I want you to focus at least two-thirds of your time on that."

"Will do, sir."

Raven scowled at him. "How are you progressing with the 'Taser as MO' angle?"

"Nothing so far, sir. We've just got a guy in Birmingham who's currently inside for armed robbery."

"So nothing?"

"Afraid not."

Raven stared at the board for a few seconds, scribbling an illegible note next to *Taser*. He faced them again, arms folded, wiggling the pen between his fingers. "DS Kelly has a full list of detailed actions for every officer, but I just want to outline our priorities for the day. I want us to find Calum Urquhart. I want to find who picked him up. I want people back at uqTech speaking to their entire payroll and ex-employees. I want to find who trapped Graeme Christie and Kyle Ramsay. I want this van found. Also, I want to find out who recorded these videos and posted them online. Lastly, I want to prevent an attack on Camperdown Park."

He licked his lips. "This is a critical case. It's not the usual type of case we'd deal with in MIT North. There are clear signs of an escalation. We don't want the next crime this group commits to involve an atrocity on a scale larger than what we've seen here or a young boy being crucified on the Law Hill. I'm liaising with the

NCA and other bodies to make sure we're managing the threat appropriately."

He took a deep breath. "Dismissed."

Vicky spotted MacDonald heading her way. She shot off in the opposite direction, found Karen in the sea of bodies.

"Christ, Vicks, you look like you need a breakfast."

"I do. I'll see you across the road. I just need to speak to someone first." Vicky went over to DS Kelly's desk.

The admin officer was reading the paper as the Acting DC shadowing him doled out actions. He looked up. "Doddsy, speak to young Keith about actions. I'm busy."

"Are you hell." Vicky snatched his paper up. "I want to raise a new suspect in the case log."

Kelly blew air up his nose. His fat lips vibrated. He leaned forward, his belly wobbling, shirt buttons straining, eyes on his paper. "Got any evidence?"

"Some. The name's Robert Hamilton. He appeared on the list of significant donors to the animal shelter on Brown Street." She held out a finger. "Not the council one."

"Right. Anything else? As far as I recall, Vicky, there were over four hundred people on that list. Shall I add them all?"

"Just that one. He owns a black saloon. An Audi."

Kelly raised his eyebrows, his lined forehead creasing further. "You know we're not necessarily looking for an exec-class one, right? They've changed the request."

"Can you get someone to run a check on his car?"

Kelly checked a page of notes. "Robert Hamilton, Robert Hamilton, Robert Hamilton . . . Here we go. Aye, he's on our list of car owners. Got two officers heading down there, probably head out there this afternoon."

Vicky swallowed. What had she got into? "Thanks." She handed his paper back.

Kelly thumbed at the ADC next to him. "You spoken to wee Keith about your actions yet?"

"Not yet."

"Well, you and Big Time Charlie are to investigate the Muirheads as suspects."

Chapter One Hundred and Eleven

Vicky opened the door to the Old Mill Café in a daze. The end of Reform Street, MacDonald kissing her. Now she was stuck with him.

She swallowed and looked around the place, smelled the familiar tang of coffee in the air.

Karen was seated in the window, flicking through a paper.

"Morning." Vicky slumped in the seat, the nerve in her neck thumping.

Karen slid a bacon roll across to Vicky. "Butter and bacon at breaking point."

"At least my breakfast will be okay today." Vicky opened the roll. Perfect.

Karen finished chewing a mouthful. "Soon as we're done here, I've got to head out to that DIY place again."

"Lucky you." Vicky tore open a blue sachet of brown sauce and squirted it onto her roll. She took a bite, savouring the liquid butter mixing with the crisp bacon.

"You feeling okay, Vicks?"

Vicky chewed faster. "Sorry, I'm a bit hung-over."

"How did you chance upon this hangover? Robert?"

Vicky let out a breath, eyes on the plate. "I went out with Forrester and MacDonald for a pint after work last night. Mum had to drop me off. I left my car here."

"You got a taxi back to Carnoustie?"

"Aye. Twenty quid."

"Oh Jesus, Vicks." Karen put her head in her hands. "You cancelled on Robert, didn't you?"

"Aye."

"By text?"

"No! I phoned him."

"You're a nightmare, my girl." Karen took a bite of her own roll. There was ketchup smeared on her chin. "If you binned him last night, I take it Wednesday was a disaster then?"

"Wednesday was good." Vicky stared into space. A draught from the door sent a shiver up her spine.

"Aye, Colin said something about you looking all ravished yesterday morning. I take it your top drawer didn't get opened?"

"Only for a condom."

"Oh my God!"

Vicky mopped up the fat from her plate with the last bit of the roll. "Yeah, there you go."

"Morning, ladies." MacDonald walked past the table, raising a finger in recognition, before going up to the counter to order.

Karen leaned across the table. "Big Time Charlie's not bad looking, actually. Total wanker, though."

"I got off with him last night."

Karen ran her hand through her hair and stared at Vicky for a few seconds. "You're a complete idiot."

Vicky looked away. "I know."

"That Robert guy sounds nice."

"He is nice." Vicky stared at the table. "That's the problem. I've never been one for the nice guy, have I?"

"MacDonald's very much the bad boy, isn't he?" Karen looked across the café. "Blue BMW, Big Time Charlie attitude."

Vicky watched MacDonald fiddle with his wallet as he waited for his latte. "I've no idea what I'm doing."

"Have you told MacDonald you've got a kid?"

"No."

"What about Robert?"

Vicky nodded. "He's met Bella."

"I said you were being an idiot four and a half years ago when you let Alan go."

"I didn't let him go. He pissed off and left me, three months pregnant. What kind of a man does that?" She hit the table. "He's a fucking worm, Karen. I don't want him anywhere near Bella."

"You're sure?"

"We're better off with him out of our lives." Vicky rubbed at a tear slipping from her eye. "Bella's better off never knowing him."

"You can be a cold bitch at times."

"I wonder why. It's how I cope. I've got a load of shit to do today so I'll be pressing the switch marked 'cold bitch' any second now." Vicky wiped another tear away.

"You're such a Dundee wifie, Vicks. You just need a kettle-boiler husband while you work in the jute mill."

"That's my family history. I'm not a Fifer like you."

"Is Robert the sort to look after Bella while you're out working?"

"I don't know." Vicky watched MacDonald again as he bantered with the barista. Was he the sort to take in a four-year-old and her damaged mother? She sighed and pushed her plate away. "I'm worried Robert's involved in this case."

Karen rolled her eyes. "Now we're getting down to it."

"I'm serious. He's into this animal welfare stuff. He's on a donation list Zoë got from the Brown Street kennels. And he's got a black Audi."

"You're serious?"

"He's been tapping me up for information, Kaz. He's trying to keep an eye on the case. I've been such a bloody idiot."

"Sure this isn't you up to your usual, Vicky? As soon as a guy gets anywhere near you, you run a mile." Karen shook her fists in the air. "I want to shake you so hard right now."

Vicky put the last bit of roll back on the plate. "I raised it in the case log."

"Christ, Vicky. You better not be wrong."

"I know."

Considine breezed past, slapping MacDonald on the shoulder like they were best mates. MacDonald wandered over to the table but stayed standing, a frown on his forehead, smile on his lips. "Morning, Vicky."

"Morning, Euan." She looked away.

"Supposed to be checking out the Muirheads, right?"

Vicky exchanged a look with Karen, her eyes wide as she stifled a laugh. "Correct."

"Finally got hold of my pal in Vice. Really cagey about why they're investigating them. Escalated it to Raven — his problem now. Hopefully sort it out, DCI to DCI."

"Here's hoping."

MacDonald thumbed back at the counter. "Considine checked their alibi. Turns out there was a dinner party but they left early. Half seven."

Vicky rubbed at her face, trying to clear her head. She thought back to her timeline, trying to zoom in and make it clearer. "Christie was attacked at the back of eight, right? So they could have done it?"

"Yep. Ferry to Fixit's about five minutes, right?"

"Did that holiday story check out?"

MacDonald shook his head. "Not yet. Summers was looking into it. Said they arrived back in Edinburgh on the morning of the nineteenth."

"So they could've been involved in the snare one, too?"

"Could be."

Considine sipped through the lid of his takeaway cup. "This about the Muirheads, Mac?"

MacDonald nodded. "Yes."

"I was speaking to Buchan just after the briefing. He finished that phone record search you asked him to do."

"And?"

"He was saying something about Polly Muirhead calling Marianne Smith a few times."

MacDonald tightened his grip on his coffee cup. "Get uniform to bring them back in."

"Will do." Considine grinned at him and took a sip of coffee.

Karen ran her hand through her hair. "What about them going to the Chief Constable?"

"Bollocks to that. Happy to take any heat on this."

Chapter One Hundred and Twelve

MacDonald stood outside the interview room, taking deep breaths. He grinned at her. "Ready?"

"Give me a second."

"Want to talk about last night?"

"No."

"Okay. I'll get it started, okay?" MacDonald opened the door and sat opposite Polly Muirhead. Fergus Duncan sat next to her. The tape recorder blared out as the door shut.

Vicky stared at the door. What the hell was she doing? This was bad news. She entered the interview room and sat next to MacDonald.

"DS Victoria Dodds has just entered the room." MacDonald leaned back in his chair, arms folded, sucking in breath.

Across from Vicky, Duncan twirled his mobile phone in his hands. He put it on the table, looked at Vicky then back at the phone. He sniffed as he adjusted his bright orange tie.

Vicky ignored the message. "Mrs Muirhead, on the morning of the nineteenth of August last year, you and your husband arrived back in the country from a holiday in Latvia, is that correct?"

"It is. We were in Riga. We flew back to Edinburgh via airBaltic. We had a stopover in Stockholm."

Vicky noted it down. Very precise. "What time was this?"

"The flight was twenty minutes late. I think we arrived just before noon."

Plenty of time to get up to Edzell, travel tiredness or not. "What did you do next?"

"We stayed overnight with friends in Edinburgh."

"Do you often stay with friends?"

"My client doesn't wish to answer that question." Duncan adjusted his mobile on the table.

Vicky ignored him. "Can you provide the names and addresses of your friends, please?"

"Is this strictly necessary?"

Vicky leaned on her elbows and rubbed her hands together. "Mrs Muirhead, you arrived back in Scotland on the same morning the first of these crimes occurred. You'd a clear opportunity to drive to Edzell and commit the attack on Mr Lethnot."

Polly slumped in her chair. "Very well. It was Graeme Davenport and Donald Cairns."

"Are they a couple?"

"They are. Homosexuality was legalised in Scotland in 1980, so you won't be able to prosecute them on those grounds."

Eyebrow raised, Duncan whispered in Polly's ear. She nodded.

Vicky folded her arms. "We will, of course, validate your movements with them."

"Very well."

Vicky nodded at MacDonald, who was sitting back, arms folded. "Sergeant?"

He sat forward, leaning over his notepad. "What were you really doing at Phorever Love?"

"We've told you. I did some *pro bono* legal work for them."

"Your employers are somewhat cagey about releasing information about these cases to us."

"It's called client confidentiality."

Duncan smirked. "You may know it as corporate sensitivity."

MacDonald poked his tongue into his cheek as he inhaled. "Phorever Love are closely linked to the crime committed at Hunter's Farm."

Duncan sniffed. "My client isn't involved in that. I assume you've checked the statement governing my client's trip to Mrs Muirhead's sister in Dunfermline?"

"We have." MacDonald leaned forward. "Mrs Muirhead, what were you really doing at Phorever Love?"

"No comment other than what's been previously stated."

Duncan tapped his mobile phone and raised his eyebrows at Vicky.

Vicky smiled, trying to ignore the threat, but acid burned in the pit of her stomach, not all of it from the bacon roll. "Mrs Muirhead, on Thursday evening, you attended a dinner party."

"That's correct."

"According to your friends, you and your husband left the dinner party at seven thirty. Correct?"

"No comment."

"Why did you leave early?"

"No comment."

"Where did you go?"

"No comment."

"You didn't go to the Kingsway East Retail Park?"

"My client doesn't wish to go on the record for this."

"You didn't go to the Fixit DIY store there?"

Duncan tapped the mobile again. "Move on, Sergeant."

"Where were you between noon and four p.m. yesterday afternoon?"

Polly blew out a breath. "I was at work, then I had a client visit."

"Where?"

"In Monifieth."

"You weren't in the centre of town by Dundee High?"

Polly shook her head. "No."

"You weren't at Dudhope Castle? Or Barrack Park just by it?"

"No."

Vicky put her pen down. "Mrs Muirhead, why were you phoning Marianne Smith?"

Polly's eyes bulged. "I wasn't."

Vicky held up a sheet of paper. "Your phone company says you were. Over a hundred and ten calls in the last year on your landline, going both ways."

Duncan grasped the edge of the table. "Polly, have you been calling her?"

She stared at the table. "It was Sandy."

Vicky struggled to comprehend. "Was your husband having an affair with Ms Smith?"

Polly shook her head. "No."

"What, then?"

"No comment."

"Mrs Muirhead, your husband's waiting for us in the next room. I'm pretty confident we can get the information out of him."

Polly folded and unfolded her arms before rubbing the end of her nose. "No comment."

"We've still got Ms Smith in custody. We can ask her. She's been in here since Tuesday, charged with some fairly hefty terrorist crimes. I imagine she might be in a more communicative frame of mind."

Duncan leaned across and whispered in Polly's ear.

She scowled at him. "Really?"

Duncan nodded. "I think so."

Polly coughed, eyes shut. "My husband is into dogging."

Vicky laughed. "It's *dogging* now, is it?"

Polly shivered. "Sandy likes . . . having sex in cars and other public places. I go along with it for Sandy's sake."

"I've heard some very interesting alibis from you so far. This takes the biscuit."

"It's the truth." Polly's eyes filled with moisture. "Christ, I've been living with this for so long."

"Why was your husband calling Ms Smith about *dogging*?"

"He'd been asking Marianne about the sites in Cupar. He found a few places on the internet and wanted to know which sites would be best to avoid being caught."

"Why her?"

Polly shrugged. "We knew her from xbeast."

"Did she go with you?"

"Not recently. She used to be into it as well but stopped doing it."

"Were you dogging at Phorever Love?"

"That was technically swinging. They have bedrooms and so on."

Vicky pinched her nose. "Jesus Christ."

"I swear this is the truth. It's the reason we left the dinner party early. It's where we were when we were supposed to be at the Rep."

"You weren't having an argument?"

"We had one afterwards. I wanted out of this whole thing."

"And you say this is for your husband?"

"Sandy has particular . . . needs. It's why we went to Riga. The prostitutes are cheap and *liberal* there."

"Assuming this is all true, you've wasted a lot of police time."

"I'm sorry." Polly rubbed at her face. "I'm a respectable member of society in Dundee. I didn't want this getting out."

"We'll need to get this confirmed, of course."

"Speak to Simon Hagger about it."

"We've already spoken to him about your movements. Is it going to be the truth this time?"

"I certainly hope so. Simon's the one who got Sandy into this whole bloody thing in the first place."

Chapter One Hundred and Thirteen

Vicky leaned against Considine's Subaru and looked back at the Haggers' house, a post-war bungalow on a decent street in Barnhill. Seagulls wheeled above them — there was a salty sea tang in the air. "Why do people who live in a house like that do something so stupid?"

"Boredom?" Considine shrugged. "She wasn't so bad but the bloke was a bit of a munter. You ever seen *Family Guy*?"

"Never heard of it. Where do they get the name 'dogging' from?"

"Isn't it from men pretending they're walking the dog but really cracking one off as they spy on couples having sex in a car?"

Vicky patted the roof of the car. "The Python sounds like the sort of car that gets dogging action."

Considine laughed. "No comment."

"You better not get caught."

"Christ, of course I'm not taking this baby dogging."

Vicky grinned. "Really?"

"I've got an old Saab for that." Considine pointed back at the house. "You were pretty bloody-minded in there, Sarge."

"I'm fed up of getting the runaround by them. Simon and Emma Hagger have a history of lying to us. They provided the Rep alibi that fell apart. We need this backed up by other sources before those idiots are let off the hook."

"You let them off pretty lightly, considering."

Vicky tilted her head towards the approaching police car. "Those two are going to give them a much harder time than I did."

"Remind me never to get on your wrong side."

"You better focus on getting on my right side, Stephen."

Considine frowned then opened the driver door. "Where to now, Sarge?"

"Let's get back to the station." Vicky got in the car and checked her mobile — no missed calls or texts. Still nothing from Salewicz.

Considine started the engine and pulled away.

She pressed dial again. "Hello?" Noise in the background, maybe a building site.

"Hi, Andy, it's DS Dodds. Are you okay to talk?"

"Hi, Becky. It's been ages since I've heard from my kid sister."

"I take it this is you letting me know it's difficult to talk?"

"Of course I haven't forgotten your birthday. You get the card? There was a message in it. Took me ages."

"I need to speak to you about the Muirheads. Was there any swinging at the camp?"

"Of course. That sounds brilliant. There are a few people here who definitely think that's a great idea."

"Were you personally involved?"

"Not me, no. Look, I'm in the middle of something. I'd better go but I'll call you later, okay?"

"Thanks." Vicky ended the call.

"Who was that, Sarge?"

"Salewicz, just checking on what the Muirheads were up to at Phorever Love. Sounds like there is some sort of swinging scene there."

Her phone buzzed. A text — Salewicz. *You almost blew my cover. Thanks for nothing. I hope it's worth it. NEVER CALL AGAIN.*

Vicky watched Dundee pass by, tempted to text the ending to *Breaking Bad* out of spite.

Her phone buzzed again. MacDonald. *Vice confirm Muirheads part of dogging crackdown. No action taken yet but sting planned for this week. Mac*

Vicky blushed. Her hand stroking his back, his on her neck. *That why they didn't want us surveilling? Uniform just going in 2 speak to them abt it now. V*

MacDonald replied. *Exactly why. Ill warn them. Summers said holiday checks out. Riga notorious for sex tourism tho. When do you fancy coffee? X*

Vicky put the phone away. She looked up — they were already at the Kingsway. "I think the Muirheads are in the clear."

"So who's doing it, then?"

"I've no idea."

The Airwave on the dashboard crackled. "Control to DC Considine. Over."

"Can you get that, Sarge?"

Vicky picked it up and answered it. "This is DS Dodds receiving. DC Considine's driving."

"Just had a call from a member of the public. Someone's found a black Vauxhall Vectra in a lock-up in Fintry."

Chapter One Hundred and Fourteen

Considine tore up the dual carriageway, heading north out of the city. He tugged the wheel hard right to overtake a supermarket lorry. "Think this is them?"

"Doubt it." Vicky stared at the playing fields passing by, rubbing at her neck. This had to be a load of bollocks. It was Robert. She just needed one of Kelly's guys to head round to speak to him. That was it.

Wasn't it?

He swung a right at the first roundabout, heading into Fintry Road. "It's still a complete shit hole up here."

"It's better than it was when I was growing up."

"Didn't think they had council estates in the nineteenth century."

"Whatever. Right here."

Considine turned at the roundabout. The buildings oscillated between long rows of flats and detached houses — most of the small gardens were filled with trampolines.

Vicky checked the maps app on her phone. "Right here. Then it should just be on the right."

"Sounds like we're going in a circle." Considine drove down Fintryside. A row of brown council houses faced into the park, balconies at the front.

"This is it here." Vicky leaned forward, pointing to the right.

Considine pulled up behind a Dundee City Council van with a police car parked in front of it. A side road, blocked off by a steel fence, led into Finlathen Park. "This must be it here, surely?"

"I think so."

A man in high-vis gear was talking to a policeman. He came over and motioned for Considine to wind down his window. "One of you DS Dodds?"

Vicky got out of the car and held up her warrant card. "That's me."

"PC Paul Arnold." He took off his hat. "Got the call from one of the guys who rents a unit here." He thumbed behind him. "He's in the back of the car. Thought you might want to speak to him."

"We'll get round to that. So, what's the story here?"

"Boy who called it in reckoned he saw a car on Tuesday when he was locking up. Saw your info request in the *Tele* last night. It's a black Vectra."

Vicky nodded. "Can we have a look?"

"Aye." Arnold pointed at the man standing next to him, who wore white council overalls with a yellow pencil stuck above his ear. "This is Jim Smalls."

Smalls grinned at them. "I manage these lock-ups for the council. We rent them out to punters to park their cars in."

Considine raised an eyebrow. "Do they store other things as well?"

Smalls chuckled. "Aye. Not sure why you'd want to lock your car away in Fintry, but then no bugger's getting in here, that's for sure."

"Who rents the one with the car in it?"

"I'd need to check on that, son." Smalls gestured across the road. "Past the gate up there. If you'll follow me?"

Vicky leaned close in to whisper. "Stephen, you stay here and take a statement off the guy in the car, okay? I'll deal with this, get this off our plates quite quickly."

"Sure thing, Sarge."

Smalls was unlocking the gate across the road. He waited for Vicky to cross before he pulled it to.

She followed him up the long drive. Halfway up the steep incline was a long row of lock-ups, thirty or so single-storey garages made out of concrete. The building backed onto the park — mature trees now covered two-thirds of the roof. "Can you unlock it for me?"

"Aye, will do." Smalls wrestled with a large chain of keys, eventually finding the one he was after. "Lucky we've got a skeleton for these."

Vicky stood watching. This wasn't their car. How could it be? She'd seen it outside Robert's house.

Smalls pulled the garage door open to reveal a matte black Vauxhall with o8 plates. "Here you go." He turned round to Vicky and then his eyes bulged at something behind her.

A hard object pressed against her back, turning her muscles to jelly. She stumbled to her knees and fell forward.

Chapter One Hundred and Fifteen

Vicky started to feel again. The tarmac dug into her cheek. She managed to twitch her fingers again.

An engine roared behind her. She looked over. The Vectra shot out of the garage, tearing off the way she'd come. As it passed, she saw two heads in the front wearing balaclavas.

Smalls was kneeling on all fours, groaning.

Vicky got to her feet. "Are you okay?"

"Bugger got me with a spanner. You got off lucky. Bloody Taser."

"Did you say Taser?"

"Aye." Smalls sucked in breath. "Zapped you good and proper."

"Did you see them?"

Smalls shook his head, one hand clutching his skull. "He had a balaclava on."

"I'll call an ambulance. I need to get after them." Vicky set off down the hill, fumbling her phone out to call Forrester. "Sir, I've got a sighting of the car in Finlathen Park. Just by the entrance on Findale Street. It was in a lock-up. I need an ambulance there and support vehicles now. I'm going to give chase."

"Vicky, can —"

She killed the call, dialling Considine as she sprinted away. Voicemail.

The path curved round to the left. The Vectra idled at the entrance, the engine revving. A figure wearing a balaclava was wrestling with the gates. He got back in and the car screeched off, heading right.

Vicky looked up to see Considine reversing his car back up the road to her. She got in, tugging the seatbelt on as Considine wrenched the car forward. "You should have just left me."

"Arnold's giving chase as well." Considine tore down Findale Street, dodging amongst the parked cars. "Anyway, that's a Vectra VXR, Sarge. Sheep in wolf's clothing. The Python will *nail* it."

"Thought this was just a car?"

"More than a car." Considine took the corner tight, sending Vicky almost flying into the middle of the car.

A thud boomed from the left, just out of sight.

Vicky peered around. "What the hell was that?"

Considine put his foot down and the Subaru careered round the corner.

The Vectra sat at the end of the road, side on, steam coming from the bonnet. A panda car was wedged into its side, the siren blaring and lights flashing.

Considine screeched to a halt. "Holy shit."

Two figures got out of the Vectra, wearing balaclavas. They started running along a lane at the back of the houses.

Vicky got out, letting her seatbelt fly free. "Come on."

They gave chase down the lane, dodging a pool of broken glass. One of their prey was starting to lag behind.

The androgynous member of the gang.

Vicky got a good look as she closed the gap between them — while the figure was tall and muscular, it also clearly had curvy hips and small breasts. Definitely a woman.

Considine accelerated, gaining ground. He lurched forward, arms coming round in a rugby-tackle.

Just missed his target's shoulder.

He reached out with his leading arm, catching her feet.

Vicky shoulder-barged into her, sending her to the ground. She leaned in hard, forcing the woman's arm behind her back.

Vicky turned to Considine, already dusting himself off as he got to his feet, and pointed down the lane. "Get after the other one!"

"Right." He shot off.

Vicky put a knee into her captive's back, tugging her hands up behind. She pulled out handcuffs, slapped them round her captive's wrists. "On your feet. Now."

The woman got up, shoulders slouching.

Vicky kept one hand on the cuffs as she reached for the balaclava and pulled it off in one movement.

She concentrated on the woman's face, struggling to place her. The woman stared at the ground.

The animal shelter. The expert in NME. The woman who preferred animals to people, who'd given Zoë the donor list.

Yvonne Welsh.

Chapter One Hundred and Sixteen

Vicky clasped her hands around a glass of Diet Coke, already empty, and looked out of the Old Mill Café window. Traffic was crawling up and down the Marketgait. The police station was starting to get the sun.

She clenched her jaw. Had she hung Robert out to dry?

"Hey." MacDonald hung his jacket on the back of the chair and sat down, clunking his coffee down on the table. "She's getting processed now. We'll get in there soon."

"I can't believe it's her. She just works round the corner from here."

"I know."

"Considine and I spoke to her last week." Vicky shook her head. "I'm going to get such a doing over this."

MacDonald flicked up his fingers. "Nobody's blaming you. We were all in the dark on this."

Vicky sighed. He was probably right. "Maybe."

MacDonald took a sip of coffee. "Other one ran off. Got three units out looking for him. Looks like he's gone to ground somewhere."

"You think it's a man?"

"Maybe."

"What about the two uniforms in the squad car?"

"Just got the all-clear." MacDonald tore open a sachet of brown sugar, tipped it into his coffee. "Uniform are bringing in Alison McFarlane."

Vicky nodded. "Yvonne's boss."

"Aye. And alibi."

"Think she's involved?"

"Maybe. Maybe not." MacDonald sipped at his drink, grimacing at the taste. "Can I get you something else? More Diet Coke?"

Vicky stared at the glass. The ice was melting and turning brown. "I think I need something stronger."

"Bacardi?"

"No, like a coffee."

"Want me to get you one?"

"I'm fine just now. I can't decide whether I want tea or coffee."

MacDonald smiled. "Definitely a Taser they got you with?"

"I think so. Have you ever been electrocuted, Euan?"

"Not something I plan on making a habit of." MacDonald laughed. "Have you?"

"Aye. I used to help Dad do his DIY. Once, when we were putting a floor in the attic, I accidentally stuck a screwdriver on a live wire. Threw me clean across the room." She tugged at her ponytail, stroking it. "It felt exactly like that. My muscles just turned to jelly. There was nothing I could do."

"Jesus. Least it wasn't a gun, I suppose."

Vicky put both hands around the can, still cool. "How did they know we'd be there? Surely it would've been easier to shift it before we turned up."

"Thought it might be bad luck." MacDonald showed her a photo on his mobile, a black box with a red display. "SOCOs found this on the back seat alongside a disposable mobile phone."

"What is it?"

"Our Tetra Scanner."

"You're kidding."

"Nope. Think they heard the call over the Airwave system saying we'd found the car. Must've panicked and headed out there. Problem is, you got there just after them."

"Christ."

"Bloody network's supposed to be secure." MacDonald shook his head. "Wouldn't happen to have a brother called Andrew, would you?"

Vicky nodded. "Why?"

"Coming to look at it."

Vicky nodded. "Is someone tracking down whoever rents that unit?"

"Considine, aye. Guy from the council, Smalls? Seemed a bit cagey about it as he got taken off to hospital." He blew on his coffee. "Got it a lot worse than you, believe me."

Vicky stared at his cup, deciding she wanted a coffee after all.

MacDonald took a big drink. "Struggling to get anyone else to help us at the council."

Vicky nodded. "They work at Dudhope Castle, right?"

"Right. Kirk's up there trying to find someone."

Vicky avoided his eyes for a few seconds. "What happened last night, Euan?"

MacDonald rubbed his face. "You tell me?"

"You kissed me."

"You kissed me back, Vicky."

"Then I got a taxi."

MacDonald gazed down at the table, prodding at some grains of sugar. "What would've happened if those guys hadn't started cheering?"

Vicky stared into her glass. "I don't know." She leaned back in her chair, tossing her ponytail back. "What do you think, Euan?"

"Was away to ask if you wanted to come back to my flat."

"Why didn't you?"

He shrugged. "You ran off."

"I do that." She shook the glass, swirling the last of the ice cubes around. "You need to know something about me, Euan. I've got a daughter."

MacDonald frowned. "A daughter?"

"Her name's Bella. She's four."

MacDonald glanced at her fingers. "You don't wear a ring."

"I'm not married."

"Where's her father?"

"He lives in Edinburgh." Vicky looked away. The nerve in her neck started up again. "We're not together. Never were, really."

"Okay."

"Euan, you need to be okay with her if we're to get into anything."

He nodded. "Quite a lot to take in, you know?"

"I know."

MacDonald finished his coffee and checked his watch. "Come on, let's see what Yvonne Welsh has got to say for herself."

Vicky swallowed down mucus, her throat tight. "I'll be a minute."

"No problem." He got up and left her sitting there.

Vicky watched him walk across the road towards the station. She got up and walked over to the counter. She looked up at the board above the coffee machine, a sprawling list of drinks she'd never had to look at before. Mocha, latte, Americano? She smiled at the barista. "Can I have an English Breakfast tea, please?"

Chapter One Hundred and Seventeen

Yvonne Welsh sat hunched over the interview room table, rocking back and forth, eyes shut.

Vicky stared at the recorders. The tapes hissed as they wound round. Which of the three was Yvonne? She could be the woman, of course, but she could also pass for the androgynous third member. She was tall and didn't have a particularly large chest, though the hips were a giveaway.

Vicky glanced at MacDonald before leaning across the table to her, trying to make eye contact. Failing. "Ms Welsh, you need to speak to us."

Yvonne kept her eyes shut.

"Do you prefer Yvonne?"

She shrugged.

"Yvonne, you're in a lot of trouble. You do realise that, don't you?"

No reaction.

Vicky looked at her lawyer, Kelly Nelson-Caird. She wrote long, elliptical paragraphs on a yellow notepad.

Vicky cleared her throat. "Yvonne, a child's out there. Calum Urquhart. You've abducted him. Whatever grievances you've got against his father, does Calum deserve what you're doing to him?"

Yvonne screwed her eyes tighter and began to rock slowly.

Vicky licked her lips. "Yvonne, we've caught you red-handed. The car you were driving was spotted at the other crime scenes. We've spoken to two of your victims and they've confirmed it was a Vauxhall Vectra VXR."

Yvonne clenched her fists. "I wasn't driving."

"Who was?"

Yvonne clenched her jaw.

"Yvonne, who was with you?"

"No comment."

"Yvonne, whoever you're protecting, it's doing you no favours."

"No comment."

"Yvonne, things are escalating." Vicky left a pause. It wasn't filled. "I don't think you wanted to get into this, did you?"

Yvonne glanced at Nelson-Caird.

"It started out as fun, didn't it, Yvonne?"

No reply.

"It's gone way beyond that now. We're investigating a murder. Do you really want to face those charges alone?"

Nothing.

"Yvonne, were you working with Marianne Smith?"

She looked up. "Who?"

"Marianne Smith."

She looked away. "I don't know who that is."

"On top of the murder, there are kidnapping and abduction charges. On top of those, there are terrorism charges. You'll face them alone. If you're not leading this, it might be a lot to take on your shoulders."

Yvonne stared up at the ceiling. "What're you saying?"

"Are you the one behind all this?"

Yvonne shrugged. "No, I'm not."

"I didn't think so." Vicky looked at MacDonald.

He sat upright. "Yvonne, it's possible we could be lenient with you. *If* you give us whoever's behind this."

Nelson-Caird whispered in Yvonne's ear.

Yvonne sat for a few seconds before shaking her head.

"My client isn't prepared to listen to any offer."

MacDonald rolled his eyes. "Really?"

"I'm afraid so."

MacDonald got to his feet and left the room, the door clattering as he slammed it.

Vicky leaned over. "Interview terminated at twelve oh seven." She hit the stop button on both recorders almost simultaneously. She shook her head, eyes on Yvonne. "You really are up to your neck in this."

Chapter One Hundred and Eighteen

Forrester crunched down on his office chair, sticking his feet on his desk. Dark purple rings looped around his eyes. "She'll swing for this, I swear."

Vicky crossed her legs, noticed a ladder in her tights. "I don't see her co-operating, sir."

"Maybe. Mac, what do you think?"

MacDonald shrugged. "Certainly seems to be deep in this. Just not sure she's the ringleader."

"What've we got on her?"

"Good news." MacDonald flicked through his notebook. "DNA from Hunter's Farm matches against her."

Forrester grinned. "So that confirms she's involved."

MacDonald nodded. "Throw the book at her, sir."

"What about Smith?"

Vicky shrugged. "What about her?"

"Do you think she's involved?"

"I don't know."

"Is it worth getting the pair of them in a room together?"

MacDonald shook his head. "Terror organisations make sure they never meet. If they do, they'll have been trained to ignore each other."

"Have we looked into any links between them?"

"DCs investigating it just now, sir. Good to have them back from Greig."

"Aye." Forrester chuckled. "Poor guy's been dragged over half of Dundee and not found a single thing. That Camperdown Park attack never happened. They've been up the Law and out to the Ferry. All they've got is a sighting of a van dropping a letter off last night. That's it. Don't even know if it's our letter."

Vicky stared into space for a moment, then noticed MacDonald's eyes on her legs. She uncrossed them. "What do you want to do, sir?"

Forrester got to his feet. "Let's see what the DCs have got linking the pair of them." He led them into the office space. Only Zoë and Considine were there. "Where are your colleagues, Constable?"

Considine shrugged. "Out speaking to people I think, sir."

Forrester rubbed at his stubble. "What're you working on?"

"Still trying to find out who's renting the lock-up, sir."

"Keep on that."

"Will do." Considine nodded at Vicky. "Sarge, there's an Alison McFarlane downstairs. Do you want me with you?"

Forrester patted his arm. "Don't worry, Constable. I'll take the interview with Vicky. You've got some important work to do."

Considine beamed at him. "Thank you, sir."

"Mac, can you get me an update from the others?"

"Will do."

"Come on, Vicky." Forrester set off towards the door, then glanced back at Considine. "You're doing a decent job with him."

"Thanks, sir."

"Still a sleekit wee bugger, though." Forrester shook his head. "I've also got him leading the interview with the idiot who posted those videos of Kyle Ramsay punching his birds."

"Think they're involved?"

"Probably not, but it makes him feel important."

Chapter One Hundred and Nineteen

Ms McFarlane, you're going to have to start answering our questions." Forrester sniffed before rubbing at his nostrils.

"And I'm trying."

"Very." Vicky smiled at her. "Please, start with Yvonne Welsh and your relationship with her."

Alison's eyes shot up. "What's that supposed to mean?"

"You work with her, correct?"

"That's right." Alison crossed her arms, briefly diverted her gaze to Vicky. "I told you that last week."

"So I gather." Forrester hefted up a copy of the case file, dumped it on the desk with a thud. He licked a finger then flicked through the pages, stopping a third of the way in. "You gave her as your alibi for the crimes."

"That's true."

"So, we now find out she wasn't there." Forrester glanced over at Alison's lawyer. "Mr Flynn, your client's now implicated in a series of serious crimes, including murder."

Flynn cleared his throat. He was young and heavyset, his thick, dark brown beard matching his hipster side-parting. His shirt was open to the neck, tufts of chest hair sneaking out. His light brown suit jacket hung off the back of the chair. "I acknowledge that, Sergeant."

"Inspector."

"Sorry, Inspector." Flynn coughed again. "My client maintains her statement, albeit without the benefit of it being verifiable."

Alison smiled as she rubbed a finger down her cheek. "I was at work, on my own."

"That's only part of it, though." Forrester leaned back, almost horizontal. "Providing a false alibi. Tut tut."

"I'm sorry?"

"It'll be interesting to see the judge's face when you use that as your defence in court." Forrester nudged the file away towards Vicky then rubbed his hands together. "You'll get charged with that after this interview, of course."

McFarlane swallowed. "I see."

"Are you involved in these crimes?"

"No, I'm not."

"The trouble is, you don't have an alibi for the evening of Wednesday the twenty-sixth, do you?"

"My client will amend her statement. She still has an alibi."

"But you've got nothing to back that up, have you?"

Flynn blinked a few times before turning to Alison. "Any work emails?"

Alison shook her head. "I was checking through the paperwork we receive from our vets, making sure it tallied with our own records."

Vicky noted it down. "On a computer?"

"Paper."

"What about for the other times in question? Start with Sunday th —"

Flynn raised a finger. "I know all the dates you're going to ask my client. She was at work on each of them."

"Each of them?"

"Yes."

"How do you know this?"

Flynn held up a Moleskine notebook. "The desk sergeant downstairs — Davies, is it? — he gave me them when I arrived."

Vicky stared at Alison. "Is there anything pinning you to a location?"

"Probably not." Alison scratched at her hair. "Sorry."

"Very well." Forrester picked up his own notebook. "I want to ask you a series of questions relating to other matters. Please answer them. Correctly would be my preference."

Flynn raised a finger in the air, then thought better of it and returned his gaze to the tabletop. "Certainly."

"Ms McFarlane, are you acquainted with a Polly Muirhead?"

She shook her head. "Never heard of her."

"What about Sandy Muirhead?"

"No."

"Marianne Smith?"

Alison blinked a few times, then her eyes widened. "I've never heard of her."

"Well, you reacted there." Forrester thumbed over Vicky's shoulder. "This is being recorded on video. That's admissible as evidence."

Alison swallowed. "I used to know someone of that name. A long time ago."

"Interesting." Forrester scribbled in his notebook.

Vicky sucked her tongue, trying to generate some saliva. "What about a Robert Hamilton?"

"No." Alison held her gaze. "Never heard of him."

"Okay." Forrester clapped his hands together and leaned forward, his mouth over the microphone. "Interview terminated at thirteen thirty-one." He got to his feet and smiled at the Custody and Security Officer. "Can you take her downstairs and get her charged? Davies knows what to do."

The PCSO nodded. "Will do, sir."

Forrester led Vicky out of the room and they paced down the corridor together. "Who's Robert Hamilton?"

"Somebody who came up on their donor list. I flagged him with DS Kelly this morning."

"Okay." Forrester started up the stairs. "Nothing I should be worried about?"

"Shouldn't think so, sir." Vicky felt short of breath as they climbed.

Forrester held the door open for her. "Reckon McFarlane's involved in this?"

"It's possible. She seems to know Marianne Smith, definitely knows Yvonne Welsh."

"What makes somebody do this?" Forrester led across the office towards his room, pausing by the door. "I just don't get it."

"Love of animals, hatred of people."

"You've got a cat, though. Why aren't you doing this?"

"I don't hate *every*one, sir."

"Aye, I suppose." Forrester shook his head. "What a bloody city."

Karen entered the room, heavily out of breath. "I've got something for you, sir."

Forrester scowled. "What?"

Karen held up an evidence bag containing a phone. "This is the mobile we found in the car. It's a Pay As You Go burner. Forensics have been all over it and found some GPS locations on there. The location map shows it was used at least ten times in the Hilltown."

"Was there an address?"

"Number one Ann Street."

Vicky briefly shut her eyes. "That's where Brian Morton lives."

Forrester scowled. "The fat boy on the scooter?"

"Aye." Vicky nodded at Karen. "How accurate is the trace?"

"To two metres, she reckons. Jenny Morgan swore on her life."

Forrester patted Vicky's shoulder. "Get him back in here. And get his bloody laptop, too."

Chapter One Hundred and Twenty

Forrester stopped pacing and looked over. "He's been in the bloody station twenty minutes now. What on Earth are they doing?"

"Deliberately taking his time getting up here, sir." Vicky tapped a foot against the door. "Shall we speak to his lawyer alone?"

"It's Nelson-Caird, isn't it?"

"Aye."

"Let's do that."

Vicky followed Forrester into the interview room and sat down next to him.

Nelson-Caird smoothed down the margins of her black notebook. "Has my client arrived?"

"Which one? You're representing Yvonne Welsh, Marianne Smith and Brian Morton. Care to explain?"

"My clients are all Legal Aid cases. As you should know, my firm — Brown and Martin — are the largest Legal Aid practitioners in the city."

"You're saying you're ambulance chasers, then?"

"I beg your pardon?"

"No win, no fee, right?"

"DI Forrester, you should be relieved this interview is not being recorded. We take our reputation very seriously and defend it rigorously."

"Cutting all that noise for one minute, how come you're defending virtually all of the suspects in this case?"

"It's just the way it works. We're a busy company and I happen to have been allocated these cases by our office workflow system. I'm more than happy to push them to a colleague but that's going to slow things down for you."

"Very well."

The door opened and PC Soutar pushed a wheelchair in, scraping the wheels on the door. Brian Morton was a dead weight in front of him, his body wobbling with the movement.

Forrester leaned forward to start the interview.

Vicky got up and joined PC Colin Woods in the corridor. "How is he?"

"Not said a word since we picked him up. He's just sat there breathing heavily. Took an age of man to lift him off his scooter."

"Was his brother there?"

Woods shook his head. "He was on his own."

"Off you go. I'll let you get back on duty."

"You don't need us to take him back?"

"Don't worry about that." Vicky flicked up her eyebrows. "He's not getting out anytime soon." She entered the room and sat opposite Brian.

Forrester spoke into the microphone. "DS Victoria Dodds has entered the room."

She passed a sheet of paper across the table. "Mr Morton, we retrieved a mobile phone from a car. This vehicle is central to the case we're working on. You might've seen it in the news?"

No reaction.

"We traced the mobile to your residence." Vicky stabbed a finger at the sheet of paper. "That's the results of a series of GPS extracts we obtained from the phone this afternoon."

Nelson-Caird picked up the sheet and reviewed it. "My client lives on the ground floor of a block of flats. How do you know it's not the first or second floors?"

"Neither of those residents are active members of xbeast. Are they, Brian?"

His head sank, flattening out his jowls as his face grew flushed. He scowled at Vicky but didn't say anything.

"Brian, do you know Yvonne Welsh?"

His breathing sped up. His mouth hung open.

"Do you know her, Brian? We've got her in custody."

Brian turned away.

"Did you use the phone, Brian?"

"No."

"Was it Yvonne?"

"I don't know an Yvonne."

"I bet you do." Vicky gave him space. He didn't fill it. "Where's your brother?"

Brian clamped a hand to his chest. "I don't feel well."

Nelson-Caird got to her feet. "You need to get him taken to hospital."

Brian slumped in his wheelchair, head rolling back on his shoulders, arms prone.

The custody officer jumped into action, wheeling Brian out of the room, Airwave to his face. "Control, this is Buchanan. I need urgent medical assistance for a Brian Morton."

Nelson-Caird followed them out of the room.

Vicky leaned over the microphone. "Interview terminated at fourteen eighteen." She got the first tape out of the machine and put it in its case.

Forrester put his feet up on the table. "Shite."

Vicky shut the case of the second tape, scowling at the open door. "It's an act. He's involved in this."

"He clearly hasn't been trapping people in cages."

"Doesn't mean he's not involved, sir." Vicky got to her feet. "Come on, we need to get closer to this."

Chapter One Hundred and Twenty-One

Vicky held open the door to their office space for Forrester. MacDonald was talking to Karen and Considine. He looked over as they approached. "Did you nail him?"

"DS Dodds made him have a heart attack."

MacDonald raised an eyebrow. "Seriously?"

"Not sure." Vicky leaned against a desk and noticed the ladder in her tights again. "He's faking it."

Forrester got out his mobile. "I'll need to cover your back with Raven, okay?" He put the phone to his head and walked off.

MacDonald folded his arms. "That true?"

"He's faking it, I swear." Vicky spun around and pointed at Zoë. "Can you check Brian's account on xbeast again?"

"What for?"

"Anything incriminating."

"Okay, well I've got his laptop so it should be easier." Zoë patted the machine then started typing, her fingers blurring over the keyboard, thumb dancing off the trackpad. "Right. Here we go." She tapped the screen, clicking with her tongue. "Well, it looks like he's definitely the one who posted the videos. There's raw WMV files on here."

MacDonald stood behind her, gripping the seat back. "This is definitely true?"

"Aye. I've sort of known for a couple of days."

"What?"

"Well, I got a match to one of the accounts posting the videos on YouTube. The IP matched the same one used on xbeast. The Met guys have better gear than I'll ever see but they still got nowhere. It wasn't until we got his laptop that I could definitely check."

MacDonald stood there, nostrils flaring. "Should've told us earlier."

"I didn't want to be wrong, sir. This was more art than science until I got his computer."

"Fine, I'll let you off. Who's doing this with him?"

Vicky folded her arms. "I think it's his brother. Brian flaked out when I asked him about John."

Forrester stormed over, hands in pockets. "Right. Raven's been in with the Procurator Fiscal. He's happy for us to offer Yvonne a deal. We can get her to turn Queen's evidence."

Chapter One Hundred and Twenty-Two

Interview recommenced at fifteen hundred hours. Present are myself, DS Victoria Dodds, and DS Euan MacDonald. The suspect, Yvonne Welsh, is also present. Kelly Nelson-Card is her lawyer." Vicky sat back in her chair, making eye contact with Yvonne. "Ms Welsh, you know this is a murder case, don't you?"

"You told me last time."

"We've just spoken to Brian Morton."

Yvonne's eyes shot up. Her mouth twitched.

"We traced the phone we found in your car back to his house. For obvious reasons, we don't think Brian's directly involved in committing the crimes, but he's certainly implicated. Not least by the fact he's been posting videos of the crimes online."

Nelson-Caird waved her hands in the air. "That pertains to another case entirely. You can't bring that up here."

"It's all one case. Just because you've got a conflict of interest doesn't mean it's invalid." Vicky tossed over the results of Zoë's analysis. "This proves it."

MacDonald leaned forward. "Yvonne, you're linked to Brian. No point in denying it."

"I'm saying nothing."

"How do you know Brian?"

"No comment."

"How do you know John?"

Yvonne rubbed her forehead. "John who?"

"John Morton. Brian's brother."

"No comment."

"Final answer?"

"No comment."

"See, we can't find John. Seems to have disappeared. Is he involved?"

"No comment."

"Well, he certainly seems happy for you to take the rap for this."

Yvonne glanced at Nelson-Caird.

MacDonald put a sheet of paper in front of Nelson-Caird. "Yvonne, this is an offer made on behalf of the Procurator Fiscal. Guarantees you immunity from prosecution for charges pertaining to these crimes in exchange for testifying against your collaborators."

Nelson-Caird retrieved the page and slowly read through it. She whispered to Yvonne, loud enough for them to hear. "I'd take it if I were you."

Yvonne's eyes stayed focused on the table. "No."

Vicky gritted her teeth. "Yvonne, you're being set up. Whether it's John Morton or Marianne Smith or someone else behind this, you're the one taking the fall for a murder. I think your heart's in the right place, I really do. From my perspective, I think you've just got in too deep. You wanted to help animals and you've ended up killing people. You never wanted to do that, did you?"

Yvonne took the sheet from Nelson-Caird and studied it. She swallowed hard then sat for a few seconds, mouth open as she thought. "John's behind it."

"John Morton?"

Yvonne covered her face. "Yes."

"What happened, Yvonne?"

She let out a deep breath. "You're right. I got in too far. I just wanted to frighten people. I wanted to get our message out there."

"But John didn't?"

"No. John did but he took things too far."

Vicky nodded. The video . . . "Like Micky Scott, right? You said something like 'This is going too far' before it was cut off, didn't you?"

"I did, aye. He'd been doing that for hours, kept stabbing the Taser at him. He didn't want me to let the owls go."

"Kyle Ramsay's owls?"

"Aye. The ones that he got to gouge at him. I didn't like him doing that. Getting them to bite him. We're supposed to be stopping cruelty, not doing more ourselves."

Vicky noted it down. "Why's John doing it?"

"Power?" Yvonne shrugged. "He got carried away with it all. He works in PR. This is all just a campaign for him."

Vicky crossed her legs under the table. "How did you meet him?"

"Through Brian."

"And how do you know Brian?"

"We were at school together. We used to be, I don't know, a couple? We were fourteen." Yvonne scratched at her hair. "Brian wasn't always like he is, you know? He used to be fit and healthy."

"But?"

"But their dad was an arsehole. He treated Brian like shit. Losing his dog was what got him into the animal rights stuff."

MacDonald leaned forward. "What happened to his dog?"

"Their parents were divorced and Brian was staying with his mother for the weekend. She was allergic to animals so Brian couldn't take his dog, Goldie. Their dad went away on a boys' weekend, some last-minute thing. He took Goldie to the Brown Street kennels."

"Where you work?"

Yvonne shook her head. "No, the council one. He thought he could just put the dog in on a Friday and get her back on the Monday. Free boarding. Goldie got rehomed."

"Did he try and get her back?"

"He did but their policies didn't allow her to be reclaimed."

"What happened next?"

"Brian was allowed to see the dog occasionally. The family lived in Monifieth. One day, Goldie got run over. Brian just fell apart. That's when he started eating to cope, until that's all he did apart from mess about on his computer."

Vicky focused on the wood grain of the table, centring on a particular knot. Was she throwing John to them? They'd given her an offer and she'd given them the mastermind behind it. Convenient. "Yvonne, we had John under surveillance when you attacked Hunter's Farm. He didn't leave Brian's flat all weekend."

Yvonne nodded. "He saw you talking to another copper at Tesco. He spotted the same car outside Brian's flat. Didn't take an expert to work out what was going on." She shrugged. "He just got out the back window. It was pretty easy."

"He was supposed to be at the Speedway when Rachel and Paul were abducted?"

"He wasn't there." Yvonne shrugged.

"How did you get the cages delivered to Dryburgh?"

"We were squatting there. John knew the security guard's pattern. It was easy to avoid him and plan around it."

"Tell us about the car."

"John's had it for years. He bought it when he lived down south. He wasn't happy when you put out a description on the TV news. Had to use Brian's lock-up."

"*Brian's* lock-up?"

"Yes. He's had it for years."

"What does he keep in there?"

"I don't know. Old computers. He was collecting them for a while, like one of those hoarders on the TV. His mum got him to put them in storage. That was the cheapest place they could find that did it long-term."

"What about when you attacked me at the lock-up?"

Yvonne held up her hands. "That was John."

"But you were there, right?"

Yvonne gave a slight nod. "I was. John heard you were going there to get the car. Mine's still parked a couple of streets away."

Vicky rubbed her forehead. "Where is John?"

"I honestly don't know. It's not like we were living together."

"Were you an item?"

"No way."

Vicky rested her head on her hand. "How were you supposed to meet up with John again?"

"He texts me."

Vicky held up the disposable phone from the car, wrapped in an evidence bag. "On one of these?"

"Correct."

Vicky put it down. "Where's Calum Urquhart?"

Yvonne avoided her gaze. "I don't know."

"Really?"

"I swear."

MacDonald took the offer back from them. "Tear this up if you're lying."

Yvonne's gaze darted around the room. "John's got a mate who lives in Fintry. He might've gone there."

Vicky stared at the mirror and nodded.

Tears streaked down Yvonne's cheeks. "I helped him abduct Calum. Maybe I can help get him back?"

MacDonald squinted at Yvonne. "How did you manage to pick him up in the middle of Dundee?"

Yvonne leaned forward. "I was off work all day. I just waited in John's van and picked him up at the bus stop."

"How?"

Yvonne nibbled a fingernail. "Said I'd show him my breasts. It was John's idea. The kid was thirteen. His little eyes lit up."

"You say *was* thirteen. Is he dead?"

"*Is* thirteen, Christ." Yvonne shook her head. "I swear he's alive. If he's dead, John's killed him since I last saw him."

"Where was he keeping him?"

"He's got a cottage near Forfar."

"What's he going to do with Calum?" Vicky held up a copy of the note from the Urquhart house. "*We're moving to clinical trials.*"

"You know what they do at that company, right?"

"That's still no excuse."

Yvonne cupped her hands at the back of her head. "I don't know what he's planning."

"Right." MacDonald held up the sheet. "How do we get in touch with John Morton?"

"I swear, I don't know. John gets in touch with me, not the other way round."

Chapter One Hundred and Twenty-Three

Vicky sat at her desk, head in her hands. "That's good news, I suppose."

"Could've sworn you'd made Brian have a heart attack. Dr Rankine reckons he was just putting it on." MacDonald picked up a report and started looking through it.

Vicky looked around the room and frowned.

Andrew fiddled with a black box a couple of desks away, his forehead creased and his tongue sticking out.

"Welcome to the team, Andrew."

"Aye. Cheers."

Vicky squinted at the box. "Is that the Tetra scanner?"

"It is."

MacDonald looked up from his report. "Taking forever and a day to get anything out of it."

Andrew scowled at MacDonald as he leaned back in his chair. "I'm not supposed to be here. I'm signed off on long-term sick."

"Yet here you are. Can't be that sick."

"I've got ME, you twat." Andrew got to his feet, tossing his screwdriver on the desk. "You know what? If this is all the thanks

I'm getting then I'm going home." He stormed off, tugging his black, waterproof jacket on.

Vicky went after him, catching him in the corridor. "Andrew, wait."

He stabbed a finger in the direction of MacDonald. "Is that who you're shagging?"

"No comment."

"If it is then your taste in men's getting worse, if that's at all possible."

"What's he done?"

"That wanker keeps pushing my buttons. I'm going too slow. I'm not getting results." Andrew shook his head. "I've got ME for Christ's sake. I shouldn't be here. I'm breaking my sick note."

"That's not as dodgy as selling pirate DVDs, though, is it?"

"Bye." He marched off.

"Wait." Vicky grabbed his arm. "How are you managing?"

"I feel like shit. I've had three coffees today just so I can look at that bloody box. I've not even opened it up yet."

"What's MacDonald after?"

"I don't know." He looked at her hand. "Going to let me go?"

"Tell me about the scanner."

"What is there to tell? They've been listening in on our calls."

"Are there more of these things?"

"Aye. Looks like they've been manufacturing them."

"How?"

Andrew raised his shoulders. "That one in your team with the Subaru who fancies himself, what's his name?"

"Considine?"

"Aye. He was up at the fat boy's flat and found a load of kit in his bedroom. He's been making Tetra scanners that can decrypt our security."

"Okay." Vicky nodded. "You can go home if you want."

Andrew took a deep breath. "I don't know, Vicks. I don't want to let that wanker win."

"You won't. Don't worry." Vicky patted his shoulder and went back inside.

Considine was chatting with Zoë. "So, anyway it turns out this Brian Morton boy was renting that lock-up. It was full of about fifty old PCs."

Vicky nodded at him. "Did they find anything else there?"

Considine smirked. "A load of tinfoil and a ham radio lab. Looks like he was a classic tinfoil hat nutter. Until he couldn't leave the house, that is."

"Were you at his flat?"

Considine nodded. "I was. After I interviewed the guy who —"

"Stephen, my brother said you found the capability to make other Tetra scanners. Is that right?"

"You're asking the wrong man. I found some components, a soldering iron and a load of wires. It was your brother who reckoned they could build something to hack an Airwave."

Vicky stared at MacDonald. "You know what this means, right?"

"Enlighten me."

"They've got more than one Airwave scanner out there. Brian's been building them."

"Right."

Considine held up a hand. "Your brother reckoned it was just the one, Sarge."

Vicky nodded. "Do we know where John is yet?"

"No idea." MacDonald shrugged. "Half the team are out looking for him. Kirk went to his mate's flat — that Speedway alibi was a load of shite."

"Bloody hell. Have you been to his house?"

"Cottage by Forfar, aye. Boy's a terrorist, that's for sure. Got the same paper as Marianne Smith, same printer too. Looks like it was him who was making the notes. Terror books, God knows what else."

"Christ." Vicky slumped in her chair. "He can't have just disappeared."

"He can."

"Ma'am." Zoë tapped her on the arm. "Brian's been sending emails to Marianne Smith."

Chapter One Hundred and Twenty-Four

Do you know an Alison McFarlane?" MacDonald arched an eyebrow.

Marianne Smith sat back, hugging her arms around herself. "No comment."

Vicky stared at her notebook, trying to focus — this was their only chance. John was out there and he had Calum. Nobody knew where he was.

MacDonald cleared his throat. "Ms Smith, I'm pleading with you. John Morton is perpetrating these attacks. With or without your assistance, we'll find out. Calum Urquhart has been abducted by John. He's *thirteen*. We're fearful for his safety."

The corner of Marianne's lip turned up. "Mr Urquhart and his family have caused untold suffering to pigs and primates. He's clearly given a chance to stop it but he hasn't taken it."

"What chance was this?"

"A note went to his work, didn't it? Do you really think I care about his son given what he does to animals?"

"You know about the note, then?" MacDonald leaned forward. "Are you admitting your involvement?"

"What I'm saying is, can you really blame whoever's doing this? Gordon Urquhart isn't the good guy in this. Who cares what happens to his son?"

"We've not mentioned his name. You do know that?"

Marianne looked away. "Mr Urquhart's atrocities are public record."

MacDonald narrowed his eyes. "Ms Smith, what if that was your son out there?"

"I made a conscious decision in my twenties to never have children. There are far too many people on the planet as it is. Just because our genes or our parents or politicians tell us to breed doesn't mean we should. The planet's collapsing under its own weight. If whoever has Mr Stewart's son kills him, is that going to be much of a loss? There'll be hundreds born today to replace him."

MacDonald slammed his hand on the table. "Where's John?"

Marianne held up the print-out. "I'll admit to knowing a Brian Morton. John?" She shrugged. "Never heard of him."

MacDonald lifted his hand again, fist clenched.

Vicky grabbed it. "Come on, Euan." She leaned over the microphone. "Interview paused at sixteen oh nine." She followed him out of the room, leaving Marianne with her lawyer and the PCSO.

MacDonald paced around in the corridor. "We're almost there. Why did you stop that?"

"We're getting nowhere with her." Vicky folded her arms and leaned against the wall. "She's involved in this and we'll prove it, given time. What we need to focus on is finding Calum Urquhart."

"What are you saying?"

"Let me get this straight — at the crime scenes, John was the man, Marianne was the woman and Yvonne was the androgynous one. Right?"

"Certainly looks that way. Yvonne's still involved, whereas Marianne dropped out after the first two." He folded his arms. "So?"

"I don't know." Vicky shrugged.

"Your brother's a piece of work."

"Sure it's not you?"

"Just trying to get him to do his job, Vicky."

"Right." Vicky stared at the floor, frowning — John still had an Airwave scanner. She stared at MacDonald. "I've got a plan."

Chapter One Hundred and Twenty-Five

Vicky held up the Airwave on the table in front of them. "Control to all units. Repeat, the suspect from Findale Place has been released without charge following an interview with Brian Morton. Morton has died of a heart attack in police custody and we still seek the whereabouts of his brother, John."

MacDonald shook his head. "This is such a huge gamble."

"I know."

"Reckon Raven will go for it?"

Vicky shrugged. "Forrester's approved it. The wheels are in motion now." She looked across the table at Yvonne. "Are you still okay with this?"

Yvonne stared at the mobile on the table next to the Airwave. "If it rings."

"It will."

"If it rings, I'll play along."

"Remember, no funny business. I'm already pissed off at you for not bringing up Marianne Smith's name. No code words here. Plain speak — yes/no as much as possible. Okay?"

"Okay."

The Airwave repeated the message. "Control to all units. Repeat, Brian Morton has died of a fatal heart attack in custody and we still seek the whereabouts of his brother, John. The suspect from Findale Place has been released without charge."

The phone lit up. A text message.

Vicky took a deep breath. "Okay. He's texting. Is that normal?"

Yvonne shrugged.

"Yvonne, is it normal?"

"You tell me. You've got the phone records."

Vicky turned to look at Considine, who was leaning against the door.

He flicked through some pages. "Usage is about sixty-forty texts to calls."

"Let's see what he's saying." Vicky picked up the phone. "*Are you okay to talk?*" She focused back on Yvonne. "This is it. Okay?"

"Okay."

Vicky replied, her fingers struggling with the buttons on the phone through the evidence bag's plastic. "Does 'Walking up to Hilltown. Free to talk' sound like something you'd say?"

"It does."

Vicky sent the text then waited, eyes locked on Yvonne.

The phone rang.

Vicky answered it, putting it on speaker straight away. Quietly, she opened the top of the bag.

"Yvonne?"

"Hi, John."

"Christ, are you okay?"

Yvonne smiled. "I'm fine. They just let me go, John."

"Why?"

"I don't know. My lawyer said it was something to do with Brian. The police told me he died."

"I've heard." John sniffed down the line. "Where are you?"

"I've just left the police station."

"Are they following you?"

"If they are, they're really good. It's really quiet here, John."

"Where are you going?"

"I don't know. I was thinking of heading up to the Hilltown."

"Why? They know about Brian's flat."

"I'm scared, John." Yvonne bit her lip. "I don't know what to do."

A pause. Vicky dug her nails into the palms of her hands.

"Yvonne, I'll pick you up."

"Where?"

"Outside the old Dundee College Building on Constitution Road. I'll be about fifteen minutes."

Vicky glanced at MacDonald, whose head was nodding to a silent beat.

Yvonne leaned forward. "Have you still got Calum?"

"He's with me. I'm just readying him now." John laughed. "Still wants to see your tits."

"Is this over?"

"It's never over, Yvonne."

"Okay. See you soon. Bye."

Vicky killed the call and got to her feet. "You did well, Yvonne."

MacDonald was already out of the room.

Yvonne nodded slowly. "Thanks."

"Why would he want to meet at Dundee College?"

"After school, John did a journalism course there."

"It's not a trap or anything?"

Yvonne shook her head. "Not to my knowledge."

Vicky pointed a finger at her. "He said he was readying him, Yvonne. Do you know what for?"

"For surgery." Yvonne shut her eyes. "He's going to experiment on Calum."

Chapter One Hundred and Twenty-Six

Vicky stood shivering outside the old college building. Its seven concrete storeys were all boarded up ready for sale. The cloudless sky was darkening.

She looked down. Yvonne's clothes didn't quite fit her. She reached down and rolled the legs of the jeans up another notch. The hoodie was baggy in the wrong places, tight in others.

Her phone rang. MacDonald. "You set, Vicky?"

She glanced down the street to the end of the one-way system to where MacDonald's team, in plain clothes, were hanging around. "Aye. Everything's hanging off me. Feel like I'm trying on my dad's police uniform again."

"Probably too much information."

"Just hope my hips and bum aren't a giveaway."

"Hard not to be distracted by them."

Headlights came down the hill. The nerve in her neck throbbed, sending pulses of pain shooting up to her brain. She pocketed the phone and put the balaclava on the top of her head, rolled up like it was a hat, covering her hair.

The van pulled in on the other side of the road.

Vicky screwed up her eyes, trying to see if it was John.

The window wound down. The deep voice boomed out. "Get in, Yvonne."

Vicky froze. Her nerve jangled hard.

The van began to drive off.

"Wait!"

It stopped.

Vicky jogged across the road and got in.

The vehicle shot off. John stared at the road as he drove. "Did anyone follow you?"

Vicky snapped out her baton. "John Morton, I'm arresting you —"

He smashed his elbow into her cheek, sending her rocking back in the seat. She clutched at the seatbelt, desperate fingers locking it.

A Taser sparked in front of her. Vicky's muscles released as the electricity tingled all over her body. Just like in Fintry.

John accelerated hard as he shouted at her. "You think you've won, bitch?"

Vicky slumped down, unable to stop herself.

Blue lights ahead of them, sirens from behind.

"Shite." John tugged the wheel to the left, heading the wrong way down a one-way street, dodging the parked cars on the single-lane road. He sped up, mounted the pavement and knocked over some wheelie bins as the road curved back round. They passed a green gate and a stone wall as they powered down the lane.

Vicky clicked her jaw. "You won't get away."

"Just watch me."

"Why are you doing this?"

"Publicity."

"Is that for the animals or yourself?"

"Both." John nudged his glasses back up his nose then stabbed her with the Taser again.

Vicky slumped in the seat once more. She could only watch as they drove. Who'd look after Bella?

They shot out at the bottom of the road.

Vicky recognised the street — they were back on Constitution Road. They'd done a loop.

Police cars shot up the hill in the direction they'd come from.

John gained speed as they went downhill before pulling onto the Marketgait, narrowly missing a car as he merged in. He darted into the right-hand lane, easing past the traffic, before cutting in again. The needle was hitting ninety. He squeezed through the roundabout, braking to avoid a crawling lorry.

Vicky felt her fingers start to respond. The light cut out as they entered the tunnel. She reached over and tugged the wheel to the left.

John looked over, Taser in the air.

The van crashed into the wall and bounced back, hitting the concrete central reservation, before going into a slow spin.

John let go of the Taser and started wrestling with the wheel. The Taser dropped into the middle of the cabin.

Vicky reached down for it.

John slapped a hand across her face, pushing her backwards.

A police car thundered into the front of the van, sending them both flying backwards. Something else hit John's side of the van.

They lurched over, down becoming up. The seatbelt tore into Vicky's shoulders, cutting into her left breast. She glanced over.

John was gone, his door hanging open.

Through the crumpled windscreen, she saw him hobbling away, stepping between the smashed police cars.

Vicky braced herself and released the seatbelt. She fell to the roof of the vehicle, landing on her shoulders.

Something jarred against her neck. The Taser. She put it in the pocket of the hoodie and shoved open her door.

She got out, noticing a deep cut to her right hand as pain started to make its way through the adrenaline. She started towards John, weaving through the cars. An officer was slumped against the wheel of the nearest one.

The other car was a dark grey Subaru, its bonnet mangled. Considine was pushed up against the windscreen. The passenger door was open.

Behind, a wall of yellow hazard lights and blue police sirens blazed out. She ran on, speeding up as she went, the turn-ups on her jeans unfolding.

Beyond the cars, MacDonald jumped at John from behind, sending them both sprawling along the carriageway.

John was first to his feet. His glasses had been knocked off. He aimed a fist at MacDonald's head as he got to his knees. The blow sent MacDonald staggering backwards and he toppled to the ground. She was almost there when John started in with his feet, kicking at MacDonald's prone body.

Vicky stabbed the Taser into John's back.

He fell backwards, his body spasming. She held it against him for a few seconds before taking a swing with her foot and connecting with his balls.

Arms grabbed her from behind. "Easy, Vicky, easy." Forrester.

Karen Woods knelt down and cuffed John.

Forrester helped Vicky over to the wall in the middle of the carriageway. She collapsed against it, focusing on the traffic in the opposite direction. Rubberneckers stared at her and the mangled cars. She smelled a fire from somewhere. "Where's Calum?"

"Oh, shite." Forrester looked back at the crumpled mess of cars.

Vicky staggered to her feet and started towards the van.

Forrester jogged ahead. He stopped and started fiddling with the back doors.

Vicky gripped the handle, pulled it open.

Calum lay upside down in the middle of the van, unconscious. He was naked from the waist up — black ink marked out his organs.

Forrester got in the back, stood on the inverted roof. He felt the boy's neck for a pulse, his eyes on Vicky. He let out a breath. "He's alive."

Vicky collapsed to her knees, tasting blood in the back of her throat.

Chapter One Hundred and Twenty-Seven

That was good work back there, Vicky. Quick thinking."

Vicky sat in front of Forrester's desk, fingers playing with the bandage on her arm. "Just glad we caught him, sir."

"Considine's fine, by the way." MacDonald stood up again, rubbing at his buttocks. His face was bandaged in places. "Shame about his car. The Python's a write-off."

Vicky grinned. "The next one will have to be the Cobra."

MacDonald laughed. Then winced with pain. "How's Calum doing?"

Forrester grimaced. "Not great, Mac. But he'll live." He shook his head. "Being stuck in the back of the van like that. Christ."

Vicky stood up and found the pain eased off a touch. "I still don't get why he did it."

"He's not talking. Not with his balls in his ribs now, thanks to you, Vicky. Laing and Greig have been in with Yvonne and Brian Morton again." Forrester chuckled. "That was a good touch, by the way. Cheeky bugger was just faking it."

"Did they get anything?"

Forrester raised his shoulders. "Nearest we can get is it was a power trip for John. The boy worked in PR. This all seems to be an advertising campaign for him. You can bet the court case will be just the same."

"I still don't get it."

Forrester leaned forward. "Marianne Smith started speaking a bit once she knew Yvonne was talking. They're part of some organisation, no names given yet. Marianne recruited Yvonne and she got Brian involved. The boy's a prodigy with computers. We could use someone like that were it not for the fact he's going away for life."

MacDonald leaned against the window. "Did he spill on his brother?"

"Aye." Forrester leaned on his elbows. "John and Brian's mother died of cancer two years ago. John had just been made redundant so moved back from London-shire to look after Brian. Marianne was Yvonne's partner in their cell last summer. She moved upstairs and became her handler. They got John in at that point. He came at them with this advertising campaign idea. Started with that snare trap, then shoving Irene Henderson in a bin. They saw they could get away with it so their ambitions grew."

MacDonald shook his head. "It certainly got them publicity."

Forrester shrugged. "Found a list of dead CCTV cameras he'd got off the internet somewhere. Also, he had some notes on other attacks. Nothing on Camperdown Zoo but they had plans for an attack on a racehorse stable, someone charged with poisoning cats in Aberdeen and the Musselburgh Racecourse."

"Jesus Christ." Vicky thought it through. "So we've stopped this escalating into a much wider attack?"

"Looks that way." Forrester sat back in his chair, nodding. "Thank Christ we don't do any whaling in this city anymore."

"Reckon we'll get a conviction?"

"They're all going away for a *long* time."

"Except Yvonne."

"Well, there's that. She'll get placed under witness protection. Someone will make sure she's not getting involved in any more shite like this."

"I think she's learnt."

"Me too, Vicky." Forrester laughed. "I'd ask you if you wanted a pint but I got such a doing last night after the state I got into. You pair can get off home now, if you want."

"Thanks, sir." Vicky got to her feet. She followed MacDonald out of the office.

He stopped just outside. "Do you fancy a drink?"

Chapter One Hundred and Twenty-Eight

"D id you catch the baddies, Mummy?"

Vicky undid Bella's seatbelt and helped her out of the car, her breast aching. "I did, Bells. For once."

"Mummy's my hero."

Vicky picked her up and cuddled her, wincing at the pain in her back. "I love you, too."

"Where are we going, Mummy?"

"Mummy needs to speak to someone. Have you been a good girl for Granny?"

"Granny said so."

"Granny might be biased. Well, if you've been a good girl you might get to meet a new friend."

"I've got lots of friends."

"This might be a special one."

"Okay."

Vicky led her up the drive and knocked on Robert's door.

He opened the door and frowned. "Vicky?"

"Hi, Robert."

The frown turned to a smile when he saw her daughter. "How's Bella?"

Bella kicked her foot out. "I'm *fine*."

Vicky smiled. "Can we come in?"

"Sure, Vicky. Come on in." Robert led them through into the hall.

His greyhounds raced through from the living room and started jumping everywhere, tails wagging and mouths open.

Bella covered her face with her hands and started squealing.

Robert tugged at the collars. "I'll just put these two outside." He took the dogs into the kitchen. The patio doors slid open and shut again.

Vicky knelt down and patted Bella's shoulders. "It's okay. The dogs won't bother you again."

"Sorry about that." Robert came through to the hall. "Come on in. Sorry the place is such a state."

Vicky inspected the living room from the doorway. Bookshelves lined three walls, all filled with novels. An expensive hi-fi sat in the corner underneath a large TV. "No worse than our place."

Robert's son, Jamie, lay on the ground playing with a Lego set.

"Jamie, this is Bella. Bella's mummy is friends with Daddy."

The boy sat up, pushing his glasses up his nose. He tilted his head to the side as he inspected Bella. "Do you like Lego?"

Bella looked up at Vicky. "Can I play, Mummy?"

"Go on."

Bella joined Jamie on the floor and began amassing her army of bricks.

Robert stared at Vicky, his Adam's apple bobbing up and down. "Do you want a tea or a coffee?"

Vicky nodded. "I'll make an exception for once. Tea."

Robert led them through a doorway into the kitchen, went to the sink and filled the kettle.

"This is a nice house you've got, Robert. Seems bigger than Liz's."

He shrugged. "It's okay, I suppose. The bungalow next to Dave and Liz's is much bigger."

"How much bigger do you need?"

"I've got a lot of books, believe me." He chucked teabags in the mugs and poured water in, before mashing them against the sides. "Do you take milk?"

Vicky nodded, her heart thudding in her chest, the nerve throbbing. What the hell could she say? How could she explain her behaviour? "Lots of milk, please."

Robert poured some in and handed her a mug, his jaw clenched. "Here you go."

"Thanks."

"This is the best cup of tea you'll ever taste, mark my words."

"We'll see."

Robert took a drink. "You've not come here to talk about tea, though, have you?"

Vicky leaned against the counter. "No, I haven't." She put the mug down and pinched her nose. "When you introduced Bella to Jamie, you said I was your friend."

Robert nodded. "That's true."

"Just a friend?"

Robert shrugged. "I'm not sure. Maybe I could be more if you just let me in."

Vicky rubbed her eyes. "I've been such an idiot."

"How?"

"I thought you were involved in this case."

He lowered his head. "Is that why the police came around this afternoon?"

"Yes."

He set his mug on the counter. "How could you think that about me?"

Vicky looked up at the ceiling. "I found your name on a list of donors to the animal shelter on Brown Street."

"I told you about that. It's what happened when Moira died. It was in her will."

"Well, I flagged it. Last night, I came here when I got back to Carnoustie, wanting to apologise for cancelling like that. I saw your car was a black Audi, which matched the one we were looking for."

"You're a cop. I get it." He pointed through to the living room. "I don't know if you've noticed but I've got a large collection of British and American detective novels. I know what you go through."

Vicky raised an eyebrow. "You don't know the half of it, believe me."

"Try me."

"When I noticed those things, I was duty-bound to report it, Robert."

"I see." He stared out of the kitchen window, along the main road in Barry. The dogs were chasing each other in the garden, tearing chunks of turf out of the lawn. "In some ways, I'm glad you did."

"How?"

"If I'd been involved and you'd done nothing about it, you'd really be in the shit."

Vicky concentrated on the rim of her mug. "One of my colleagues tried to kiss me last night."

Robert tightened his grip on the handle of his mug. "Was he successful?"

"I was drunk."

"You were *drunk*? I thought you were working."

"I had been working. We went for a drink afterwards. Things got out of hand and I had to get a taxi home."

533

Robert put his mug in the sink. "Right."

Vicky grabbed his arm. "Robert, I'm a mess, okay? I'm fucked up. I have this commitment phobia thing. It's one of the things I still have from my relationship with Alan, I guess. I can be a cold bitch. I have to . . . I have to put this switch on in my head when I go to work. I have to keep work and home separate. Otherwise, I'd —"

"Vicky, what're you trying to say? Are you letting me down gently?"

She put a hand on his shoulder. "I'm saying if you'll have me and work through the shit in my head, then I want to give it a go."

Robert stared at the floor. He didn't say anything for a few seconds. He nodded. "Okay."

Acknowledgements

Thanks for reading SNARED — I seriously hope you enjoyed the book and Vicky.

It wouldn't have been possible without the help of a lot of people. In chronological order . . . Thanks to Kitty for helping with the initial idea, alpha reading and constant moral support throughout; to Pat, Geoff and Rhona for the invaluable feedback on the initial draft; to Allan Guthrie for helping tear the book apart, for teaching me to write properly and for being the best agent I could hope for; and, last but certainly not least, to Emilie and everyone at Thomas & Mercer for having faith in me and the book.

Ed James,
East Lothian, October 2014

About the Author

Ed James is the author of the self-published Scott Cullen series of Scottish police procedurals, featuring a young Edinburgh Detective Constable investigating crimes from the bottom rung of the career ladder he's desperate to climb. The first book, *Ghost in the Machine*, has been downloaded over 300,000 times, hitting the Amazon UK top five and US top 50. In order to write full-time, Ed gave up a lucrative career in IT project management, where he filled his weekly commute to London by writing on planes, trains, and automobiles, managing to complete three full-length novels in just seven months. He lives in East Lothian, Scotland.